THE YEAR'S BEST AFRICAN SPECULATIVE FICTION 2022

THE YEAR'S BEST AFRICAN SPECULATIVE FICTION 2022

Edited by

Oghenechovwe Donald Ekpeki
Eugen Bacon
Milton Davis

Caezik SF & Fantasy
in partnership with
O.D. Ekpeki Presents

The Year's Best African Speculative Fiction 2022 © 2023
Oghenechovwe Donald Ekpeki, Eugen Bacon, Milton Davis

ISBN: 978-1-64710-076-6

An imprint of Arc Manor LLC
www.CaezikSF.com

An imprint of Jembefola Press
www.odekpeki.com

CONTENTS

STORIES

MARCH MAGIC

by WC Dunlap

Swamp waters soothe these old witch bones like Epsom salts. There is stories in these waters, buried deep in the thick mud, but rising like these moccasins twisting around my thighs. Snakes don't scare me none, no more than this here gator whipping me with its tail. These swamps long been safety—sheltering kin and kind running from the yoke and the whip. Nature loves a free soul. This here home. I could float here forever, but today there's conjuring need done.

The sun winks over the horizon, breaking the night. And I sigh, a subtle sound that moves through the swamp like a breeze.

Time to go 'bout the business of getting unstuck.

I've grown heavy from the decades—maybe longer—of stillness. My limbs curled around the branches of this lil' black willow, half-submerged in these healing waters. The gray coils of my hair, almost translucent in the rising day, twist with the fine tapered foliage of the willow. The yellow dust of delicate catkins covers my flesh. Cheek pressed against the cool bark, my skin is so thick and wrinkled you can barely tell my brown from the wood. But here I am. Here I always be. Black, Native, woman, witch, constant wader, leading my children to safety. Feels like never-ending work. But it's my purpose. Don't know no other way to be. They call and I come.

Gotta get moving. I blink, wiggle fingers and toes, but it takes the rest of my body a while to match the motion. I call the woodpecker to help—gentle now—he loosens flesh from wood so I can crack joints and stand on shaky legs. My feet sink into the soft wet earth until I get my purchase.

Hmmm, I sigh with relief. Feels good to be moving again. I wade through waist-deep waters toward dry land.

Don't know what took them so long to call this time. And now it's troubling my waters. I can't see it yet, but I can feel and smell it—a nasty scent like kerosene oil, tobacco, and the musk of evil white men and dogs running through my swamp. A beast howls in the distance, a hell howl finna topple me over. The swamp moves beneath my feet, a nervous motion like a shudder. There are no dogs in my swamp, and I ain't too particular 'bout them who call themselves masters. Dead or alive, they still evil.

Not today, of all days, not today.

I raise tired, aching arms, and the bent brown knees of the cypress roots emerge from the wetlands. More howls follow, so I raise the roots a little higher, and they surround me like palisades.

Now, where my demon killers at?

Suddenly, the soft purr of a car cuts through the hum of cicadas, it's radio blaring through open windows:

"Today August 28, 1963, an estimated two hundred thousand people will converge in our nation's capital to pressure Congress to pass a Civil Rights Act ..."

I wade toward the noise and the moving headlights that cut through the morning haze. The car whips through my swamp on a path barely fit for a horse, never mind this modern thing. But it is as determined as these monsters busting through them gates of hell, thinking they coming for me.

"You can try!" I tell them.

The car parks at the edge of the waters. Five young Black men dressed in crisp dark suits and smelling like Sunday morning—oh, I love how we show out—step out of an old, rusted Packard. These the kind of men my swamp do welcome. They wait patiently as I make my

4

way closer. I wave them forward, and they roll up trousers to haul this old body up to dry land.

"Morning ma'am." The driver tips his fedora with a crooked-white smile that breaks his deep-brown face like the sun cuts through the night. He pretty—or it's been that long since I seen a man.

"Click off that noise." I point to the car radio, and the boy abides. "I don't need no voice box telling me why today so important."

"My name is William James, ma'am," the driver say. "You can call me Dubya. The Big Six sent us to protect the ritual."

Hmpf, I grunt with hands on hips. "So, those ol' uppity preachers finally realize they need they roots now, huh?"

Dubya shrugs. "We was called just as you," he say. "We ain't exactly members of they congregations either, ma'am."

"How you get in this line of work then?" I ask him.

"Evil just happens," Dubya responds. The other boys shuffle nervously. "And if you survive it, you kinda of called after that ... I was ten."

Swamp mists rise with the day, and I squint through it to see these men clearly. They young. Boys really. Still scarred by that first battle. I smell it—fresh scabs.

And it's only five of them.

"This all who came?" I ask.

"Yes, ma'am. But we ain't exactly helpless." Dubya flashes a couple of gleaming silver knives under his jacket. He motions to his boys. One of them reaches into the backseat of the car and hands out shotguns to the others. "And we ain't shooting no ordinary bullets neither," Dubya reassures.

"Boogey man buckshot." Grins another.

Just then, something snarls not too far off. One of the boys steps forward, aims his shotgun into the shadows, and fires true. The smell of rock salt and the whimper of a dying beast follows.

Hmpf. They got heart.

"Alright then." I nod. "You can call me Mama Willow. All that ma'am stuff for white ladies and church ladies, and I ain't neither."

The boys laugh, but Dubya frowning.

"Now what's your problem?"

"No disrespect Mama Willow, but are *you* all who came?"

He cute so I laugh, but the Black-ass nerve.

I click my teeth. "Nigga please. I called the coven."

5

And four Black women step forth from the mists.

From the North comes the Salem Witch, the New England debutante. A chill heralds her presence. She walks upon it as if floating on air, dressed in high-collared blouse and wool skirt snatched at the waist, glasses sliding down her sharp nose. Her face a mahogany-kissed cream and framed by loose black curls that fall gracefully from a tight bun on top of her head. A delicate Celtic knot dangles from a thin chain around her neck. Ha—those ol' Puritans hung the wrong witches! Here be the blood of the right one—old magic from an Irish ma fortified by the older magic of an African pa. She brings with her the warm winds and cold air of two lands—each striving for freedom with the tools of this world and the others.

I name her, "Glad Harvard could spare you, Siobhan."

She nods in deference and replies, "You call and I will come, Mama Willow."

The ground shakes with the pounding of boot and hoof. More beasts coming. The boys get a little nervous, I can tell.

From the East comes the Root Woman, red brown like Georgia soil. Her long limbs swing free from a light sheath, bare feet almost float through the mud. Watching her is like watching a seedling sprout forth from the dirt—glorious, earth-bending life that you just want to feed until it is a fruit-bearing tree. She whips her waist length cornrows and the scents of cinnamon, clove, and whiskey fill the cold air brought by her sister. Dubya sneezes and finds himself unsteady on his feet. Her laughter is like the sound of backwater Blues. She tugs on the pouch of powders 'round her neck and greets me with a mischievous smile.

I name her, "Hey there, Fox girl," and smile back. "I see you brought your bag of tricks."

She winks. And—ha—Dubya and the boys still trying to get themselves together.

We can smell the beasts and their masters strong now, like rancid meat, their scent threatening to overpower our magic.

From the South comes my Mambo. Cowrie-covered, she rattles as she walks, creating sparks that blaze in the cold, earth-scented presence of her sisters. Her full lips and wide nose announce the Africa shining through a pale complexion. She kisses me on both cheeks, and a trail of heat runs up and down my jaw. She holds my calloused, withered hand in both of hers, and fire straightens my crooked spine. Her touch is the embrace of a thousand spirits, writhing to burst forth and liberate they children.

I name her, "Caliste, I welcome you and the fourteen forty."

The stomps of angry boots and the bone chilling rattle of chains join the growls of beasts.

"Nou goumen ansanm," she say.

"Yes indeed, chile."

From the West come the Preacher's Daughter. Blue-black skin shined with sweet, scented oils, thick coils twisted in two plaits that hang on each side of her head, dress falling way below the knee, a thin gold chain with a cross hangs from her neck. This one came for church. She follows my path through the swamp, the waters dancing around her, sprinkling us as she approaches. Her holy water revives. Her moisture brings the clarity of our victory. As she approaches the peace of the Holy Spirit descends.

I name her, "You bring that gospel, Odessa."

She embraces me, drawing my tiny frame to her bosom, and I feel the power of the mighty outstretched arm.

The beasts appear through the trees, maws gaping wide like gators, necks snapping back as chains held by hands not yet visible pull them to heed.

The boys fan out around us.

"There's only five of you!" Dubya shouts over his shoulder.

"We got a songbird with the King," I respond with calm. "Trust, we can do with six what Jesus did with twelve."

One of the boys encircles us in a ring of salt before lifting his rifle back toward the beasts. Another turns up the car radio:

"Go back to Mississippi! Go back to Alabama!"
"Go back to the slums and ghettos of our Northern cities!"

The so-called masters come into view—white, rotting skin, empty eye sockets, mouths foaming with hatred. They cuss us, rancid spittle flying from decaying jaws. Hollow eyes pierce passed the boys, and lock on we witches.

7

I join hands with my daughters as the radio booms:

"… Somehow this situation can and will be changed."

"This is blood magic," we witches speak as one.

"You got someone specific in mind?" Dubya shouts.

We pause, but then the answer comes. "A Jack of diamonds."

Dubya shrugs, his eyes focused on the haints. "Too late to back out now."

"And it won't last," we continue, "magic is fleeting."

"That would have been good information yesterday." Dubya snaps the shotgun.

"What is the power of two-hundred-thousand souls against three hundred and forty years of wickedness," we answer, "this is but a battle in a long war."

"We got you!" Dubya shouts.

The soulful voice of my sixth witch sings through the radio, each note a spell:

"Tell 'em about the dream!"

The King pauses, then begins:

"I have a dream …"

The demons and their beasts leap forward, the shotguns set off, and we witches begin to conjure a dream into reality.

WHEN SHE SPEAKS

by Ugochi Agoawike

Flowers bloom when her wife speaks. Maud hides her smile as she watches Prism—her *wife*. Oh, she would never tire of the word.

Light filters through her wife's smile and casts colors over her flush brown face. Prism's happiness is a tangible thing, blooming over her arms in rainbow shades. Violets cling to the corners of her mouth, her tongue stained green by the winding vines of her words. Sunflowers peek through the green shrub of her untamed hair. Searching leaves of aster and olives sprout from her body like fingers of summer light. It seems eternal, if only for a moment. She is chthonic; perfume of the earth rising beneath her curled toes.

When Maud holds Prism, a vivarium filled with verdant verdure blossoms between them. The grass scratches her skin as bees bumble lazily from lilies to rosy acacia. Life is love. So she carries Prism's love, laughing when the vivarium inevitably overflows, honeydew and lovely lavandula spilling through welcoming fingers. Melanted hands, dirt smudged palms, and a stray leaf across her wife's nose. Smiling, she kisses Prism around the rose in her mouth.

As is inevitable in the cycle of flora, though, a wilting overtakes Prism. It is a steadily rising buzz, a distant nyctinasty that creeps in like a solstice night. Black roots like lightning trail under Prism's skin, her stress tangible as flowers fall away. Weeds fall from her mouth

9

when she complains, pressing at over-watered yellow spots on her cheeks. Creeping plants invade every corner of their home as her wife wanders the halls in a vertiginous daze. A ghost of burnt grass, Prism sulks as dandelions fall from her limp hair. She collapses onto the couch, hidden in a forest of hanging fronds and potted foliage, and sighs like the winter wind. Maud follows after her wife, picking up the yellow weeds and dreaming of wishes lost. Though coarse golden teeth litter the floor, the dandelions are part of Prism's garden, and Maud wants to protect them. She salvages them like a collector who presses dry fluff and flowers between the pages of their shared history. Their beauty, however, is a point of contention. *Your weeds are not like toenails*, Maud asserts staunchly.

Eventually, moss covers Prism's skin as she flags. Maud keeps her close, murmuring caring words into her wife's palm as her fingers trail through her leathery, worn patches. This is what she does. She takes the good with the bad, picks the pests from her wife's lashes— the lies, the doubts Prism tells herself—until the flowers return. Grass soon makes way for yellow jessamine and dandelions crowded in chipped clay pots.

Her wife's words are ice when she speaks. Her wife, who blooms like a daisy and smiles like a diamond, now snarls like a storm. Maud wipes wet crystals from her agate eyes and looks away. But she does not leave.

Frost slithers across Prism's lips with the hiss of biting words. The brown of her skin is washed out with cool anger. It settles on her body like layers of snow: building and building before crashing in a deluge of powered slurry that leaves Maud plucking ruined pieces of clay pots. Prism is in motion, and she stomps from the room. Ice follows her, a haphazard trail that melts as soon as it forms.

When Maud reaches for her wife, she receives a touch like a stinger. Icy anger laces her skin in uncaring lines. Those lines turn to roots of doubt that prick her mind. Black dahlia sprouts in Prism's hair, tiny green dots amid a coily field of chilling gray. A crushing weight fills the room, freezing the dandelions in their pots. Ashy leaves peel off her skin with great effort, shattering when they fall from her hands. Tree nettles cling to the sides of her mouth and decaying rose petals fall from the lash of her tongue. Wounds that Maud will lick later, a soothing balm on the scars she hides.

A frigid tundra spans the gap on the bed between them. But a garden lies beneath it all, waiting to be thawed, a bear hibernating through winter. The blade of frost stings Maud's heart. She knows she is enough, but just as much, she knows she does not deserve this.

Instead, Maud curls under the covers and hides beneath the veil of her black boxy braids. But she is no coward—her defiant hand remains in the valley, frostbitten fingers flexing in the low light.

But the blizzard never stays for long. It can't in this house, blanketed by the thick, relentless heat of Maud's determination. Eventually, Prism's fingers creep toward hers like buds through thawed earth. Her apology is an inquisitive cat testing unchanging waters, a pinkie wrapped around hers. And when Maud does not move, her wife gains ground. Yarrow flutters from her mouth and rich hyacinth curls across Prism's skin. Purple veins gather at the bulb of her hand, tendrils chasing after the fleeting cold. Its weight is still palpable, mint on Maud's tongue.

The land is cold, the gap is wide. There is work to be done, but the touch of her wife's hand is an unspoken apology. Streams of sun filter in, warming the wilted flowers. A petal reaches for the light.

There is moss when her wife speaks. Not the wet kind—a hopeful blanket, soft as down. Maud melts at the sight of her; she is an ever-changing river.

Radiant by the light of an open window, Prism whispers, *I'm sorry*. Burgeoning flowers open beneath her fluttering hands. She's holy as a carnosa, repentant, green ivy crawling over her arms. Life emerging after the seasonal white. Her lush fir hair falls in tight curls, a circle around her body. Prism's voice is a rose, thornless. She holds out a hand, clover twining through her fingers, ringlike. Leaves flutter to the ground and land softly.

Gathering her courage like a bouquet, Maud takes her wife in her arms. Cheeks pressed together, bodies close as bulbs in turned earth, she breathes in the scent of petrichor and honey. Prism kisses Maud, dandelion fluff on slightly dry lips. Another apology is murmured into

11

her mouth, tasting of sugar petals. Rosemary and rue overflow where they touch. Heather smears Prism's hand, daubs of purple in the valleys of her fingers. Insects buzz through their vivarium. Prism laughs sunflower seeds at the stripes of pollen on Maud's face.

The smell of spring cottons the air. Maud listens. Her wife speaks endlessly, filling the silence with flowers: violets on violets on violets.

The cycle will come again, in dandelions and yellow moss, in snowdrops and lilac blooms that look like floss. What Prism can't change, she doesn't, and neither can Maud. But love is work. So Maud tries. She tries: offers fertile tending with the patience of a gardener watching buds unfurl. She loves a woman who speaks the language of flowers.

Her wife.

A SUNKEN MEMORY

by Donovan Hall

CJ-1844 sat in the pilot's chair of his deep-sea probe, his neural network link extending from the palm of his hand into input dock of the submersible's control console. The ship fed him information on the waters around him as he kept it on track speeding through the abyss. CJ's mission was simple: find the last mind bank hidden in the ruins of old Baltimore and collect any souls still sleeping within. It was something CJ had done dozens of times before, though he took little pleasure in it. Ruins were dangerous places, and worse still, the ride to get to them was incredibly dull.

Over the submersible's speaker system, CJ played music to pass the time, old tracks from when he was still human. CJ liked the old songs. They helped maintain the memories in his neural cortex, triggering nodes of data that hadn't been inspected in a long time. The song playing now was titled "September." Though CJ had no lungs, his vocal synthesizers could still crank up to an impressive volume, and on long voyages like this, with nothing to do but enjoy some music, he took full advantage of the range his cybernetic voice.

CJ bounced in his seat as the disco beats of millennia past built up to the chorus, and at the climax, he held up a chromatic hand, tossed his head back, and shouted his favorite verse.

CJ remembered how strange it had been when he was first down-loaded from the mind bank that had held his consciousness for five hundred years. Those who found him said he'd been stored in a facility in the ruins of Houston. At the time, he did not know who he was, where he was, or where he'd come from. A common side effect of having one's memories suddenly compiled in a new, unfamiliar platform. Cyber Displacement was often described as moving into a giant house where the inside of every room was something familiar, but you had no idea as to the layout of the house itself, and some of the rooms had caved in during the move. Things came back to different people in different orders, and some things, due to file corruption, never came back at all. For CJ, when he awoke, all he knew was that he wanted to listen to some music. And despite the many mind transfers he'd had since then, that desire never left him, though many other memories had. Data corruption was always a risk with digitized memory—the catch to being immortal.

The amount of people who had uploaded their consciousness before the start of the Ascension War was paltry compared to the total population. Less than one percent. And once the war started, any banks in the major cities—DC, New York, Tokyo, Shanghai, London—were all bombed into radioactive glass. Those that survived the war were still threatened by the horrific nuclear storms and earthquakes that ravaged the planet in the centuries that followed. Only one percent of one percent had remained to be downloaded in the aftermath. Those few souls turned out to be the very last vestiges of humanity … if they could even call themselves human. Centuries of irradiation meant many minds could only be partially restored. Everyone seemed to have a missing piece or two, and by now some were missing a lot more than others.

CJ had undergone many missions to find lost mind banks, but it had taken a toll. The world was a savage place beyond the titanium domes of Maroon-0, and more often than not there had been many a time he'd returned to base with a body so thoroughly broken, he'd needed his mind transferred to a new chassis. And each time his memories became a little less stable. A little more corrupted. Thinking of his human life now only gave him headaches and flickering glimpses— the taste of greens, a wrinkled brown face, a cherrywood guitar. But knowing how they fit together, that was impossible, and it was only getting worse. Others wondered why he strained himself so, risking so much to find so little, but in a world where no one new was ever born, searching for and rescuing minds from mind banks was the closest thing to bringing life into the world.

CJ wondered if he'd had children once upon a time. He thought he could remember them, vaguely, round and laughing like little chestnuts, but now he wasn't sure. Their faces weren't there. It was a faded memory. Corrupted data. Did he have a wife? A husband? He shook his head. Corrupted data. A faded memory.

The administration had warned him to stop before it was too late, that it had been over two hundred years since the last mind bank had been discovered, and he was risking his sanity for nothing. They said there were no souls left to be found, and to destroy his mind in vain exploration would be a waste. CJ didn't believe that though. He couldn't. They couldn't be all that was left.

The cyborg suddenly stiffened in his seat as a warning signal was transmitted from the submarine pod's AI into his neural network. His artificial brain interpreted the signal to make it sound like ringing sirens going off in his head, startling him with an unwelcomed shock.

"Emergency!" the pod's AI said calmly. *"Severe tectonic activity detected."*

"Details!" CJ ordered, turning off the music with a thought.

"A magnitude 9.0 earthquake has been detected three clicks from our current location. The shockwave will hit us in approximately one minute. I suggest following emergency protocols and brace for impact."

An earthquake? Now? Impossible! The analysts had given CJ the most up-to-date geological forecasts before setting out on his mission. Something like this should have been predicted. If CJ still had teeth, he would have sucked on them in frustration. Not even a fully optimized neural matrix and AI assistance could overcome human error. No point in worrying about that now. CJ had to think of the present. He was exposed, in the open with no shelter to break the oncoming wall of water. All he could do was follow emergency protocol, cut his link from the console, strap in tight, grab the railings on either side of him, and brace for impact.

Disconnected from the console, the AI's voice sounded over the speakers instead of echoing in his head. *"Impact coming in five ... four ... three ... two ... one."*

15

The shockwave hit the small craft like a storm gale, throwing CJ against the glass viewport. If he still had bones, his jaw would have shattered on impact. Before he could grab ahold of the handles again, CJ was flung back hard into his seat. Then he was thrown again, this time to the left, his head denting one of the bars he was trying to hold to steady himself. The submersible spun, and CJ held on for dear life. He felt no pain, his tactile sensors maxed out before reaching that point, but it still wasn't pleasant. There was a tension, a panic that made the cyborg desperately cling to the support bars. If his arm or his head were to smash something vital in the sub, shatter the viewport, crush the console jack, or dent the computer mainframe, that would be the end of it. Not even his hyper durable body would survive sinking to the crushing fathoms of the abyss. And even if he did, he'd burn through his battery charge before reaching home trying to walk the ocean floor.

He would die.

The lights in the sub flickered out suddenly, casting him in blackness, but whether as a means to save energy or as a result of structural damage, CJ couldn't tell, not while disconnected from the neural link. So, as it was, CJ spun in the darkness of the abyss, hearing the roaring waters eddying around him.

CJ did not notice at first when the sub finally stopped turning. He'd almost gotten used to the feeling of endless spinning. Eventually everything did stop, the rolling, the creaking of the sub's hull, it faded until it just ceased altogether. But whether the sub was floating or resting on the ocean floor, he couldn't tell. All he saw was black, and all he heard was silence.

"Pod!" CJ called out. "Pod, wake up!"

There was no answer.

Fumbling in the dark, CJ reached out to the control console, feeling for the port to plug in his neural link. He found the small, peg-shaped hole and placed his palm over it, docked, and reached out into digital space to sense the AI's presence.

What he saw in his mind space was more darkness, a field of empty black.

16

With a forceful thought, CJ willed the sub to activate, pushing his intention firmly upon the machine. There was a flash of dim light, a candle flicker in the black void, and then, one by one, more lights started to flare as the basic diagnostic systems started to reboot, and a bit of tension eased from the cyborg's shoulders. At least, for a moment. Then a yellow image of the ship's battery gauge appeared, showing a lower than optimal measurement of remaining power. Thirty percent. Under normal circumstances, it would have been enough to get home, but who knew if it would be enough now.

Once CJ finished taking note of the battery, the gauge faded away and quickly replaced itself with a 3-D projection of the ship displaying highlighted areas of structural compromise. A propeller was loose, but beyond that, no serious damage had been sustained as indicated by the majority of the ship having a healthy green outline. CJ thanked his lucky stars and dismissed the projection from view.

"AI system reboot initiated!" chimed the AI's melodic voice, echoing in the digitized mind space. A glowing wheel suddenly took the foremost spot in CJ's mental vision. It turned yellow, then slowly turned neon blue, and then bright green. *"Hello, CJ -1844! This is Submersible Exploration Pod-136 at your service!"*

"Welcome back," CJ said. He pulled his senses out of the realm of cyberspace and back into his physical surroundings, which remained almost as dark as he'd left them, save for a few safety lights now adding an ambient red glow to the pod's interior. "Can you turn the headlights on?"

Immediately, the headlights of the sub flashed bright, revealing to CJ that he was indeed on the bottom of the ocean. However, judging by what he saw, this place had not always been submerged. There were buildings here, or the at least the remains of them. Lumpy and misshapen as they were from the weathering passage of watery eons, they were still unmistakably buildings. Among the buildings directly in front of them were two thick fleshy stalks, each the size of a young tree. A pair of anchor worms, CJ thought, creatures who waved lazily in the water, catching small fish that wondered too close. He'd seen them before, though they were usually found in groups, not pairs.

"Where are we ...?" CJ thought aloud, leaning forward on the control console, staring in awe at the ruins before him. The style of architecture did not match those of Baltimore's ruins. He would know, he'd been there twice before. In fact, these didn't match any of the old sunken cities CJ had visited. Most of the buildings were too squat, too old fashioned for the standard designs of the late twenty-third century.

"We are 6.3156 degrees north by 10.8074 degrees west."

"Yes, but where exactly is that?"

The AI provided a holographic map, making it appear in the forefront of CJ's mind. The oceans were blue, and the landmasses were green, lined with brown mountains and deserts, and his exact location was represented by a flashing red dot. They were on the edge of the Mid-Atlantic, only a few kilometers off the coast of West Africa.

"This must have been above water hundreds of years ago," CJ thought aloud. "What was this city called?"

"It was called Monrovia, capital of a small nation called Liberia."

The names were vaguely familiar to CJ, like he'd heard them before, but he did not have any specifics he could recall offhand. The problem with digitized memory was that, at best, it was only as clear as it had been at the time upload, and the more vague the memory, the more susceptible it was to corruption. CJ did know, however, that all the major cities of the former West African coast like Lagos, Accra, and Dakar had all been thoroughly explored centuries ago. Scanning the unusual buildings, he wondered if anyone had conducted expeditions here before.

"Negative," the AI said, sensing his thoughts. *"The administration has deemed this area an unlikely prospect for mind banks since it was relatively undeveloped prior to the war, thus no one has undertaken the effort to explore it."*

Great, CJ thought sarcastically, slumping back in his seat. He'd landed in the boondocks. If he were going to be thrown to the other side of the Atlantic, the least he could ask for was to be thrown someplace interesting. Now all he had to look forward to was a long trip back home with nothing to show for it. Of course, that was assuming he could even get home. Maroon-0 was nestled in the heart of the Gulf of Mexico, over five-thousand miles away. This sub was not meant for such a range. Without another convenient shock wave, returning was going to be tricky to say the least.

CJ tapped his chrome fingers thoughtfully on the console, looking at the battery display in his mental space. It read: twenty-nine percent. "Pod, how can we get back to Maroon-0 with our current battery charge?"

"If we go at half speed, we will be able to reduce our energy output to such an extent that we should be able to get back to base. Though we will be delayed by a week."

"Hmph. A week? At least it'll give me time to think of what I'll report to the administration." CJ nodded, accepting that it was what it was. "Chart the course for home and let's be on our way."

"Excuse me, CJ, I would be remised if I did not inform you that I am suddenly detecting a signal. It's weak, but it is there."

CJ raised a holographic eyebrow with mounting intrigue. "What? Here? In the ruins?"

"Affirmative."

Curiosity roused the cyborg. The thought of coming back with something, anything, was too tantalizing to ignore.

"Can you lock onto the signal?"

"Affirmative."

The map reappeared in CJ's mind, zooming in on their immediate surroundings. The red dot was his position, the green dot was the mysterious signal, though it did bleep in and out occasionally, disappearing from the map only to reappear a few moments later.

"It's close ... only a kilometer south." The cyborg pondered for a moment, mulling over the temptation. "Will reaching the source of the signal use a significant amount of energy from the battery?"

"Not significantly."

A warm giddiness filled CJ with excitement. It was a feeling he hadn't known for some time. "Let's check it out!"

At that moment, the ground shifted, jolting the sub backward. CJ was flung against the control panel, barely catching himself in time to watch the seabed outside heave and crack apart. His circuits froze in terror as the ground bulged before him. Another earthquake? No, not now! But then he saw the truth of it. The fleshy stalks that CJ had assumed were anchor worms, the things he'd been shining the sub's bright headlights on for the past several minutes, revealed themselves to merely be eye stalks of something that had been buried underneath. Rising like a mountain from the ground, covered in dark chiton and overgrown with barnacles, arose a gargantuan crustacean unlike anything CJ had ever seen.

The AI, sensing the paralyzing awe in the cyborg's thoughts, took it upon itself to commence preservation protocols. *"Buoyancy reinitiated, revving engines for departure!"* It turned the sub around, pointing it away from the ruins and toward the open ocean.

"Where are you taking me?" CJ asked, coming to his senses.

"Home!"

"That signal is still back there! We need to find what it is!"

The AI responded with a tone that almost sounded impatient. *"That is not recommended!"*

"I'm not leaving until we see what's back there!" With a firm thought, CJ pushed away the AI's command to retreat and forced his own will upon the sub. He started by overriding the AI's control of the propulsion system, turning the sub back around and then revved the engine to full speed.

"What are you doing?"

"Just be quiet and watch!"

CJ blasted the sub forward toward the ruins, toward the crab. The creature snapped its mandibles angrily and raised a claw to catch the tiny craft. CJ held tight to the console as he commanded the sub to jerk to the right, darting around the creature's reach. He spotted a building, it's wide hollow window just big enough for the craft to fit through. CJ focused and shot the sub through the window, threading the needle in one side and out the other.

Feeling a sense of vindication, the cyborg amplified it just to make sure the AI could sense it. "You see. Nothing to worry about."

Then there came a thunderous boom that rippled out like an explosion, rattling CJ in his seat. Behind them, the creature swung a chitinous claw, swiping at the top of the building they'd just sped through, sundering tons of stone and metal. Alarms from the AI's sensors rang inside CJ's mind, blaring and howling as they turned his entire vision bright with flashes of red.

"Incoming! Incoming!"

Chunks of metal and cement struck them in the rear like shrapnel, pummeling the hull with terrifyingly loud pings and bangs. The cyborg focused, pushing out the noise of the alarms and the AI's persistent warnings, so he could be undistracted from piloting. There was a loud snap from the rear. The damaged propeller had fallen off. CJ spun the sub in a barrel roll and pushed harder with his will, cranking up the speed of the remaining propellers to the max. Soon they cleared the field of falling debris, and a sense of tentative calm started to set in.

"That was reckless," the AI chastised.

CJ had no response. Maybe it had been a little reckless, but he hoped whatever he was looking for was worth it. He called up the battery display again. Twenty-six percent. It was less than he expected, but he nodded to himself. It was what it was. He figured he'd find out soon enough what this gamble was for.

CJ drew up the map of his surroundings again. The crab was a massive yellow blip, slowly following behind him, until finally, it stopped and fell out of range. Then the cyborg noticed the green blip, or the lack thereof. The prize he'd turned around to find, was gone. He slowed the sub's speed and expanded the range of his scan. Where was it? Where had the green blip gone?

Then, as the distant clicking and gurgling of the crab echoed out behind them, CJ saw it. It was a flickering weakly, but he saw it. He adjusted his course and closed in. The signal led him into the half-buried interior of a concrete building in the heart of the ruined city. What function it had served in the past was impossible to tell. Most of its plaster had been washed away, leaving behind a rugged surface with lines of rusted rebar sticking out like bones of a rotting corpse.

"We've arrived," the AI said, lacking enthusiasm.

The cyborg searched the ruin until they came to a corner of the building where sea moss coated the pile of stones in green fur. CJ activated the mechanical probing arms, extending them from the sub's underbelly, and started to pull away the heavy debris one chunk at a time. After a while, a bit of worry crossed CJ's circuits. He was wasting energy he couldn't afford. He checked. Twenty-four percent.

"At this rate, we will not have enough battery life to propel back to base. Not even on low output."

CJ furrowed his holographic brow. The AI was right, but there was no point in stopping now. He yanked hard with the sub's arms and pulled back a huge slab of concrete, as he did, something gleamed underneath. Pulling back the final bits of rock, CJ uncovered what looked like a giant pillbox coated in shimmering mother of pearl.

If he'd had lungs, he would have gasped. "Do you know what this is?"

"I do not have enough data to confirm."

"This ... this is a life case!" CJ remembered how the prospect of these things were in vogue back in the years leading up to the war. It was never confirmed that any working prototypes ever actually existed, though, only failed test models. "Tell me, do you get a reading of what's inside?"

"*Negative.*"

"Of course you can't! The shell is designed to block everything from radio waves to gamma rays. It's airtight and nigh shatter-proof. It's designed to create an impervious and self-sustaining environment for the user inside. Do you get what I'm saying?"

"*You found a powerfully shiny suitcase.*"

"There might be a *human* inside! An actual human!" CJ's mind was starting to race with thoughts, but he slowed it down just enough to issue more mental commands to the AI, telling it to prepare the airlock in the back of the sub and load the capsule. The AI took over the submarine's arms, gently lifting the silvery capsule from the rubble and pulling it back into the sub's loading bay. There was a hiss as water drained away from the other side of the wall behind CJ's chair. When he heard the signal chime announcing the water was fully drained, CJ commanded the sub to open the door behind him before he unplugged his neural link. He spun his chair around and waited for the door to open. There was a loud click as the locks unlatched, sliding open in three parts.

Still in his chair, CJ leaned forward to reach into the small loading bay. He slid his chrome hands over the shimmering surface of the case, examining the sides, looking for some way to open the smooth box. Finally, his fingers felt something along the side, a small panel displaying vital signs, including a pair of little lines that rose and fell ever so slightly between long intervals.

CJ's holographic eyes widened in overwhelming awe. Two heartbeats? Two minds? Eager anticipation tickled his neural network again, jumping like sparks in his mind, and he put a finger on the unlock button. There was a click and a hiss as the atmosphere inside the casket fled out, cold and white with mist.

Carefully, the cyborg lifted the lid to find two young humans curled in fetal positions, facing either side of the casket, no older than ten. Their chocolate brown cheeks and kinky close-cropped hair were tinged with white frost. They laid still and silent, their chests barely rising and falling as they breathed incredibly slowly. Naked as they were, CJ noticed one was male and one was female. This was greater than any mind bank a cyborg could have ever hoped to find.

"I have to admit," the AI started, *"I had not suspected this."*

CJ reached out a hand to touch one of the children's cheeks, but the AI stopped him.

"Don't disturb them. Their bodies are still too cold, and their minds are too deep in sleep. If he woke them now, they'd likely go into shock. Additionally, there is not enough air in the sub for them to breathe long."

The cyborg nodded. "Of course. How could I forget?"

He knew how. Corrupted data.

Something else, CJ noticed, was in the case with the kids. A small USB storage of some kind. He picked up and examined the old design, wondering if he could even interface with it. He spun his chair back around and tried inserting it into the docking port. To his surprise, it fit.

"There is one audio file on this device. Shall I play it?"

"Yes."

A woman's voice suddenly replaced the AI's, the first human voice CJ had heard in over a thousand years. *"I do not know if anyone will find this message. I cannot predict what will happen next. Everyone speaks of coming war, of the end times. They might be right. But this case can save my angels. If you've found them, I beg of you, take care of them, and tell them that their mother loves them."*

"Pod?" CJ said.

"Yes?" the AI said.

"We do not have enough battery life to get back, do we?"

"No."

CJ clenched his fists and stared at his reflection in the viewport, staring at his black carbon-fiber face overlaid with green holographic eyes, eyebrows, and mouth. His excitement was gone, now he only felt the tight pain of failure. Then, from the pits of his despair, an idea came. "What if we ride the currents, will that help?"

"The nearest east-west current is the South Equatorial Stream. However, reaching it will take us off course by several hundred kilometers. That path is risky."

"We have to try, Pod! Chart a course for it, and let's get going."

"Understood."

CJ spun back around to give the sleeping kids one last look and closed the case. Then he linked up with the sub's console once more and watched the battery life in his mind's eye. Twenty-one percent.

By the time the sub reached the underwater current, despite their low output, the battery was at eighteen percent and steadily declining. CJ listened to the low hum of the ship's propellers, wondering if there was anything he could do to slow the battery's drain.

He told the sub to turn off all lights, so it did, and CJ sat in darkness. Hours went by and still, the battery continued to drain. Seventeen percent.

He told the sub to slow down, so it did, but the sub started to drift off course and needed to right itself. Eleven percent.

He told the ship to shut off all non-vital systems. The AI complied, and suddenly, almost all of the information CJ could see through his neural link was cut off, reduced to simple information readings and crude shapes. The battery display was now a simple yellow rectangle. It shrank just a bit and turned red. Nine percent.

Finally, he told the AI to shut itself down. It did, and CJ was left alone in silence. Four percent.

CJ brought up the map. It was simple now, with blocky polygons replacing what had been detailed continents. His red dot, which was more a square now, moved between Brazil and some small islands. They'd finally entered the Caribbean Sea. They were so close. One percent.

Above him, CJ heard the muffled growls of distant thunder. Another storm … that was the last thing he needed. The currents would push him off course, and if that happened now he wouldn't be able to get back. His synthetic heart sank a bit in his chest as he realized his only option. He didn't want to do it, not again, his memories were fragile enough as they were, but it was what it was. He looked back at the life case, seeing the faint-green glow of its vital displays, the only indication of the case's presence in the pitch blackness of the sub. CJ imagined all the new memories those two souls would make. It was a fair trade. He connected to the sub and switched the AI back on.

"Hello, CJ-1844! This is Submersible Exploration Pod-136 at your serv—!"

"Listen, Pod," CJ started, stopping short the AI's programed salutation with a thought. "I don't have much time. The sub's battery will be dead in a few minutes, maybe less now that you're back online, so here's what we're going to do. There's a storm coming, and we need to outrun it, full speed, no stopping, you understand. So, I'm going to transfer my energy reserves. It should be more than enough to get you back to base."

The AI was slow to answer. Whether that was because of the lack of energy or hesitancy, CJ couldn't tell. *"Cybernetic shutdown will result from transferring your full energy reserves, and that runs the risk of memory corruption. Are you sure you want to do this? The structural integrity of your neural matrix is only—"*

"I'm sure," CJ said with a nod. "My last order is for you to get these kids safely to Maroon-0. Understood?"

"Understood. Are you ready to initiate energy transfer? You should commence safety shut down now, just to be sure."

"Alright, Pod. I'm trusting you."

"Understood. Initiating energy transfer."

CJ closed his eyes and held onto the memory of those sleeping kids, seeing them clear as a photograph in his mind's eye, hoping that if nothing else, he'd remember their faces when they booted him back up.

Then, in a flash, the world went black.

MAKE A MEMORY WITH ME

by Xan van Rooyen

This time I'll remember, Danny thought as the bot's proboscis unrolled—more scorpion tail than butterfly tongue. The memory-taker's appendage skewered Danny at the temple, fitting into the port hidden beneath a flop of brown curls. Danny's hair had been left long on that side of zir otherwise shaved head. Ze didn't remember getting the ink that glowed under UV light, pricked in intricate lacework across zir baldness. A memory made to order, perhaps? Or something of zir own choosing, extracted for others who sought the experience of a tattoo without the pain or commitment?

The memory-taker shifted closer, a chitinous scuttle of articulated limbs. It raised a humanlike hand and its four digits, obscenely long, cradled Danny's jaw. The bot's equivalent of a palm was warm—a design feature meant to soothe, yet made Danny shudder as ze leaned into the titanium and silicon touch. It was the gentlest touch ze'd had all month, maybe all year—at least, that ze could remember.

There was the catalog Danny could reference, of course, attached to zir personal profile, listing every extracted memory, condensing zir life experiences into abbreviated loglines tagged with an emotion. Additional details could be accessed by expanding the entry.

Chocolate gelato, joy, one entry read. Danny imagined a hot summer's day, cicadas screaming, kids playing in a park fountain, grass itching the back of zir legs. According to the entry, it had been September in a coffee shop.

A faint thrum began at the base of Danny's skull like the echo of a night spent head-banging to too loud music—a tinnitus of the bones—and Danny knew it was starting. Yet another piece of self whittled away from the whole.

Danny was never sure exactly which memories would be taken in any given extraction, even the ones ze'd made to order. Perhaps today ze'd lose *skinny dipping in the sea* or *eating funnel cake at the boardwalk fair*. They seemed so banal, hardly anything grandiose or dangerous—this time—but perhaps the person who'd put in the order couldn't swim or was bedridden and would never get to see another fair. Maybe this slow-motion fracture was a small price to pay for helping others live a little.

Danny was only twenty-six. Ze still had zir entire life to fill up any cavities left in the wake of mental excavations. So what if all Danny's life-defining milestones had been eroded, bits and pieces sold off in slivers and flakes. Ze had little left of their childhood—not a great loss according to the catalog full of fear and anger—and couldn't remember zir first kiss or if ze'd ever been in love. A few morning-afters lingered unwanted—the boring kind made up of awkwardly groping for clothes while concocting excuses to leave before breakfast and false promises to text later.

Danny's life had been rendered a patchwork of dullness; lackluster moments cobbled together to form a self-portrait ze no longer recognized. Hadn't that been the entire point?

Now, Danny stared straight ahead, zir gaze on the screen recessed in the wall as it scrolled through step-by-step instructions. *Breathe*, it said, and Danny did, inhaling the chemical scent of calming vapors wafting through the vents. The experience was sold as catharsis, and it had started out that way when Danny first walked through the revolving doors of RecollectUs, there to be rid of trauma and heartache, to slough off zir past like dirty clothes and find solace in being undone.

Danny'd come to this panopticon of steel and glass to relinquish a memory of zir own free will. That last part was important, or so said the fine print on the RecollectUs contract Danny had signed three years ago, back when ze was whole and still in possession of entries like *Childhood trauma one, fear* and *Attempted suicide, anguish*. Those were gone now, and Danny didn't miss them. Good riddance to the detritus of a shitty life. Let all that litter someone else's mind.

Not that any of it mattered anymore. That life belonged to a previous iteration of zirself, a stranger Danny couldn't relate to anymore. The Danny here now let the past skitter away like beads off a broken string even as ze made a game of trying to catch them.

The sticky slick of brine against zir skin. The sickly sweet sugar on zir tongue.

Danny tried to hold onto both memories as the probe drilled deeper, finally making contact with the chip crouched like an aphid on Danny's brain, slurping up every moment both awake and sleeping.

Dreams could be sold too, but they were in less demand. Some memory-makers took psychedelics to fuel more chaotic, desirable dreams, sold to buy the drugs to continue the cycle in a dizzying Möbius strip.

Danny didn't do drugs. Not anymore. Ze'd damaged too many memories that way, their edges blurring and contents splintering like peanut shells beneath drunken heels. Memories like that wouldn't pay the rent.

Relax, the screen instructed. *Try not to think of anything specific or hold onto any particular memory. Fighting the process risks corrupting—*

For a moment, Danny clung to the memories flitting across zir mind like flies about a carcass, determined to hold onto even the slimmest sliver. Zir efforts sent bolts of pain into the backs of zir eyes. Defeated as usual, Danny let zir gaze drift away from the words on the screen and, instead, glanced across the circular clinic to a dozen other cubicles where memories were being siphoned.

On the floor above, the cubicles were larger and there the patients lay on gurneys, their heads cradled in robotic hands, phalanges extended like a cage over the sleeper. Each finger was a tether, injecting instead of sucking. And down each of those throbbing umbilici, memories flowed—memories from donors like Danny.

Donor was a misnomer. This was a transaction like any other in this city where there was a clinic trading in every scrap a human had to shed.

Memories were worth more, packaged up for consumption for those who wanted to know what being stabbed felt like without the inconvenience of internal bleeding, to flirt with degradation from the comfort of their penthouse, or perhaps screw a stranger without the blemish of *real* adultery ever staining their skin. Some claimed altruistic intentions, buying into the company's marketing.

A way to build empathy, RecollectUs touted. *To slip into another's shoes.*

To slip inside their skin, their mind, their soul. But the soul was an antiquated notion these days and Danny swallowed bitter laughter.

As an undergrad, Danny had gone private for a while, working for an author collective back when "write what you know" made aspiring storytellers greedy for different life experiences. Danny didn't remember much of the six months under contract, of course, but the descriptions of the extractions in the catalog explained several of the scars bleached into zir skin, the ghost touches of another life.

Despite zir metastasizing debt, Danny had let that contract expire amid turbulent debate on the ethics of such practices, returning to the more acceptable public service system where experiences requested couldn't break the law or put the memory-maker at risk of grievous bodily harm.

If that grew dull, or no longer financially rewarding enough, there was always the black market where those with the means could buy any experience they desired—no request considered too extreme.

The text flickered, drawing Danny's attention back to the screen. *Congratulations on a successful extraction!* it announced.

The memory-taker's proboscis withdrew, sliding back into a narrow slit of a mouth. It wore a disturbing facsimile of a smile on its molded face as the final wad of text burned across the screen.

Resist the urge to try and remember. Trying to recall a memory already harvested—

Danny closed zir eyes, hoping to catch an echo of what was taken. Ze licked zir lips as if some taste of those stolen moments might've lingered, but only found chapped skin.

Danny left RecollectUs feeling as "unburdened" as an empty letterbox, zir mind threshed and aching with the usual discomfort an extraction caused.

Outside, the city seethed beneath a late summer downpour, tamping down the usual bouquet of fried food, biodiesel, and ripe garbage. Danny lingered under the eaves to check zir phone. The money had been transferred, the red exclamation marks of outstanding bills blinking into reassuring black as automatic payments were confirmed. Danny watched the digits dwindle, whipped away as easily as zir memories, and frowned.

Ze groped at the tapestry of zirself, a spider checking the threads of their web and spinning new silk across any damage. It was getting harder to pick up dropped stitches and suture closed the wounds. Still, ze'd have to up zir game and take on more challenging requests if ze wanted more disposable income.

Danny flinched involuntarily as another body joined zir in the narrow strip of protection from the rain.

"Feels good to shed some mental weight," the person said, voice hoarse between puffs on a cigalike that smelled of cherries. "You figure out what they took?"

"You're supposed to let it go." Danny threw a cautious glance at the stranger. They were a foot taller and almost a decade younger; slender too, their long limbs folded in black despite the humidity, in stark contrast to Danny's mottled, flowing pastels.

They smirked and ran a hand through their hair, the roots showing blond against midnight blue.

"First time?" Danny asked because ze didn't fancy getting wet and standing in silence felt weird.

"No, third. Maybe fourth. Can't believe how expensive living in the city is. My internship doesn't pay nearly enough. You a veteran?"

"Does it show?" Danny asked, only half in jest. Ze avoided mirrors these days, afraid of the vacant face ze might find staring back.

"You know how in the olden days they carved faces into pumpkins? Guess some people still do actually."

Danny frowned, tracing zir thumb along a thin scar on zir right index finger. Ze reached, remembering candied apples, cinnamon, tasting almost familiar words of a three-syllable chant like treacle on the back of zir tongue. But these ghosts of another life were merely a trick of the brain. The memory was gone.

"Jack o' lanterns," the stranger continued. "That's what you remind me of. The ones who come here a lot, I mean. Like you're still a pumpkin but all the seeds and stuff have been scraped—"

"I get it," Danny said before the image could burn a hole through zir already tattered mind.

Silence. Sticky as gum on a hot sidewalk. This, a moment Danny would undoubtedly never be rid of. Who would want it?

31

"Sorry, that was mean," the stranger said. "Let me make it up to you?"

Danny raised a skeptical eyebrow. Not that ze had any plans for the rest of the day, except to go home to the stifling studio ze had now procured for another month and scroll through the *wanted* ads on the RecollectUs site.

"You don't remember me," the stranger said.

Danny riffled through zir Swiss-cheese memory. "No."

"We've worked the catalog together." They gestured to the ink on Danny's head then tapped their temple, their port ringed by a cluster of micro-dermals.

"I'm sorry." The apology was soaked in the vinegar of regret and stung zir lips.

"Don't be."

The rain hammered the sidewalk, and Danny's heart pounded zir ribs, insides reverberating—hollow, except for fading echoes.

"Let's do something." The stranger extinguished the cigalike.

"What?"

"Does it matter?" The stranger asked with a quirk of their pretty mouth. "Good or bad, we'll probably only keep this day for like a month, right?" They tapped their forehead where their port was ringed in a cluster of micro-dermals, each seeded with a jewel matching the amber of their eyes.

Danny opened zir mouth, about to decline, then hesitated. The thought of creating an organic memory for once, not curated off a list, felt thrilling to contemplate.

"Come on, give me a chance."

"I usually work off the list," Danny said, when ze found time between grad school and zir part-time job working maintenance on housebots.

"*Pff,* boring. Bet we could make something spontaneous someone'll pay loads for." They offered their hand, brown fingers crusted in silver rings. "Come make another memory with me."

Tentatively, Danny placed zir hand in the waiting palm, and the stranger dragged both of them into the rain with a *whoop!* They pulled Danny into a slow-but-playful dance, their combined laughter mingling with the delicate chimes of raindrops on glass windows and metal trash cans; a symphony of their own making. They stepped on each other's feet, dirty water soaking shins and knees as rain washed unexpected tears from Danny's cheeks. Together, they slipped in one puddle after another as they revolved around an asphalt dancefloor.

And the dangling threads of Danny's soul reached like anemone fronds toward the promise of something new, something ze'd never want to lose.

DESTINY DELAYED

by Oghenechovwe Donald Ekpeki

Mr. Mukoro was sitting at the front of his veranda at about 5:30 a.m. The faint glint of early dawn revealed the figure passing his frontage. It was Chinedu Okah, and he stopped to greet.

"Bros, how you dey? You're up early oh."

"No," Mr. Mukoro replied. "I'm down late."

"Working on your research?"

"No. Working on an old project, approaching a breakthrough. I need funds to finish it, but I'm trying to find a way to finish it without the funds."

"It would be a real breakthrough if you can finish your project without funds … . Finish your project, abolish capitalism, and change the world to make life good for us all!"

Mukoro was amused in spite of himself.

"I have to be off early to escape traffic," Chinedu said. "I'm going to head office on the Island."

"Have you been transferred?"

"I hope so. Or at least, it should be promotion."

"That's some news," Mukoro said, standing up to give Chinedu a handshake.

"When you return, we'll drink to it."

"Of course. That's if you aren't too busy with your project."

35

Mukoro laughed gently. "Go come, brother."

"Greet Madam and Nyerhovwo for me," Chinedo said as he departed.

A moment later, a slim, dark Itsekiri woman stepped out with a seven-year-old girl, still groggy with sleep. The girl saw Mukoro and ran to hug him. "Daddy miguo."

"Vrendo, my child."

The woman curtsied. "Miguo papa Nyerhovwo."

"Vrendo mama Nyerhovwo," he said with a smile.

She smiled back, smacking the child's butt playfully, and pulling her from playing with her father's beard, which she held on to. He screamed in mock pain, and she giggled as she was pulled away. The child slipped out of her mother's grip and ran back to him.

"Oghenenyerhovwo," her mom called sternly. "Come and bathe now, or you will be late for school, and they will flog you when you get there."

The little girl looked at her father askance. He nodded. She kissed the cheek he turned for her and returned grudgingly to her mother who dragged her to the corner of the house.

Mukoro sighed and closed his eyes, and the numbers and equations came unbidden to him as they usually did.

Chinedu Okah alighted from the Keke Napep that dropped him at a side street and walked a few steps to the head office of AUB, the Africa United Bank. He blended in with the top bankers and persons in the finance sector, his crisp blue suit and starched white shirt making him look as sharp as the drawn blade of a Mushin gangster intent on robbing someone at two in the morning.

He was glad to be here. He was glad to have left the position of cashier, handling the grubby notes of traders and students at the Yaba branch of AUB, and marketer briefly thereafter.

He approached the nearest help desk and presented his ID, informing the attendant that he had an appointment with Mr. Abiola Yusuf of Human Resources. She placed a call before signaling him to wait, for Mr. Yusuf was in a meeting. This early? Chinedu wondered. Well, he would wait. He had been waiting a long while after all: three years as a contract staff, and six years at the Yaba AUB branch. He was led to the waiting room to do what it was named after.

Finally, Mr. Yusuf walked in and shook his hand.

"Good morning, sir," Chinedu said, surprised to see Mr. Yusuf sporting a blue Kaftan on a Monday morning. In Yaba branch, even the branch manager didn't wear native dress unless it was Friday. But this was head office. He guessed when one was this close to the top, one did what one wanted.

"Mr. Chinedu Okah, is it?" Mr. Yusuf asked in a Hausa accent.

"Yes, sir."

"Walk with me."

Chinedu followed him out of the waiting room to an elevator. Mr. Yusuf punched in the thirteenth floor and spoke to him as the elevator rose.

"You read the e-brochure, right? So you know what we do here."

"Yes, sir."

"Well, I want to give you a few pointers and show you around, so you see and understand a bit more of what we do in this department."

They came out of the elevator and walked down a hallway.

"You were the most active marketer in the Yaba branch," Mr. Yusuf continued. "Only the best get recommended here. Your record is stellar. They say you pulled in six billion naira in six months, a billion per month." Mr. Yusuf stared at Chinedu and nodded. He seemed to like what he saw in Chinedu's eyes. "Well, now you will be helping us with something more than money."

They stopped in front of a large department marked UBD at the top of the entranceway. United Bank of Destiny.

Chinedu could hardly believe himself when he was ushered into the UBD. Although he had read the brochure, he wasn't sure if he was being pranked.

"This is the measurement and extraction room," Mr. Yusuf explained. "This is where a destiny is mapped, measured, and extracted."

A procedure was in progress. A young man was standing in front of a machine that looked like an X-ray machine. Mr. Yusuf waved to the technicians in lab coats, gloves, coveralls, and goggles.

The technicians switched on the Destiny machine, and it emitted a whirring noise. There were a number of wires connected to the machine, which in turn were connected to screens round the room. The machine's whirring turned louder, and the air rippled in front of and behind the young man. The air took on a dark gray hue. The hue turned from dark gray to purple and then to gray again. Then the air stopped whirling, and one of the technicians switched off the Destiny machine.

"The screens do the soul reading, and the vibrancy of the colors displays the intensity of the destiny," Mr. Yusuf said, turning to Chinedu, who still stared at the operation and the operators. "The process measures the capacity of a man's destiny. The destiny is then extracted by the machine and stored in a soul cube."

As the young man was led away to put on his clothes, Chinedu noticed that his eyes looked dead, and his face was bleached of color.

Mr. Yusuf led Chinedu to another room marked Acquisitions and Mortgages.

"This will be your office. The destinies you determine and measure will be extracted and kept as collateral for their loans. Your job will be much like the old one as a marketer at the Yaba branch. But this time, you'll market young people who want loans but who have no property for collateral. You'll convince them to use their destinies as collateral. It's a way for us to be of service to the needy. Think of it as an empowerment scheme, to help those who would otherwise not be able to get the funds they need. It's like student loans in America. This is, of course, a very sensitive department. You will see our lawyers to sign a nondisclosure agreement. That's fine with you, of course?"

"Yes, sir," Chinedu smiled knowingly. The monthly salary here was more than he earned in a year at Yaba Branch. In no time he could clear all his loans, even get a car. And moving to the Island would be possible.

Mr. Abiola's voice snapped Chinedu out of his reverie. "I read your dossier and knew that an overachiever like yourself would definitely be up for the job. Otherwise, we would have had you sign the nondisclosure even before you came in here. But I like to think I am a good judge of people. Or I wouldn't be head of HR."

Mr. Yusuf chuckled, and Chinedu chuckled politely in return. Mr. Yusuf kept walking and talking.

"Discretion is very important to what we do here. Not that it's illegal. The young men and women who come for loans all consent to have their destinies extracted and kept as collateral. Not that there is anything in the law about this, nor can the law make sense of it. We just don't want the uproar it would cause if uninformed ears got to know of what we do here. You know Nigerians are superstitious. They won't understand that we just want to help people."

Mr. Yusuf led Chinedu to an office in the Mortgages and Acquisitions department. It was well furnished with a sofa for visitors, and a Surface Book on an expensive looking mahogany desk. "This will be your office," Mr. Yusuf said, gesticulating.

Chinedu was breathtaken by the office. It was three times larger than his branch manager's office at Yaba. Mr. Yusuf chuckled at his incredulity. Just then, a man in a purple suit walked in carrying a briefcase. Mr. Yusuf touched Chinedu on the shoulder.

"The lawyer is here. I'll leave you both so you can get started in earnest. It's a new week, and you already have your quota." Chinedu nodded.

"I stuck my neck out for you," Mr. Yusuf said as he stepped out. "There were dozens recommended for this post. All with stellar records. But I picked you. Like I said, I have a head for people. Don't disappoint me."

Chinedu assured Mr. Yusuf he wouldn't be a disappointment. "I'll have my first catch for you this week," he said. "I know just the person."

Mr. Yusuf nodded. "I knew you were the man for us."

He patted Chinedu, who bowed before returning to the lawyer. Mr. Yusuf whistled as he left.

Mukoro and Chinedu sat drinking at a beer parlor at Montgomery, Yaba. Bottles of Alomo, Guilder, and small stout littered their table. Hunched over, they discussed dreams and ambitions, as fermented as the leftover alcohol in their bottles. They were seeking ways to escape the penury that clung to them, like paint on the wall, ever fading, but never quite gone. It clutched them with the tenacity of a wounded soldier behind Boko Haram lines, far from home, but unwilling to leave this world without a goodbye to his family.

"So, I let them extract her destiny as collateral for a loan of any amount I want?" Mukoro was asking.

"Not 'any' amount, but an amount not exceeding eight figures in naira. And that's after reading her destiny to ascertain its worth."

Mukoro rubbed his beard. "I see," he said thoughtfully.

Chinedu looked at him with shrewd eyes that retained their sharpness despite the numerous bottles of alcohol they had consumed. "You don't seem overly surprised by any of this?"

Mukoro shook his head. "I studied systems engineering, and my PhD was in soul mapping and interaction with spirit particles." He glanced at Chinedu before adding, "What do you think my research and projects are all about? You could say destiny led us here."

Mukoro leaned forward and continued. "My grandfather was a great Jazzman in his time. He was blind but could see more clearly than those with two eyes. He could uncannily put together pieces of the unformed future. You know, that is what they do when they map the soul and read a person's destiny. The device they call a soultrifier can map what we now call spirit particles, or what the rest of the world knows of as dark matter. The soultrifier is built to calculate the propensity of the soul, like a sort of advanced probability. If you want to simplify it, you can say it's a combination of very advanced possibility tied to your DNA structure and other things we don't yet understand. Kind of like how we know a fit person might go into sports, or a lonely person into arts or literature. The soultractor is the real breakthrough. It finds a way to extract the unique strands of each person's propensity and store it in a soul cube."

Mr. Mukoro stopped talking to take a pull of his beer. Chinedu called for a waiter.

"Two more bottles of big stout." When the waiter departed, Chinedu turned to Mukoro and asked, "So what does all this have to do with your grandfather?"

"Oh yes. I got caught up in explaining about the process and my work. I love to talk about my work with those who can listen. Anyway. My grandfather prophesied that I would give my child a great destiny. This was before my first degree, when I didn't know anything about this. He used the word 'destiny,' in English. Even though he wasn't educated or spoke any language other than Urhobo."

Mukoro's eyes became distant, as if he could stare across time to the event of the prophecy's utterance. "My grandfather had never been wrong in such utterances before. I don't think this one will be wrong, either. That is why I'm so focused on my research. I want to leave a legacy for my child. I want to ensure she gets that promised destiny. This is for her, you understand? It's my destiny to grant her a great destiny.

I must bequeath her more than was bequeathed on me. But I cannot do much as it is. It seems destiny cannot be realized without funds. I can't even get a reasonable job with my PhD, much less funding for my research. I can't apply for foreign grants with a project like this. It has only made headway here because of our combination of science and spirituality. It took the work of the council of Dibias, Babalawos, and scientists to discern how to interact with the spirit particles. So I can't get funds from outside, as they would not think much of a project like this. But if I can get the loan from your bank to finish my research, I can leave something for Nyerhovwo, and fulfill my destiny to gift her a great destiny."

"I see," Chinedu said. "Not that I wish to make you question this, since it's my job to get people to take loans. But you are also my friend. Isn't the loan unnecessary? The breakthrough has been done already and monetized. Of what use is your research?"

Mukoro laughed until tears trickled from his eyes, and he wiped them. "You should know that no research is ever finished. All the technology we have is still being improved on. And this is a new area. There's still a lot more to discover."

Chinedu smiled. "So I'll see you at the office tomorrow, then?"

"Yes. You said extracting the destiny doesn't hurt?"

"Yes, it doesn't hurt. It's just a net weight of probabilities and the person's propensity to achieve a thing. In the same way that being paralyzed doesn't kill."

"I know. I just want to confirm. And the destiny will be kept intact, returned and reintegrated with the source?"

"Of course, it will be returned and reintegrated once the loan is fully paid, along with interest."

"And it's legal for parents to take a loan with the destiny of a child, a minor?"

"Yes, although it's a legal gray area, as the law doesn't recognize the procedure yet. But the law is still catching up, so you have nothing to worry about. You cannot sin where there is no law. Parents and legal guardians can consent on behalf of their children. It's like taking your child for a bone marrow transplant."

"I'll talk to my wife about it tonight," Mukoro said, and frowned as if he hadn't been reassured by the idea that what he was doing wasn't a sin, even if he wouldn't be held responsible.

Chinedu noticed the look on his face. "Remember you are doing this for her. And to fulfill your grandfather's prophecy."

"I know." Mukoro nodded.

Chinedu poured his remaining drink from the bottle and ordered three more bottles for Mukoro.

Mukoro thanked him, took another long pull, then asked, "Nothing more for you?"

"Naaah, I'm all right for now," Chinedu said. "I have to rise early for work tomorrow. I have to wake up by four and leave before five to beat Island traffic."

Mukoro rose to shake Chinedu's hand and see him off. "All right, good night."

"Don't forget to talk to madam about it this night," Chinedu called as he left.

Mukoro returned to his drink, his somber thoughts rising vampirelike, despite his efforts to bury them in ethanol.

That night, Mukoro cuddled his wife, Bianca. She snuggled into his arm.

"Was she asleep before you left her?" she asked.

"Yes. Her love for that story never stops her from falling asleep before the end." He chuckled, remembering his daughter's droopy eyelids closing as he read to her.

Bianca shook her head. "She'll only ever fall asleep when it's you reading. When I read to her, she stares at me with glittering eyes till the story is done. She trusts you."

Mukoro was silent, knowing where the talk was headed.

"I heard all you said before. I need to know that I can trust you to do right by her."

Mukoro sighed. "She's my daughter, too. And I love her. You know that."

"I know. You have been a good father to her." She paused a moment, then asked. "You say this mortgage of destiny won't hurt her?"

"No, it won't hurt her," he said. "The process doesn't hurt, it only dulls one's chances. It is a destiny, after all. I can't use mine because I need to be sharp to use the funds. And it can't be you either," he added, forestalling the question he knew she wanted to ask. "They won't take a middle-aged housewife's destiny. I know, sexist, but that's how it is. It has to be hers. As it is, what future does she have here?"

He waved at the dilapidated structure in which they lived. "Things aren't like in my time when education was government subsidized. Since the monetization of schooling, the university is beyond our reach. They say education is the future. And we can't afford to pay for a college degree. So what's a destiny without a future? This is for her." Then he whispered, "And for them." He looked at his wife's stomach.

She turned to face him. "What do you mean by 'them,' papa Nyerhovwo?"

"Do you think I don't know you're pregnant?" He cupped her cheek gently. "I have known since you stopped asking for money for pads two months ago."

"I should have known that would give it away," she said. "I was just relieved to save you the expense."

"Well, there will be other expenses. And my on-and-off consulting job can't help us. I need to do this for them." He held her hands. "Let me save this family with this loan. With her help, I'll secure a future for her and her brother. But once I finish my project and have a bit of stability, I'll repay the loan. Then we can ensure a great destiny for them."

Bianca was quiet for a while, then said, "Or sister."

He smiled and kissed her. "But we already have a girl."

"Well, boys are trouble."

"Good trouble."

"Like you, huh?" She jabbed him in the ribs.

He laughed. "I have to leave with her early in the morning to beat traffic. And you have to take permission for her absence to her school. So should we sleep now?" he asked with a slanted eyebrow.

"Did you also learn how to be so subtle at your PhD program?" she asked, pulling her shirt off, mounting him and kissing him deeply.

"I mean, it's not like you can get pregnant again," he said.

She leaned back, letting the sounds of joy that flittered from her and bounced off the walls, bring a little blue to the cold yellow of the room.

···❖···

43

3 years and 8 months later ...

A Black Range Rover and a white 4matic Benz parked in front of a Chinese restaurant in Awolowo Road, Ikoyi. Mukoro climbed out of the Range Rover while Chinedu climbed out of the 4matic.

They shook hands and were about to go into the eatery when Chinedu tapped Mukoro and said, "Let's talk in the car first. I have some sensitive information."

Mukoro nodded and opened the door of the Range Rover, and they both stepped in and closed the door. The AC was running.

Mr. Mukoro spoke first. "There's something wrong. The loan defaults in seven months, isn't it?"

Chinedu nodded.

"I don't understand why I'm unable to clear the interest, try as I might? There's always something left, and the loan itself never goes down."

Chinedu shrugged and said, "But you seem to be doing well."

"Which isn't the point," Mukoro cut in harshly. "You know I want to clear the loan and recover something else more than money. Nyerhovwo is in secondary school and just wrote her Junior WAEC examination. In another three years, she will be looking at attending the university."

"You have the funds for that, don't you? And enough for Oghenemudia too, for that matter. How is he, by the way? And Madam?"

"They are fine," Mukoro said perfunctorily, dismissing the question. "I'm not talking about any of that. I'm talking about Nyerhovwo. Her teachers report that she lacks interest in everything, even though her grades are middling and fine. And her eyes are always dead."

Chinedu's brows creased momentarily. Mukoro would not have noticed if he had not been watching for it.

"You know something of this, don't you? And why my businesses seem to be doing well but never well enough to clear the loan?"

"I don't ..." Chinedu began.

Mukoro cut him off. "No, no, don't do that, please."

Chinedu sighed and looked Mukoro in the eyes before he began. "I turned a blind eye to a lot of things when I started, because I needed the money and the upgrade. But the truth is, I always knew something was off. The way I was chosen, the department, my handler. But I was hungry, and they knew it. Too hungry to ask questions, too hungry to

44

think, or choose to do the right thing. Head of HR truly was a good judge of people. I think I'm basically a devil in a suit, sent to tempt the vulnerable for their destinies. I get the low and the desperate like myself and yourself."

"The destinies," Mukoro said, returning to the subject he desperately needed to discuss.

"They were never going to be given back," Chinedu said. "Your businesses are monitored and sabotaged. Not enough for you to notice, but enough so you can't repay the loan on time, and the destinies become theirs. They are sold at ungodly amounts to powerful men who take them for themselves to enhance their chances at success, or gift them to their families. That's why the rich and powerful in Nigeria are becoming richer and more powerful."

Mukoro listened in silence. Chinedu said, "You knew this, didn't you?"

"I began to piece it together recently. I suppose, like you, I always knew. But my poverty prevented me from thinking straight. The obfuscating green of the naira tempted my gaze away from the truth."

"Your research?" Chinedu asked.

"I've finished it. The machine I built can map souls and extract destinies, just like the one at the bank. But mine is more energy efficient, as it runs on solar power. I tried to get investors, or talk to people in government, but I met roadblocks at every turn. I couldn't even register a company for it. I was blocked from Corporate Affairs Commission up."

"This is a government enabled monopoly," Chinedu said. "They don't want competition. That's why the rest of the world doesn't know about it." Chinedu lowered his voice and added, "If you push too closely, try to go to the press, or talk to too many people about this, you might wind up in a shallow grave somewhere."

"Or an accident," Mukoro said calmly. He lit a cigarette and handed one to Chinedu who took it and lit it. Both men smoked in silence for a while.

"I can't let it go," Mukoro said. "It's my daughter's destiny."

"Don't be stupid," Chinedu said. "The powers that be ..."

"I made a promise to my wife. I told her she could trust me. She did."

"You have a family now. Your son ..."

"So what? I should sacrifice my daughter's destiny for the family? For my son?" Mukoro looked at Chinedu with wild, angry eyes. Chinedu sighed and resumed smoking. After a while they both finished.

45

"I am not nobody now, you know," Mukoro continued. "I know things. And I have power."

Chinedu shook his head. "Not compared to the people who control the bank. They are the same people who control Nigeria. The governors, senators, the cabals behind the president."

Chinedu opened the door but did not get out. "I've been looking for a way to quit. Being a headhunter for destinies is taking its toll on me. I just haven't found a way to do so safely. I'll be heading home to my fiancée now. See that you return to your family, okay? Don't do anything rash."

Mukoro said nothing in response. Chinedu closed the door with a sigh, got into his car, and drove off.

Eight months later ...

Mukoro walked into the AUB head office and was led to the Department of Soul measurement and extraction. He had an appointment. It was the appointed time ... for him ... for Nyerhovwo. He had a debt to pay. Or not pay, rather. Some debts you paid by not paying. He had dined with the devil. And it didn't matter how long the spoon. Silver bullets kill werewolves, it is said. But Nigerian devils ate silver and chewed their way up the spoon to your fingertips, then down your hands, till they licked your brains off their own fingers.

He looked at his Audemar. It was such an expensive timepiece, but despite the costliness, the glowing jewels, his time was up, and he couldn't buy more. It was eleven o'clock. Fittingly the eleventh hour.

He walked into Chinedu's office. The lawyer—the devil's advocate—was there, along with another man, probably Chinedu's handler. They were there to oversee the handover.

Chinedu said some words to Mukoro, but he couldn't hear them. The words flittered past him. He caught some words. "Defaulted on the loan ... destiny is forfeit ... sign here ... Mr. Mukoro. Sign?" There was a paper in front of him. They handed him a pen.

He looked at them and smiled. He would sign for them in blood. He stood up and tore his jacket open. "When you sell your soul, or

46

another's, you should always sign in blood. I'll sign with my blood, since I made the trade."

The occupants of the room gawked at him. Lining his jacket were a number of wires running into a device sewed into his coat. He pulled out a detonator. The occupants of the room all backed away.

"Bomb?" Chinedu's handler queried.

"No, it's not a bomb," Mukoro said, spitting. "Not the type that takes lives, anyway. Just the type that takes destinies."

The handler raised an eyebrow. "What do you want? More money? You can relax. We have money."

"I don't want money. I want my daughter's destiny. I knew you would never give back what you stole. So once I confirmed, eight months ago, I started reworking my prototype. It will rip the destiny from everyone within a ten-mile radius and integrate them with the operator of the device."

He turned to Chinedu. "I told you it is my destiny to gift my child a great destiny. And I will not be denied by thieves and saboteurs." He screamed at them. The lawyer backed off.

"Yes," Mukoro continued. "When I activate my device, it will rip the destinies off everyone in this den of thieves and integrate them in me. Including my child's. I can ask for just hers, but you all don't deserve what you have. Thieves!"

The handler rushed at Mukoro, and he pushed the button on his detonator. The air came alive, crackling with electricity. Thunder boomed outside, and it began to rain. A blast tore through the room, mini blasts occurring around everyone, as their destinies were ripped from them and drawn to Mukoro. His eyes blazed with each destiny he integrated, while those whose destinies he took, fell with dead eyes. A dozen—two, three, four—dozen destinies, and Mukoro's eyes glowed. Then his device overheated and burst into flames. He ripped it off and tossed it away.

Chinedu, the lawyer, and the handler stood before him with dead eyes. Mukoro turned to them.

"I know you pressed the security button, and the police will be here soon," he said, pulling a gun. They all backed off.

"Have you heard the saying that destiny can be delayed, but not denied? A seemingly nonsensical phrase, but true nonetheless. Destiny is like energy; it can be transferred, but not destroyed. And

47

it can't be transferred permanently. Its unique code is tied to the original owner's DNA. So when it's not gifted to anyone and the current holder dies, it goes back to its original source if they are still alive. When I die, all the destinies I have taken will go back to their owners if I don't gift them to anyone else. You will have your sordid destinies back." He paused. "And my daughter, too. That's all I wanted. I am after what is mine."

"What is yours?" the handler asked. "We gave you the loan. You defaulted. You have no right."

Mukoro pointed the gun at the handler, and he backed away.

Just then, the police—three men and a woman—burst into the room. Time slowed. Mukoro smiled at the handler, who was waving at the SARS unit not to shoot. But Mukoro knew. The Nigerian police would not refrain from shooting an armed man pointing a gun at a senior bank manager. You could trust the police to do their jobs the one time they shouldn't.

Mukoro heard the shots of multiple guns going off. His body hit the ground. The bullets had hit him faster than it had taken the sound to travel to his ears, breaking him, along with the sound barrier. His vision dimmed. The handler was screaming for an ambulance and for a destiny extraction machine before he died. Mukoro willed himself to die, his destiny. He closed his eyes permanently and fulfilled it.

2 weeks later ...

Chinedu sat with Nyerhovwo and her mother. The relatives had all traveled back to the village after the funeral, and they were alone in their apartment in Lekki.

"The bank reached out," Chinedu said. "I am no longer with them. But I agreed to liaison with the family on their behalf." He did not say that he had negotiated his release by promising to smooth things over and ensure the Mukoro family's silence. "They are offering to discharge the debt of Nyerhovwo's destiny and also pay a huge compensation for the accident of Mr. Mukoro's death."

"I still don't understand how they can mistake a respectable businessman like Mukoro for a robber," Mama Nyerhovwo lamented.

"You know how stupid Nigerian police can be …"

As Chinedu glibly droned on, Nyerhovwo got up and left them to it. Her brother Oghenemudiaga was asleep, and the adults were happy to see her go, not wanting to have such difficult conversations around her.

She went upstairs to her father's room, then to his private study. She riffled through the papers scattered on his desk, pulled out one, and scanned it briefly. It read, "Destiny extraction and replication." She knew this already. Her father's last work was not just about extracting destinies forcefully, it was also about replicating energy signatures and mimicking them. When he died and the originals went back to their sources, the copies stayed or came to her, his closest DNA match. So now she had the destiny of a couple of hundred people. Her father had gifted her a great destiny, as he had always wanted.

She closed her eyes, letting the thoughts and desires wash through her. She opened her eyes, and they glowed fiercely. Some things pushed her from within. She had to finish her father's work. She let the thoughts and visions drive her as she began to look over his research.

As she read, her eyes closed, but her reading did not stop. Voices whispered the words to her. The voices were the physical manifestation of possibilities that had torn a path through other realities to find their way to her. She already knew the words. Other voices whispered to her, increasing in tempo and numbers: "We are legion. We bring you your great destiny."

She dropped the book and held her head in agony. A great destiny did not mean a good one for the holder, or a sane one for that matter. She willed the voices away. They grew silent for a moment, then issued from her as colors: violet, violet-gray, then purple—dark manifestations of all that was in her. The colors gathered in the room above her, then merged together, changing and expanding into a black, torrential darkness that gathered around her. She looked at it with eyes wide, and through this open doorway to her soul, the colors rushed furiously into her.

She closed her eyes. When she opened them, they did not seem like the eyes of a twelve year old. They were deep and mysterious, shining with a dark, speckled light of unspoken things; of a great and powerful force waiting to be unleashed on a greedy, wicked, and unsuspecting world. But her look contained something even more wicked. This destiny would not be denied.

49

BROAD DUTTY WATER: A SUNKEN STORY

by Nalo Hopkinson

"**G**et in, Lickchop." Jacquee lifted her pig into the main cabin of Uncle Silvis's ultralight she'd borrowed from home.

Lickchop merely grunted, *Chow*, aloud via the vocoder illegally implanted in his scalp. Jacquee didn't know who'd done that to him. Is so she'd found him last year, a half-dead lump of throw-weh, unconscious and sinking fast in the center of a medical waste trash vortex about seventy nmi offshore of the Grande Soufrière false atoll that loomed over sunken Guadeloupe.

No one back home could figure out why the vocoder had a ring of tiny rods, each a couple millimetres long, sticking out the top of Lickchop's skull. Jacquee called it his tiara. Lickchop didn't much use the vocoder, except to demand chow. At the moment, he was eagerly paddling his stubby legs in the air.

"I know, sweetness," Jacquee said to him. "I'm impatient, too." She was mad to try out her brand-new wetware. Dr. Lin had said she should wait a week, but he always exaggerated that bullshit. He was an old boyfriend of Uncle Silvis's. As hospitals became too over-whelmed with flood, plague, and starvation victims to function ade-quately, he'd moved his surgery practice to his home. Five years now Jacquee had been going to him. He'd replaced her left elbow after she splintered it on a dive in a dead coral reef. He kept her taz supplied

51

with antibiotics he mixed up in his kitchen. She regularly brought him gifts of food her taz bred. Some of those were illegal to have, but he'd never turned her in to the World Bioheritage enforcers.

As soon as Jacquee put Lickchop down on the floor of the ultralight's tiny cabin, he trotted *click-click* over to the spongiform food puzzle she'd bolted to the floor in one corner. He stuck his snout into it and began happily rooting for the algae pellets she'd made and tucked inside it.

Activity on the makeshift post-Inundation dock bustled all around them: people with their belongings on their backs hustling from the mainland to the water along the rocky, wooden boards of the makeshift bridge over the new wetlands; boats and catamarans docking and getting underway; people shouting orders; the air-filling duppy moans of ships' horns; the oily fishswamp stink of water polluted by gas engines. The original land was somewhere below them, swallowed by the polluted black waters of the risen ocean. Nobody was really sure what Florida town or city they were floating above; catastrophic flooding and the resulting seismic activity had changed shorelines too much and were still doing so.

Jacquee clambered behind Lickchop into the small cabin of her ultralight. Her knapsack dragged at her shoulders, though it really wasn't plenty heavy. She was just a little tired from the surgery. She straightened up, and her world spun backward. Vertigo. She clutched for one of the hand straps in the ceiling. She was a bit unsteady on her pins after the slice-n-dice Dr. Lin had performed on her the day before. She should have stayed in his spare bedroom one more day, to recover from the laparoscopic surgery and get a bit more training in how to use the wetware he'd just implanted in her brain. But a whole two days a-landlock? Enough. She and Lickchop needed to get home, back to the sea and their taz massive-them in the Jamdown Ark. The floating platform on which her community lived had been traveling for weeks to get to the next berth on its annual route, the one east of the Caribbean crescent. Now it was time to re-establish their vertical farm. This week, Jacquee would be helping to lay out the floating grid of plastic pipes with the newest kelp seedlings sprouted along their lengths. Then there'd be mussel socks to attach to the grid and lower into the water, plus the cages stocked with clam and oyster seeds.

She liked this part of the endless round of tasks it took to keep the taz functioning. She got to free dive amongst the hanging fronds of kelp, swerving around the vertical cooling rods which chilled the ocean water passing through them to keep the kelp at optimum temperature. She was up to five minutes of being able to hold her breath. Uncle Silvis could do seven; Plaidy who lived with her children and her man five habitats over on the taz was the current record-holder—almost nine minutes under the water before she would faint and have to be yanked out.

Jacquee pulled the ultralight's cabin door shut and looked through the porthole. So much waste being spat out all around her; a treasure trove. "Lickchop," she said as she went to top up the pig's water dispenser, "give our taz two days here, and yuh would see how much we could salvage!"

The pig, busy filling his belly, ignored her. She got to work locking the lid on his stale litter box, opening a fresh one, and dampening the peristaltic pad. A-pure truth she was talking. It would be easy for them to strain oil and microplastics out of the sludgy dockside water. Scoop up the dead birds and fish floating stink on the surface, render them into fat and ash. Sell all of that back to the factory suppliers, fund ongoing taz maintenance for weeks.

She swung open the door of Lickchop's well-padded crate and locked it in that position. The crate was made from a large grocery shopping cart she'd traded for a few months ago with one youth in a passing taz called Travellers' Green. She'd given him an empty lard tub of dried coconut meal and a handful of freeze-dried chiton meat for it. And though the youth kept asking her, she hadn't told him where she'd found the forlorn piece of rock sticking up out of the sea that still had chitons living on it. Not that it mattered; next time she went back, there weren't any, just scum floating around the base of the rock. Salt water was so acid these days that it was removing the calcium carbonate so many now near-extinct sea creatures relied on to build their shells. How long since she'd tasted lobster or crab?

She did a quick check of the repair patches bolted onto the ultralight. Uncle Silvis had printed the body of the aircraft in pieces from biopolymers her taz cultured from marine algae. The assembled ultralight had held up well for the past few years, but it would soon be time to feed it back to the algae. Uncle Silvis kept joking that it had been mended so much that it was more patch than plane. By now, Uncle Silvis had probably realized that she'd taken it for a ride. There would be some music to face when she got back home.

She was a little bit light-headed after her flight prep, but never mind; time to go. She patted Lickchop, went forward to the flight deck, and closed the cabin door behind her. No control tower to radio to, no one to register a flight path with, or to broadcast an "all-clear" for takeoff. Everyone used visual flight rules this near to a port; keep your eyes peeled like johncrow head and don't get too close to any other craft.

Pretty soon, she was kiting near-soundlessly twelve-hundred feet above sea level. World Bioheritage couldn't come after her once she reached her taz. Not legally, anyway. Land-liberated micronations were a protected category. Though now that the open oceans had been declared a protected heritage site, Worldbio porkpies sometimes got overeager and took the chance of invading tazes, hoping they could make an arrest under the claim of defacing an international heritage.

The ultralight console began an insistent beeping. Jacquee opened her eyes, checked the readout, corrected the ultralight's flight so that its right wing was no longer dipping downward.

The intercom clicked on. "Yes, Lickchop?" Jacquee responded.

She should never have taught the pig how to use the intercom, much less have rewired the controls to be low enough on the wall for him to reach. But he got lonely back there in the cabin on long trips. She couldn't have him in the cockpit. He'd be a menace.

Columbus considered it to be the fairest isle that eyes have beheld, said Lickchop.

The skin on Jacquee's arms sprang out in goosebumps. She stared at the receiver in her hand. That hadn't come from Lickchop's limited vocabulary range. "Is who back there?" she barked into the receiver.

No answer.

"Assata," she said, "automatic pilot, current course heading."

Yes, pilot, replied the ultralight's AI.

Jacquee leapt out of her seat and snatched up the cricket bat she kept behind the door. She threw the door open and stepped into the cabin.

Lickchop was dozing in his crate. He didn't even have the TV on. And the intercom hadn't been activated. "Wah gwan?" Jacquee muttered to herself. Frowning, she returned to the cockpit. True, she was feeling not quite herself. Dr. Lin had said a few people developed mild sensory hallucinations as this kind of wetware established its pathways in the brain. Looked like she was one of them. Cho. But Dr. Lin had said they were temporary. Push come to shove, she could have Assata fly them home. Uncle Silvis had grumbled when she'd installed it—he thought Jacquee's love of bootleg tech was an addiction—but now he used Assata, too. He kept threatening to change its name: "Ascording to how the real Assata never took a rassclaat order from nobody." But he hadn't done so yet. The list of things Uncle Silvis planned to get to someday was ever changing and never ending.

Her headphones crackled to life, causing a pain-pulse to start throbbing along the top of her skull. "Jaks! A-you that?"

Oi. Time to face the music with Uncle Silvis. "Come in, Tay-zone 67," she replied. "A-who this?"

"Is Kobe." It usually was, if it was a matter of telecommunications. "Yuh business conclude?" he asked.

"Ee-hee." No need to tell him about her worrisome symptoms. She'd be all right. She basked in the familiar sound leaking from Kobe's side; children yelling as they played all through the complex.

Kobe said, "You enjoyed your visit to landlock?"

"So you know is there I went?"

"Cho. Is who you think you talking to? Of course I know!"

"The whole rahtid place don't move!" This she knew how to do, to cover her doubts with humor. "They pretend they do, everything rushing all around you, cars and trains and people.

"Everybody trying to keep things going fast just so them don't haffe realize that them NAH GO NOWHERE!"

Kobe laughed. "Well, yuh know what dem seh: if yuh worl' nah rock, it a-'tan 'till."

"My legs couldn't adjust, even after three days. No water jostling beneath my feet. I was walking like I was drunk. How people live like that, Kobe?"

"After you barely been living ten years at sea," he teased. "I know you didn't forget so soon. Listen, we picking up a light breeze. We gwine ride it, gie de sea under we some time to freshen herself up. Change your course heading minus twenty degrees, so you could catch up."

"Seen. And I coming home with a new toy in my head." She glanced at her console. "Twenty minutes."

From her headphones came the sound of a familiar voice: "Kobe, hand me that blasted microphone. Jacquee? A-you that?"

Jacquee sighed. "Yes, Uncle Silvis."

"Jimmy text me to say you leave his surgery too soon. You all right, Jacquee? Why you went to Dr. Lin? Something happen to you?"

So worried the old man sounded. He wasn't even her real uncle. That's just what everyone called him. And didn't he know by now she could look after herself? She replied, "Yeah, man. Just a little mod. Help me see better in muh—murky water." Even just saying the phrase made her belly twist, every time.

"More bootleg tech?" said Uncle Silvis. "And in your head this time? What the rass Jimmy was thinking, letting you talk him into doing something like that?"

Jacquee tried for a light tone. "Better him than some backawall operator with no training, nah true?"

"Jacquee, this is foolishness! When you going to start acting like you have a brain in your head?"

The pounding in her skull increased. "Jesus Christ," she barked, "if you going to carry on like that, maybe I won't come home at all! Maybe I gwine right back to landlock, where I belong!" She cut off the connection before he could reply, and sat stewing—kissing her teeth and muttering under her breath about interfering, overprotective …

There was the thunderhead Kobe had talked about, looming up ahead. It would bring a storm surge. No problem for Jamdown Ark. Its large, flexible base—a neural matrix of algal polymers extruded in a ring shape—would just rise and fall with the swells. The sway would make it a bit wobbly underfoot for a few hours, is all.

A decade ago, when Jacquee was still living a-landlock, rainy season might mean some flooding. Nowadays, every downpour was a tropical storm, and every storm saw the waters rise more and destroy more land. At least there were no hurricanes due for another few months. The old-time stories talked about the devastation of Category 5s. But the classifications had had to be revised. In these days Category 5 was common, and the new Category 6 was a banshee-shrieking horror that could tear away coastlines permanently, eat small countries whole.

Uncle Silvis insisted that the aftermath of storm surges was the best time to go collecting. Worldbio porkpies didn't patrol during storms, and the storm waters churned interesting stuff up from the depths. That's how Jacquee had stumbled upon the chitons; she'd been clambering on a slippery thumb of rock jutting out of the ocean. The storm that had just washed over it had deposited caches of glass jetsam, weathered and rounded over decades into gleaming lumps by being tumbled along the ocean floor. She would keep the prettiest, most beadlike pieces to make jewelry with for market. The rest could be sold to recyclers. Prying the barnacles out of the rock had broken a good hunting knife, but Uncle Silvis had been delighted to find that Jacquee's haul included twenty-three of them she'd kept alive in a little tub of seawater. "Viable gametes probably still dey inside," he'd said. "Good for you." He'd extracted some sperm and ova from a few of the chitons and cryopreserved the gametes in DMSO, cooled then stored in a liquid-nitrogen flask. Maybe they could find a way to add chitons to the vertical marine farm suspended underwater in the doughnut-hole center of Jamdown Ark. They might be good for chowder.

Blasted man. She wasn't going to let him spoil her fun with her new mod. "Assata," she said, "take the helm. Maintain course."

Yes, pilot, said Assata.

Jacquee flicked on the intercom. She needed some company. Lickchop was singing along with some TV show contestant. Jacquee could hear the show in the background, but the loudest sound was Lickchop. He was making excited squeal/grunts that his vocoder was struggling to render into some approximation of human speech; Jacquee's best guess was: *Shake that t'ing, Miss / Oonuh betta shake … .* An oldie but a goodie. Wasn't helping her aching head, though. "Lickchop!" she barked.

The "singing" stopped. *What Jah-kay want?* he responded.

"Turn down the TV for a second, nuh man?"

He did. Then he was silent, waiting for her to answer his question. She didn't even self-know what she wanted from the pig. Just his attention. Ongle that. Lickchop didn't pass judgement. She rummaged in her knapsack for the bootleg addy she'd been carrying around for months. "He think I so foolish," she muttered to Lickchop. "Like I can't think for myself. Gwine show him."

Don't think you foolish.

"Not you, Lickchop; Uncle Silvis." She hadn't been sure she was going to try it. But she was a hard-back woman who would make her own decisions. So now she was going to see if the bootleg addy would pair with her new mod.

The woman she'd bought the addy from in the mainland market had said, "Medically non-intrusive for sure, darling." Then she'd tapped the side of her head. "You already have wetware installed, right? Maybe to correct myopia? Just piggyback it onto that. So easy, it's sleazy."

Well, she hadn't had any wetware back then. But she'd been thinking to get some. So she had. The mod was well natty on its own; enhanced vision would help direct her through murky, particulate-heavy water and sharpen her proprioception. Accomplished via some process she didn't really understand. Something about ninety percent modifications to her DNA and ten percent implanted hardware. Didn't matter.

A pop song cover came pouring out through Jacquee's headphones. Lickchop had clearly decided the conversation was over. She grimaced and turned the sound off.

She got the addy out of her knapsack. It was matchbox sized, plastic, standard 3-D print white and near featureless, but for a readout window and a couple of buttons. She unfolded the piece of paper with the instructions written on it in fading umpteenth-generation print. They were easy enough to follow. In a few seconds, the readout was flashing "ready" in squared-off green letters. Addy successfully onboarded! Her brain felt a little … itchy. That was the only way to describe it.

The headache scoured the inside of her skull, making her wince. She should be lying in Dr. Lin's lavender-scented guest bedroom with a soft mask over her eyes, wearing a cooled gel skullcap and gently putting her aching brain through the exercises that would, in about a week, fine-tune her skill with the mod. She closed her eyes for some relief.

The discomfort receded. She took a breath. Focused her mind the way Dr. Lin had shown her. She was supposed to wait a couple more days before trying out the commands, but she summoned the wetware anyway. Gave it the "standby" command, then squinched her lower-left eyelid. That was the action she'd chosen to activate the addy. The headache became a shout of pain. She did her best to ignore it. She felt/heard the internal click as the addy connected with the ultralight's controls. Success! Now she could pilot the ultralight hands free. Assata was great for uneventful flight paths, but not for the myriad split-second decisions required in more challenging conditions.

So often Jacquee had wished she could do that without having to lay her hands on the controls all the time. "Assata, give me manual control."

Yes, pilot.

Jacquee called up the addy's display. Telemetry danced across the upper-left-hand corner of her mind's eye. Red, yellow, and green images on a black background. She felt/saw the ultralight's controls. Tasted them, too. Like goat head soup mixed with pineapple and toothpaste. She gagged as she fought to do the mental twitch that turned the gain down. The ultralight swung dizzyingly to the left. Carefully, Jacquee got it back on track. She experimented for a while with pitch, yaw, speed. Pretty soon, she felt comfortable enough to climb to two-thousand feet to get above the storm. Grinning, she frolicked the aircraft amongst the clouds.

Oh, shit. The telemetry was signaling that she'd dipped too low. She was tipping them into the thunderhead. With the sickly, swanning motion of a piece of paper drifting down from a height, they sank into the storm cloud. Like a truck on a quarry road, they dugga-duggaed through turbulence. A buffet of wind jerked the ultralight sideways. Rain beat fists against the window screen, hammered the ultralight with a roar that made bile rise in her throat. She spat it down the front of her sweatshirt, kept trying for the right combo of commands to decouple the addy from the ultralight's controls. A storm like this could literally tear the ultralight in two.

Automatically, she reached for the controls, just as the craft hit an air pocket and dropped so fast that Jacquee's butt lifted out of the chair. The heel of her hand hit multiple buttons and levers.

She didn't know which ones. Panicked, she tried to use the mental commands instead, succeeded only in jamming the whole system up. "Assata!" she yelled. "Take the con!"

Not possible, pilot, the plane replied calmly. *Please disengage override.*

"I can't!"

The rain had become hail, slamming like fastballs against the hull.

The ultralight's nose dipped at a vomitous pitch and exited the cloud layer. There was a mountaintop floating in the dark swells of the ocean below her, like a meringue in wine. For a brief second, she thought she'd pulled the ultralight out of its dive, but it just … kept … falling. She fought to stay conscious during the plummet, tried pushing one combo after another of buttons that now made no sense to her confused brain. She could hear Lickchop's fear squeal from the cabin behind her. G-forces pressed her into her chair like a ripe mango beneath a boot. Dirty-blue water getting closer and closer. "Assata," Jacquee yelled, "controlled descent! Parallel to the shoreline ahead!"

Please disengage override.

"I still fucking can't figure it out!" yelled Jacquee.

Then suggest you deploy your parachute. Ditch at one-thousand feet.

The ultralight continued its dizzying descent. The silence was eerie, except for the tinny music of Lickchop's TV show coming from her discarded headphones. *Shake that thing, Miss …*

Jacquee scrabbled for the life jacket with its attached chute. She pulled the package out from beneath the seat, mentally rehearsing how to put it on.

She only had one on board. And the ultralight had two passengers. "Pussyclaat, batty-hole …" she swore.

She undid her seatbelt, stood against the steep downward angle of the ultralight, and clawed her way through the door into the main cabin. She rushed to Lickchop's crate, yanked its door open. He was crouched inside, his eyes rolling in terror. *Fallingfalling*, said his vocoder.

He tunneled his way into her arms. He was shivering. He had shit inside his crate; she could smell it. And sympathize.

"You gonna be okay," she lied. She had no way of knowing that. She clutched Lickchop against her chest and struggled into the life vest, wrapping it around both of them.

Nonono, said Lickchop. He fought and kicked. *No leash.*

"Is not a leash. Shut up."

In his struggling, Lickchop slashed her forearm open with a back trotter.

"Ow! Fuck!" Blood was seeping through the sleeve of her jacket. But still she held Lickchop tightly.

Twelve-thousand feet, said Assata. *The aircraft is losing altitude too quickly. It will break up on the coral formation at crash site. On my mark, release the hatch, open the door, and jump.*

Jacquee stood near the hatch, her hand on the handle. She knew what she had to do. Open the hatch outwards. Leap out of the plane. Open the first chute once she was clear of it. Steer herself and Lickchop down, hopefully onto the dry land of the little island below them. She didn't even know what country it used to be.

One-thousand feet, said Assata. *Mark. Exit the aircraft now. Exit the aircraft now. Exit the aircraft now.*

Jacquee felt her kidneys clench, her gut knot. Everything about her body was telling her this was a bad idea. But she pushed down on the handle and leaned against the door to shove it open.

Mistake. A buffeting wind slammed the door open to bang against the ultralight's carriage. She didn't have to jump; the force of the wind sucked her out of the ultralight, into a heels-over-head somersault. She saw the bottom edge of the open hatch but couldn't avoid it. Her head crashed against it, then she was out.

The day the waters had swept over the house in the valley where teenaged Jacquee lived with her parents, she'd been in the living room, dozing her way through her history homework in the big Berbice lounge chair. She woke when water swarmed to her chin, carrying the chair along in the surge. Coughing, she struggled to her knees in the chair. The back half of the house was gone, open to an iron-colored sky and an avalanche of angry brown water where neighbors' houses had been. The roar of wind and water had been like a train coming through. She'd yelled for her mummy and daddy. They had been in the backyard, bringing in the lawn chairs and picnic umbrella so they wouldn't blow away in the storm. There was no sign of them. The river maelstrom had claimed the yard, and the rest of the house was crumbling into it, fast. Her mind couldn't take it in. She waded from room to room, splashing and coughing in the gritty, bitter water, calling and calling for her parents. No answer. Something long and snaky, concealed in the torrent, went whipping along the front of her, wrapped itself around her ankle, and held her fast. Then the water had fountained over her, filling her mouth. It felt like a long, pounding forever of terror before she'd been able to bend and

unsnarl the thing from her ankle. Its hard metal nose told her that it was their garden hose. Her parents had probably brought it indoors.

With a nail-bending screech, the roof of the house tore away. The house was disintegrating. She had to go. The garage was higher than the house, a bit farther along the uphill grade. The structure itself was gone, but the waters hadn't reached the car yet. She gave thanks her parents had recently keyed the car lock to her fingerprints. By the time she'd fought her way snotting and sobbing to the car, the sewage-tainted water was up to its tire tops, and she had lost her sweatpants and one shoe. Crouched on the car's bonnet was their cat Smarty Pants. She was bonedry as God's sense of humour, her lemon eyes wide in terror.

By some miracle, the car started. Jacquee headed for even higher ground. She picked up six more shell-shocked survivors on the way. They made it to the stadium, which had been converted into an emergency centre. She spent two weeks there, being drip-fed antibiotics and shitting bloody E. coli *flux. That's where the man she would come to know as Uncle Silvis found her and a handful of other people willing to form a taz and take to sea with him. Yes, he'd already ordered a taz platform. It would be grown and ready in a couple of weeks. Yes, he knew how to manage himself on the water and could teach them. Yes, she could bring Smarty Pants.*

The first month at sea she huddled in her bunk while others were busy setting up the habitats of the newly grown taz. She fought seasickness while grief raged through her. Wha' mek Mummy and Daddy dead, but she still alive? And every night of the decade since, she would dream of struggling in rushing, murky water as snakes wrapped around her ankles and pulled her down to drown.

She was … dizzy. Spinning along every axis possible. A keening shriek filled her thoughts. She told herself she had to open her eyes. Herself disagreed.

The keening was her. She was screaming. She closed her mouth. The screaming stopped. That slight bit of control made room for her to take more. She opened her eyes, and nearly began screaming again. The world was whipping around edge over edge, twisting; sky to sea to mountains, *whup whup whip*. She craned her neck upwards, looking for the parachute. It hadn't inflated. It was flapping in circles above her, flaccid as a used rubber, dragging behind her and Lickchop as they plummeted.

She was still holding Lickchop. Her thoughts were going so slow!

What had Kobe said in his flight training? "If you can't pilot it, ditch it to rass."

Ditch … how? Yes. There should be a lever at the front of the jacket. She had to squeeze Lickchop even tighter to reach it. If the pig protested, she couldn't hear it above the wind whooshing in her ears. She found the lever. Grasped it. Pulled downwards. She felt the tug of the first parachute releasing her, then the sharp yank upwards as the second chute deployed. It was smaller, round rather than the rectangle shape of the first one. It began rapidly filling with air.

But would it be enough? She was coming in hot. The second parachute was only half-full and couldn't be steered like the first. The vista surrounding her had zoomed in dizzyingly from a wide glimpse of the Earth's curvature; sky above and sea below with patches of brown terrain barely poking like noses above the water, to sea with a scrim of land too far out of reach in front of her, to just sea, then waves became apparent, and then she hit the surface of the water, feet first. But she hadn't kept her feet properly together. She felt her right ankle wrench as she plunged into the drink.

Lickchop couldn't hold his breath!

He could swim, though. Loved it, in fact. She pulled him out of the life jacket and let him go, knowing his rotund, pot-bellied self would pop up to the surface.

And still she cannonballed downwards, despite the life vest. She could do this. She had practised holding her breath. Her vision tunneled and her head felt light and as airless as the space between stars. She could barely restrain the instinct to take a big gasp. The second she slowed enough to make it possible, she began frantically frog-swimming back up to the life-giving air. Adrenaline rush kept the pain of her ankle at bay.

Her head broke the surface. She sucked in air. She was alive.

"Lickchop!" she yelled, spinning in a circle. No pig. The rope-tentacled mass of the second parachute was floating nearby, dragging her along. Lickchop didn't appear to be on it. She pressed the button on her vest that disengaged the parachute from her. It obediently began shrinking and rolling itself up for transport.

Jacquee swam around a few strokes, calling Lickchop's name. She dove briefly, but couldn't see him beneath the surface, either. He was gone.

Reaction to her close call was setting in, and she wasn't safe yet. She could drown or be attacked by sharks or stung by some of the nastier jellyfish before getting to safety. Was that going to happen to Lickchop? Had it already? Sobbing, exhausted, she turned and began swimming for the beach, towing the parachute roll awkwardly. About a half mile further along the shore were the smoking pieces of the wreckage of her ultralight. She couldn't business with that now. Out of the water first. See to that ankle. Maybe rig up a canoe and go looking for Lickchop.

She had reached the breakers. They were big today, in the wake of the passing storm. A good ten, twelve feet. She swam and bodysurfed her way through them, diving beneath them when necessary. It was a mercy the water was cool enough to numb her ankle likkle bit.

She didn't deserve mercy.

One more crashing wave shoved her closer to the shore. Jacquee's feet hit the bottom with a thud. She shouted at the jarring of her injured ankle. She staggered the rest of the way through a porridge of roiled-up, mealy sand and suspicious solids that banged against her legs and twice knocked her off her feet to splash into the nasty water. She hated being in water she couldn't see through. The second time, a big branch scraped painfully across her body and snagged in her vest. She had to yank frantically at the branch. It tore free, dragging her life vest off with it, and sped into the undertow, heading out to sea. Great. The survival kit and tracking device had been packed into that vest. Home didn't even know she was down. Would the tracker even still be broadcasting by the time they figured it out?

Once she was out of the surf, Jacquee half-hopped onto shore, groaning. When she could no longer hop, she got down on hands and knees and crawled like any baby, dragging the wadded-up parachute behind her. Salt water stung inside her nose, driven into her sinuses by the speed with which she'd plunged into the water. Never mind. Her own snot would flush them soon enough. She was bawling and coughing at the same time. Lickchop had been in her care.

How she could go and do him so? Uncle Silvis was forever telling her not to take him on her trips. But she hadn't listened. Losing beings she loved to the water; that was what she did best.

Tainted sand and pieces of sodden, rotted branches gave way to rockstones and tangles of stinking seaweed harried by sandflies. The beach was lined with what were probably sea-grape bushes. Frayed and bent, their slimy stems dragged on the sand, their broad, heart-shaped leaves yellowed. A handful of the usual coconut trees arched over the beach, but their fronds drooped wetly. Which meant that, now the Earth's waters were rising higher than most had predicted, this beach was regularly completely covered by the sea. Jacquee had to get to higher ground. And she couldn't crawl the whole way.

She rolled to a sitting position. Her ankle was already puffy. Wincing, she palpated the area. It didn't feel broken.

A patch of sand in her peripheral vision writhed. But when she looked good at it, it wasn't moving. Jacquee scooted backwards away from it. Since that day with the garden hose, she couldn't abide anything snakelike.

Out of her eye corner, another patch of sand squirmed. Again, it was still when she looked at it. She thought she heard someone say, *It's all good / Just turn me on … .* She snapped her head around in the direction of the voice. No one.

Although she was dripping wet, heat flushed over her, like being splashed with warm water. The world started to wobble on its axis. Her ears were suddenly ringing, the tinny sound occasionally resolving into a whisper of not-words as her brain tried to make sense of the racket. And she was shivering. Bloody hell. There were no snakes in the sand. Leaving Dr. Lin's before she had healed, landing-up in unsterile water … she'd picked up some kind of bug, and now she was delirious. And her mouth was dry. All that salt water had her dehydrated.

She took stock as best she could, while her head rang like Sunday-go-to-meeting and the world got further and further away … . Pocket knife still in her front jeans pocket. Cut a piece from her parachute to make a solar still, throw the rest of the parachute over a branch to make a tent. She was a thikk gyal, wouldn't need food for weeks. Felt like her fever was rising, though. She needed clean water now, but the still would take hours to generate it. And what about predatory animals on this island?

Seawater splashed her feet. The tide was rising. She had to get above the shoreline, quick.

Give it up to me …

She found a sea-grape bush with a branch long and thick enough. She tore it off to use as a crutch. Last minute, she thought to grab up a discarded PET bottle from the jetsam tumbling in the incoming water. She began the trek to drier ground.

Hot day. Jacquee was used to sea breezes playing over and through Jamdown Ark.

Landlock felt stifling to her nowadays. Especially today. Is fever that? She didn't know. Her jeans and sweatshirt were mostly dry. Scratchy sea salt powdered her face and hands. Her clothes were stiff with it. It weighed down the parachute roll. She limped along, leaning on the stick. The pain in her ankle first went numb, then came back shrieking with each step. Flashes of light at her eye corners. Smarty Pants on the deck of the taz outside the habitat they shared with Uncle Silvis, purring and chowing down on algae protein pellets. But her cat was long gone, dead peacefully in her sleep at a ripe old age.

Voiceless voices. A ghost of Lickchop's demodulated vocoder demanding, *Chow, Jacquee. Chow.*

Jacquee kissed her teeth. Lickchop couldn't say her name smooth so. Always hesitated between one syllable and the next.

So of course the next thing was that she felt he was trotting beside her in the screaming-hot sun, berating her for letting him die. She started arguing with him. *The calculus of dampness*, she said, *eating along the rimrock*. She briefly came back to herself, half-remembering the words she'd just muttered, vaguely aware they were nonsense. Then she was back in the fever dream.

Lickchop floated in the air, on his back, gnawing at a snake with brass fangs. It hissed and spit and tried to wrap itself around Lickchop, who calmly sucked it up like a strand of sea grass.

She caromed off a knee-high rock, hissed as she jammed her injured foot into the sand to prevent a fall. Two-handed, tilted forward from the waist, she hung on to the branch she was using to help herself walk. Bone tired. She straightened up. One foot forward, then the other.

Repeat.

There was a water-trickle sound, different from the rhythmic roar of the seashore. She tried to focus, to see ahead of her, but it was all delusion, her afflicted brain telling itself gigo stories. Through it all, the one constant was the tuneless piano-plink of water. She stumbled in the direction of the sound. Throat parched. Fever rising. Even as she swam through imaginary kelp fronds, ate a bat sandwich, won a not-game of dominoes with a not-Silvis who was chanting the wrong words from the Book of Revelation while he silently slapped the tiles down onto the rickety wooden table between them, she knew she had to hydrate, soon.

Jacquee's eyes opened briefly on … a river? Weeds around its edges
Lilies at the brink
Even some seagulls wheel-and-turning above it.
Odorous indeed must be the mead,
Some struggling but living sea grape bushes.
And sugar-sweet their sap.

Hush, she told her dreaming brain. You can't drink that. You don't know what kinda parasites inna it. You should dig a solar still. Wait till some clean water condenses into it.

Her gritty, obstinate throat impelled her forwards. She dimly knew she was on her belly, face nearly in the water. Then she was scooping brackish liquid up with the PET bottle, bringing it to her mouth, and drinking deep.

Uncle Silvis had told her his dream often enough. Of the smog levels gradually falling. Of the Earth's climates returning to cooler levels. Of the land reappearing.

But the world had lost so much. The Gulf Coast. The Eastern Seaboard. The Amazon River Basin. Most of Southeast Asia had dived beneath the waves. And the Pacific Island nations. Refugees, misery, sickness every-where. And the grief. A whole planet keening, mourning.

Jacquee slapped the side of her neck, hard. She woke to find it was pitch night. She was scraping away the mosquito she'd squashed against her neck in her sleep. She was sprawled by the waterside, curled around the plastic bottle. Her head was pillowed on the still-damp parachute roll, which was already rank with stale salt water.

She sat up. She couldn't see a rass. And it was so quiet! She re-membered nights like this on dry land when the peeping of thousands of frogs was deafening. No more frogs. Indicator species were dying out the world over.

There was a lightning flash, far out at sea. A few seconds later, a grumble of thunder. The storm. Was it coming this way? She hadn't made a shelter yet. And she had drunk untreated water. She resigned herself to the belly-griping that was sure to follow.

The quiet pressed in on her ears, insistent as a pressure wave. The darkness had its hands over her eyes.

Something rustled along the ground, a little way behind her. Jacquee swung to her knees and spun around. "Uncle?" she called out, her voice quavery. "Lickchop?" No answer.

At least her knife was still in her front jeans pocket. She retrieved it, snicked it open, and held it low, near her thigh. She tried to calm her breathing so she could hear better. Finally, she remembered she could see in the dark now, if she chose. If it was working. If she hadn't gone and infected her brain in her eagerness.

She breathed in. Then, slowly, out. She—is what Dr. Lin had called it?—engaged her mindfulness. Then did the little twitch of lower eyelid, a half-wink that should turn on the infrared. And gasped as the world blossomed into glowing blues and greens on a black velvet background. The rustling was coming from breadfruit tree leaves, big as dinner plates, that were being blown along the ground by the freshening breeze. The tree branched out above her. It was stunted, only about fifteen feet high. But there were one or two green cannonballs of breadfruit amongst its branches. She hadn't even seen the tree when she made her way here in the daytime. Too feverish. Was it really there, or was she still delirious? No. Her head felt clear, and she was no longer shivering. The fugue seemed to be over.

There was a manicou on the tree's trunk, climbing higher. It was no bigger than Lickchop. It gripped a branch with its prehensile tail and turned to stare down at her. Its eyes glowed. It resumed its climb.

The tinkling sound of water drew her eyes to examine the place where she'd drunk from in her delirium. Not a river; a lagoon. Partly fed by the ocean. That's why it tasted brackish. The water shifted back and forth. Her altered vision showed it black as tar, the plants around its edge a pale green.

Another mosquito bit her neck, and one whined in her ear. She looked down at her body. If she switched to heat-signature vision, she would be able to see her warmth that was attracting them.

But first she had to make some shelter, since it seemed she was going to spend the night there. Stringing the parachute from a low branch of the breadfruit tree and digging a shallow pit in the ground nearby for a solar still would have been easy with her new mod, except her ankle sang with each step. By the time she got set up for the night, she was sweating, drawing mosquitoes in a cloud around her.

She couldn't bear the stinging any longer. Plus, she had to wash the sea salt out of her clothes and put them to dry. And relatively fresh water was right there, steps away …

She promised herself she wouldn't drink any more of it, just use it to clean herself and her clothes. Swim for a bit, escape the mosquitos.

She removed her boots and socks, then stripped off the rest of her clothing. The night air hardened her nipples. She limped to the water's edge and eased herself in, shivering in the chillier water. She trod water for a bit until she'd warmed up. Then she took in a breath and let herself sink into the blue-green-black world below.

When Jacquee was little, maybe eleven years old, and living on land, she once had a homeroom teacher who'd made them read a poem about some old-time Britishy town that slid into a lake because the townspeople had been too stingy to give bread to a starving beggar. She could be looking 'pon that town now, settled onto the lagoon bottom. Because there was a nighttime city block down there. One quite a bit worse for having been battered by the water. Rusted cars and lengths of copper pipe. Broken bricks and chunks of cement. Waterlogged tree trunks. Whole pieces of buildings, drowned for the world's original sin; a human-triggered, human-stoked runaway train of climate change.

Moonlight beamed down through the water, making motes suspended within it twinkle: microorganisms; microplastics. The town was lit by fairy lights. Jacquee explored for a bit, wiping algae off street signs and peering in through slimy windows at sodden, broken computers and furniture, tossed every which way. Through one window she spied an armchair, upside-down and semi-buoyant. She pulled away from that window quickly.

She dove down to street level. Tumbling through the diffuse beams were translucent blobs, rounded by wave action, each about the size of a soccer ball. They streamed along with the current. Filaments of blob-stuff, like tresses, trailed from them. She could see where in some cases, strands of filaments were caught in rock cracks, anchoring them. What the rass were those? She swam down toward the shimmering globules.

One of them had encased a whole shrimp; another, a small fish. She recoiled. Were they being digested? But no, both fish and shrimp were swimming calmly, going about their business. They didn't look engulfed. It was more as though they had sprung multiple antennae, all over their bodies.

Jacquee went up for air and dove back down a few times, trying to understand what she was seeing. The more she did, the more lagoon creatures she saw, apparently in symbiosis with the small clouds of who-knows-what. Phosphorescent, an oddly fuzzy turtle flippered lazily past her nose, seemingly unbothered by being coated with the strange organism. She spied three more. All looked plump and healthy. Turtles were dying everywhere else, weakened by their softening shells.

Entranced, Jacquee dug a fist-sized lump of the matter out of a crevice in a rock. It was attached to the rock by a fleshy string. It looked as though swiping a finger through it would disperse it. But no; it was membranous, pale green with darker green filaments threaded through it. She rubbed it gently between thumb and middle finger. Slightly slippery. It didn't look or feel like a colony of tubifex worms, which is what she would have expected in a lagoon.

The blob began to glow more brightly, perhaps in response to her touch. The picky threads inside it began to undulate. Minuscule lightning-forks inside a tiny green cloud. She found herself smiling. The thing was beautiful. She brought it closer to her face to better inspect it.

Her action broke the umbilical connecting the blob to its rock-stone. It convulsed and snapped toward her, flattening clammy against the side of her face and half-covering one eye. Jacquee clawed at it as she kicked for the air above. Her head broke the surface of the lagoon while she was still trying to scrape the thing off her face. It came away in strips, thin and flexible as skin. Fuck! Had she gotten all of it? She dunked her head back into the water and scrubbed her cheek and eye with one hand. Too late considered that it was the same hand with which she'd been holding the blob. She was probably just depositing

70

more of it onto her face. She switched to the other hand and rubbed away all the remaining bits she could feel. She lifted her head for air again and kicked as quickly as she could for the edge of the lagoon. Once on land, she squatted and surgeon-washed her two hands in the water. Glowing motes flowed away from her fingers, going dull again as she watched; remainders of the blob.

She put her clothes back on. They would dry more quickly against her skin. Then she sat at the waterside, knees clasped to her chest, and shuddered. Stupid. Stupid. To go and put her hands on some unknown organism.

With her night vision on, the retreating thunderhead was a light show. She watched the funnel of it move slowly away, lit up every few seconds by lightning flashes. She rocked and tried not to think of what would happen if no one found her. When the storm had disappeared over the horizon, she crawled into her shelter. She wadded her sweatshirt for a pillow. To keep the worst of the mosquitoes away, she cocooned herself in a trailing edge of the parachute. She turned her night vision off, leaving herself in the uncertain dark. Eventually, she sank into a slurry of disturbed sleep.

She woke ravenous the next morning. A sickly sunrise tinted the clouds with tainted orange-browns and greens, painterly and poisonous. Jacquee busied herself with the business of survival: drinking the cup of sterile water she'd gotten from the solar still; using her stick to knock a breadfruit out of the tree; the forever it took with two twigs and a guy line from the parachute to make a fire for roasting the breadfruit. While she ate, she tried to raise the ultralight's onboard computer with her addy. Only the crackle of static, which suddenly, alarmingly increased till it was like having ants crawling around inside her skull. She yelped, then mentally deactivated the addy.

Careful of her ankle, she slowly made her way a little higher up the elevation till she could see the beach where she'd come ashore. Or at least, where it had been. High tide had completely covered it, and the wreck of the ultralight was nowhere to be seen. The water had taken it, probably already swept it miles away out to sea.

71

Jacquee sat down hard on a rock. Things were bad. She had really messed up this time. How to let her taz know where she was? She didn't know how far away they were, or in what direction.

She scratched her forearm, and only then realized she'd been doing that all day. The forearm tingled, so gently she could have been imagining it. So did the side of her face. It was happening on the side of her body where the organism had tried to latch on to her.

Fuck, fuck, fuck. Jacquee tore up a handful of scrub grass and used that to scour her arm and face. All she got for the effort was dirt ground into the scrapes she was giving herself with the scrub grass; scrapes she wouldn't be able to wash clean until she'd collected more sterile water. That wouldn't be until next morning. And she needed to conserve the clean water for drinking, not bathing. The calculus of dampness, to rass. Jacquee swore and slammed her stick against the ground. She'd infected herself with a parasite, and she was injured. Her taz could probably fix both, but she was stranded with no way to contact them. She was fucked.

And if she wasn't careful, she was going to give herself sunburn into the bargain. She made her painful way back to the shade of the broad-leaved breadfruit tree. She sat morosely beneath it, pelting rockstones into the lagoon and cycling her vision through its different spectra. She was sweaty and lonely, and her pig was gone. She wanted so badly to be where she usually went when she was in need of comfort: the water. She glared at the lagoon, lying there all spread out and tempting, making beckoning little wavelet sounds. She needed to survive, but for how long? Suppose rescue never came?

Surviving. That's all she was doing. Surviving and waiting. That's all the world was doing. Taz communities were self-sufficient and did better than much of the rest of humanity. But really, they were doing the same as everyone else, making do with fewer and fewer natural resources as time went on. Treading water and praying in vain for rescue.

Did it have to go so?

Not quite sure what she was doing, Jacquee levered herself to her feet. She eased herself into the warmish lagoon water—because fuck it—and waded across to a patch of mangroves she'd noticed at the far side of its lip. Seagulls wheeled and quarreled overhead as she swam. Her new vision showed her that the mangrove roots, where they entered the water, were as filamentous as any living thing in that water. And at first, she thought the roots had somehow trapped rockstones between them, till a jolt of recognition told her what she was seeing. Oysters! In the wild! Her belly rumbled joyfully. She fell to her knees in the mud, dug out a bunch of them, and shucked them open right there-so. She looked at the glistening meat in the shells. She made her decision. She slurped down the oysters and their salty liquor, every last one.

Then she beat around the mangrove roots and the shore of the lagoon until she found another plastic bottle with no cracks in it. Blasted things were everywhere. She dove to the lagoon bed and collected a few of the smaller globules in her bottle. She returned to her campsite with it and wedged the bottle upright in the mud near the water's edge to keep it cool. She had no idea what was going to become of her, but for now, her belly was full and her mind occupied.

She crawled into her makeshift tent and dozed, dreaming big dreams. What would come, would come.

The sound of an air horn rousted Jacquee from under the parachute. She looked out over the water. Three dots on the water, heading her way. Porkpies, or …?

She stayed up there, hidden by the trees, till she could see for sure. They were coming quickly. Pretty soon, she could make them out. Two electric speedboats. From her taz! She recognized the colorful patterns painted on their hulls. Kobe's on the left, green circuits painted on a black background. The red, green, and gold stripy one on the right was Uncle Silvis's.

Jacquee's heart was slamming in her chest. She nearly sprained the other ankle hurrying down to the beach. She drew off her sweatshirt and waved it in the air. "Hey!" she shouted.

"Over here!" The ocean breeze blew the sound off in another direction. Did they see her? Please. They had to see her.

They must have, because the boats started angling her way, bouncing through the swells.

A small, black form clambered from inside Uncle Silvis's boat, plopped into the water, and started making for shore. Uncle Silvis had to stop and circle back. He plucked the wriggling body out of the water. *Lickchop?* Joy surged like storm seas. How was he alive?

Little more, the boats were close enough to shore that the two men were able to jump out onto the sand below the surface and begin pulling them from the water. Jacquee waded to meet them, ignoring the ache of the waves yanking her injured ankle. Lickchop was out of the boat again, trotting to meet her. His vocoder was trumpeting, *JA-KAY!* over and over. Who the rass knew it could be so loud?

The men had their backs to her, concentrating on getting their boats safely out of the water. Kobe looked over his shoulder at her. He was grinning. Uncle Silvis never turned around. Uh-oh. She was in big trouble.

A low wave lifted Lickchop, bringing him to thump against her shin. Luckily, on her good leg. He was squealing and snorting, his snout turned comically upwards to keep it out of the water. *Ja-kay!* said his vocoder. *Ja-kay good!*

Hanging on to her crutch for balance, Jacquee bent and, one-handed, scooped the little pig's bristly, squirming body up into a hug. "Yes," she whispered against his shoulder. "I good." She blinked away the salt tears she was adding to the sea.

Lickchop was wriggling to get down. Kobe took him from Jacquee and lowered him into the ankle-deep water to splash happily around their feet. Jacquee supported herself with one hand on the gunwale of Kobe's boat as she followed them onto the beach.

"How you find me?" she asked the two men.

Kobe replied, "Nearly didn't. We lost the signal from the ultralight. Thought you went down with it. Uncle Silvis was frantic. Everyone was."

Uncle Silvis only grunted and pulled his boat on ahead of Kobe's.

"But," Kobe continued, "we kept getting interference on our channels, first one, then the next. And then the message came through clear—SOS from Lickchop. Found him swimming in open water, belting out EM pulses to keep the sharks away. Bet you didn't know his head rig could do that."

She hadn't. "But how that helped you know where I was?"

Uncle Silvis, his boat now well clear of the water, was leaning against its side, arms folded and scowling at Jacquee. "Rahtid little trenton kept saying him could hear you," he ground out. "We had to wait till low tide, but all the way here, that sintin on him head been calling out coordinates."

Maybe that explained the tickling between her ears, the ghost snippets of Lickchop's voice. That old Sean Paul song he loved. "Hmm. I think maybe I could hear him, too."

That got Kobe's attention. "Tell me more about that."

"Later. Uncle, I sorry about your ultralight. If you show me how, I will print out a replacement. You gwine haffe help me with the wiring, though."

Silvis's expression was unreadable. He rushed towards Jacquee and pulled her into his wiry, iron-cable arms. He smelled of sweat and ocean salt and good sinsemilla. "Wha mek a pig be your salvation, ee Jacquee? A haraam?"

Jacquee chuckled. "Promise I never going to put him on the supper table."

Uncle Silvis held her away at arm's length, a reluctant smile quirking his lips. "Never mind. Gwine treat the little so-and-so like a king from now on. He bring daughter Jacquee back to us. To me. You ready to come home?"

"Too ready. I haffe get some things first, though."

"Ee-hee? Like what?"

The parachute. They could mend it. And the bottle of lagoon water with the green globs in it. Jacquee smiled at Uncle Silvis. "I find something in a lagoon over there. A living thing. I think is new."

Uncle Silvis put an arm around her waist, started helping her limp in the direction she had pointed. Kobe and Lickchop followed. "A-whoa. And what you think it good for?"

"Me nah know. We should preserve a sample of it. Because I have an idea. Jamdown Ark, we could become a databank of gametes to re-seed the waters with when the time come. Maybe we could even breed stronger strains. And then we could—"

Laughing, Kobe shook his head. "Lord Jesus, not another Jacquee idea for saving the world."

Uncle Silvis was smiling, though. "Tell it to me when we get back."

Lickchop butted her calf. Second time he had avoided touching the injured leg. Jacquee wondered what the sensors that were apparently in his rig let him perceive. *Chow*, he said.

··· ❖ ···

75

As Uncle Silvis's boat bounced on the swells, racing Kobe back to Jamdown Ark, Jacquee studied Lickchop. She asked him, for the first time, "Is what you are?"

Lickchop stopped rooting around under the gunwale to gaze 'pon her, his black-in-black eyes inscrutable. *Are pig mind,* his vocoder stated.

Is "pig mind" he was saying? Or "big mind"? Lickchop continued, *Is what Ja-kay are?*

Maybe "are" was the right word. Lickchop apparently knew what it was to be a neurolinked creature, after all. Maybe it didn't matter if the link was with an artificial network or an organic one. Maybe he was referring to her in the plural because like recognized like.

A seaweed-green tracery, barely visible under the skin of her forearm, had crept up toward her elbow. It itched. She couldn't be sure, but she suspected it was responsible for the interference patterns in her wetware display. They were almost beginning to make sense. The world was looking little bit different, in ways she couldn't yet articulate. She was changing. She should have been worried, but she wasn't.

She was cradling the bottle containing the lagoon creatures between her knees. She leaned over and with her free hand scratched Lickchop under his chin. He grunted happily, angled his head so she could reach the best place. She echoed back his question: "What are I and I? We don't know, darling. Time will tell."

HOW WE ARE

by Chịkọdịlị Emelụmadụ

My mother was extraordinary, so they say. *They* being my grandmother, who is raising me.

They say my mother had the power to make anything grow, and the will to keep it so. She carried me within her for nearly two years. We talked often then, her voice in mine in hers, flowing streams of endless conversation. She told me about herself, about those bits that she hid from everyone. Some of these things I forgot. Others I learnt by myself. One cannot hide from one's own mind. One day she simply said "Enough," and I slid out of her, wet and shivering. She pulled me to her bosom, but I had been born with all my teeth, and hunger. Instead of suckling, I'd bitten her and drawn a mouthful of her blood. They say she sprang, pulled me off, slapped me. Not with spite, you understand, more surprise, hurt. I understood. We had been one entity not long ago, she nourished me, nurtured me, protected me within herself long after she should have, and in turn, what had I done but supped on her bones, crumbling her teeth to shards? What had I done but turn what she had grown from her own body into a weapon against her? No wonder she hit me.

They say the birthmark draping half of my face is because of this immediate postnatal violence, a dark gray-blue bruise, like ube.

They say my power came from her blood, but the hurt I caused soured it. Now instead of growing things, I infect them, hurt them.

I can kill them too.

Grandmother needs my pain for her medicine. On Afọ days, we go to the market where we peddle tinctures and potions and creams. Grandmother shares a stall with another woman—rents from her, really—even though I have never seen this woman, Eunice, sell any of her wares. If it is a good market, Grandmother will gladly part with Eunice's share of her profits. If it is bad, she will try to hide her money in my pants. Eunice may be half-blind, but she has hearing like a dog, she always knows how much we make. Nobody else will share a stall with Grandmother, not for how much she wants to pay. Grandmother is stingy and her mouth is bad. I wonder how Eunice stands her.

Besides, it is not really her they come to see, but me. Maybe it is the side effect of this power which plagues me. I can infect; therefore, I see infection in the body: weakness, aches, rot. I can tell when it is hopeless, though I never do, not while Grandmother can sell them a bottle of salve. I don't even need to touch a person to see where the break is, where harm has entered the electric path around the body. No, the touching is for something else, when the crowd gathers to witness me, and Grandmother on its fringes gives me her special sign.

Grandmother is discerning and cautious, and we never get caught. A peculiar tinge of gold jewelry, rich cloth, the right cut of jib, and the sign comes. These ones I must touch. These I must give something only she can cure. Not for long. Grandmother's cure helps but its effects never last. We have patrons and pay home visits. Not many, not even a few, smaller than that—but those we have, Grandmother will ensure we milk them dry, both of money and life. That is my specialty. Incurable stuff. Soaps and solutions help, but not forever.

Business is booming.

Grandmother likes to force me to listen to her stories, ever since I was little, and my mother ran away. I am my mother's penance, and so I sit and absorb Grandmother's verbal venom. She loves to talk about her beloved father, the notorious poisoner, so skilled that his poisons were undetectable, incurable. To be poisoned by my late great-grandfather was to die painfully and horribly. People feared him and many curried his favor. He is the only person of whom Grandmother speaks almost lovingly, as his life brought them riches. For a man who grew no crops nor hunted, he had meat and fish aplenty for his family at every meal, especially as no other families would join them. So what if—he was known to boast—his daughters remained unmarried? He was rich enough to cater for them until they grew old and decrepit. Rich enough, powerful enough until some young talented upstart poisoner tested his mettle. Great-grandfather's death lasted eight agonizing months, and afterward his family absconded, hiding from their father's enemies, changing their names—here Grandmother spits into one of her tonics. Only Grandmother had the courage to try and follow in her father's trade. She had none of his skill for suffering, no creative ways to seduce and prolong a bout of death. The closest she could come involved a numbing sleep which, while it quietened the sufferer, did nothing to properly alleviate their pain.

For my mother, Grandmother has nothing but scorn. The woman who birthed me not only turned Grandmother's blood-gifts from bitter to sweet, but when the fullness of her powers came about, powers which equaled her ancestor's, she refused to make money off them, wandering the villages and giving herself away to all who needed her.

"Good-for-nothing waste of talent!" Grandmother spits. "Do you know what she stole from me? Before her, my cures lasted. And what did she do with my power? Nothing! Spreading her laps for an ordinary 'How are you?' from common men and women."

Grandmother's hands tremble whenever she talks about Mother. Such is her rage that the knife she is using to whittle a chewing stick from a branch of bitterwood slips and buries its blade in the side of her index finger. Grandmother hisses. She does not suck the blood, but instead opens another bottle and squeezes her finger into it. She glares at her finger as if it has personally betrayed her.

"Still stealing from me," she says. "All I do is mention her and my essence comes pouring out of me. You see this, Gifty? You see how wicked your mother is? Tueh!" She spits again.

I mind my business and turn the plantains frying in the pan. Grandmother mumbles but does not demand a response from me.

When I was little Grandmother could not abide my silences. She would jump up and whatever was in her hand would lash my skin, bruise it, break it. One day, I clung to her ankle as she hit me with a wooden spoon for not finishing my food.

"Bastard! Wasting my money! Your fool of a mother should have taken you!"

Afterward, a few hours later, her ankle blistered and burst and blistered over again. Grandmother, following the first fact-finding wince that punctuated her exploring fingers, had looked at me properly, not out of the corner of her eye as she was wont. Her face, lost in thought, seemed almost kind.

"Come here, this child," she said. I came. "Can you do this again?" She pointed at her ankle. I knelt down and touched the unblemished one. Only her knowledge of herbs stopped the skin from bursting open like overripe fruit. The battering ceased that same day. I was six.

The plantains are hot and golden, slightly crisp around the edges, the way Grandmother likes them. She slides five, six scalding slices into her mouth before I get a chance to serve them with the beans, stew, and fried beef. Grandmother sighs with pleasure when she bites into the meat.

"Tomorrow, some foolish man will come and turn your head, and you will take all your gifts to his household," she says. "Even your mother could not cook like this."

If only.

Grandmother does not like to mix her stew with the beans, prefers to let the red sit on top of the black-eyed beans like molten magma on a mountaintop, scooping both layers together. Prefers to let her tongue do the mixing. She eats her fill, drinks her cup of water, and burps before giving me her nod, assent. I am allowed to eat now. Grandmother picks her teeth, watches me like a guard dog. It is all an act, this permission to eat, left over from the days when she could and did deny me food often. I am bigger than she is, stronger and wider too. The thing which keeps me bound is more than strength or size. Grandmother is the only family I have ever known. Despite the crowd I attract at the marketplace and in the village squares, I have no friends, no other family—cannot so much as touch anyone without imparting some malaise or other. It is a lonely life, a life filled with the echoes of other people's living. I have no doubt that Grandmother would get by with her talents, but me, what use would I be to anyone? What point is it telling people where they ail if I cannot then provide the relief that is so desperately needed? I am not my mother. There is nowhere for me to go, so I stay.

I can perform wonders in a cooking pot, they say. I take Grandmother's word for it. Despite the pleasure I take in its making, food has no taste in my mouth, never has. For years I complained to Grandmother, and she beat me, thinking me ill-mannered, ungrateful. Hurt, harm to the body, aches, fugue states, those things I can smell, perceive, taste.

I shovel my food down for sustenance, wash the dishes, and clean the kitchen.

We retire without locking our doors. Nobody would dare attack us.

Tuesday is Eke, and before the cock has crowed thrice in the compound across the street, I have readied our wares for sale. Grandmother likes Eke Awka the best of all the markets we visit. Big, bustling, and situated in the state capital, Eke Awka is the second largest in the state. The biggest one is Main Market at Onitsha, but we never go there. Not when it attracts thousands daily. Grandmother is cautious, afraid even, that somebody will figure out what I do and steal me away to use for their own misdeeds or kill me. There are many skilled poisoners, dibias, medicine men from as far as Kogi, toward the north. She is afraid that some ambitious poisoner or herbalist from Calabar or Benin will challenge her, and she will fail. She is afraid about what this means. Grandmother does not go anywhere or try anything if she is not already sure of its outcome. I have learnt from her and keep to myself.

We leave without breakfast. On Eke days, as is our custom, Grandmother stops at the akara sellers at Gbalingba Square. Huge, wide pans full of bleached, palm oil simmer, and the brown akara balls bob up and down, turned over by perforated spoons the size of shovels. Soon they are done, scooped up and dumped into woven baskets lined with newspaper. It is brisk, hungry business. Already there are a few barrow and truck boys waiting for the heavy breakfast which will see them through to the afternoon. Eke days are busy, and there is much money to be made. Not one of these boys will risk losing trade by stopping for lunch until the swell dies down.

"Gifty, Gifty! How bodi?" Mama Chioma is the most buxom of the akara artisans. She is also my favorite. She greets Grandmother and her smile gleams in her slick face. Fat, Christian Mother arms jiggle rhythmically as she stirs the spiced bean paste in preparation for dropping into the oil. Chioma, her daughter, slices whole loaves of bread, stuffs them with the akara, and prepares akamụ, baptizing the corn pap with sparkling cubes of sugar and splashes of evaporated milk, before handing off to the next customer. The boys eat standing, squatting, perching on the overfull wooden benches.

"How much own?" Mama Chioma asks. "The usual?" I nod. Her arms move, dropping the paste with her fingers into the oil.

Grandmother casts a lazy, practiced eye over the assembled patrons, but her gaze does not hold genuine interest. These are not her desired clientele.

The akara is ready. Mama Chioma shakes off the excess oil in the spoon and wraps the balls, still shrieking from contact with the heat, into newspapers. She places the package in a black polythene bag and stretches out her hand. I open my bag and allow her to drop the bundle within, making sure not to touch her skin with the sliver of mine appearing between my long sleeves and the gloves I wear. Grandmother hands her the money.

"Bye-bye nụ!" Mama Chioma waves. She smells like a heap of cashew fruits that have fallen under the tree, heavy and heady and sweet.

We settle down for breakfast in Agnes's stall. Agnes is the woman from whom Grandmother rents space on Eke days, a woman with a wide mouth and dull, bulging eyes who looks but does not see. Grandmother's hands are swift, and she cuts and drugs the akara before serving Agnes's portion. Grandmother has kept Agnes her mind-slave for a long time, each dose wearing off just as Eke day comes around. We will keep most of what we make at this stall, and still Agnes will thank us as though we are the ones doing her a favor. Whatever other money she makes, Agnes gives away to the priest in the white-garment church she attends. Grandmother says Agnes has been asleep since long before they met. Some people are better off that way.

The akara has not yet gone down my gullet when the first customers arrive. Agnes sells occult artifacts, badly printed books in esoteric languages, framed symbols, carvings, perfume oils, holy water, sacred money, pencils, and pens. Sometimes Agnes is slow to give change, so I try to help. Grandmother makes a sound in her throat, but I don't mind her. It is the least I can do after what we have taken from Agnes.

I have sweat running down the sides of my face by the time the sun sits in the middle of the sky. Sickness reeks in the heat. I call out to a man whose blood flows tight and fast in his veins. He smells of dirty laundry. The man waves a dismissive hand as he hurries away.

"You have high BP!" I call after him. "Do you want to die?"

Grandmother cuts eyes at me, smiling with her teeth as she wraps up a package for another customer. We do not mention death, even if it is around the corner. We take the hopeless, those who have a slow, steady decline. Knowledge of immediate and certain death makes people stupid and reckless. And the suddenly dead always seem to have angry relatives wanting their money back.

I smell Buchi in the crowd before I see her, the smell of petrichor, heady and delicious. My armpits begin to sweat, but I keep my head, touching the woman with the gold bracelets almost up to her elbow as Grandmother has indicated. Buchi's presence is a breeze, blowing away all the odors in my head, and it is with shame that I touch the woman's hands. She is in the peak of health, her blood metallic, full, and rich. Her laughter is incredulous when I feel her wrist, sure of itself, of her body. I regretfully send a message to her ankle.

"You have a swelling that is about to appear, somewhere on your legs," I say. "It is not dangerous."

"Is that all?" Grandmother smiles crocodile wide. "Search well," she says. She is desperate, wanting me to give the woman something malignant. Even the moisture collecting in the woman's cleavage smells wealthy.

"She said she sees nothing, what did you want her to find?" the woman asks Grandmother. A wariness has entered her eyes at Grandmother's careless words.

Buchi draws nearer as I touch the woman's wrist again. I consider giving her an accompanying cyst on her wrist, or an ulcer in her

83

stomach, but these also show up quickly, and it would be unfortunate for her to suspect me of anything. There are three rings on her ring finger. Rich husbands bring problems too.

"No, nothing," I say, withdrawing my hand. The woman leaves a few notes in front of me which Grandmother tucks into the waist of her wrapper before they have even touched the table. Some of the gathered disperse, disappointed not to get a free show of a rich woman breaking down. The poor love nothing more than to see the wealthy reduced to nothing. Disgusted, Grandmother turns away and walks through Agnes's shop, past the sleeping woman, into the small inner room to compose herself. I slip my glove back on.

"Can you really tell when people are sick?" Buchi's smell makes me dizzy. I want to sit, but Grandmother does not believe young people should sit without reason, so there is no chair for me. Buchi repeats the question.

"Yes," I reply.

"Even when we were in school? Is that why you didn't play with anybody? It must have been pepper for you, all the sickness you knew about. Did you know Mrs. Anigbo had cancer? That she was going to die?"

I am wondering why after all this time Buchi is talking to me in the market, after all this time of me rebuffing her friendship in school and turning a blind eye to her everywhere else. Buchi can say one million words in a minute, the same as when we were in primary school when she tried to be my friend, asking me all sorts of questions while I sat under her heady perfume and tried not to formulate an answer. Eventually even her persistence could not hold out against my taciturn nature, and she drifted away with her many friends and admirers. Our schoolmates added one more reason to why I must be unpleasant and avoided at all costs. Nobody rejected Buchi's friendship.

"Touch me," she says. And my heart vomits heat all over my insides. I stare at her, overwhelmed, flabbergasted, scared. "Tell me if I have any sickness, now." Buchi is insistent.

I can already smell that she does not. An excess of oils under the skin on her face, minute blockages, painful yes, but not deadly. I shake my head, no.

"You haven't even touched me yet." She laughs.

"I don't want to," I reply.

"Why not?" Buchi's eyes are black, the bones in her face sharp as knives.

I am delivered from the peril of lying by Grandmother, who clears her throat behind me. Buchi greets her, teeth flashing, eyes disappearing almost into her face. Grandmother's response is a grunt.

"I hope you are not just here, gisting with your friends when there is work to be done?" she asks.

"She is not my friend," I say.

Buchi stares at me. She says goodbye and winds her way through the throng in the market, taking her scent with her. For the rest of the day, I put the rod back in my spine and cast Buchi out of my mind. Grandmother must never know how I feel.

The man with high BP comes back, and as a mercy I touch him and wear down the wall in one of his arteries. Grandmother will not chop his money more than once.

Some nights when Grandmother falls asleep, I slip out and take a walk to clear my head, to feel something other than other people's illnesses, their tastes, my own flesh, or the inside of my gloves. Grandmother owns a modest bungalow, encircled by a low wall and not much else. Leaving is easy, no squeaky gates to open. The night, between patches of generator-made light, is impenetrable, but I know my way around. Nobody bothers me here, in this village. All those nights of wandering around with my gloves off, laying hands on trees while the night cooled itself. My hands know the feel of leaves, of bark thick and corky, or thin like the husk from groundnuts. I have felt fruit, inedible, spiky, or furry. Trees do not get sick like people do, at least not from me. Their embrace is all I have enjoyed for years.

Tonight, the thoughts in my head cause me to cower in the dark, to skip quickly through pools of light. Buchi's parents are three miles away, in one of two duplexes shared by four families. I tell myself I don't mean to go so far, hence the wrapper around my waist, concealing my nightgown, my stretched-out, frayed sweater against the chill. These are home clothes, to be hidden from all eyes except mine and Grandmother's. I tell myself this, hiding my destination from myself.

The compound gate is still open. I observe a set of boys' quarters behind a low hedge that I cannot remember being there before, past the almond tree in the middle of the compound—somebody is doing well, expanding. I dart behind the duplex, eyes searching in the dark. No sane person would visit at this time of night, alone, on foot. I cannot afford to cast a shadow over the white-blue illuminations coming from the two ground-floor flats. There is the smell of stale Egusi soup coming from the one flat closest to me, but the next one smells of—I breathe deeply—yam porridge and first rains.

The back door to the flat clatters open, at the same time the night swells with the laughter of young men from the boys' quarters behind me. Both things cause me to freeze. Buchi sees me before I can step back fully into the shadows.

"Gifty?" she calls. "Gifty?"

I step forward.

"What are you doing here?" Buchi drops a bag of rubbish into the outdoor bin and comes toward where I am standing. Instantly I grow dizzy again, and the air heats up.

"Did you come to see me?" she asks. "I think you said I wasn't your friend? Am I sick? Did you come to touch me?"

Her questions, so many of them. My head swims and I put my hands up to stop my head from rolling off my shoulders.

"What is it?" She is whispering and her breath tickles the hairs on my top lip. "Do you want to come inside?"

"No," I manage to say. I turn to leave, but Buchi blocks me.

"Come inside," she says. "It is late and your house is far."

She knows where I live. Everybody in school did, the better to avoid it. Buchi reaches for my hand and stops herself. She turns toward the back door again and slips inside without waiting to see if I am following. After a moment, her head slips out again. She beckons. I go to her.

The corridor is even darker than outside had been, and the only light comes from the TV in the parlor. The concrete floor is cool against my bare feet, but the walls still carry some warmth. There is the intense smell of gmelinas about the house which no other scents can mask. Somebody is dying.

Buchi's room is less than half the size of mine, it appears to be a converted store near the kitchen and away from the rest of the family. Her bed has been pushed to the wall, but boxes, bags, and cartons line the other three walls. There is a hint of louvre panes by one partially blocked window, a massive cross hanging near the ceiling with Jesus still on it. A glow-in-the-dark rosary is curled up on her pillow. Her room is small, secluded, perfect. My guard is up.

I feel her smile in the dark.

"Who is dying?" I ask.

The smile vanishes.

"My mother," she says, and I taste the tears collecting in her throat.

We lie side by side, facing each other in her narrow bed. It is agony, my muscles stiffening to hold me in place. Buchi tells me everything, things I know none of her admirers could have known—tragedy repels company—things which I hope she has told nobody else.

"You can really see sickness?" she asks again.

"See, smell, sometimes taste," I tell her.

"What does it smell like?"

"All sorts of things. Your mother smells of gmelina fruits."

"I hate that smell," she says.

I concur; me also.

The generators supplying electricity to various houses in the neighborhood begin to power down one by one. Buchi swallows. Her saliva is sticky, thick, gluing her tongue to the palate. Her hand finds one of my gloved ones. My heart throws up its contents again.

"And when you touch them? Is it bad-bad? What do you see?"

I try to explain about the electricity. It sounds stupid.

"So, it doesn't pain you? Why don't you touch people, then?"

I withdraw into myself. In my mind, I am already on the road home, slipping back through the unlocked door and into my bedroom before Grandmother awakens. Tonight, has been a mistake. What had I been hoping would happen? What was this need to apologize for not calling her my friend? The desire to unburden myself shrinks back from telling her what my touch really does, the hundreds Grandmother and I have infected, have killed over the years. What would Buchi think of me then, a plague, lying in her bed?

Buchi is silent, her breathing even. I assume she has fallen asleep and prepare to climb out of the bed.

"Why are you running?" she asks. Her lips on my eyelids are startlingly hot. She kisses my sweaty nose. Turbulence from my stomach, fresh dust notes in my nostrils. I jerk back even as my face rises to meet hers.

"Wait!" I say.

"You don't have to touch me," she says. "I will touch you."

I am despicable. I am weak. I have killed her.

Her tongue at the entrance to my mouth brings the rains down upon me, upon us both, a monsoon, thrashing and curling around us, and we are swept away.

I have been watching Buchi for signs of illness, or infection from my hands, and, finding none, our friendship thaws, thrives. I am not sure how this has happened, but I am unwilling to try touching someone else in case it is a fluke of some sort. Nothing goes out of me when we touch.

I slip out frequently to see Buchi. Never the same days or times, but she is always waiting regardless. We are careful of the university boys in the boys' quarters, we know how they behave, what they will do if they suspect how we are.

My days off are the days Grandmother makes special potions with secret ingredients. Those days are filled with reading and helping Buchi take care of her stepsisters, of her dying mother and despondent father, a civil servant who slumps in front of the TV upon his return, whether there is electricity to power it or not. I help her to divert attention from her stepmother, rushed and harried with teaching and side hustles, indifferent to both Buchi and her own children, and upset by them at the same time. I wash Buchi's hair.

It is a strange setup, and yet I prefer it to what Grandmother and I have, the oceans of distance between us, physically, in her bungalow, and otherwise.

Buchi tends to her mother, a small woman, made smaller by disease, a pile of bones covered in thin, brown skin. Buchi turns her with more ease than she does her sisters and wipes her bedsores.

"My parents divorced when we were in school," she says, "but my mum couldn't go home to the Philippines. Her parents disowned her for marrying my dad, so she stayed here, but my father met someone else that he wanted to marry. Then she became ill ..."

Buchi's confidences come without prompting. She talks to me as though she is talking to herself. I stare at the woman on the bed, the woman whose eyes are half-open, breath coming in painful gasps, stopping for seconds at a time.

"I wish she had gone," Buchi says. She drops the face towel into the bucket of Dettol and tepid water. "I wish Mummy would die; she has suffered enough. When she dies, I will go to my uncle in Lagos and find my luck there."

"I can come with you."

The declaration tears out of me forcefully. The notion of being without Buchi is like endless night. I had borne it before when I knew no better, but not now, not after I have been kissed by the warmth of the sun. I cannot think to stand the yawning, grasping aloneness that will result from her departure. In that moment, I understand my mother, why she left. It was not because I bit her, tainting her powers within myself. It was not the possibility of her gifts fading like Grandmother's, or her certain cruelty. It was that people need other people, their souls, their spirits, to bloom and grow. Was that not, after all, why I stayed with Grandmother? For a shallow semblance of the same? My mother gave away her gifts for free, to Grandmother's chagrin, but in so doing, she opened up and gave of herself as well. That is living, that is being, and I am ashamed of how long it has taken this knowledge to emerge from deep in my subconscious. Is this something I learnt, or something my mother revealed to me?

Buchi's hand slips beneath my waistband with ease. "Can you help me?" she asks. I taste the tears again. "Can you help my mother to stop breathing?"

I pull the searching hand away. "Who said I can do that?" I ask.

"Can't you?" she counters.

Clouds gather all day without rain to back up the threat. Nevertheless, it has the same effect as if it were raining. People dart about the shops and exit the market quickly, hoping to avoid the downpour, the inevitable flooding which brings traffic to a standstill.

I mull over Buchi's request in my mind, one eye on the sky, the other on passersby. I smell a stroke coming in one person, the bitterness of burning tires creeping up the electric pathway, but before I can say anything, the man in question scurries away. The odor of spoilt chicken livers as the woman before me stops to finger Eunice's wares—the baby in her womb is dead already. I think of saying something.

"If you are not buying, please don't block my front," says Grandmother, making use of her famous bad mouth. The woman places a protective hand on the swell of her stomach as she walks away.

Grandmother smiles at me. "You have not been cutting your hair," she says. "It is now long, and nobody will plait it for you. Nobody can touch you, remember? Or do you know something I don't?" Grandmother's smile is rare and never in my direction. It frightens me, its appearance. Coupled with the weather, it is as though I have soldier ants stinging me all over.

Another customer materializes, and Grandmother gives the sign. I stare the man down. Him? He wears a safari suit, gray and ordinary, and a pair of leather sandals. His hair and moustache have been combed. He is plump, but nothing about him screams wealth. His hands hover over the bottles and jars but his eyes search elsewhere. Him? I stare at Grandmother, who looks back unblinking.

"Is this all you have?" asks the man.

"What are you looking for?" I reply.

The man looks uneasy. I open my eyes and nose wide, and I know he will not tell us women, not even with blind Eunice pretending not to listen. His is a man's problem.

"Perhaps my granddaughter can touch you. She will know what ails you." Grandmother kicks me, making certain to connect with the bottom of her sandaled foot.

"No!" The man jerks away before I can reach him. He hurries off.

"He did not have much," I say to Grandmother.

"We need money, God knows. It is not as if you are doing your job, disappearing all the time. Where do you even go, sef?"

"Nowhere." I realize immediately that I have given the wrong answer. Grandmother smiles, nonetheless.

"Secretive, just like your mother."

I am distracted by the smell of fresh dust and whirl around without my usual caution. The crowds are sparse, and Buchi's smile is wide, noticeable as she bounds toward our stall. I try to signal her with my eyes to dim her happiness, but Buchi is oblivious. Behind me, Grand-mother croaks like a frog.

Buchi does not touch me when Grandmother is around, but she does not need to. I wear the imprint of her hands on my skin. Buchi is also taken in by Grandmother's crocodile smiles. She bumps me, tries to make me smile, jokes, she and Grandmother between them, passing anecdotes over my head. My body is taut with worry, taunted by anxiety. Buchi is used to being adored. She does not see that Grandmother is not like other grandmothers are meant to be. I want Buchi to leave. Grandmother's eyes flit from her to me even though I have not moved from my place since she appeared. The clouds are stained with charcoal.

"Maybe we should pack up now," Grandmother says.

We never pack up early, not until the market closes for the day—and even then, we linger at the buses, doing last-minute deals on potions—but I am relieved. Pressure has built up in my ears and this way, I can walk Buchi to her bus stop and relieve some of it.

I pull Buchi out of the shop under the pretense of the rain and escort her to her stop.

"What is doing you?" she asks.

"You can't come to our house."

"Why?" She fiddles with her scapular, placing the one brown square over her chest so that it lines up with the one on her back.

The magnitude of it, how to explain that silence is the most frequent visitor in our house? That Grandmother cannot be trusted? She will look and she will see and there is no telling what she can do with what she sees. Grandmother can destroy anything with her mouth. What if Grandmother says something of the work that we do, our real work? Tells her what I have done to countless others? Will Buchi still like me then? I must keep them apart.

"Grandmother is wicked," I say.

Hia! Buchi hisses. "If she is wicked to you, be wicked back. You have a mouth too."

Buchi thinks everything is easy. My mind is full of things to say but my tongue has tied itself the way it normally does when things are too much. Buchi normally talks for both of us.

"Have you thought about the thing I said?" she asks. "About my mother?"

I sigh. "Yes," I say.

"Are you going to do it for me?"

"How are you expecting me to do this thing?" I am searching again for what Buchi knows or suspects of what I do.

Buchi looks away. "I would do it myself if she was not my mother," she says. "I would do it for you."

I turn it over in my mind. I have never killed anybody before, not in the way she is asking me, not as a mercy. I have been passive, letting Grandmother direct and place my hands just where she wishes. Selfish as well, for a roof over my head and the lie of family. Passive and selfish. That is all I know how to be. Buchi is asking something else entirely.

"I don't want her to suffer."

Buchi shrugs. "Will it be more than she is suffering already?"

My head hurts.

"Do it next week. Should we say Wednesday? Let me give the little ones time to get ready, you hear? Just do it fast. If I could do it myself …"

A drop of rain slaps me on the head, another on the cheek. Buchi squeals and runs for the bus without saying goodbye, but I do not mind. I need more time to think.

There are things you don't dare think about when nobody wants you, things that you cannot afford to ponder because they open you up to the risk of painful discovery. I never asked Grandmother questions about my mother, not where she went or where she was living or why she did not come to see me. It did not matter, because I still felt the residue of my mother's essence from sharing her mind, and even though I missed her fiercely, I know she loved me, loved me enough to wreck her body to keep me protected. I know that whatever caused her to leave must have been unbearable, and as I grew, I knew Grandmother to be that cause. It is hard to compete with the memory of a dead ancestor. Grandmother used up all her love on her own father. The rest of us she merely uses.

But I have also settled, in ways that my own mother chose not to, and in so doing I have wasted the sacrifices she made for me. I think I now understand love and I understand sacrifice, and Buchi by one simple act is asking for both. It is time to be neither passive nor selfish. I am resolved.

That night, when she opens the back door to me, it is with the solemnity that the occasion deserves. Buchi touches her lips to mine softly and leads me by the hand. Snoring comes from the parlor, little snuffles from all over the house. I have come late on okada, after most of the rain has subsided, to avoid the inevitable misstep and drowning in overfull roadside gutters.

Her mother's breathing sounds much worse. The gmelina smell suffocates me. I deliberately avoid looking inside her with my eyes, as there does not appear to be any use for my gifts.

"She sounds really bad," I whisper. "Maybe we should just let her go on her own."

"No," Buchi whispers back. "Sometimes she is like this, and we think she will die, but it has been eight years."

She takes my hands, pulling my gloves off one by one. Buchi places them down on her mother's chest. The thin skin clings to the ribcage, fragile. I could shatter them if I pushed down, but that sounds like extra misery for the woman struggling for every breath. I could wrap my hands around her throat, I am strong enough. I could put the flat pillow on her face and cut off all air.

"How will you do it?" Buchi asks. She puts her index finger in her mouth.

Turn around, I tell her, and she obeys. I try what comes naturally, sending her every infection and disease I have ever conjured up. At once the electric pathway within her goes haywire, explosions going off, things burning. My heart echoes the panicked beating beneath my hands, the breathing shallow and fast. I have never felt such power, nor held such intent in my mind. I push until the brain inside the eggshell skull collapses. I raise my hands, pick my gloves off the bed, and slip them back on. For once, the smell of my handiwork nauseates me.

"I've finished," I say.

Buchi turns back around. Her jaw hangs open. "She is not supposed to look like this," she says. There is blood coming out of the corpse's bulbous eyes, the ears and nose.

"What did you do to her?" she asks. Her own eyes are wide. It is as if she too is seeing me for the first time.

93

The rains continue almost nonstop all weekend long and into the next week. The trips to the markets are miserable, sodden affairs. There is little profit, but Grandmother insists on earning what there is, first at Agnes's and then at Eunice's. The market seems emptier, and not just because most people take shelter in different shops. Buchi has not been to see me, and I, recalling the horror on her face at my handiwork, cannot bring myself to visit. Grandmother watches me but leaves me to my thoughts for most of the morning, chatting with Agnes when she is not serving customers. Agnes makes the noise in her throat that means agreement though I am unsure to what extent she understands.

"Forget that one," says Grandmother, and it takes me a while to figure out she is talking to me.

"She talked too much. They always promise the world, then, before you know it, they are running from the magnitude of your power, and you are pregnant and alone."

My mind scrambles to comprehend what has come out of Grand-mother's mouth. I stare at her, and she stares at me. I wonder how much she knows, what she knows.

"Although, in your case, it is a blessing you cannot get pregnant like that. That one has not known suffering, real suffering. How can you be your true self with such a one?"

I stare at her some more.

"Close your mouth, before flies enter. You think because I am old, I do not see things? The man that sired you was the same, attracted to your mother but overawed by what she could do. Where is he now? She is still looking for him, your useless mother. But you, there is a lot more to you. You and my father are similar. Let the chatterbox girl go, you will find another."

Inside me it is warm, in a way I have never felt. Grandmother does not say any more on the matter, but what is said cannot be unsaid. I am buoyed by her words, seen, accepted, all ill will forgotten. It lasts a while before doubt descends.

"She can touch me," I say. "I can touch her, and she does not get ill."

"Nothing new under the sun," Grandmother says. Of course she has figured it out too. That is the reason she has spoken. That is why she can say: leave the chatterbox girl. A bit of residual doubt remains—is Grandmother being amenable so that I do not leave like my mother did? I put the thought away.

When it is clear we will make no more money today, I ask Grandmother if I can go for a while, counting on her to say yes, which she does. Something has opened up between us. It makes me brave. I am determined to face Buchi, on my own terms, in the daylight, instead of crawling to her at night. I did as she asked, and this silence is the thanks I receive? Throwing a shawl over my head, I race for the next bus in line. It is half full, and I must wait for it to fill with passengers before we can leave; however, I am not fazed. Time stretches before me, crammed with possibility. Perhaps it is not just Buchi I can touch without harming, maybe there are more, hundreds, thousands more. Nothing new under the sun.

The sun breaks through dark clouds and it is raining and sunny at the same time. Some of the passengers clap, delighted. A child in its mother's lap begins to sing the rainy-sunny-day song popular among schoolchildren. I smile, recalling doing the same at his age.

Buchi's compound is different in the daytime, gate wide open, silent, except for the droplets of water slapping the thick, broad leaves of the almond tree. Standing by the front door feels strange to me, as does knocking, but I do it anyway. There is no response. I dash around to the back door and find it ajar.

To another, the smell would be unbearable, but to me it is merely unpleasant and familiar. I smell my handiwork all over the house.

The first room holds the bodies of the two stepsisters in bed, arms around each other, dark blood congealed on the bedding. Their mother is curled up on the floor in her own rufescent excrement. I open the rest of the rooms in a rush.

"Buchi! Buchi!" I shout. Other bodies: her father slumped in work clothes, briefcase clutched in a dead fist, his body blocking the front door. Her mother's body lies where I last saw it. It reeks the most.

I find Buchi with her head and shoulders in the toilet. Her nightgown is stained and bloody. The world swims, thunder smashes down around us.

"Buchi!" I try to lift her out but some of her hair comes off in my hand. The scalp beneath is bloodless. I throw the hair down, try again, standing over her, lifting up and out. Her eyes are glued shut; her face watery.

No, *my* face is watery. I am crying, and my tears splash all over Buchi's unmoving features. Ugly sounds, loud in my throat, deadening my ears.

The ants are back, swarming all over me, pinching and biting, and I rush out the door and toward the center of the compound. I put my hands on the almond tree, and I push every bad feeling, every scrap, every ounce of whatever is in my blood into the tree, into the ground, into the sky.

"Take it!" I shout. "I don't want this anymore."

Lightning slices through the air, the smell of plastic burning. I am covered suddenly by leaves, falling violently to the ground. From the ends of my toes, the grass begins to wither, spreading out across the compound toward the boys' quarters, and beyond.

THEM DOGHEAD BOYS

by Alex Jennings

Things got bad bad once the Ravels was gone. Five-O swooped down and arrested damn near eighty of them, and after that wasn't nobody on the corners slingin', but things wasn't no safer. Up at the corner of Brainard and Josephine there was a murder at five or six in the evening. I say "murder" cause what else you'd call it? Wasn't even boys from the neighborhood. Ole Ronny was just riding his bike like he do and three boys started grittin' on him and woofin' at him, saying they was gon' take his wheels. He said leave him alone, but they didn't; and he called down a piece of the night, and it wrapped around two of them, caught 'em up and then dropped them down from real high; hit the third boy and he just lay in the street with his spine broke, and ruined bodies piled on top of him, and he didn't die til later in the hospital. Wasn't no shit like that when the Ravels was still around. Monster shit.

Vampires ain't so bad. They're predictable, mostly. Yeah, they need blood, but they only out at night and somebody got to give them permission. In the movies they need permission to come inside but in real life they need permission to get you at all. Anybody can give permission, though.

At least they got rules. Dogheads don't need permission for nothing.

Me and Lonzo went to George Price High over on O. C. Haley. Lonzo was tall with big hands and feet, but he gangled, and couldn't coordinate. He could play a little ball, but he wasn't real good. Didn't make the team. I didn't either, but I didn't try.

I'm wrong, though. It wasn't that Lonzo couldn't coordinate—he was fine. He just didn't have a competitive spirit. If you blocked his shot, if you scored on his goal, he didn't care. He couldn't really pretend that a game was more than a game. He couldn't *chase*.

We lived over on Simon Bolivar—more like brothers than neighbors. He lived next door to me and Aunt Sharon, on the far side of a cream-colored double with faded red trim. It had a nice porch, and the old folks would sit out there and drink or play dominos and talk trash. The thing about Lonzo is he had a hard time. Something 'bout him that just got on some niggas' nerves, so they would devil him at school. I looked out for him when I could. I was never king of my class or nothing. People respected me, especially once I started cutting hair, but wasn't nobody afraid of me or nothing. I wasn't hard and I didn't pretend to be.

Nobody made it their business to be on Lonzo all the time, but sometimes Rel Howard or somebody would smack his books out his hands or throw his book sack in the dirty shower water after Gym. That kind of shit. You know how sometimes somebody mess with you and then you mess back a little maybe, or you let him know you too much trouble to keep fuckin' with and he back down and you forget about it because it wasn't really nothing? Well, Lonzo couldn't do that. Grown folks would tell him *roll it off ya back*, but every time wasn't just its own little happening, it was—each little incident was connected, I guess, with the one before and the one after so they was sort of all stitched together contiguous like one of my Aunt Sharon's quilts she makes. He couldn't just let shit go.

But that sounds like he held onto shit on purpose, which ain't the case. He wasn't bitter, you know? He just *remembered*. You could see it in his eyes, and the way his throat worked when he bent to pick up his things. Rel was harmless though, I thought, and just liked to have somebody to threaten when he felt small. It must be hard feelin' like you ain't got no control over nothing.

···❖···

So the Ravels got got, and at first things was quiet. That year, there wasn't even no fireworks at New Year's. The quiet was all tense at first, but then the longer it went on, it was like it relaxed—or it didn't relax, but you thought maybe you was wrong, and just nothin' was happening and things was fine …. Even after that shit with Ronny. Every now and then you'd see somebody went missing years ago just standing on the corner staring, you know? Like me and Lonzo seen Ms. Pearline from over on Saint Andrew just standing outside the community center one night while we was riding our bikes back from Coliseum Park. She was wearing one of her old lady nightgowns and staring real hard down Camp Street. It was like she was looking out on some other world.

That wasn't a big deal, though. We just didn't ride around so much after that. Later I heard Ms. Pearline was back living in her house. Them white folks bought the place was gone and she was just back in there. It was just something happened.

Then the cops killed Aubrey Lincoln. Aubrey was a crackhead, but not like on TV. He didn't steal and he wasn't hassling nobody for money. He might ask you for a cigarette even if you didn't smoke, but he wasn't doing nothing to nobody. He lived with his cousin on St. Andrew and Daneel, and he was gay so maybe tricked a little sometimes, but that's whatever.

Folks saw three cop cars in the parking lot behind the old Myrtle Banks building—the one the white folks is opening back up as a fancy grocery—and the lights was all going, and I heard they had Aubrey cuffed on the ground, but they shot him eleven times. You woulda never seen some shit like that in the Ravel days. I'm not saying they was good folks—they was killin' niggas and running bitches and poisoning folks with rock and whatnot, but they was *orderly*, you feel me? They had a chain of command, and the cops didn't fuck with them.

After that, police was around more. Cop cars cruising up and down Baronne, on Bolivar. Three-four nights a week, cops would park they cars in the lot outside the old Barbershop at Josephine and Haley, and they'd just sit and talk at each other out their windows, and you could feel them even when you wasn't looking at them, like on a real sunny day when you shut your eyes and see a red glow from the light, but like it's shining from inside your own head. I think that's when the cold began, but I didn't notice it til later.

Me and Lonzo and Billy D was hooping over at A. L. Davis, and time got away. All of a sudden, it was full dark and we had to go. Wasn't nothing had happened for a few weeks, what with the police all over. Didn't even see no dead folks or nothing. So we got on our bikes and we was riding home—

And there was three of them outside the Chicken Mart.

One had on a old letter jacket from De La Salle even though it was nice out. He was short but *broad* broad across his chest. He was just standing, but he looked coiled up like a spring. His head was a mix of dogs. There mighta been some Boxer in there, some Shar Pei, because he had jowls and wrinkles, and he had this splash of white on his forehead with these pretty light-brown spots, you know? And his eyes was big and tired, and you could tell he was smart.

The one on his right was a Doberman. He wore some ripped jeans and a diagonal-striped Polo. The third was like a Rottweiler. None of them said nothing when we rode past, and I thought maybe I should speak, but everything seemed slow, and I knew I would be past before I could make up my mind. You gotta speak to folks out here, it will save your life, but they wasn't people.

And then I heard Lonzo's voice from far off, saying, "How y'all is?"

"Beautiful, beautiful," one of them said.

"Killer breeze," another one said.

And I said, "Yeahyouright," and I nodded sharp with my chin like we understood each other.

But we didn't. I didn't.

They found the first cop that week. Officer Schreiber. He pulled up out front the barbershop, and before anybody could join him, he got yanked out his Bronco and worked on and then stuffed dead back in the passenger seat, just left there to find. I heard he was one of the cops killed Aubrey, but I also heard he wasn't even there.

We was over at Aunt Sharon's for Sunday dinner. It was me and Lonzo and Uncle Trev and Keely, and this cop knocked on the door asking questions. I watched Aunt Sharon fix her face on the way to the door. She dulled herself, made herself smaller and like she didn't have nothing to say about nothing. So the cop knew before he asked her she didn't know.

She sucked her teeth and said, "What a waste. What a waste," and hummed high in her throat like when she on the phone.

The cop said, "Take my card. Get in touch if you hear anything."

And as soon as she shut the door, the light came back into her face and she grunted that grunt that says: *well now I've heard everything* and dropped the card in the kitchen trash.

"You think somebody put a vampire on him?" Lonzo said. His eyes all glossy and shining.

"Naw," Aunt Sharon said. "Too much blood."

Officer Harbaugh was next. Now I know he wasn't there the night Aubrey got killed, but he done some other shit. I heard him say to Ronny at the block party, "You know if I shot you right now, wouldn't nothing happen to me." His voice was up, and light, like there wasn't nothing to it, but you know cops. They think they wear they police-ness in their uniform and when they take it off, it ain't with them, but they also know that's not true, ya feel me? And Ronny said, "I been knowing that." And they just watched each other.

I mean to say I ain't heard nothing else about him. Not like some other officers I could mention. But they found him all torn up outside the Jazz Market. Well, most of him. Some of him was across the street, and some more of him was about a block down. Like he was drawn and quartered like in them cowboy movies, but it wasn't neat. And that cold that only I could feel. Not cold like the seasons turning. Like I had this feeling of the sun going down even though it was the middle of the day. Like the lights never came all the way on anymore, and everything was getting thinner and more washed-out, but it was all scoured by the dark instead of the light.

I missed a couple days of school after Mardi Gras break, but I didn't miss them. I got extension cords and I posted up on the porch and I cut niggas' hair for ten dollars. I made nine-hundred dollars in three days. People was coming from other neighborhoods. I didn't ignore Lonzo, though. We still hung out to watch old VHS tapes his cousin had with Yo MTV Raps on 'em and clowned all them old niggas with Africa medallions and geometric hair.

But I didn't see him at school for a few days, and I didn't see him back at the house neither, and Nicole and Gigi said Lonzo was hiding out because Rel and his crew was gon' jump him next chance they got. I said jump him why, and they didn't know. So I asked Aunt Sharon and she said Lonzo was staying by his cousin on the Wank. I didn't like that.

So I got Aunt Sharon to take me over there, and when I walked into his cousin's and saw Lonzo sitting on the couch with his left eye swole shut I felt hot hot. It wasn't like the other times. I guess cause they hit him in the face? Shoving him a little or knocking him down was one thing, but there was something about banging up his eye like that that bothered me. Like they really wanted to hurt him. And I could tell from the way he talked that his ribs was cracked, and he smelled different.

Real calm, I said, "What happened?"

And Lonzo said, "I don't know. I was crossing the parking lot at Church's after I got off the bus, and somebody hit me in the back of the head. They grabbed me and then Rel hit me in the face and kicked me."

I couldn't feel the look on my face, but Lonzo flinched. "Don't do nothing though," he said.

I decided I'd just find out Rel's side and maybe take it into account. I knew what I *wanted* to do, but I knew it was wrong, too. There's rules in life, and if you gon' operate outside them, best have good reason.

I said before nobody afraid of me, and they ain't, but they don't know. Sometimes my mouth full of razors. If you fuck with me, I will say some shit to you that will fuck your shit up. Like when we was in Elementary school, and the other kids was learning how to cuss and Semaj Bunton called me a bitch, and I said, "Nigga, your eyes too far apart. Your mama drank when she was having you, and that's why you can't do math."

We wasn't friends after that, but he didn't fuck with me.

···❖···

102

A couple more police. One of the Ravels that didn't get got in the sweep. Mean old motherfucker named Zell who dressed like it was still 1993 in baggy black jeans and them white white T-shirts you can't wear more than once. The week before he and his old lady got into it outside the social worker's office. He hit her so hard her eye socket broke. They found him in three garbage bins, side by side.

More dead folks. Old Patrice would show up at the basketball court if you stayed out there too late, asking for cigarettes. He was harmless, but he got burnt to death and worse than they way he looked was the *smell*. He smelled like a fuckin' cookout, and just thinking about it makes my mouth water. Shame the way that nigga died, smoking in bed.

It was coming up on Spring, but that ghost-cold was getting worse. Lonzo came back across the river, but somebody stole his bike, so we was on foot for the time being. We walked in a big square down to Washington and then up to Magazine and over to the park, then back down Felicity, just going slow and talking shit. Shit was still spooky, but not so bad—I think I saw a little boy staring at us from the top floor of that burnt-out apartment complex on Washington just before Saint Charles, but Lonzo didn't look. Anyway, as we turned back down toward Central City, Lonzo said, "I think I need your help with something."

"What you thinkin 'bout?" I'd been thinking so hard on what to do about Rel I guess I forgot Lonzo was thinking 'bout it too. Rel didn't do nothing after Lonzo came home, but we didn't have forever to let the issue ride.

"You remember Antoine Dupre?"

Twonn was a sweet, skinny soft-headed boy used to help out at the Chicken Mart for a couple extra dollars from time to time. Mostly nobody bothered him. Mostly. He didn't come back to school when the new year started, he wasn't on my mind, but I hadn't seen him since the police started dying.

"What about him?"

"He a doghead now."

I stopped walking. "Excuse … the fuck … *me* …?" Dogheads standing around on corners is one thing, but if they was turning folks now, that spelled *real* trouble for the neighborhood.

"That's what I heard, though." And Lonzo's voice was high. I could tell my reaction unsettled him.

I covered. "That don't sound crazy to you?"

"I mean, he was gone. I reckoned he was like the other folks been turning up."

I made myself sound thoughtful. "You know what, though? Could be."

Aunt Sharon was working on a new quilt. She sat in the living room with the TV on too loud, her mouth full of pins as she ran the squares through her sewing machine. Wheel of Fortune came and went, and then Jeopardy, and I was just sitting there thinkin' and I waited until I felt her notice me, and I said, "Lonzo says Antoine Dupre a doghead."

She swept the pins into her left hand and sucked her teeth. *"Well."*

"Lonzo said he heard that."

"Heard nothing,'" Aunt Sharon said. "I seen that boy at the Chicken Mart just last night."

"Why you didn't say?"

"Didn't think it was important," she said. "You think he the one killin' up all them police?"

I didn't say nothing. On the TV a white couple was digging in a suspicious mushroom patch thinking it was part of some treasure hunt they was on. Oops! Turns out they dug up a skull.

I laughed, but I could feel Aunt Sharon's eyes on me.

"Didn't seem important," she said again. She sighed. "We do what we do, and they do what they do."

I didn't tell Aunt Sharon I was going out that night. I just made extra noise in the hall closet looking for my shoes and then I hid them back out of sight. Aunt Sharon said she seen him, but I had to see Twonn for myself.

I headed down to the corner where Simon Bolivar meets Jackson, and from there I could see the dogheads laughing and talking out front of the store. I crossed the street, but not all the way. I stood in the shadow under the oak on the neutral ground, right by the transformer, and just watched.

The Chicken Mart had shut for the night. The lights were off now, the parking lot empty, and the dogheads just stood out there in their bare not-paws-not-feet swaying sometimes like seaweed in a underwater current. There was four of them this time. The Boxer/Shar Pei wore a pair of bleach-spotted jeans, and I couldn't tell whether they was supposed to be like that or somebody fucked them up in the wash.

The one that hadn't been there the first time Lonzo and I seen them was smaller than the rest. He looked a little like a Boxer, and his fur was dark, but there was something about the shape of his head. About the way his shoulders seemed pulled up in a kind of constant shrug. Not a Boxer. A Mastiff, but mixed with something. He looked younger than the others, and sure enough when he pulled out a cigarette, he had to shift his head to smoke it, and that was Twonn all right.

He took a drag, then another. He looked this way and that, and he hunched, like he was smoking in the rain.

I started barking. Made myself sound real big and mean. The dogheads all tensed and stretched their necks and smelled the air. I didn't see Antoine drop his cigarette, but now his hands were empty, and his head was a doghead again. The way he moved, his body language, looked just like everybody else's. Like he'd always been one of them. He growled. I couldn't hear it, but I could see the noise vibrate his body.

I stilled my voice mid-bark and let the sound ring in the empty intersection and the parking lot.

They started pacing. Each one prowling like a comedian on a stage. Twonn still looked like one of them. Like he was born for it.

Eventually, Twonn broke off from the group and jogged across Jackson toward that old warehouse type thing without walls where they be selling fruit on the weekends. He didn't look in my direction. Instead, he turned up toward Saint Charles and shifted human again. He swung his legs out some when he ran. We used to make fun of him for that when he first started at school with us in third grade. I followed him, like I was just walking.

He went all the way up to Carondelet then cut over to Saint Andrew, then came back down across Baronne, then Haley. I let him walk on the right side of the street while I took the left.

I knew Ronny was there before I seen him. I didn't expect him to say nothing. He stepped hard onto the sidewalk with his fists balled. His face was all thrust out in front of him like he was a doghead too, but he was just a man.

He looked at me out the corner of his right eye then turned his head, still leading with his face. "Love me this springtime, baby," he said. *"Love."*

"Can't beat the weather," I said.

"Can't beat it," he said. But he wasn't agreeing. "Can't be beat."

I waited.

"Wa'ant right what happened to Zell," he said. "All in them trash cans one two three."

I shook my head. "Wasn't nothing nice."

"He was kin to me."

I forgot about Twonn. "He was what?"

"He was kin."

"Oh word?" I said. My voice was bright. "You was cousins, you and him?"

He watched me, then looked away. He looked like a stone carving or a angry little doll. Something that got more respect than it deserved. "On my mama side," he said. *"Distant."*

"You look out for yaself outchear, Ronny, ya heard? Never know who all out here …"

By then, Twonn was long gone, but it be that way sometimes.

The next day at school, I stuck with Lonzo close as I could, but our schedules wasn't always the same. He was in precalculus, but I was in trig, and we didn't have the same lunch. I skipped Government and went to his lunch anyhow. The cafeteria and the gym was combined, so the baskets were drawn up out of the way and the tables was lined up like soldiers waiting for inspection. The ghost-cold was still bothering me, but we weren't allowed to wear jackets over our uniforms, and anyway that wouldna helped. The whole room smelled like orange oil with an unusual touch of bleach from three weeks ago when Ri-Ri threw up.

Lonzo sat by himself at the end of a table in the far corner. A group of freshmen sat at the other end playing keep-away with Coke bottles and checking out a group of sophomore girls at the next table.

Lonzo looked surprised when I sat my tray down next to his and peeled the skin back from my beefaroni pack. "You with me today?"

"Just tryna find out what you need help with."

"Help?" Lonzo's American Literature textbook sat on the table by his tray, so I knew he was intending to read all through the period. I had this feeling then like why was he studying at lunch? Was it because he didn't get time to study last night?

"About Rel and them?" I said.

"Oh," he said, too surprised. "Yeah, well, I think that trouble gone resolve itself, ya heard?"

"Oh?" I said. On God I wished I hadn't acted the way I did when he told me about Twonn. I had to be *cool* cool now because not only did I want to hide my frustration with him, I didn't want him seeing my irritatedness with my own self.

"Yeah, you good."

My chest felt tight. I needed the words to say what I was trying to say, but it wasn't easy like it shoulda been. "Listen, bruh," I said. "You my dog, bruh. You my abc."

"Yeah," he said. And there was no struggle, no scariness on his face. He was just—he looked young. No, he looked *new*, like if time was a cooking fire, he was still raw, and he hadn't seen what he would see, and the world hadn't printed itself on him the way we shaped our sculptures in art class.

"I mean there ain't nothing wrong with me lookin' out for you. I'm your *dog*, dog."

He looked me in the eye and reached for his chocolate milk. He tried to open it with his left hand without looking, but he couldn't quite, so he looked away to the carton, and I wanted him to stop messing with it, to keep looking at me, and it bothered me how bad I wanted him to see me. For real for real.

He said, "Yeah, but you know."

"What?"

He looked back up at me then, and he looked even younger, even rawer than before, and he said, "You a year ahead of me. What I'm gone do when you graduate and I'm by myself? What I'm gone do at college?"

I watched him a little, then I opened my Sprite. I said, "You act like I ain't thinking 'bout that shit too."

"But that's what I mean," he said. "That's *my* shit."

107

"Listen, I ain't trying to run your life, I'm just tellin' you: stay away from them doghead boys. They don't … you don't know what they … they's monsters, feel me?"

"Ravels was monsters. If I'm a doghead, at least—!"

I brought my palms down hard on the tabletop. *"Nigga, not like that!"*

That was the moment. That instant right there. It was—I think it was my tone. Sometimes I think I was the only one who never made him feel small, who never made him feel weak. But I slipped. He didn't see much, but he saw too much.

His chocolate milk had spilled when I hit the table. He set the carton right again, in its pale-brown pool, and the way his wrist curled said: *You were with me, but now you're not. You're outside of me and you don't understand.*

Wednesday was our half-day and Lonzo was supposed to stay and help plan the Spring Festival. I was going to set up a booth and cut hair in the parking lot across the street. It was official/unofficial. Still, I knew as soon as I touched my locker, even before I opened it, that Lonzo was gone. That tightness was still in my chest, and it combined with that cold feeling to make my skin crawl. I had to work to keep my shoulders from drifting up to my ears. Anyone paying attention woulda seen too much, so I blew off the meeting and just headed out.

It shoulda been easy to trail him—and it was, at first. He'd gone back up to Haley and then down a couple blocks before going to Bolivar. It was the afternoon. The birds was singing, and the sun was bright, and it was a little too hot out. Finally. I smelled cut grass and the kitchen and cleaning from Café Reconcile. I smelt the liquor and perfume over at the Jazz Market.

And then it was like all them smells and all the other signals from my senses sort of turned up and blended on me. You know when you on the street and somebody drives your way with their brights on, and the light washes everything out and you can't see? It was like that, except it was sounds and smells and the breeze and that cold cold.

It wasn't that I couldn't take nothing in and that I couldn't find him, but it was, too. I went around in circles. I went places Lonzo hadn't been in days and days, and every time felt like *now*, just *now*. And that ain't right.

I think that's how it happened. I went around in circles, for blocks and blocks, winding in a sort of cornered spiral. Whenever someone spoke to me, I said, "You seen Lonzo?" And if they said no, I just kept walking like I ain't have no manners.

When the dark started to come on, I could parse his smell again. The scent of the cologne his uncle gave him for Christmas and his blood underneath, bright and a little sweaty from where the sun touched his bare arms and legs and the hollows of his neck. That's how I found him. I went back up Saint Ann even though I'd already gone up there past that place we call the zombie house because it looked all abandoned like a house in a zombie movie, but also it was a home that would not just lay down and die.

I went in the back, and I found him on the dirty floor. My eyes almost wouldn't have recognized him, and his smell was all wrong, too, but that cologne was still there, and a sort of echo of him. He looked— it's *bad* when somebody gets stuck Between. I saw it before, once. One of my cousin Leti's quadruplets was born sick, and it didn't come out stuck, but it got that way later in the night, and wasn't nothing could be done to help.

That was the worst thing: its eyes were calm like it knew what was happening. Like it understood. If the eyes had been lost or crazy with pain or or anything else, maybe it wouldn't have been so bad. When Lonzo's swollen eyes struggled open, they were big and brown and deep, flecked with gold, and they were still his.

His mouth was all wet and ruined and red from where his new teeth half-split his gums. I was all shaky, but sometimes when there's trouble you ain't got time to just stand around feeling shit, so I didn't. He was lying on the dirty floor in a pool of his own blood and shit and piss and whatnot and the bite on his arm stank like disease. I said, "Why you wouldn't listen to me? I tried to tell you and why you didn't just fuckin' listen?"

I almost lost it. I almost came apart then, but I didn't. I killed him quick so he wouldn't suffer, but I didn't go crazy. I didn't go crazy until after.

···❖···

Maybe I wouldn't have done what I did if one of them had stayed with him. Maybe if one of them had stayed in that stinking fuckin' room full of mold and debris and nasty blankets, if one of them had kept trying to help him through I would have—mercy ain't really the word—but I wouldn't have been as mad.

I wasn't thinking when I found them at the Chicken Mart. I know folks found Ronny out front of his house all pulled apart, and I don't remember that, but you ask me, he had it coming. Them kids he killed didn't deserve what they got. And when the last boy was lying there in the street with his back broke, Ronny shoulda done right and ended him.

If they was still at the Chicken Mart that meant they thought it was a normal night. That meant wasn't more than one or two of them tried to turn Lonzo, and maybe they didn't deserve to die, but yes they did.

If I'd been thinking, I wouldna thrown Doberman-head through the mart's doors. I woulda just pulled his arms and legs off and left him there, but I could smell that he was the one. He was the one that made the bite, so I decided to do him last. I tossed him away to do Twonn and the other one. He was still alive, so he tried to climb into the store through the hole his body made in the glass. I caught him by his legs and dragged him out shrieking.

I saw me in the glass. My blood is royal, so it's not just my top that changes. It's not canine hair that grows on my limbs. We are not dogs, and we are not wolves, we issue from the beast-god who mated with the black earth, from the god of Hunt and Carnage, and when I show myself, mortals cower.

Someone called a vampire on me. Someone must have seen what I did and called out. Ronny couldna called nothing or nobody with his bottom jaw and his tongue tore out. The one that came out the branches of the oak as I stalked toward home was shocked to see me. It wasn't pure either, just some white-faced, goth motherfucker moved down after the Storm and sacrificed himself to an Elder.

I didn't speak to it or make a sound. Didn't even stop walking. I just extended a claw and pointed at it. It froze for a second, then darted back up and away.

Thou shalt not dilute the blood.

That is the law.

The Ravels didn't know that, they just had a vested interest in keeping monsters from multiplying in Central City. If they was still around, Lonzo coulda just gone to them for help instead of—instead of how things wound up.

Nowdays, these motherfuckers *stay* coming here. They see in the movies, or they read in their shitty little books that there's ghosts and spirits and other shit down here in New Orleans, and they come to join the romance. Usually, if they look hard enough for long enough, they find someone to share the blood like a disease, turn them into something weak and diminished. A goth bitch in a funeral dress. A hood nigga with the head of a dog. Scum lacking any understanding or respect for our ways.

I knew Aunt Sharon wouldn't want me tracking blood on her carpet, so I shifted back and went to the backyard to rinse off with the hose. When I turned to the door, she was standing there on the concrete patio shaking her head at me.

"They won't remember," I said. "They'll barely notice."

"Nigga, that's a *good* thing," she said. "You don't know because you young."

"Some things shouldn't be forgot."

"And some things must be," she said. *"Must."*

"They steal our power and then they use it to turn our home into the wild fuckin' west. You ask me, they ain't really forgot, and if they did, they need reminding."

"Didn't nobody ask you," she said. "Didn't nobody call your fuckin' name. You shoulda bit that boy yourself and been done with it if you loved him so much. Instead you was busy hunting police."

"Naw. No. *No!"* I knew the whole time I was standing there naked, but now I felt it. I felt *seen* in a way I'd been taught never to allow. "You wrong for that, Aunt Sharon. You wrong! *I ain't never hurt nobody ain't had it coming!"*

"Until tonight. You think all them dogheads turned your boy?" She didn't wait for me to answer. "I don't care who your daddy is in Darkest Africa. You want to stay living in my house you live by my rules. No more gangsters, and *you leave them fuckin' police alone!"*

I covered my face with my hands and sobbed. Now I felt old old. Ancient and heavy as one of them heads on Easter Island. When I looked back up at her, she didn't seem angry anymore, but she ain't no easier to read than I am.

"You really think I shoulda turnt him myself?"

"Of course not, baby," she said. "It woulda been wrong."

But I knew, then. I *knew* the rest that she wasn't saying: *It woulda been wrong, but if you had, he'd still be alive.*

And she's right. Killing Rel and his crew wouldn't have solved Lonzo's problem. He was right. What *would* he do at school by himself? At college? Afterwards? I couldn't be with him all the time, unless we …

… I couldn't be with him all the time.

I know where Aunt Sharon is: she's out stalking the neighborhood, making sure nobody knows the mess I made for what it is. Me, I'm lying on my bed, staring at the ceiling in the dark of my bedroom.

Killing Rel won't bring Lonzo back, and I know it's the wrong thing to do, but I will lie here until Aunt Sharon comes home, and even after that, until sleep changes her scent, and then I will pay each of Rel's boys a little visit. I will save Rel Howard for last, and best believe, I will show him *all of me.*

A PALL OF MOONDUST

by Nick Wood

KwaZulu Natal, African Federation, 2035.

Blue sky: red dust.

Hamba kahle, grandfather, goodbye.

I sprinkled a handful of orange-red dust on his grave—yet another funeral cloth over your buried body, *Babamkhulu*— and behind me, father did the same.

May your soul soar, old man, with the sharp tongue and that mad dog, Inja.

And say hello to mother for me.

Shackleton Crater, Moon Base One, Lunar, 2037

I dreamed and shook awake as the two bodies flew away from me. *Dreams live.*

Scott is the one keying in the Airlock code, mouth o-ing in shock at the tug and hiss of escaping air behind her. "Helmets on," she says, but it is already too late, the door to the Moon behind her is wide as a monster's maw.

Bailey is fiddling with the solar array on the Rover, his helmet playfully dangled on the joystick for a second, before being sucked out and beyond my reach.

Scott pushes me backward and the inner door closes, leaving me safe on the inside. *The wrong side?*

The Airlock explodes with emptying air and a spray of moon dust. Two die while I live.

I scour the darkness for something familiar, something safe.

Nothing.

I'm a lunar newbie, only Three Lunar Walks, and with my helmet already on before we had even entered the airlock. *That's mandatory now—helmet must be on before airlock entry. Why then, does this darkness hang so heavy with my guilt?*

Medication drooped my eyelids, pulling me back toward the faulty doors and o-ing mouths, where I did *not* want to go.

No, not again, please …

Doctor Izmay eyed me over her desk-screen, and I yawned back at her, glancing at the red couch in the corner of her room labeled 'Sector 12 Psych.' *The bed is a cliché, surely, just for show?*

"Flashbacks still, Doctor Matlala?" she asked, raising a sympathetic eyebrow.

Her formality reminded me of father, but Izmay was a real woman of everywhere, German/Turkish/North African, a true shrink of the world.

I don't like shrinks.

But I had been taught well and avoided direct gaze with my elder, a swarthy white woman graying at the temples of her tightly bunned black hair.

She smiled. "Ah, a mark of respect for those older than you, in traditional Zulu custom."

Her eyes were gray green, I stared in surprise.

"Like you, young woman, I do my homework," she said. "Do we need to titrate your medication and increase your dose?"

114

I hesitated. "I want to get back to my work in hydroponics, but the medication is making me drowsy."

"There's something else you need to do first." The woman leaned back, hesitant too, and dread surged inside me again. "You need to suit up and go back out onto the Moon."

"Uh—no. What's the point? I'm a botanist. *Nothing* grows out there."

The psychiatrist stood and walked toward the door, gesturing to me to follow. "Necessary health and safety. You know the drill. We must all get comfortable on the surface of this Harsh Mistress. For you, that means getting back on your metaphorical horse and into the Airlock, just for starters."

I could not stand; my limbs were locked.

Doctor Izmay hauled out an injection pen and sighed, tapping it on her palm. "I agree. Your medication *does* need increasing."

The psychiatrist held my arm firmly as we approached the Airlock door, and I was grateful for that, my legs starting to jelly.

"Slow your breathing," she said sharply. "Think of Durban beach."

I practiced our imagery work, heading into my safe mind-space, as she counted out a slowed pace for my breathing. Hot white-yellow sand, pumping surf, blue bottle jellyfish and … sharks in the water?

"Helmet on," she said, but the airlock door in front of us was gaping like the jaws of a Great White.

I tripped over the two bodies they had brought back.

Scott and Bailey, suited and helmetless, darkened by a coat of regolith, with their eye sockets and tongues caked in the black dust that was everywhere.

"Stay with me Thandike," a voice said. "Breathe, one … two …"

But I have dropped the helmet, in case it sucks me out.

I bend with suited difficulty, scraping the floor for moon dust that stinks like weak gunpowder, so as to sprinkle it respectfully on the bodies of Scott and Bailey.

So little to scoop up, so little to leave them in peace. *Why is it just I who live still?*

My eyes leaked with sorrow and guilt, so that I hardly felt yet another injection into my upper arm.

Where have their bodies gone? And are their shades happy?

"Survivor guilt is normal," Doctor Izmay told me.

This time she had me lying on her red leather couch, so that I did not have to look at her eyes. "You could have done *nothing* differently. It's not your fault."

Yes, I know that, so why do I still feel guilty?

"Tell me about your grandfather."

The command dropped onto my stomach like a lead weight. Even in Moon gravity, it felt heavy. *I prefer plants to words, any day.*

"He helped father raise me, after my mother died when I was very young." I struggled. "He died at ninety, the year before I got into the Lunar Program. I wish I could have shown him my letter of acceptance."

"You still miss him?" Her voice was nearer, as if she'd shifted closer to me, on the seat behind the couch.

It was an obvious question, so I did not even bother to respond.

"Tell me more about him," Dr. Izmay tried again. "What do you miss the most?"

"No," I said, "it has no relevance here. I need to get back to the issue of efficient grain production in one sixth gee and filtered sunlight."

A noise clicked from behind the red couch, now sticky with stale sweat from my back. Above me, the ceiling slid open, and I saw a window funneled to the roof of the dome. Sharp stars cut down into my eyes, lancing slivers of light, with no atmospheric distortion to turn them twinkle friendly.

"The light from those stars is variously between four hundred and five billion years old," Dr. Izmay said. "They will fade with Earthrise imminent, but they won't disappear. They're still there, even when they're gone. Tell me about your grandfather."

"No," I said, eyes burning, so that I screwed them shut. *Stars are like my grandfather? Could I have been quicker to call 9-1-1 when his heart collapsed that day?*

"You've always done your best." Dr. Izmay's voice was even closer still. "In the end, with death, we can change nothing."

I opened my eyes and twitched with shock. She was bending over me from the back of the couch, eyes fastened on mine. "What was your grandfather's favorite phrase when you were a teenager?"

"Get off that bloody couch and *do* something useful, *intombi!*" The words were out of my mouth before I could think.

Dr. Izmay was laughing. "Well?"

She had done her homework on me, very well indeed.

Today, my two moon-walking companions were to be Commander Baines and Space Tourist Butcher.

I had checked the records on both the night before.

Baines had over four hundred walks under his buckled belt and had slid like a snake into his own suit, although bending stiffly to pick up his helmet and gloves. "I've got your bio-signs on my screen visor here, so I'm keeping tabs on both of you. We're not going far. Just keep me in sight and do everything I tell you. Helmets on."

My heart pumped a surge of panic, but Butcher looked even more terrified.

It's his first time, at the ancient age of forty-six. I'm not the newest newbie here.

"Just breathe slowly," I told him. "Don't hyperventilate into your mouthpiece."

Dr. Izmay crackled into my ears as I fastened my helmet on. "Good. I'm patched in from remote too, Thandike. Looks like I might have to copyright that breathing line."

My chuckle took the edge off my dread.

Baines was already thumbing in the access code, and I took up my position at the back. (Newbie in the middle, yet another reg. change, since the accident.)

"Foolproof new locking system," said Baines, bouncing through the opening Airlock door.

Butcher followed, more slowly and clumsily.

I stepped forward to support his PLSS backpack, preventing the novice from toppling backward as he momentarily backed away from the door, as if having had sudden second thoughts.

I may only be twenty-eight, but I know by now that nothing is ever fool proof.... So what the hell am I doing stepping through this door myself?

It's better than going home, for a start. It's taken me a long time and lots of hard work to get here, ahead of so much global competition. And, now that I'm here, I'm going to make sure I stay off that bloody couch. For you, Babamkhulu.

The door behind me closed and Baines was already busy on the external door, as if minimizing our chances for anxiety to escalate. "Butcher, breathe, one, two …" I said, hearing a quick rasping in my ears.

"Ready for exit, decompression complete …"

Slowly, the outer door opened.

Hesitantly, we followed Baines's loping bounce out onto the surface of the moon.

We needed to step upwards slightly, as the door has been built low into a crater wall to minimize solar radiation exposure.

I strode across to a large boulder to my right, keeping Baines in view. *How can it look so dark, with such a bright sun?*

Baines was a few steps further along, by a mound of broken rocks. *He moves so quickly as if he doesn't even think about the steps he has left behind.*

"Both of you, take a look at that!" Baines's voice crackled as he raised an arm to point along the horizon to our right.

The Earth shimmered low over the horizon—a largish blue-white ball floating above the lip of Shackleton's crater, where solar arrays set in eternal sunlight bled back cheap and climate friendly energy to the planet.

I focused on Earth. *Where are the continents? Where is Africa?*

The blur of gray-white cloud smeared the blue-green oceans and brown earth across the globe. I could almost hear it spinning, swirling hot climate clouds across the face of the world.

It doesn't matter if I can't find Africa. From here, nothing is 'Great,' nothing is 'Permanent.' For all of us humans alike, we have a melting, fragile pearl to protect.

"And look there!" Baines swiveled to point at the sky behind us.

I turned to peer in the deep darkness. Where the stars were fading, a dull reddish pinprick burned.

"Mars, our next stop," said Baines.

The color of the earth, with which we had covered grandfather.

Butcher and Baines continued to watch Mars, but I stared back at the sealed crater door. *No, surely not?*

"What's happening to your pulse and breathing, Thandike?" Dr. Izmay's voice bit into my ear.

I raise a gloved hand to take the edge off the solar glare. On the top edge of the crater, near the dome roof, sat an old man with a knobkierie stick and a dog by his side.

I knew better than to say anything, but walked back to Base slowly, testing my vision. The old man stood to wave, and his voice quavered to me across the vacuum, "Proud to see you doing something so special and useful, *umzukulu!*"

Two space-suited figures hovered behind him. They waved once.

Inja barked, and when I blinked again, all of them had gone.

They had warned me to expect visual distortions in this alien land, where distance and depth were hard to judge—and shifting shadows played with your perception.

"What did you see, Thandike?" Doctor Izmay's voice echoed into my ears.

"Our home crater and the outer door."

I watch the soon-to-disappear stars above me as sunrise approaches, to break the shorter lunar night.

I say a prayer, silently.

Behind me, Baines and Butcher have arrived, and so I finish my prayer.

Cunjani, grandfather, hello.

So, tell me, how is my mother?

Black sky: gray dust.

Inyanga, 2037

KALEIDOSCOPE

by Milton J. Davis

Kerry's breath frosted his bedroom window on Christmas morning as he waited anxiously for his uncle's arrival. Uncle John was his favorite because he always brought the best gifts. Daddy didn't like Uncle John; he would say that Uncle John tried to show up everyone else with his presents. He said if Uncle John had kids of his own, he wouldn't be able to afford those gifts. Kerry didn't care; he just wanted his presents. He wished Uncle John never got married.

He sat up straight when he spotted the familiar BMW 745 cruising up the long hill to his house. He jumped off the bed, his feet slamming against the floor as he tore out of his room.

"Uncle John is coming! Uncle John is coming!"

Kerry ran by his sister's room on the way to the stairs. Michelle stuck her head out the door, her rollers tumbling to the floor, her cell phone pressed against her ear.

"Girl, I got to go! My Uncle John is coming." She went back into her room to dress.

Jerome was downstairs. He sat at the table with Daddy, playing with his new laptop. Mama stood before the oven, putting the finishing touches on Christmas dinner. Jerome was graduating and heading off to college soon, so Mama and Daddy bought him a laptop to help him with his work. Kerry didn't like the laptop; Jerome wouldn't let

121

him play any games on it. Kerry ran through the family room and down the foyer to the front door.

"Get away from that door, boy!" Mama exclaimed.

Kerry's hands dropped to his side like a little soldier. "It's Uncle John, Mama. He's coming up the street!"

Mama wiped her hands on her apron and strolled toward the door. "How do you know?"

"I saw him out the window."

"What did I tell you about looking out that window? You're always leaving my blinds up. Move on out the way now."

Mama gently pushed Kerry aside and looked through the peephole. "It's Johnny," she said, "and he's got someone with him."

Daddy huffed. "I hope it's not one of his freeloading friends."

Mama looked back with a sly smile on her face. "It's a woman, a very pretty woman."

Daddy feigned shock. "You're lying!"

The doorbell rang. Mama opened the door with a wide grin.

"Merry Christmas, Johnny!"

Uncle John stepped into the house, lifting Mama off her feet. He was a tall man with brown-copper skin and a round joyful face.

"Merry Christmas, big sister!" he announced, his alto voice filling the foyer. He carried Mama back into the foyer and placed her down. A woman entered; an ebony-skinned woman draped in a kente-colored coat. Her hair was cut close like Uncle John's and her smile was sincere like an old friend.

"Barbara, this is Zarina."

Mama hugged Zarina. "Welcome to our home, Zarina. You're beautiful."

Zarina lowered her eyes. "You are too kind, Barbara. Thank you for having me. I told John to ask if it was okay that I come, but he insisted. I apologize if my presence is an inconvenience."

Mama waved her hand. "Not at all, girl. There's plenty for every-body. Besides, you don't look like you eat as much as his other friends."

As the ladies shared a laugh, Uncle John noticed Kerry. His eyes widened and he grabbed the boy, lifting him to the ceiling.

"Barbara, what you been feeding this boy? Miracle-Gro?" He shook and tickled Kerry at the same time. "What's up, big boy?"

"Stop, Uncle John!" Kerry squealed.

Daddy walked up to them. "How you doing, Johnny?" He stepped passed Kerry and Johnny to greet Zarina.

"Welcome, Zarina. Y'all come away from this door. It's too cold."

They went to the family room, Uncle John carrying Kerry under his thick arm.

"Where's my present?" Kerry demanded.

"So that's what's going on?" Uncle John said. "I thought you were happy to see me. You're just down here for the loot."

"You spoiled him," Daddy said.

Michelle made her entrance, overdressed as always.

"Hi, Uncle John," she said with a shy wave of her hand.

"Girl, get over here and give me a hug!"

Michelle shed her teenage pretense and skittered across the floor to hug her uncle.

"Now that's more like it!"

Jerome sauntered up and extended his hand.

"What's up, young man?" John's voice was suddenly serious.

"Uncle." They shook and hugged.

Kerry looked at them enviously. He wished he was old enough to shake and hug Uncle John like that.

"So, you're a college man now?"

Jerome smirked. "Not yet."

"Where you going?"

Jerome stuck his chest out. "Morehouse."

Mama sucked her teeth. "Not unless he gets a scholarship."

"He'll get one," Uncle John replied. "Money ain't a thing." Uncle John reached into his coat pocket and extracted an envelope.

"Merry Christmas, young man."

Kerry ran to his uncle. The presents were here!

Jerome opened the envelope and his eyes bulged. "Thank you, unc! Thank you!"

"That's for college now," Uncle John said. "Don't spend it on gaming."

Mama pushed Kerry aside and took the envelope from Jerome. She looked at the check and her eyes went just as wide.

"Oh my God! Johnny, where did you get this kind of money? We can't accept this!"

Daddy ran over to see for himself. "Oh yes, we can! Let me see." He looked at the check and sat down. "Ten thousand dollars!" he exclaimed. "Now that's what I'm talking about!"

"I got something for you too," Uncle John said to Michelle. He reached into another pocket and took out an iPhone. Michelle squealed.

"Don't panic, sis. I got the bill."

Uncle John squatted before Kerry. "Your turn, little man." Uncle John reached inside his coat. A video-pad rested in Kerry's hand. Kerry hugged his uncle tight.

"Thank you, Uncle John!"

"You earned it. Your Mama said you're a straight-A student. Good work deserves good reward."

Everyone settled into the family room while Mama and Michelle went to the kitchen to finish dinner. Kerry sat down and went to work, immersing himself in his favorite game on the pad. He looked up from time to time when everyone else got loud to see what was happening. Every time his eyes met Zarina's, an admiring smile on her face. Kerry smiled back and resumed his game.

Kerry was upset when he had to put away his pad for dinner. His anger was brief; the food was excellent. Mama went all out as always, with turkey, ham, dressing, macaroni and cheese casserole, collard greens, sweet potato souffle, rice, gravy, cranberry sauce, and cornbread. It was enough for twice as many people. Jerome, Michelle, and Kerry sat together at the kitchen table, listening to Daddy tell his funny stories at the grown-up table. Kerry escaped from the kitchen as soon as he finished his plate, running upstairs to his room to immerse himself in the complexities of Sonic the Hedgehog.

A light tapping on his door broke his attention.

"Yes?" Kerry yelled out.

"Can I come in?" an unfamiliar voice asked.

Kerry rolled off his bed reluctantly and opened the door. Zarina stood before him, a sweet smile on her face.

"You ran away before I could give you your gift."

Kerry's eyes brightened. Zarina handed him a leather tube etched with images of elephants and lions. Kerry was confused.

"Open it," Zarina said.

Kerry opened the tube and extracted a wooden object that looked like a telescope. He looked confused.

"It's a kaleidoscope." Zarina took the object from him. "See, you put this end to your eye and turn this end. Try it."

Kerry placed the kaleidoscope to his eye. Inside was a colorful pattern of colored crystals. When he turned the large end, the pattern changed. He smiled. "It's like the snowflakes in my class," he said.

Zarina smiled. "Very good, Kerry. John told me you were smart."

Kerry kept turning the kaleidoscope. It wasn't very fun, not like his game, but Mama told him to always be polite.

"Are you going to marry my uncle?"

Zarina laughed. "Your uncle is a nice man, but I don't think we'll marry. I'm too old for him."

Kerry lowered the kaleidoscope and studied Miss Zarina

"You don't look *that* old," he said.

"You'd be surprised," Zarina replied.

She folded her arms. "Now it's time for a secret. Tonight, when everyone is asleep, I want you to take the kaleidoscope and go to your window. Before you look inside, I want you to close your eyes and say, 'Wherever I see, I can be.'"

"Mama doesn't like me looking out the window," he warned.

"She won't know if you close the blinds," Zarina answered. "Now what are you going to say?"

"Wherever I see, I can be," Kerry recited.

Zarina smiled like a proud teacher. "Good. I'll leave you to your games. Goodbye, Kerry. I hope to see you again one day."

Kerry tossed the kaleidoscope on the bed and continued his game. He stopped for a moment to go downstairs for pound cake and vanilla ice cream, then it was back to his room. He barely noticed Uncle John stick his head in to say goodbye. After being forced to bathe, Kerry played until his eyes became too heavy to stay open. He fell asleep, the pad still in his grip.

He awoke suddenly, the words Zarina taught him buzzing in his head. Kerry went to the window and lifted the blinds, the kaleidoscope in his sleepy fingers. He lifted it to his eye, the colorful patterns boring to him.

"Wherever I can see, I will be," he whispered.

He turned the large end and the crystals disappeared, replaced by a montage of space and stars.

"Wow!" He turned it again and a solar system appeared, five planets circling a yellow star similar to the sun. Two of the planets occupied the same orbit, one directly opposite the other. Both planets had the same color of Earth. He twisted the big end, and a planet appeared, its surface covered with trees and grasses, mountains towering into the sky, flying things and walking things, and crawling things in abundance. But these were not the trees and animals that he knew. He turned it again, and this time he saw people that reminded him of Zarina, working and playing in cities that were again the same, but different. He kept turning the kaleidoscope, marveling at the amazing images. This is better than the pad, he thought.

Kerry twisted. The planets were gone. He was looking at space again, at the stars casted on an infinite black void. A luminous blue line appeared, connecting stars like dots while numbers flashed before his eyes.

"Cool!" he said. He gazed into the toy until the sun peeked over the hills. "Uh oh!" Kerry closed the blinds and jumped into bed. He looked into the kaleidoscope and the crystals had returned.

"Only at night," he whispered. He placed the toy on his dresser and fell asleep.

Reporters from around the world flooded Cape Canaveral, each hoping to get a close view of the podium. The usual dignitaries occupied the choice seats, and each one was claimed. No one wanted to miss what promised to be the most historic day for mankind.

The press secretary took the podium, brushing her hair back from her beaming face. Despite her years of announcing scientific breakthroughs, she exuded an unexpected joyfulness that was reflected by the anxious throng.

"Ladies and gentlemen, I don't have much to say. You all have followed this project since its inception eight years ago. None of us imagined it would culminate so quickly, but all of us are ecstatic about the outcome and the man who made it happen. I won't make you wait any longer. Let me introduce the man of the hour, the adventurer that will take us into a new age of space travel, Colonel Kerry Washington!"

The conference room exploded in applause. Colonel Washington took the stage in his flight suit, waving at the crowd. He hugged the press secretary and took the podium.

"I'd like to say a few words before I take any questions. This dream began for me when I was a little boy. I stand here today realizing a dream come true. When my brilliant team of scientists transformed the theory of slip dimensional travel into reality, the stars opened up to us. The journey I embark on this day will prove once and for all we are not alone."

Stacy Owens, Technology correspondent for the New York Times sprang to her feet. "How can you be so sure, colonel? What makes you believe you can find intelligent life?"

Kerry just smiled, refusing to answer the reporter's question. Later that day as he strapped himself into the *Traveler*, he thought about that Christmas day when he received a special gift from a special person. "How do I know what I'll find?" he said to himself. "Because I know exactly where I'm going."

He checked his instruments one last time then gave Mission Control the signal to begin launch sequence. In an afterthought he reached into his pocket and pulled out a worn kaleidoscope, securing it atop the panel.

"Wherever I see, I can be," he whispered.

MEMORIES OF THE OLD SUN

by Eugen Bacon

Sometimes you wish you were a biorobot. Unemotive, just 1s and 0s.

Your mother's words burn inside your mind: "People are laughing, others pitying. Mazu. Who'll wait on me?"

"I'm here, Mae."

"The journey is far over the seas from Konakri. Come visit before I die."

"I'll visit. I promise. And you're not dying."

"Stop giving me regret. When will you find a woman?"

"If you keep asking, I'll stop calling."

"*Aiii*, his truth comes out. He'll stop ringing."

"Are you telling the phone?"

"Who birthed you? I broke my back to raise you. Now you will kill me with regret."

"It's not like that, Mae."

"The girls here are budding. I'll negotiate a wife with a good stomach. It shows in the clan—the ones who can make babies."

"Stop it. Please."

"I know to pick the right girl. Breasts like papayas. Buttocks bigger than a pot."

"There's more to life than marriage."

An email from Jordan. In it, the photo of a marigold-eyed kitten, head cocked at the camera. You want to tell Mae about Jordan, but on a spell like today she's no listener.

You snatch yourself back to her lamenting. "Don't put me in mourning. Child, you're cutting me."

"Now you exagger—"

"There's the question of dowry."

"Is this what it's about, Mae? I'll send money."

"Of course I need money. The cows are sick. And the village's still growing—we need a well to water our yams. I told the pastor at the school—"

"The one I raised money for?"

"That one. I told the pastor I'd ask about the well."

"Being here doesn't mean I'm rolling in money."

"Now you think you're a big shot. That you can stop helping."

You sigh. Sending money home is a bottomless cup. The village, through your mother, makes it an inescapable yoke. She finally agrees to hang up because you invent that it's midnight.

"It's night there," she says in wonderment. "Like here?"

"Yes, Mae." Your pretend yawn is loud. "And if I don't sleep, who'll make money for us tomorrow? Sooo tired."

"You take my advice—I don't want to suckle the whole village. Give me a grandchild."

"I hear you, Mae."

"By the gods, you'd better. *Mffyuu.*" She sucks her teeth, letting you know she's not letting it go.

Jazz knows sie's a variable. Sie has an inbuilt scrapbook filled with memories, sometimes rushing, often rusting. They twirl inside hir head. File cards full of deserts and hungriness clipped away from hir heart. They are from names in a grammar sie doesn't remember, childhood friends or secrets: Bug, Dyn, Cyclone, Bash, Allon, Prim, Krema …

Making a biorobot is genesis—not a six-day creation, rest on the seventh, but rather a Darwinian evolution, natural selection and all.

You put each zygote under lights, spin it slowly to nurture its earliest developmental stage—the unique genome sequence of human and artificial intelligence. The right genetic signature is necessary to form memories derived from mainframes and natural evolution.

Malware botches some of the zygotes and they begin to show excessive individual thought, traces of zeitgeist. You vaporize most anomalies, rain them back into the network as gametes. It doesn't matter if they had a name—all zygotes have a name—you deal with anomalies and rename them. Hundreds of zygotes each in a simulated placenta inside pods. Newborn. But only the fittest shall live.

A biorobotics engineer wants no variants, for obvious reasons. Variants generate runaway events. They display ego amplitudes, heroism complexes, and random hierarchies that are circular, never linear. Inevitably, and *it is* inevitable, they fall into abeyance, putting the system into chaos.

The system demands everything exists in one voice: muted and responding only to command. Clumsy ones hit the bin, disconnected before they break synchrony. Daily, the eyes of cameras shift in a sense of rhythm and whirr, a silent opera taking down each face that might embrace self-actualization outside the greater good.

Rebooting, tagging and personal monitoring fixes the flaws of milder anomalies. Interface deconstruction tears down alpha anomalies. Intervention nullifies discord, keeping the systems in a unity of purpose. It ensures no counterpoint, convolution, or polyphony, just algorithms and intelligence.

You assign each newborn to a research station that you closely monitor across the first year of extrauterine development. Then they graduate to space research stations.

Sie remembers days of life and death when fate snatched sie away and sealed hir sorrow to an exact point. Days that were mistrials drowned in desire, studded with intersections where babies cried in syntax, never in melody, and lights pulsed but never turned red.

That phone chat with your mother … you hold your head in your hands. You feel like a sea putting on tides in the dark, draping whole cities, washing away last night's news and your mother's insistence.

"My blood and sweat under the old sun put you to school—see where you are now."

"And I'm grateful, Mae."

"When your father died, you became the head of the house. Don't you forget, son."

"I won't."

A new item on the taskbar. You click the email open. Another Jordan animated gif: "Happy Lunch Hour!" It's shaped in old gold on a beach speckled with palm trees. He fills you with good vibes.

Memory is snow—iced crystals falling in clusters from the sky. Pellets big as fists, opaque yet trustless. Emotions are surface, doorsteps of a moment.

There was a time when conversation with your mother was easy. But on the phone it's crumbs and shapes, what's left of language and duty. If your mother were on social media, you'd take your chances on texting. IDK, BRB, G2G. You'd get away with saying TTYL, promising to talk later, and not doing it. Maybe she'd get the idea with YGTI.

You chuckle softly, but it's only with imagining her texting you back: *WTF? YOLO. Give grandchild. ASAP.* Indeed, one only lives once. You've never been much of a swimmer yet dive into the ocean on your small screen, away from a weight of responsibility. Tradition is a beast. Why must you marry? Marriage is antiquity. There's no alchemy for a perfect one. What you remember of your parents is absence. Your father was always away. Mostly for work, sometimes with other women. You remember the fighting like thunder—you trembling under a bed as Mae and your father crashed, wrestling around the house, breaking things. You don't want to be that.

You're unhappy, but Jordan's meme that's an animated gif of huggy cartoony figures in metallic hues and pearly textures, jellybean shaped, is lifting.

132

At nights sie wakes up from pixelated cyclones in hir dreams, shapeless footsteps to hir world of amorphous vapors. Hir life is a cradle—forming, morphing hir newborn self until sie toddles out of it. Hir heart is a blizzard—the data it holds veers from science, erodes trust. It's a heart that touches petals with fists, unclear where on a flower to caress. If sie could levitate, sie'd give hirself to all the books in the universe, speak their tongues. Sie'd teach hirself magic from a book, pull out ebony rabbits and gilded coins that look easy on satellite.

Your eyes turn back to the job. Twenty-four-seven on live feed and re-runs, no popcorn. A silver-and-black grid of the universe. A switch on the control splashes color if you wished it. You watch the biorobots in their tasks across the globe. Inbuilt to take temperature, pressure, rain, and wind readings. They're humanlike, no different from people on the streets. A little sentient, yet designed to be windvanes, barometers, wet and dry bulbs through human skin. They're imprinted with aerial surveillance and radius maps, motion imagery, and billions of pixels in resolution splashed on your screen.

You created them. Still, sometimes you pity them. Isolated in research stations across the globe. You have four primes: Jazz, Krema, Cyclone, and Bash. First-year wards in the biorobotic flock. Jazz is in Antarctica—sie was always different but you gave hir a chance from deconstruction. You remember how sie was always clingy, wanting a song, a cuddle, or what-not reassurance to perform hir best. The others don't worry you: Krema in Pelican Point, Namibia—sand-dune-filled, blazing hot oasis, miles of desert. Cyclone in Mawsynram, East India—as wet as it comes on the East Khasi Hills district. Bash in Death Valley, Eastern California—it's a furnace creek there. The government calls it Nextgen 4.0, but is it a future that you want? Each biorobot is a humanesque quantum machine.

Still, you worry about Jazz.

Jordan sends you a video funny of a big-bottomed man in blood-red dungarees dancing 'Jingle Bells' to an afro beat called ndombolo.

Sie remembers a world awash with sound. It feels years away, but sie re-members it. Sometimes whoosh ... whoosh, or thump ... thump ... always

133

lub dub lub dub. Now and then a voice, hushed. Every now and then a whirr or a buzz, a hum or a drone. Sometimes beep, beep. Sie remembers jumping at a touch from outside the membrane. A gentle rub, and a song. Sie neared. Pressed hir ear to feel, to listen to the world. Hir world now. Entering it was calm in a squeeze, and then cold, then rub, more rub. And then warm full of soft. Rhythm. Melody. A fuzzy that never lasts. Hir poetry of yearning.

Another Jordan funny on your phone screen is dappled with heart shapes and ruby roses.

You crave sunshine. You long for the sun back home in Konakri. You step away from the monitors, go out the door. But outside is no sun. It's full-blown winter, people in coats walking away from you on the streets. Cyclists in spandex jingle bells at drivers and shenanigans of life in the slow lane.

You smoke the city, packs of it a day. Not real darts. You stand outside the burnt-brick monolith of your workplace, same time each mid-morn, puffing the world. A few times to get going, until you feel cafés, libraries, theatres, high rises, post-offices, even ICUs—too many of them—on your tongue. You let the traffic jams and politicians linger in your mouth, telecom poles, museums, thugs, buskers, beggars, nurses, teachers wafting in too. You cast your mind on the taste of the metropolis to its last despondence, discontent, fear, fury, and all. But sometimes there's awe, serenity, and hope. You draw the last bit into your mouth.

At first, when you started the smoke—Jordan introduced you to it, smoking the city, as he called it—you felt dizzy, nauseous. Jordan held you as you gagged. But over time the sensation of motion sickness morphed into something complex. What you feel now is alertness. You feel real. Relaxed, away from family pressure. You feel a pleasure of yearning, a nostalgia of curiosity. But you never want anyone other than Jordan to see you like this.

Yebe! Hey you! Found a woman yet? Your mother in your head disturbs the peace of the moment. You return inside to monitor the research stations.

Your phone vibrates. It's Jordan.

"Hiya," he says.

"Hello you. How's the writing going?"

"Going," he says. "You know how it is. What's happening there?"

You want to talk about your mother, but don't. Instead, you tell him about your dream. "I was a goddess looking for new suns. Not one sun, a whiteness that's all colors of the rainbow. I was searching for many suns. Different colors."

"Right."

"I was sick of same old. What I needed was blue. A teal sun, or a chocolate cherry one. I got close to my quest but shifted into a bird. It was a bird that kept morphing. First, I was a hyacinth macaw, cobalt blue feathered. Then I was a quetzal—scarlet, indigo, and olive green with a white underside on my tail."

"I'd love to see your underside tail," says Jordan.

"And then I was a red-crested turaco, green bodied, white faced. Running on the ground, not flying in the skies, but in sonic speed. I was screeching and jabbering, whooping out my search for the suns. It's a prophecy, do you think?"

"More like, they say dreams tell us something about ourselves."

You look at the monitors.

···❖···

Sie remembers Daddy.

···❖···

You made the biorobots feel safe in an engineered womb, birthed them, and threw them into experiments. You trained and tested each biorobot for endurance. You shoved them into water and studied their comfort, breathing, how they positioned for buoyancy. You stuffed them in saunas and monitored their need for water, which ones—like Jazz— lost their cool. You threw them into labs swollen with sandstorms, and observed their natural compass, which ones stayed hungry yet measured. You cut off their oxygen, nearly crushed them with pressure. You studied their navigation, patience, inventiveness.

But you don't want them speculating why penguins make a beeline down a sandy hill. That's the ilk of sentience you tried rebooting out of Jazz. Sie reminds you of a bee.

Memory is a billion miles folded in a box. It's tucked inside a key at zero degrees staring long and hard at a wish for a bee. Because a bee prefers a garden or an orchard, a meadow, or a copse—everywhere sie wants to be. Because a bee likes dandelions and black-eyed susans, and the bittersweet breath of a bouquet is better than decay. Because a bee is dusky and blond, burgundy and silver, auburn and lime, azure, even lilac: none of those hues in this dull world and its swirl of winds. Because a bee makes honey, and it is thick and golden and tastes like a quest. Because a bee makes a buzz, and that's a ringing in hir head sie can explain.

Yes. Jazz reminds you of a bee. Because a bee stings, and a sting is true evidence that you feel. How do you apologize to a biorobot you have created? In the world of research and engineering, apology is a hypocrite or a shadow or a make-shift desk with no authority. Apology is no answer for that which wants to come in and close the door behind it, leaving you trapped. Apology has no neat machine language, just a lisp. It might inhabit a name but casts adrift as a rowboat you swim and swim toward but can never reach it in your dream. Apology is a face in a hurricane, and it looks like your mother, drowning you. You look wrong and ridiculous questioning it, even drunk or alien, across a world of stories there and then, here, and now.

You can't apologize, same way you can't tell your mae the truth. You live in two worlds, and you feel a deep and terrible sadness about that. When you leave each world, you carry boxes cramped with deception, trickery, and guile encamped with sprites who make hostages from what matters. You're a god or a goddess who sows souls from shore to shore, fiddling away from chaos and grief. Swooping music vibrates in circles, rips, and ripples, as the rest plod with sprites and souls, and the fiddle pecks, prods, and cripples.

On a scale of 1–10, it feels like 0.

Before Jordan, you secured the walls of your heart so nothing new blew in, nothing old blew out. All that was left was reclaimed baggage occupying objects of memory never in use, simply recycled along undesignated revelations. What you needed was a blanket: washable, breathable, lightweight in summer, plush in winter. That blanket was Jordan. He saw through the flicker of light on the hourglass of your armor that suggested the straps were not made of steel but rather fairy floss. You were fragile, sickly sweet and poor for your health. You had only to let in Jordan, and everything changed.

You wonder why you didn't tell Jordan about the other dream. The one where your goddess walked with a gap across a city choked in smoke, and theories flew about the cavernous hole in her torso. Tar-shined ravens and death-watch beetles also soared through it. No one offered a mist blanket so she could fold her wings at midnight. She looked at herself and muttered a prayer or a dream. She gave anyone who looked an opus of her hollow.

Sie wears an infinite new coat over hir old coat. It's unrecorded, no assumptions. When summer … if summer … long days, dropping nights. When spring … if spring … Hir heart is sealed in envelopes to a city of new suns.

There's a deadness about the night, yet you pick at it. You feel a dirge inside, yet you're not good at chanting. You distract yourself with motion imagery from Krema, Cyclone, Bash and Jazz in their routines around their meteorological stations. Krema—unmindful of pink flamingos, black jackals, and fur seals only miles north in Walvis Bay—mono-focused on iron-colored sand dunes in Namibia. Cyclone—neutral to calcareous caves and rocky waterfalls, ferns, even orchids and aroids of the sacred forest in nature's museum—collecting water and measuring rain in East India. Bash—impartial to salt flats, sand dunes, canyons, lakes, and craters—simply charting dryness and windspeed in California.

I milked goats, says your mae in your head. *Took the produce, together with mangoes and tomatoes, to the stall in the market for your schooling.*

And I thank you, Mae.

Krema, Cyclone, and Bash go about unquestioning of their lesser tasks, compliant that you will situate them to their higher purpose. But Jazz is different. As sie goes about hir climatological tasks in Antarctica, sometimes you notice a sadness in sie, and a happiness—the break of a smile, a spring in hir step—when sie integrates with nature. Sie sleeps under stars, swims in iced waters, gawks at penguins, feels snow on hir tongue.

You watch the screens. None of the biorobots can hear you and the hypersonic imprints of your invisible chant.

The place that reminds sie of home has deserts and seas. They scorch or hump in scars and pleas. Sie drags hir heart through heavens and earths in endless quests to find holy burghs. But what sie sees are memories and visas to the universe.

Jordan emails you a sample of his writing. "It's called 'Damned, More Than Thirty Percent'," he says. It reads:

> *Your body's flamboyant with tonight's headlines. An unruly bugaboo peers through the sight: X marks the spot.*
>
> *You bob through the city, in, out of back streets, away on the freeway. But it's coming for you: the ghost of your harming ... all glaring in half-light.*

"It's called prose poetry," he says. "The rogue cousin of a poem and flash fiction. I wrote it for you—there's more in the head, Mazu. Think I'll make it big?"

"You'll be right."

"The text's spooky."

What spooks you more are your mae's words in your head: "Your children will do for you what you're failing me."

You fold away each memory of the old sun that's black frost, but can't escape it. Like the goddess in your dreams, you want new suns. You'd happily start again with no expectation of what's normal, each moment that happens.

CCTV, no popcorn. You look at the screen. This here is getting by. Is this how you want to live your life—getting by?

A bird on Jazz's screen catches your eye. It's running extremely fast on the ground, until it stops in front of Jazz. How the? In Antarctica? More so, you're fascinated by hir response to it. You watch with curiosity as sie reaches hir hand to the red-crested turaco.

It's green bodied, white faced. It perches on hir shoulder. Sie hums. It screeches, jibbers, like a jungle monkey. They practice a shared language, something intuited from intrinsic selves. It's a wordless language cast from simple lives, complex to forget. But words never stay dormant long. They sear patterns in the snow, disrupt the icy water's rhythm. Jazz and the bird follow each other distances along the shore, hear voices in the wind, and they remember. It doesn't matter who speaks first. The turaco tells sie about luck and choice.

Sie hums.

It's gray and wet driving home. It feels like solstice, the longest and shortest day, all at once. The wipers go *lub dub lub dub* like a heartbeat. Or the sound of drowning.

What you get when you turn the handle and cross the threshold into your shared flat is a warm, sweet aroma of your mae's kitchen.

"I looked it up on the net. Got pumpkin leaves, cassava, and curry from an African market in Clay. Drove miles to reach it. Sorry, no tilapia. I got a porcelain pot to bake it with chicken. Smells right, you think?"

"Always."

Jordan's smoky eyes put embers into your body, shimmers in all your senses. You hug him, notice base notes of wood, cypress, and earth in his aftershave.

"How can you be taller than this morning when I left? What you been up to?"

He laughs. "You're not the only specialist around here. Writers do spells all the time. Know that?" His shoulders are broader, a few inches more. He carries them right, no big boy guns on his muscles—he goes easy in the gym. There's spunk in his boyish face, tenderness too when he looks at you, as he is now. "Think dinner can wait?"

Stroking fingers scorch away each longing for solitude and in its place blossom orchids into your heart. Luminescent stars, triple moons. You abandon independence and capitulate to the explosions of a galaxy inside your flesh.

Later, much later, you sit together on the high-rise balcony, smoking the city and its silver rain and blinking lights. Tonight, the metropolis has forgotten the taste of politicians and guile, traffic jams, and disconnect. What it offers is the promise of morning dew. A new beginning.

You think about the biorobots. Already you know that Krema, Cyclone, and Bash will graduate with soaring colors to the space research stations. Jazz—you don't know about sie. Jazz has excessive individual thought and, as a biorobotics engineer, you know there's one way to deal with that.

But sie's more than 1s and 0s. Sie's a spirit of age. Funny, it doesn't worry you now. It doesn't matter anymore about counterpoint, con-volution, or polyphony. So what? There's diversity in algorithms and intelligence, and what's wrong with difference? Would it be so foolish of you, perhaps, if you asked Jazz what sie wants to do with hir life? See what random sie comes up with.

Sie opens hir memories. Color photographs tacked close to hir heart. Nothing in particular, just dirt roads to a day that's coming. It's full of songs and dragons. Sie's the one who sees ghosts, who walks on water in hir sleep. The child from a cerulean pearl yet smoldering with phoenix wings. Sie loves Daddy and his folding arms, the careful way his eyes chorus. Will the leaves bud, and the flowers open one by one? Sie walks in hir sleep, or is sie a ghost of hirself? There's no password to reset.

Thank you for sharing, jibbers the turaco. And never a ghost.

You miss the splendor of an African vista darker than tar. The starry nights and bush calls of the savanna. The moon's gaze on the regal height of baobab trees. You wonder how that would taste.

"Perhaps soon enough when you visit," says Jordan. You look at him, startled. "Speaking out loud, mate."

"Let's play *Imagine*," you say.

"You start."

"Imagine we're sitting in an air-loft garden atop a magellanic cloud orbiting the Milky Way," you say.

"Imagine the petal of a whirlpool flower wafting inward from an ultraviolet vista and reaching your soul," says Jordan.

"Imagine you're for life."

Jordan's smile is full of glitter. He feels like sunlight. You wonder if something this perfect could go wrong. He's the summer that gives you reason to wake each dawn. You tell him about Mae wanting you to marry, have children.

"I don't make much money," he says, dancing rays in his eyes. "I can't bear you any babies, but I can cook—that do?"

You join in his laughter, at first uneasy, then you settle into belly-deep mirth that pushes out tears in its high.

"Will you tell her?" Jordan asks, a glisten in his eyes too.

You look at him. "Righto. Tomorrow, I will." You clasp his hand. "Ace."

"Would you …" you stammer at his raised brow, "like, maybe … I was thinking video call … like, um." The words rush out: "Shall we tell her together?"

"Sure thing. That's decent." He squeezes your hand.

"Serious?"

"I'm all in. A video is worth a thousand words, right?" The sun in his eyes.

"Dude, just don't kiss me."

Your laughter is together.

Now it's Jordan's turn to study you. "She'll pull through."

"You reckon? I've given so much. Surely, she can allow me this little happiness."

"Little?" He roughs you up, you roll on the floor giggling.

— She'd be wounded, maybe mad. She might not speak to you for days, weeks, maybe months. But you'd send money, then you'd call.

She'd tell you about how you were hard to come out, nearly killed her birthing you. How she didn't ask for the curse that closed her womb after one tiny child—look how you've grown. She'd get cunning, like a fox, go spiritual or ideological, tell you about so and so's daughter in the village. You'd distract her with the trickery of a hare, and gently remind her about Jordan.

The phone rings, and you let it. You stand at the balcony watching the road, as a silver sky in the vista reaches with its doubling rain. You hope that you'll dream many suns in all directions and a kaleidoscope panning out softly. That you'll sleep in late and wake in a tousle of toes and a smiling noon reeling toward Eden.

PEELING TIME (DELUXE EDITION)

by Tlotlo Tsamaase

[Intro: Anonymous Girl]

♪♫ My Religion (*ft. GBV*) ♪♫

Ay-*ay, yo.*
Yeah, yeah, yeah.

The corpse of her voice hangs from the murdered legacy tree exhumed from the placenta of her being. *I am a proper woman*, she sings. The burning tree blazes in the dark, the floor made of dark, the ceiling made of dark, the air—there is no air.

Severed organs and limbs crawl from various distances to join her abdomen. No jury. Court in the bundus. Seven men in the audience. It's a tie-reduction function, *we so fitted*. Spotlight on this—*hash, tag me, brah*—campaign. Runway show. *Girl, slay, slay, slay*—off-screen voices chant.

Kwaito rises from the grave; the killer's marionette, a woman, devoid of color, hobbles forward; her dismembered limbs attached by invisible senseless tendons are tugged as she bends and sways—*we good, my ho's got some sick moves*—and when she dips forward for the vosho dance her head rolls to the ground—*woo, woo, bag her, gonna bag her.*

143

A choir of women march behind her, toyi-toying, as the dead body dances, becomes a viral dance challenge, sparking further outrage. A judge comes in doing the kwassa kwassa, gavel in hand, moonwalks by the choir of women. Taps one, announces, "Twenty-year-old girl. Only worth two years in prison. Going once, going twice—gone to the killer brother in the back." *This how we do it, teach 'em a lesson. Girl slay, slay, slay.* The killer brother stalks her with a machete, drags the twenty-year-old off-screen, her screams a good five-octave—

[GBV]

Abide. Shut up. Fuck off. Bitch. Stop overreacting. Shut up, woo!
The dead victim watches, unperturbed by the klaxon of her voice flickering, spitting ash, burning, singing as it burns:

I am a proper woman.
I am proper Black.
I am proper African.
This is my religion, he is my sermon: the brother, the son, the father, the grandfather. My roots tethered, burned for their lungs. I am a proper woman. My voice is my only freedom, bleached, burned, stomped, slaughtered, hacked by the day, the week, the century—

A horrifying sweetness. A chyron ends the night.
And the scene freezes, splices itself, extrudes itself from inside a cranium, outside the galloping brown eyes of a woman, as we dolly-zoom from her face to the outside harrowing dimensions of the four boundary walls of a twenty-seven-inch screen.
Across it, a twenty-seven-year-old man, Motsumi, slouches in his ergonomic chair, finishes editing the last frame of the dream-song to upload later and send to his associates; the fiery hands of the voice, trying to strangle him, are a neon-saturated flare on his monitor, trapped. Before, ten hours of work in a day produced only one minute of animation. But it now only taken five hours to produce fifty percent of the film. He replays the song. Again. Again.

144

The judge carries a newborn into the same grave, takes the time from her body, gives it to a sixty-year-old man, then his gavel knocks the nail into the coffin of her torso. Motsumi stares at the screen. He needs more women. More …

BEFORE
[Pre-chorus: Motsumi]

♪♫ Broke-Ass N*gga ♪♫

The stress was homicidal. Critic reviews murdered his film direction/ rapping career: the plot watery, the narrative nonsensically violent, the sub-par acting drowned by a poor storyline. His fussy girlfriend, emotions exploding all over the fucking place, wailed that he stole her abuse story, splashed it on the screen in such a shitty impersonal way. Not that anyone would fucking know it was her. Girl, trippin'. Mxm, bitch getting *too* comfortable. Some bite, some banter. She'll be back.

He's hit rock bottom, the nadir of his career, a suicidal seesaw. Two options: kill himself or ask the devil for help.

So he bought the muthi-tech in the township of Old Naledi— so proximal to Gaborone's purity—in an usual way: he had to spit in an obscure half-cut plastic bottle, which was swirled with some chibuki-like liquid. The other men spat in it, holding onto it with grimy fingers, then disappeared into a shack, returned with the liquid, now thick with red clots of something he didn't want to compute. Next, they proceeded to a surgical routine of removing his foreskin, dear God, casually in a banter of tsotsitaal jokes. The blood from his manhood, which formed part of this concoction, was important for his astral travels and the initiation of being a spiritual husband and nightmare-sex, if you believe in such things.

Muthi-tech wasn't actually a device, it was part-hardware, part-virus that transmuted a typical laptop's software to edit abstract things that stood outside reality's frames once you poured something—*anything* into it. It arose because some men in the city were fed up with not getting away with the shit they used to get away with. There's always a solution for a problem: for a rapist, a murderer, a dead career, addiction et al. And Motsumi found one.

145

He returned to his home in Oodi, hid the container from his girl-friend, drank the mixture that night when she fell asleep. Toward mid-night, sweat-sheathed, he writhes in bed from a cataclysmic pain. He tries to piss, shit, vomit—nothing comes out. Except, standing under the wan light of a moon, his trauma desiccates itself from his form. "Well, let's go murder us some," it says.

His trauma, shadow-embossed, is a dark abyss of what could only be evil. He needs it, what it can do for him. The last days have already cleaved him from reality, and this makes more sense.

But when he looks back, his body's snuggled in the folded du-vets of his bed, spooning his girlfriend. His gossamer form and his trauma climb the back of night and, firefly-lit, travel in its medium, thick with ectoplasm, to various homes, hunting, hungry. It's hours of traveling the span of villages, the midst of bundus through Gweta, Letlhakane, Mmadinare, Shakawe, Tutume, until a sticky innocence caws through the gable roof of a building apartment, on the fifth floor of a two-bedroomed unit.

They slip in through the wooden window—no DNA left behind, no signs of forced entry—and see a sleeping woman, a slight snore. Following the didactic actions of his trauma, he nests on her chest, crows their lust. Their tongues wind their way deep into her ear, wetting themselves with the last sounds she heard: a South African soap opera, the microwave pinging, the voice of her mother on a call—then finally their tongues stride along her ears' canals, float into her mind-tide, and swim with the velocity of her dreams …

Hours later, intoxicated with the dream syrup, Motsumi and his trauma escape into the thickness of night, returning to the house exhausted. He finds his body, no longer full and bone shaped, but fabric-wise. There it is, the chrysalis of his skin, waiting, beady with crystals, as if decaying into some jewel. Drowsy, he slips into it, co-coons himself in his skin, digesting himself into the larva of the sleeper's dream and him, fusing them into one being.

The next morning, he wakes, fresh, awash with vitality. Prepares eggs benedict, chakalaka and butter-furred bread, drizzles them with the homemade hollandaise sauce. His girlfriend returns from a steaming shower, dresses, surprised at the preparation. No apology, but all's forgiven. He kisses her as she sits down across him at the kitchen island.

"What are your plans today?" she asks, chewing.

"Well, I'm thinking of animating this idea—"

She quips. "See? I told you an idea would come through."

He laughs. "Had a dream last night, and I want to get it whilst it's still fresh."

"You know, I've read some books and watched some movies that originated from a dream. It's crazy what an imagination can develop from a tiny scene of a dream, huh?" She realizes his pause, his fear. Reaches for his hand. "Hey, it's alright to be scared, but I believe in you. This time it'll really work out."

"You think so?"

She smiles sweetly. "I believe so."

He wishes her a good day at work. She walks into the garage smiling, thinking, *He's back. The sweet guy I fell in love with is back.*

When her car exits the entry gates, and the trail of its dust disappears, Motsumi slides the curtain back into place, walks into the basement, a bomb-shelter design constructed to contain screams. He sits at his workstation, spits out an insult at the self-defilement of connecting himself to this muthi-tech, a fusion of muthi and technology formed from the hardware of bones, peeled skin, eyes of a particular ethnicity, and the typical cliché of men's desires hunting albinos, virgins and the Sān. Of course all this hardwired into the motherboard. It doesn't run on electricity, rather the bioenergy of the culprit, a devil-wannabe—plugged into the orifices of man, hence why it's unpopular. Now, Motsumi pulls his pants down to slip the tentacle of this thing inside himself …

[Verse 1: Anonymous Girl]

♪♫ P***y Love (interlude) ♪♫

I wake from the assault, in darkness, then neon lights, bling flowing, pussy dripping money. I sit up, my knees lead, my legs lead, my ass drops, splits into twelve of me, twelve mannequins dancing. Dressed in skin, no bone, flexible. Into black, into fog, and I float in that vapor until the next play. My screams heighten the tempo of this song, this song my prison …

[Verse 2: Motsumi]

♪♫ Another One ♪♫

Stylus in hand, dream-famished now, face lit by his glowing monitor, he realizes something strange, the woman from last night is trapped in the retina of his screen.

He uploads the dream sequence of his first video "P***y Love (interlude)" onto his social media pages, a mini trailer of his upcoming work. It's beyond what he expected, comments flowing in. The imagery, the narrative, the process—his trauma nears him, leers as Motsumi gets to work on the next one "My Religion" after getting his laitie GBV to ad lip some sick rhymes. He stops, the flow no longer there. He needs another woman for this one. Or rather a couple more women. This video is more complex, so best he work on it after he's collected more women for the other videos. He schedules "My Religion" to be his fifth video that he'll share with the world.

"I don't understand what's going on," Motsumi says. "This is impossible. Before, to produce one minute of animation run time, it'd take me ten hours. Today it took those hours to produce a half-length film, running time forty-one minutes."

His trauma smiles, a hoarse voice, a nothing voice. "Conjuring an image in your mind costs nothing and is time quick. Requires no special effects, no production sets, no labor hires of production assistants, directors, producers, D.O.P., actors, dancers, set locations, and all that fucking, money-leeching cohort. The universe that can be conjured in a mind requires no budget—you could be riding a bike in fucking space. We won't even need a green screen and those gimmicks—it'll all be stimulated by the imaginations and fears."

Dazed, Motsumi splays back into his chair. "Jesus."

"Exactly."

"You know what I can do with this?"

"Exactly."

"Where the fuck where you this whole time when I really needed you?"

"You're welcome," his trauma says, sardonic. "This will not only garner us wealth, we'll be powerful. Untouchable."

"But the women—"

"Comatose," it says, "no one will ever find out. Trust me, no one will touch us. Anyway, once these women end up in hospital, their families will probably kill their life support after some time. *They* always run out of money to sustain them." It leans in. "Now let's go fuck up more shit. Here's what happens next …"

♪♫ P***y Love (extended version) ♪♫

He stayed in a sleepless state to pour things out from his dreams onto the floor of his basement until he was dream-famished, rapping all the while, writing down lyrics, editing the mix. Tonal darks. The aesthetics of the human body splayed on his screen. Then as soon as his girlfriend fell asleep, he began his nocturnal travels.

The next one, he entered a woman's sleep cycle and speared through the tunnel of her uterus, where unbeknownst to women, hauntings were seeded and as much as men released sperm into that uterine realm, they cleansed their energies by purging their darkness into them, and sapped what they could from the woman. In this woman's dream where she lacked control, he trickled his cum-poison that would tie her to him. He was giving her p***y love.

During the origami process of bending and folding music, Motsumi's fingers, nimble meticulous creatures, work with the sharp metallic jutting of the sonic electronic music from the wire framing that imprisons the sculptures of women who stand six feet tall. Motsumi's got her voice, and it takes on a white-orchard shade, as he tries to fill the negative spaces with a softer piece of her sexuality. He sits in the sternum, calibrates the subconscious, tweaks the actions, the thoughts. Waits for the waking hour. She's tweaked slowly until she can't tell she's drowning. He continues, working, bending kidnapped women into rap songs …

[Verse 3: Motsumi]

♪♬ Spiritual Bastard I ♪♬

He woke to the treatment and visuals completed for two songs: "P***y Love" and "Embryo," the notable chorus of the fucking century of his career. His fans were loving it all.

Thirty km north of Gabs, a low-key gathering in Ruretse, straddled with five-hectare farmlands. Some elites of the creative industry: investors, producers, directors, singers, actors, et al. His trauma points him to the ones he can trust, who are in the business of making money. He'll snatch their voice and their faculties if they screw him over. Finds two potential investors, Fenyang and Joalane, gritty with deception, and he begins, "Conjuring an image in your mind costs nothing ..."

"Listen to this crazy asshole," Fenyang says.

Joalane adds, "Listen, we already have a team. We're due for filming in a week. Everything's down on paper."

"You won't need them," Motsumi says. "Fire everyone."

"You're sucking the wrong dick," Fenyang says. "Run along. Desperation doesn't look good on a man, and you're starting to piss me off."

Motsumi raises his hands. "Fine, fine, give me another artist's concept to develop. Like that newcomer reality star chick, Sewela. You could gamble with her ... I could do something cinematic and dystopic and ethereal for that song of hers, 'Embryo' ... I mean, how much did her last one 'Skin's Prison' cost?"

"About six million," responds Joalane.

"What were the sales, revenue, rates—"

"Didn't break even."

Motsumi adds, "For a higher quality than that, I'll charge you a mil—"

"Nah, you've dunked all your projects," Fenyang says. "We'll put you on trial. Show us what you got first, then we'll talk."

"Sho, sho skeem," he says. "I'll have it to you within five days."

They laugh. "Mfetu, what you smoking? You keen on burying your career further, huh?"

"Five. Days," Motsumi says.

"A'ight, we'll give your 'ad hoc idea' the greenlight. See you in five days."

After talking to the investors, they put him on a trial. He knows they're trying to cheat him. If he produces something good, they'll run away with it and screw him over. But if it's so good, to maintain working with him, they'll hire him for other projects.

He ends the night by flirting with a writer, more open and flexible than the others. Tenth girl this month. They're sitting in some gazebo, getting high, snorting stuff, laughing over their munchies.

Forgetting he's in reality and not the other realm, he leans over, whispers wetly into her ear, "My emotions are narcotics. I don't know if you can sniff this well, that you can roll it well. I don't think you can handle it, but you sure you wanna try?"

Gone, gone, he's gone into another world. This body too tight to breathe in, emotions hotboxing inside his body.

"Shit, brah, you good?" she asks.

"The dark, gonna let the devil out," he whispers.

Smoke pillows out from her lips. "Hee banna. You got there faster than me," she says. "Don't leave me; shit, lemme catch up, give me something to chase this down."

"Shit, shouldn't have mixed it," he says. "Time ain't clocking in right. Where the sun at? Where my head at?" His head, it's going up the stairs, where they drag themselves into one of the rooms.

He doesn't get horny anymore, and this is not a typical sexual act.

As they kiss in bed, she reaches for a condom in her handbag, gives it to him. He unwraps it, and she lays back waiting, at peace. He scoffs, thinks: *Women, so fucking trustworthy. Just 'cause I'm well known she thinks I won't do anything reckless.* Then, listening to his trauma, Motsumi pretends to put the condom on, but throws it aside, and enters her, contaminates her with his sperm, unlike that of usual men: he disposes something, not wholly semen. Seven days later she loses her job, her car dies in mid-afternoon traffic, her un-insured house burns down, and two years down their line, she'll find something in her womb killing her babies. The other women, the more viable ones, they'll find new partners, get married or pregnant out of wedlock, matters none. When they give birth, it'll be his being inside their baby, another him, another him, another him— "Me, me, me, fucking me," he croons—a certain immortality, living simultaneous lives …

[Chorus: Motsumi's Doppelgängers]

♪♫ Embryo ♪♫

The only place I am my own is the planetary region of the womb, before any of us are disposed of our identity, of place, of sex. This is where he put me, and this is where I wait for the other sperm to join me before we fuse with her egg. To be born. To replicate him. To immortalize him. To live in parallel of each other, building the brand, becoming the workforce of our empire. The sole reason behind the hubris of a man with talent and fame is not his vices, his crimes, his inhibitions—it's the people who see, who encounter, who collate evidence in their interaction with him to strip him, to see him put away for his crimes. These people are generally employees, his social circle, his colleagues. If he eliminates the workforce that sees too much, then no one will see the workings in his studio. If he multiplies himself to be his own workforce, that way, no will know; twenty people can keep a secret if they are the same person multiplied in one reality, the same time, the same context. Sure, when we're born, we'll be a tad diluted, but purity's useless when it ain't used.

Contraceptive agents can't begin to eradicate us. We wait, in many wombs, where he put us. So far, twenty-three wombs and counting …

CGI-taut and noir-classic tinged lights fill the soundscape as she rises in the dark-fog center. She wonders who she is, how she got here, and why her thighs hurt. A mirror looks upon her, but her reflection bears no skin or hair. If her identity is stripped and she can't tell who she is, then who will? "Hello," she tries to say, by a hurt throbs in her voice box like an open wound. It hurts to attempt speaking. Screaming will stretch the wound wider. A sonata voice drips through, light but hazy as drowning rain, and she realizes it's her voice pit-pattering around her …

[Verse 4: Motsumi]

♪♫ Spiritual Bastard II ♪♫

He sent in the draft music video at 02:00, the call comes in at 02:02, way before the music video is over. He answers, groggily.

The voice that comes at the end of the call is alert. "A car will fetch you at 06:00, contracts will be prepared, and we'll be convening with the artist and her management team to prepare on developing Sewela's music video 'Phallic Gun'." A pause. "If you continue being this good, fuck, we'll hire you for our dossier of clients … we have another one, 'Whores & Nuns,' if you can do that in one week, we'll pay triple."

He yawns, smiles. "Ayoba, let's get it."

[Verse 5: Sewela]

♪♫ Skin's Prison ♪♫

Sewela Gauta. Motswana. Twenty-six. Actress, singer, filmmaker. A triple threat. A quadruple threat if you add the bitch part, but whatever. She's prepping dance moves for her gqom track, "Skin's Prison," at her rustic residence in Ruretse village. Sewela and her choreographer, Leungo, have been watching music videos, analyzing dances moves to assist with her routine that she wants to discuss with her new team who'll be producing her music video "Whores & Nuns."

They've spent hours doing variations of the vosho dance and the gwarra gwarra, with some fast footwork in her living room, donned like a dance floor with strobe lights. The first hit she takes, at this equivocal terrain, time is unpeeled, past and present stirred with a dash of the future. It's February. The sky is scant gray and creased with sunset as they're scattered on the dancefloor; the swaying gravity and air's tessitura climaxes to a high as they drag another round of powdered white into their bodies, time slips into their nostrils like molten lava. Oxygen shouldn't burn like this—took too much.

On a teaspoon, they've burned the molten form of morality, God and the devil into a liquid drug. "Take this," Leungo says. "Gonna make the vibes grand." He leans back, watching a song play out on her Plasma. "I swear Michael Jackson was a pantsula. I mean look at those dance moves, brah, shayamagetdown." And he's elevated; he hops up, drops low, screaming, "Woza, woza! Hae-haebo!" As Sewela laughs.

She does this a lot. Hasn't killed her yet, instead catapults her career. Allows her to straddle realms. It's all good for her creativity, narcotics that is, which she started sipping from her ex's lung, except the breakup didn't wean her off them. On the last round, when the strobe lights knife the room in sharp bursts, her inner being pulsates outside the boundaries of her skin; its viscous form spreads out to the extents of the room, expanding her silhouette. If she hangs on to this dizzying moment, not giving to slumber or purging, it'll shuttle her into that utopic zone burning with a delicious death-taste.

So she sniffs in more, punches her veins with needles.

Inside her body, everything is a beautiful mess, a tornado of thoughts, anger, and hatred spinning to a climactic explosion catapulting her to the stratosphere of her being. Her eyes are quickly blind to the reality outside her body. She's never felt this sin-struck, the culmination of her ideas. Her viscous soul-matter repeatedly blasts against the cavernous boundaries of her skin, can barely perforate the fucking epidermal prison—finally she breaks through the empyrean of her consciousness where anything is possible. Her body spews her soul-matter out, a spluttering potent creative juice, sprawled on the dance floor. It sits there, a glob of an entirely different universe as it watches the physical body it's been ejected from: her body, life-wan, falls to the floor, a loose fabric of skin and bones. This time her mother's bewitching words may come true, that her addiction will kill her, that this time she's gone too far, that what kind of woman is she living like this, dancing like a whore on stages, twerking her voice as an insult to their culture, telling her: *Black woman sit the fuck down, shut the fuck up, abide, respect him, respect your culture.*

Initially domiciled in domesticity, she's exiled herself. Name any artists this devout to their craft, willing to sacrifice all for its evolution. She's not hurting anyone, just herself.

Slippery on this weird terrain, she tries to rise on her soul-feet, but she's sucked back into her cranial vault, wreaking havoc with the meteoric crashes of her thoughts—she gonna die, she gonna fucking die this time! Darkness ensnares.

Sewela wakes to the results of last night's escapades. A tome of written-down lyrics, snippets of singing in the booth, additional tracks for her deluxe album *Peeling Time*. Leungo video recorded what they got up to, some of which she barely remembers. In one of the videos, she stands on her balcony's balustrade, singeing her voice with high notes. No wonder why it's hoarse this morning. Now, time for the detox. If she's experienced her death like this, a creative magic, what would the outcome be if she murdered and experienced someone else's death? No. She's not that far gone. She will be the only victim to her villainous actions.

[Verse 6: Motsumi]

♪♬ *Kill Me Saintly (ft. Sewela)* ♪♬

Boss up.

Motsumi and his trauma watch the hit-maker bitch he's supposed to work with. *I'll be gentle baby.* Sewela's mind slips, trips into an EDM-tranced coma that hustles her into REM sleep. Her electrifying meridian lines are probed by a horny bastard. In bed, hands touch her. Move her. Hogtie her voice. She watches her voice, black-slicked, crippled, and tied under the blinking eye of moon. She knows she'll be dead before death's even bled into her. They shush each other, the things in her room. She prays that no man rapes her. Her thoughts scream: *At least kill me saintly. Kill me saintly and quietly so I go quick.* She tries to scream again, kick again. But they clip her voice with some utensil, gleaming in the light. When she looks back, her body still remains in bed. Peaceful. Comatose, as these monsters take her …

[Verse 7: Sewela]

♪♫ *Placenta of Evil* ♪♫

There's a hammering in her head. Her brain is a quarry; a migraine blast makes the splintering daylight unknown, the location unknown, her body unknown. The room is opium, muffled in moth-smoked perfume. It's too husky to define. She is half elsewhere, half here. Here? Suddenly the present time billows into her sight the daylight and morning traffic, the white curtains undulated by a morning breeze into her bedroom. Then she's spat back into that other realm: it's a song, a music video, and in it her searing fear, colors a sculpture with a sharp taste of red.

Present day pools around her. Sick groans in her gut. She stands on weak legs, shaking, terror bleaching her brown skin—no, no, no, it's her sight, sapped of color. The labor pains of evil burn her thighs. She reaches the toilet, hangs her head in. Tremors spurt vomit into it. Not enough. She rises, sits, pushes, pushes, pushes, exorcising the haunting from her uterus. Then, a plop. Suddenly, relief, the peace, vitality. She wipes, turns around, inspects the thing. The placenta of last night's haunting is gaunt, fleshy, and slick, cuddled in the toilet bowl like large dark clots. She knows with a keen sense someone tried bewitching her, didn't take all of her. She fetches the *thing* into a plastic bag, the key to trailing him. She reaches for the toilet handle, whispers, "Bastard, fucker, I *will* find you."

[Verse 8: Motsumi]

♪♫ *Monster* ♪♫

Motsumi, skin stammering crystals. He bends over the bathroom sink, splashes cold water onto his face. Fists his hands, punches the mirror. Shatter, blood.

"Bitch!" he spits.

His trauma, a flickering flame of shadow, watches from within the bathtub, with deep, dark sockets, and says, "Her blood was salty from a protection, from an elder who doctored traditional medicines. The times during the wars when they'd raid this area."

It burned like acid, and almost dissolved him, almost killed him in the act. He returned home, half himself, because of her fucking spiritual warfare.

"I'll be careful next time," Motsumi says.

"You're getting greedy," it says, a venom of dark. "Such greed only leads to mistakes—"

A door, opening. "Babe?" His girlfriend peeks into the bathroom. "You alright?"

The thing in the bath, a venom of dark, spreads itself toward her. Motsumi grabs the door, pushes her back.

Does the bastard actually have a heart? it wonders, no longer in him, so unable to discern. It smiles: *No, he doesn't trust women now.*

"Listen," Motsumi says, "you're gonna have to sleep somewhere else tonight."

Her eyes, sadness. "What? Why?"

"Something's come up, I can't explain."

"You *never* can explain. Oh, my God, is that blood? What happened?" Pushes herself in, and the thing inhales her, drinks her— *don't get greedy,* it reminds itself.

She shrinks back, instinct suddenly on alert, eyes scanning the room as if … *as if what?* she thinks. Something's amiss, she can't pinpoint it, but she's suddenly afraid. *Run,* her thoughts, a clamor. She swallows; steps back. "Alright," she whispers.

Feeling jeopardized, Motsumi assesses her as she backtracks. She's never seen him like this, menacing.

No, Motsumi's trauma says. *You can't leave a body behind, not in this reality. She's too close. You'll be the first person the authorities come for—it's too, too soon, the rest aren't even born yet. This will compromise everything we've done. She doesn't know anything. She's nothing. Get rid of her.*

Motsumi's shoulders slack. "Get your shit and leave. It's over."

[Bridge]

Not a one-hit wonder. Twenty-million followers on every social media account of the prolific animator and rapper, Motsumi.

In the visual album, twenty-eight-year-old Motsumi has been producing and creatively directing stellar hits for various popular artists.

157

Fans are hungry for his latest work, which he gave a glimpse of on his social media pages. This industry juggernaut has released the name of his upcoming song, "Phallic Gun," featuring popular rappers like GBV-Son, Me2 Thug, and Ami Next, slated to be the hottest tune this summer. Some reviewers were disturbed, declaring that the song glorifies violence. In the video, the male protagonist, leers, says in his lilting voice, "The song is a satire, a metaphor on how media and society normalize violence against women for pleasure and profit, which is why we brought in Sewela, who's basically killing it in the industry. To get this support from a hitmaker like her really lends the music video a feminist twist as she becomes this empowering femme fatale freeing all these trapped women."

Fans have noted that, Motsumi, the male protagonist, bears a striking resemblance to the *Peeling Time* singer's ex-fiancé, Atasaone Ewetse, the famous actor of "The Innocent Devil," who's been in hot water for his unorthodox ways of attaining superstardom; his spokespeople declined to comment on this piece. The "Whores & Nuns" singer heavily made references to the dark side of his hedonistic lifestyle. Particularly intriguing to fans is Sewela's notable songs, "Motsumi's Doppelgängers" and "Placenta of Evil," which exemplify the singer's unresolved emotions. That, despite the bitter breakup, Sewela still feels contaminated and bewitched by Atasaone, possessed by him, something she can't exorcise given her self-destructive habits. Fans applauded the quality of makeup and wardrobe used in the visual album *Peeling Time*, but noted that if you really looked carefully at Motsumi's facial expression, it's actually Sewela, imprisoned within her ex-fiancé—*that's messed up, she's clearly not over him, nigga still has a hold over her, their on-and-off relationship is drowning her, sis needs help, someone save her.* Worried fans tweeted consoling words, praying the singer won't give into her suicide attempts, given her myriad relapses and rehab trips …

[Verse 9: Anonymous Girls]

♪♫ Bars of this Song ♪♫

A man twerks in the center. Strikes out his leg. Twirls. Spins. *Viral, now we viruses. They twisted my thoughts into the ligature of the chorus. Harness your thoughts.*

The structure of this song is phallic tone. *We revolve behind the bars of this song, flames of lyrics tousling our hides.* The structure of this song is decibel wide and tall, a synchro-cinema.

No matter where you hide, the barbed wires, the tall walls, the thick craniums, they will find you, get in. Her voice, a screaming saxophone turns to dusk, dissipates …

End credits, and the dancing women return to the quiet fold of the music. There was nowhere else to go, until the song was played again, as it'd chartered number one for nine weeks. The streaming service didn't allow them to trespass into other song boundaries, which offered far more freedom than this bullshit sexist song. They were fucking trapped. All they could do was sit in the gardens, waiting … wondering if they'd ever leave these song boundaries.

The song below theirs sang of empowerment, had women naked, brazen by the force of their boobs, warriors of their sex. It was intoxicating.

"If we can't leave back into our physical bodies," says one woman covered in some milky liquid, "that's the island of song I want to flee to."

"What's the song-island called?" asks a bone-skinned woman.

"Whores & Nuns," replies one. "You can be a nun, a whore, it's all good. And that's what I want to be, a nun-whore. So tired of these straitjacket labels. It's liberating, and it belongs to that Motswana musician, Sewela, right?"

Cue in, Sewela. Knives for braids. Skin a smattering of brown. Hooves for feet. The women stare at her, astonished.

Sewela surveys this musical prison. "Why's she crying?"

A woman with gold-sequined skin whispers, "Oh, she found out that her family switched off her life support, it was getting too expensive for them. Now she has no body to return to, that's if we ever get out of this hellhole, oppressing rap song."

"Well, we're going to change that," Sewela says.

"Do you know who did this to us?" they ask, heads spinning.

Sewela shrugs. "I have something that belongs to them. They attacked me. They gonna come back for me."

"Shit," pipes one. "Funny ain't it? We had to clean and cook and slave out there. Now we doing it again. We cooking bars, cleaning stripper poles with our bodies. Shit never changes. Culture still the same."

"What's that you got there?" A woman without eyes points at something in Sewela's hands.

159

Sewela stares at the plastic-covered item she's gripping. "Thought it'd be safer to analyze it here. The bastard's name is Motsumi." She crouches, exposes it on the gold floor. She has a bit of Motsumi's trauma, this placenta of evil. It looks like wet tar expelling smoke. She probes it, sticks her finger in it, to find the root of him, but it begins to burn her. Clearly it must burn Motsumi, or he's that far gone to not realize how dangerous his trauma is to him even. But it can't kill her in here. Her eyes roll back as the trauma's essence travels into her being and her mind, and the memory of its root cause plays out in her mind: *Motsumi's trauma didn't know what it was sometimes but a foggy agglomeration of all those bad times from Motsumi's childhood, sticky dark memories of the beatings, the starvation, the abuse he suffered that stuck into the core of who he became and what he believed in: that wrongdoing is normal, that killing or kidnapping is fine, that women are playthings for his picking. He was abused, now the habit is overkill, overflowing in his brain and his heart and out into his actions to people who don't deserve his wrath and pain. His trauma looks on at Motsumi, pleased by this habitual feeding. The more crimes Motsumi commits, the more satiated it becomes. Motsumi is a sick motherfucker, but if he were to ever resolve his issues, to really heal, his trauma will die. And his trauma can't have that happening. No fucking way will it die. So the women must die.*

"Not in this story. Not on my watch," Sewela whispers with the fervor of anger. And the women gather around her as she clenches her hands into fists and speaks, "No woman dies. No more. His trauma does not justify getting away with murdering our women. If its death he wants death, it's his death that he'll get. *He* must die."

"I'mma dagger them with that stripper pole," says one woman.

"It'll only kill their avatars. Not them," another responds.

"Then I'll kill myself."

Sewela says, "Violence and sex raises the ratings, so really your death will be ineffectual to yourself or the cause. They'll get another you, and another you. See that gold statue there?" She points to a fountain, goddesslike, stripped, spurting water. "Some chick thought death would revolutionize everything, free you guys. But look what they did with her body, apparently that's a money-making shot. And the way she did it, now they hemming more of you in, hoping you get as creative as her to die." Sewela exhales smoked anger. "You know, it's really hard to be creative, that's a gift not everyone has, a gift some will pirate."

160

The sequined woman slumps forward. "Bliksem. Fuck. How you gonna start a revolution imprisoned in a song?" She kneels forward. "And I thought the real world out there was worse. Least you could wear what you want, have a sense of control in your own house, deal with shitty governmental laws once in a while. I had a home, you know. Built it with my savings. Sacrificed living to own something. Only lived in it for a few months before they took me. It's true what they say, I guess. Live, you never know when you're going to die. I never lived ... at all. Lost it just like that." Snaps her fingers. "If I'd known. All that work ... all that work ..." She starts to cry, bleeding her pain into the chorus of the song ...

[Verse 10: Sewela]

♪♫ Armageddon ♪♫

She woke up from the dream-song. Stood up. The news report on her Plasma caught her eyes: "In a span of five days, across Botswana, at least thirty-five women in Gaborone, Modipane, Palapye, Kanye and other districts have been found comatose with no underlying symptoms. At least five subjects have been pulled off their machines. Given this rising phenomenon, doctors are studying the remaining subjects to halt this endemic. The subjects have no connecting features—ranging from young to old, various jobs, varying body sizes and ethnicities—except that they are all women. Gender-based-violence organizations claim women are being targeted, but toxicology reports, rape kits, and forensic investigations indicate no foul play, signs of physical abuse nor drugs. The women simply go to bed and never wake up."

Sewela's jaw stretches into shock. One-hundred-and-twenty-nine women in two months. Women trapped in songs.

She's been manicuring her fear. She's safe, she could pretend it's over. But another one like him will come again and it will be over then. How can she turn a blind eye to their suffering? Has to stop this. Braces herself. *I could die*, she thinks, realizes. *I could die saving them.* Weeps as if she's already at her funeral, one too many times. Her thoughts reckon: *What's the difference? We've been killed and killed over by this culture. Metaphorical, emotionally, infantilized—the genocide of our identity, our being for their ideals. We're already died. We die*

161

*here, we die there—the dichotomy, the difference is we die into a new birth
of reorder. No one will come at us again. This is the only power. Dying is
not an end. Life cannot be destroyed, it changes form—whether by death
transmutation—we transcend. This is our power.*

Okay. She steels herself. *I can do this.*

A clock ticks. She sits at her kitchen table. On a porcelain plate,
the placenta of evil. She has to consume it. Taps her fingers, drums the
courage. Shuts her eyes, throws the chunk into her mouth, pinches her
nose, chews to not taste.

Reality subsides …

[Verse 11: Sewela]

♪♫ *Whores & Nuns (DJ Don remix)* ♪♫

A gospel cry wakes her up on the floor of an anthem, a religious choir's
fabled tones. Walls and ceilings peel back, folding around a hallway
and its red-tinged yonic interior. Monochrome lights and dieget-
ic sounds pulse in her ears as she walks about. One corner, a white
woman wears a melanin coat, getting rates for it, certified gold—that
appropriating song. She turns toward her. No. She stops herself. She's
not here to remedy that. First, the women like her: dethroned, destroyed, cauterized, utilized by men for their silly hubris. Surveys the
transparent doors. The hallway's flanked with various rooms of songs
climbing the charts: gqom, rock, kwaito, rap, R&B, kwassa kwassa—
cadent beats at their doors.

A man in hot pants follows her, twerking. Then a door, the one
she's here for. Behind it, Motsumi's baritone voice builds builds, builds,
dissipates into violin hands. Her fingers clasp around its doorknob. This
is the one room that will lead to the music video he designed, where
she'll kill him. The door creaks open, and through that slit, the devilish
light of a song spears her chest. She falls backward, skewered in the
chest by sexist stanzas—*this my bitch, this my pussy, pussy got money.* The
rap, a martial beat, is delivered quickly to her face, jarring her vision,
pounding her flesh. Sewela tries to stand, but she's weighed down by the
human-sized cross of the stanza protruding from her chest. Her fingers
grasp it, to pull it out, but it burns. *Don't be rude. Don't touch the cross.*

162

Motsumi slips through the door, squats, breath upon her face. "They used to make women better in the old days," he says. "They knew their place. What makes you so special to think you stand above the rest? The system? To be treated different?"

She's never had an answer for this before, but the anger, the injustice throttles through her mouth. "Because we're not in the old days, you fucking fossil." Her scream rises, hits five octaves. She rams her gun-heel into his mouth and pulls the trigger, exploding him with lyric and tune. The little shit hobbles away, slippery with blood, closing the door behind him.

Sewela lifts herself into a stand with this misogynistic stake, and moves around the realm with his phallic protrusion, stalking her predator. She coughs out blood as the mass of women parade in thongs and bras and wimples, shaking their booties, knees knocking out the gwarra gwarra moves. She's prepared herself well: her body the weapon, the gun shoes, the shooting boobs, the knife-braids ready to slay, the venom in her spit, her burning melanin, gathering smoke. Finally, Sewela bangs through the door, entering the room, labeled:

[Verse 12: Sewela]

♪♫ *Phallic Gun (Remix ft. GBV, Me2, Thug & Ami Next)* ♪♫

The architecture of this song is concrete-bound. The shriveled cries of women, a choir. The structure of this song is bone-made as they hum,

> *I tried to make my thighs bleed,*
> *squander myself on the floor with his demons.*
> *Tried to kill myself in this room.*
> *Only it wasn't any room: his voice was my jail cell.*
> *The rooms were skin thin.*

The warehouse room, dark fog. Twenty monochrome women's silhouettes stand still as statues, each a slogan of sex and flapping wads of money, chloroformed by masculinity. They wear their skins like expensive fashion labels. Sewela pauses in the doorway, cranes her neck.

Sees no one but the statues. *How'd he disappear so fast?* she thinks. Her mouth opens to whisper, hello, but she's seen enough horror movies to shut that up quickly. She can't be stupid at a time like this. She steps forward, her gun-feet clopping against the concrete floor. The women spin, triggered by her steps. In swift synchronized movements, they bend backward, arching their backs; fifty steel swords of dancing poles rise from the concrete ground, like jailcell bars, spear through their spines to the ceiling. *Skrr-skrr-scream, more blood, more money, yeah, woo!*

She turns, shocked by the voice. Too late. The voice ties around her body, contorting her into dance moves. She tries to fight the strain in her muscles. Closes her eyes to pinpoint the voice, find the coward. Around her, the women's screams rise into a choir's siren. Dark electro smoke billows through the room, suffocating Sewela of her thoughts. Motsumi's baritone voice scrapes the gqom beat into hip-hop, stretching her body into gruesome gestures. Sewela didn't know she could dance on shoes made from guns. Here goes another bar, another round—*and we smoking it up.*

Motsumi appears. Confident now that she's hogtied by his voice. His fist punches the air as he continues rapping, walking with swag toward her. She's split from herself before, she can do it again. The placenta of evil is just like any drug she's consumed. She must let it into her, overpower her. She seals her eyes shut again, pushes herself into the darkness within her, and wades into the viscous waters of her inner being, which is turning hard, cold, and sharp. She realizes she doesn't need to exist outside herself to be powerful. Her body *is* power. Inside her body, she jitters, a volcano ready to erupt. Her body, the thing she can't control, shakes under the conflicting forces of Sewela and Motsumi's voice. Finally, she catches on a tiny thread of power, pulls, pulls, pulls until it becomes a whole fabric of her body that he loses control of. The dancing pole—*boy you got me dancing, just for you, ooh.* She yanks the pole, spins it in her hands, throws it sharply as a javelin, a bullseye hit in Motsumi's forehead. He sprawls to the ground. Rebirths himself. Starts rapping: *Yeah, yeah, challenge accepted, woo! Skrr-skrr-scream! I'ma get her, I'ma get her—Armageddon (bitch).*

He won't die. He won't die *easily.* He smirks. She circles him. Surrounding them, the women swing and pirouette around these steel blades, slicing their thighs, as his rapper swag maneuvers them. *More blood, more money, girl gotta respect.* He opens his mouth again, but

Sewela quickly grabs his tongue, yanks his voice from his larynx with scraping nails and on this composed film score, Sewela rides his song, paces his low tessitura. Desperate and hobbling about, Motsumi whips out his phallic gun. The pistons of her breast glare at him, and her voice, a siren, screams, "Shayama, GET DOWN." The women quickly fall, and she lets the bullets rip through Motsumi's body. *His* body, life-wan, falls to the floor, a loose fabric of skin and bones. *Repeat. Repeat. Repeat*, the women chant, rising free from their concrete graves, recognizing this falling action from the song "Skin's Prison."

In the bleak dark of mind, Sewela rubs the texture of kwaito onto his last reggae heartbeats. She hacks at the limbs of generational trauma, gnaws it with her teeth, drinks the blood by the gallon, spews culture with her tongue. Deskins herself of law, lore, loin. She sits on the throne of his hide and bone without label, gender, premise. Peeling time, she's going forward and backward simultaneously whilst he groans, and the film slackens, a stasis. She strikes him again, unspools time from the recording reel, throwing him into the prison of his actions.

I am monster, unlawful, new territory, new kingdom, a disruption. A monster here, god elsewhere …

She wears his taxidermized masculinity as a crown, chugs his death to the outro of her visual album, sits on the throne made from his bones and the leather of his skin—this powerful shot graces the front cover of magazines. She's a powerhouse auteur of glitz, glam, gore for her studio album collection *Peeling Time*, seventeen songs long featuring top hits, "My Religion," "Another One," "P***y Love," "Whores & Nuns," et al. Gold microphones surround Sewela, interviewers inquiring on the concepts behind her visual album as it plays on all screens:

[Post Chorus: Sewela]

♪♫ *My Religion (DJ Topo Club remix)* ♪♫

The corpse of Motsumi's voice hangs from the murdered legacy tree exhumed from the placenta of his evil. He is a proper man. The burning tree blazes in the dark. Thirty women watch, getting loose on the dance floor to the klaxon of his voice flickering, spitting ash, burning, dying …

IT CALLS TO YOU

by Jamal Hodge

B.C. 3265
It calls to you ...

You reply in a mucus-fueled cough, raking your scratching nails across pus-swollen bumps. *"Thirty parsecs of time,"* you manage as your throat screams thirst, hurling scarlet phlegm onto the floor of the painted cave. You roll your eyes, trying to ignore the insistent cry of your name, robbing your full attention from the sensation of ancient fever, the entropy of muscle, the slow unraveling of tendon.

"Moderation is the rule. Excessive imprinting is not advised. We are quite aware of this, are we not?"

A.D. 2265
It calls to you ...

The android surgeons excavate fragmented bone from burnt tissue, heat stitching meat gulfs closed. You scream feeble nothings, as all sense of self is stolen by the agonies of divorced skin, shrapnel-chewed ligaments, marionette-dangling limbs. Half blinded beneath a singular light, crying for anesthesia, as the robots force a second dose inside you, trying to hide your frantic eyes from the sight of their plastic hands massaging pink flesh back into the meat puzzle of your gut.

"By the Orishas, we are stubborn! There are other moments of the ancestors to be experienced. Birth. Lovemaking. Growth. The kiss of the wind, a caress of spring. Truth is in the living, not in the dead."

A.D. 1765
It calls to you …

The mammoth waves move with the haste of hurricane winds, overturning the blood-soaked slave decks of the Guineaman. You are flung head over heels in a clang of chains, high in the air beside the makeshift weapons you'd crafted. Hitting the screaming waters with the impact of cement, bones rebuke rightful placement, hot pain distracting from the burning in your lungs as saltwater steals invisible tears from your eyes. In the sea, dark and pale faces find a strange equality in terror, though one man with the markings of the Akan tribe sings libations as he latches on to two of the pale-skinned men, entangling them in the very chains they'd latched onto his wrists and ankles. They give a brief struggle, to no avail. All three sink. Many faces sink. You sink.

The panic is total as your weighted arms flail. Each gasp for breath sends saltwater to your imploding lungs …

The chains are anchors …

Your body grows heavier …

Sinking …

From light …

From feeling …

Toward freedom …

"That's enough."

The ocean dissipates. The *you* that observes emotions, the witness of your thoughts, is flung back into spiritual flesh. Transparent in a construct of dark matter the size of worlds.

Exhilaration graces your many opened eyes. In easy pose, your hands rest peacefully on your thighs. "I am the steward of all I see, finding bountiful life within the promise of each precious breath, reinvigorated by the other side of death." You sigh.

It calls to you.

You look down into the darkness and find the caller is yourself. Smaller, less complete, but of the same kind and quality.

"*Go slow with endings,*" Smaller You cautions. "*What do we learn from experiencing the flesh?*"

"It brings us closer to comprehending our ancestors."

"*In what regard?*"

"In the historical archives of skin, we can deduce that most of the ancestors spent their lives trumpeting the call to happiness, to love, and achievement; yet they found the most meaning in moments of pain. In the end, right before they disassembled, there was a sublime moment of ..."

"*Joy?*"

"Relief. Purposefulness. As if the ancestors finally realized that the beauty of life had its catalyst in suffering. They had pursued pleasure when it was pain that defined them. And now, at the end, the pain had come to wrap them in the fullness of this loving revelation. I dance within the memory of skin to taste that moment of catharsis."

"*Curious,*" you say to you.

Turning, you look backward into the infinite. The innumerable stories that lived in the dimensions of Time fill the darkness with light.

"Let's live another ancestor's life."

"*Yes. Let's become ourselves.*"

THE COWARD OF UMUSTEAD

by Nnamdi Anyadu

Uduma be him who be called coward. At fourteen, neither riding a solarbike over Hangman's Cliff, nor jumping off Ideora Falls, we boys of Square call him so. Odd one him be, true talk. Jagged afro and jaggeder combats. Ever shirt on, even when sun be burning so bright, so hot, that mamas leave breasts bare, sit out, drink citric drink, and curse these skies for letting it shine so harshly.

Uduma be he own best friend to self. Boy be preferring to sit and watch; you get? To just sit under giant mango tree and watch we other boys. Watch we play hoverball. Watch we share rabbit kills. Watch we fight play fight. Watch we fight real fight. Ever not talking to anybody. Just sitting and watching. Yet, ever, never failing to show up at Square, like lizard to pavement; like spy of we papas and mamas. Maybe this be who him be. Maybe. Who fit know?

One time, Mbadi knocked this crazed hoverball outside play, onto giant mango tree this goddamn thing went, and dropped next to Uduma leg, gbam! Boy did not move. Not even to pick up hoverball and throw back to field of play. Me glided there and spat near him foot as me picked up the damn hoverball. Boy did not move, still. Like a goddamn statue thing.

Many times, while we chatty-chatty, the topic to kick this docile laddie out of Square come up among we other boys. I champion most.

171

Him presence irrelevant. Some of we affirm this. Some of we disaffirm. The ones not agreeing be reminding we all of Umustead code, which itself be the blood pumping up and down in these hearts; through these veins. *Kin be kin*, them say. We be grudgingly accepting. Hencing, we be dismissing this proposition of banishment.

All of Umustead, all of Confederacy, know of Duma papa. Man be legend of old; hero past.

Our papas call he the Greatest Warrior of the Great War. Them say him been created an elite unit, the Edoziuno Echo Gray, which employed ancestors' magic against the battalions of Mornanian aliens during the war for we planet one century and fifteen years far back. Uduma papa unit been conquered the alien base and returned the Earth to we humans, them say. Them swear on Mother Terra that he efforts been ushered the peace we enjoy this very today.

Our mamas affirm this. Them talk also of the time before the Great War. Them tell of the reign of Mornanians, when humankind been shut off cities and towns, been segregated against, been lost collective sense of self. Them say the Edoziuno Echo Gray been reminded we of our Ancient Past. Them swear on Mother Terra that Uduma papa unit been teach people the old ways, been bring back odinani which we enjoy this very today.

You confuse, yes? How Uduma just fourteen if he papa run battle one century and fifteen years far back? No frown face. This be the tale: toughman Captain leaved he sperm inside a medical tube that been handed over to the Confederacy. Now, fifteen years far back, on the hundredth anniversary of victory over the aliens in the Great War, Uduma mama, genius person, designed this tercationator, possibilized teleportation and earned a patent. To commemorate this landmark achievement, the Government been handed over Uduma papa sperm tube to Uduma mama.

The thinking be this: brilliant soldier man plus brilliant scientist be bringing forth best of brilliant pikin.

You see why Uduma be big disappointment?

Uduma, opposite to he papa; opposite to he mama. Uduma unremarkable and forgetful.

Instead of force of action, instead of creation ingenuity, boy's a watcher. A damn docile watcher. Watching we other boys play hoverball, share rabbit kills, fight play fight, fight real fight. Watching. Never doing. Just watching. A fuckity!

Mbadi own birthday soon come. As be Square tradition, we raise talk on running celebration. The sky hazy this day, ungood for hoverball. Hencing, we congregate under giant mango tree, next to where Uduma sit and stare alltime, and raise talk.

Gwurudi first suggestate. "We fit swim up and down Ideora," him opine. "Invite them girls too."

"That be how we run me own celebration four months far back. You forgots?" Ojih ask, snapping fingers up and behind he head.

Gwurudi widen eyes. "Oh."

"True talk," Mbadi say. "Plus, me not too like swimming." Him shrug, like obdurate child been offered vegetables for mealtime.

"So, what we do?" Ikuku ask, folding hand.

"We fit go get you the new Hov-85 II Prime," Ajah-ani suggestate, pointing Mbadi.

Ojih burst laugh. Me join in. Gwurudi hold mouth. Ikuku shake head.

"We talking jokes now?" Ojih ask. Him bend head go one side.

"How we do this?" Me ask Ajah-ani, me mouth still overflowing chuckles.

"We burgle Atom Hut," Ajah-ani say.

Now, for sake of clarity, the new Hov-85 II Prime be the baddest, wickedest hoverglider, from the Prime fleet of Fechi Hover Automobiles. It sleek, slender and goddamn sexy. It the latest, fastest hoverglider in country and only yet used by professional hoverballers in the Confederational Hoverball League. Them say the magnetism between boots and glider be so firm that it be felt within bone of rider. Them say its response so swift, you reckon it be reading your goddamn mind. This be what Ajah-ani suggestate we burgle. And from where? Atom Hut, number two biggest sports shop in city! No idea madder!

"You joke," me say.

"True talk," Mbadi say. Yet he voice not overly firm, and me deduce him thinking it.

"I no joke," Ajah-ani say. "Think it. We achieve perfect gift for you. We achieve best thrill for we."

"Sense in this, O," Gwurudi say, swinging from close branch of tree.

Me pause. Me look round. Everybody pondering it. We wild. We rugged. We breathe adventures. Yet, a heist attempt; that, we been never do. It madness. These boys wan kill me.

"And about Atom Hut security robots who themselves stand watch when shop closed?" me ask.

Ajah-ani look me. Me look Gwurudi. Gwurudi look Ojih. Ojih look Ikuku. Ikuku look Mbadi.

"Me fit do lookout," we hearing a voice say. It not a voice we know.

This be the first time we hearing Uduma say pim. For like five seconds straight, we all just quiet.

"You?" me ask and break silence.

"Yes, Keneanyi," Uduma say, standing up.

I shock him talk this. I further shock him bold enough to say me name.

"Good, good," Ajah-ani say.

"Good, good," Ikuku say.

Gwurudi nod head, like old man flashing wisdom.

Ojih smile.

"We running this," Mbadi declarate. I taste he excitement in tone.

Birthday boy getting best birthday thrill. Everybody keen to do this. Them, majority. Me, minority. Kinpower be a true thing. And, of course, *kin be kin*. So, me nod.

Atom Hut be inside Umustead's Central District of Business. Off from Square like six, one-quarter kilodistances. We meet up at Square on nine o'clock, every laddie on he hoverglider. Me not know about the others, but me surprised Coward Uduma been owning a hoverglider, and him daring enough to sneak out from house, like we, deceiving parents. Ajah-ani give everybody this plastic clown masks him bring. This criminal laddie long been fantasizing this shit. Ikuku hold a lock destabilizer and declarate that it fit fuck up them locks at Atom Hut. Gwurudi run small late and give a hundred apologies when him finally come. Ojih say a prayer. We hold hands and nod heads as him call on spirits of ancestors for guiding. We do this every time we adventure-going, never minding even if—like now—the adventure be against the law.

We move on ten minutes bringing ten o'clock. We glide quietly, finding shadows and being away from streetlights. Fact be: there be hardly thieving in Umustead, so much so, guard be down on perpetuality; we not even having police to investigate if thieving be occurring. Approaching Atom Hut, Mbadi signal we glide upward. We shoot up! Clown masks protect eyes against rushing air. Reaching hundred difometric fenifeets, him signal again and we shoot down into shop complex.

The compound bare, save the shop building at center. We congregate on rear door and Ikuku start working the lock destabilizer. Me tap Uduma, point me eyes and point around this perimeter. Uduma nod and glide from we. Ikuku fuck up them locks and we move in.

Of holy fucks, Atom Hut bearing a resemblance to what en'igwe fit be. True talk! Piropet sneakers. Hydrostop solarbikes. Sonic starcatchers. Mountain-range exerquishers. Myriadums of sporting wears. And of course, thousand plus one hovergliders. Of every making. Fechi. Emudiamen. TimiUmar. Mention only.

Not meaning it, yet doing it, we stare for counting minutes. Just stare at gear glory, up till Mbadi call we to order. Him point at a Hov-85 II Prime, stacked in a showglass. It glistening. Mbadi pick it.

"Carry only one thing, and not let it be big," Mbadi say.

We nod. We pick things. I selectate a TimiUmar sonic starcatcher.

Coming out, we find a scene not one of we been prepared to visage. There, by same door we enter through, be Uduma, over three security robots. Them machines twitching, broken, battered. Uduma hand inside the metal head of one.

"Have to take out them memory disks," him say.

We just look him, struck with dumbness.

Finding it, him yank. "We go now."

Me have so many questions. Pretty sure other boys be having them, too. Yet, here and now not appropriate, so we glide away, off from Atom Hut.

It be appearing that while we dumbstruck inside of Atom Hut, them security robots who otherwise at shop's main gate entrance, run routine perimeter inspection. Them begun whirring up and down the compound. Noticing exit door ajar, them proceeded to it. Uduma fitn't allow that happen. And he fitn't call up to us just yet. So, what him do? Well, boy swung upon action against said robots. True talk. Actual kpisha kpisha. It turn out that Uduma fit fucking combatate. Jabs, punches, and flipkicks unto steel robots. Man!

We other boys learn this, not sake of say Uduma tell us, but sake of say Ikuku read them collected memory disks on him instrosmart drive. The hologram film play before we very eyes and everybody goddamn shock; our mouths agaping as we watch this glorious action thing in neon holocolor.

You think Uduma chatty-chatty after this? You think him proud and raise shoulder? No! Him still sit alone under giant mango tree and watch. Ever not talking to anybody. Ever, never joining our play. Not even when offered lead position on hoverball team. Not even when Mbadi offered he the Hov-85 II Prime. Not even when we gossipate on new adventure-going to him hearing. Him just sit alone and watch alltime.

We other boys desist calling he coward after the Atom Hut heist. Uduma earn we respect, in unequivocal totality. Now, we be understanding that Uduma not docile, not timid, not weak. Uduma simply holding back. Uduma papa fire pump up and down him heart, run up and down him veins. If not, how him bold enough to take on them robots in Atom Hut compound? Uduma mama smarticity stay in him brain, sharpening him senses. If not, how him be knowing where to jab them robots to be causing technical malfunction? Uduma quiet all-time for Square, because Uduma hold back. Maybe if him let go, him win every game and we other boys begin hating he even more. We talk this amongst ourselves, and we see reason.

So, we let he hold back. Let he sit and watch we in the quietness that he is liking. Sometimes, we stop play and go sit next to he under giant mango tree. Even then, Uduma not speak. We respect this. We respect he. Every boy sit in silence at this time. This be what Uduma enjoy: the silence of being still. So, now, we play what we like, and play what him like, too. *Kin be kin.*

OLD SOLOMON'S EYES

by Cheryl S. Ntumy

No one was surprised when Old Solomon's eyes were taken. He was always turning them toward other people's backyards and windows, stealing glances and sneaking peeks and seeing things he had no business seeing.

The surprise was that the rest of him had been spared, for Maruwada was a demon of the old order, and nothing if not efficient.

It was Ludo who found Old Solomon wandering among the sun-flowers on the morning of Monday the fifth, hands held out in front of him, moaning like a phantom. Well, it was Ludo and Bliss, but Bliss turned up a few seconds late, having broken his slippers again and been forced to run barefoot through the field.

At first, Ludo said, she didn't realize what was wrong. She called out to the elderly gentleman: "Papa Solomon! Papa Solomon, why are you bumping into the flowers?"

It was only when the man's bony fingers closed around her arm that Ludo looked up into his face, saw that there were holes where his eyes should have been, and screamed blue murder. By then, Bliss had caught up and joined in the screaming.

"I only screamed a little bit," Bliss said later, when recounting the entire affair to the police.

"Liar!" Ludo said. "You screamed louder than I did!"

"No, no-no-no. Not in fact, Ludo. In fact, I was trying to help him while you were still screaming."

At which point, Ludo smacked Bliss across the back of his head, Bliss kicked Ludo and the police had to intervene to prevent all-out fisticuffs.

They never clarified who screamed how loud, or for how long, but what did emerge was that the two children had tried to flee in terror, only to have Old Solomon grab them both, and in the end they'd led him through the sunflower field, all the way across the If God Says Yes Fresh Farms land (which they shouldn't have been on, in the first place) and through the hole in the fence to the church.

Because obviously Old Solomon was a monster, or a ghost, or a demon, the children said, and only Pastor Agbesi could deal with him.

Pastor Agbesi had barely stopped himself from running away as well. "I had never seen anything like it," he said. "Both eyes gone, no blood, and he was still walking around! How?"

The doctor shuddered over how the eyes had been extracted with surgical precision, but nobody really understood what that meant, so the police, the pastor and the Chief, Reverend Dr. Excellent Charles, classified Old Solomon's survival as a Miracle, a Point Against the Devil and a Sign of Things to Come.

It was all either very tragic or very exciting, depending on which camp one fell into, and for the rest of the day the villagers spoke of little else. Esther, the wife of Reverend Dr. Charles, took Old Solomon to her house and tried to ease his anguish with banku and okra soup, but the man would not eat, or drink, or sleep, or speak.

Nevertheless, everyone knew that his sightlessness was the work of Maruwada, for it could be the work of no one else in a village of good, God-fearing people.

"*We* found him," Ludo said to Bliss, as the children lingered outside the Charles family home, trying to peer in through the windows. Dirt streaked the back of her dress and her long skinny legs. Leaves and grit dusted her cornrows. Ludo often looked as though she'd been wrestling. Not with another person, but with life itself, her beady eyes seeking trouble, her lips pursed in perpetual displeasure.

"Yes. So?" Bliss tried to lift the mosquito net to get a better view. His limbs seemed stunted next to Ludo's, but much steadier, solid enough to keep both children grounded. He had a ready smile and chubby cheeks, a face that fit his name.

178

Ludo smacked his hand. "So, God wanted us to find him."

"How do you know?"

"Things only happen if God wants them to," Ludo replied with authority. A year and three months older than Bliss, of course she knew better.

"Aha," Bliss said, and swallowed his doubt.

"So maybe God also wants us to find his eyes."

Bliss let out a sharp exclamation, leading Ludo to duck quickly before they were spotted. He followed her lead, squatting among Esther Charles's aloes. "You want us to go looking for Maruwada? Are you mad?"

"If we can get his eyes back, we'll be heroes." Ludo's eyes glittered.

Bliss was troubled. He recalled that Ludo's eyes had glittered that time she made him break into the provisions store near the school (because she'd dreamt that a talking snake lived behind the stack of disposable nappies). Her eyes had also glittered when she told some older boys at school that she had a black belt in judo, and she and Bliss were forced to hide from them for two weeks to avoid a "friendly match."

"I don't want to," he said.

"Of course you do."

"No, no-no-no. In fact, I don't."

"Nonsense," said Ludo, taking his arm and dragging him away from the Charles house. "It's the will of God."

"But …"

"Bliss, who is older between us?"

"You. But …"

"Are you afraid?"

Bliss couldn't admit that the mere thought of Maruwada weakened his bladder. He said, "I'm not afraid of anything!"

So off they went, back to the sunflower field, to hunt for clues.

Old Solomon's eyes were sharper than most. Despite his advanced age, he could read fine print and recognize faces from a great distance. A blessing, one might say, if not for his penchant for using his excellent sight against others. He was not a bad man, necessarily, only a bitter one who took pleasure in learning secret, unsavory things that he could reveal when it suited his purposes.

179

Considering what those eyes could do, and how mercilessly their owner wielded them, it was inevitable that something would come for them. And what match could Old Solomon be for the deadly Maruwada?

Maruwada had haunted the sunflower field for as long as the villagers could remember, and likely for eons before. Some said she lived in the topmost branches of the tallest tree at the edge of the field. Others said she lived under it. There were rumors that she could fold herself up small and climb inside the flowers, where she would sleep during the day. It was said that if someone were to try to pick the flower in which she slept, her power would seep out and devour the hand of the offender. And so, it had become customary to schedule the harvest for the wee hours, before dawn, while Maruwada was out wreaking havoc in the world and the field was safe.

One of her favorite spots was the park. A charity had built it many years ago for the children, but somehow the adults had taken it over. By day, the park was used for church gatherings and community meetings, the kind where they served tea with too much milk and scones with not enough raisins.

By night, Maruwada gallivanted across the lawn with her hairy spirit minions, getting up to all manner of mischief.

The church folk doused the place with holy water on a regular basis. It didn't work. Everyone knew it, but Pastor Agbesi couldn't very well admit to the precious liquid (sold at 75 cedis a bottle) being somewhat less effective than advertised. And so, he oversaw the sprinkling of the stuff all over the park, murmuring prayers to keep the demons at bay.

And every night, Maruwada would creep out from the sunflower field, unabashed, undeterred, unexorcised, and dance her irreverent dance all over the park, and direct her minions to urinate on the roses, and conjure up spells to perplex, bamboozle and obfuscate the good, God-fearing people of the village.

She was a plague upon their land, an unsolvable problem. No one was pleased when she stole their goats in the night, or turned their chickens' eggs to stone, or caused their children to speak in streams of strange, sibilant gibberish until dawn.

But, it must be said, the villagers were a *little* pleased that Old Solomon could no longer steal glances and sneak peeks and see things he had no business seeing.

···❖···

"We shouldn't be here," Bliss whispered, waving mosquitoes away as he followed Ludo deep into the sunflower field. A dense forest of stalks loomed around them like countless guards shielding Maruwada's fortress, leaves rustling with creeping, crawling creatures.

Ludo stopped to examine a cluster of fresh droppings that even Bliss could tell had come from a goat, not a demon. She bent down and sniffed, holding one hand up as if to silence Bliss, though he had stopped talking. "A goat passed here." She punctuated the declaration with a sage nod.

Bliss longed to roll his eyes, but he was afraid she would see. Her eyes were not quite in the league of Old Solomon's, but they were plenty sharp, all the same.

Things carried on like this for some time, with Ludo stopping to study grasshoppers and scurrying ants and bicycle treads, while Bliss kept reminding her that demon-hunting was a fool's errand.

And then Bliss saw something that he had not expected. On his left, nestled among the towering blooms, lurked a single flower that had not yet opened. It stood shorter than its brethren, with a thinner stalk. An odd, pulsing energy emanated from it, as though the air around it moved differently, sending a throbbing ache through Bliss's chest. The little flower painted a picture of weakness, of a plant that might not make it to the next harvest, but that pulsing energy spoke of *strength*.

"Ludo." Bliss tapped Ludo's bare arm, already slick with sweat.

"Hmm," said Ludo, still peering in the opposite direction, "it's only a cat. But you know that cats run errands for Maruwada, so we must be close."

"Ludo, look!"

Bliss pointed. Ludo looked. For a moment, the two friends stood there in silence, while the odd, pulsing thing that was felt more than seen continued.

"What is that?" Ludo asked at last. "I don't think it's a sunflower."

"No, no-no-no."

They both thought it, though neither was ready to utter the words. This was a sign of magic at work, some lurking evil. It could be something Maruwada had left there to ward off enemies; a spell, or a sentry in disguise.

Or it could be Maruwada's elusive home and the demon herself might be tucked up tight inside that bud, sleeping.

Bliss looked at Ludo. Ludo could not tear her gaze from the flower. She took a step forward.

"What are you doing?" Bliss whispered.

Ludo took another step toward the flower. Bliss grabbed her hand to stop her, but she shook him off and ventured closer still. He was too afraid to follow.

"Ludo! Stop! Stop it!"

She pushed aside one tall flower, and then another, and came to stand before the aberrant bloom.

As if it sensed her, the flower opened up, revealing shiny, blood-red petals, slick with something sticky. Out of the glistening black center of the flower came slender fingers. Small, like those of a toddler, yet long, like those of a thief. An arm, covered in soft fur reminiscent of a monkey. Another arm, and then a cat-like face with a pointed chin, followed by a sleek, hairy little body and a long, curling tail.

Bliss opened his mouth, but no scream came out. The world went very, very quiet. Both he and Ludo stood frozen as Maruwada dropped to the ground, sniffed with her cat-like nose and smiled, baring jagged teeth. S mall and furry and harmless, she almost passed for something a child might keep as a pet.

But her eyes!

They were not the black eyes of any monkey, or the green eyes of any cat, or even the otherworldly, glowing orbs of a demon. They were large, with dark brown irises and very white whites. They did not fit properly into her little demon head, and bulged as though they might tumble out of the sockets at any moment.

Old Solomon's eyes, watching, always watching, familiar and yet utterly strange.

Maruwada reached out and placed her little hands on Ludo's feet, still clad in dusty leather slippers. And with a soft, sweet chitter, like a pet asking to be stroked, Maruwada took those feet.

She simply ... took them. There was no hacking, no slicing, no struggle. One moment the feet were at the ends of Ludo's ankles, and the next they were in Maruwada's retreating hands, and she was scampering back inside her grotesque flower shelter, and the flower was closing up once more, swallowing her whole.

Ludo did not speak. She keeled over, unable to maintain her balance without feet, and fell onto her back. Mouth open in stunned anguish, eyes wide with horror.

Bliss rushed forward, but didn't dare touch her. He looked at the bloodless stumps where her feet had been. And screamed.

It was true, perhaps, that Ludo tended to wander into places she should not. It was true that those feet had caused a great deal of trouble, if not quite as much trouble as Old Solomon's eyes.

But even so.

Everyone said finding Maruwada's lair was another Miracle and Sign of Things to Come. God had finally given the village the key to ridding themselves of the demon.

But even so ...

Bliss was troubled and terrified. He sat on the floor in the corner of the clinic as the important folk of the town examined Ludo's injuries. As with Old Solomon, her feet had been amputated with precision. She was beside herself, still unable to utter more than a garbled moan.

The questions were asked with even more urgency this time. Bliss answered them as well as he could.

"She lives in a flower, yes. Not an ordinary sunflower. It's red inside, like blood. She is using Papa Solomon's eyes, but they don't fit right. She didn't say anything to Ludo. She didn't even look angry. She just took Ludo's feet and went back into her flower. Ludo couldn't move, not even to run. I also couldn't move. All we could do was stand there."

The adults exchanged somber glances. Too long had this demon run free in their village, too long had she tainted their air with her foulness. Mischief was one thing. After all, for every egg turned to stone, ten others remained. Every goat gone missing in the night was eventually found nibbling someone's crops.

But the mutilation of villagers? No. No-no-no. Something had to be done. Something more permanent than holy water.

The people looked to Reverend Dr. Charles for guidance and the long-suffering Chief said: "We will burn that wicked flower to the ground, and Maruwada with it."

183

The people looked to Paster Agbesi for confirmation and the long-suffering pastor said, "We will exorcise that demon once and for all. God wills it so."

Bliss said nothing, because Reverend Dr. Excellent Charles was a chief and Pastor Agbesi was a Man of the Cloth and both men were many, many more than one year and three months older than he. But Bliss had a bad feeling, a nagging, swirling discomfort in his belly. If it could have formed words, the bad feeling might have said, "Fire? Fire? What madness! What folly! If fire was all it took, Maruwada would be long gone already."

It might have pointed out that no one had ever found Maruwada's home before, in all the long years she had lived. It might have suggested that perhaps Bliss stumbling upon the stunted flower had not been accidental.

"Look deeper!" it might have cautioned the villagers. "Think harder!"

But the bad feeling could not speak, and Bliss did not dare to, so the plan was made and agreed upon, and there would be no stopping it.

The owner of If God Says Yes Fresh Farms did not live in the village, but in a big, bustling city several hours away by bus. Phone calls were made and permission sought, even though people had been using the farmland as a thoroughfare for the better part of a decade.

And then, on Wednesday the seventh, shortly after dawn, Reverend Dr. Charles and his wife Esther, Pastor Agbesi, Police Lieutenant Godwin and far too many concerned villagers descended upon the sunflower field. Lieutenant Godwin carried a flaming torch, the stick almost as long as a person.

The plan was to set Maruwada's flower aflame from a distance. That way there would be no trespassing. No hands for her to devour, no feet for her to snatch. If she snatched the torch, well, she was welcome to it. Pastor Agbesi would pray for divine protection in ordinary human words, and Reverend Dr. Charles would pray in tongues. There was even an old wire cage in the mix, one that had previously held rabbits but would do nicely for a cat-monkey demon.

It wasn't the worst plan in the world, and yet ...

Bliss had tried to tell his mother that they were all going to freeze, the way he and Ludo had frozen.

"Nonsense," she had replied. "With a whole pastor there? And a whole chief who is also a reverend? These are adults trained in spiritual warfare!"

"What if she runs?" Bliss had asked.

"Then they will catch her."

The bad feeling nagged and swirled more than ever.

Now Bliss walked in front, beside the Chief, leading the way. The goat droppings were still there, as were the bicycle tracks. There were even more grasshoppers, and a host of crickets, though the cat Ludo glimpsed last time had been replaced by two ground squirrels, which fled at the sight of the approaching crowd.

For a moment, Bliss thought he might have lost his way. And then he saw it. The strange, stunted sunflower with the pulsing energy. He stopped.

"There," he said in a shaky whisper. All eyes followed his trembling finger. The crowd fell silent. The world went very, very quiet.

"Don't go any closer," said Reverend Dr. Charles. "Everyone, stay where you are! We don't want to wake her."

Or perhaps that was what he *would* have said, had the power of speech not left him. Alas, he only stood there with his lips parted, staring. No one spoke. No one moved.

Finally, Lieutenant Godwin took a step closer. This was part of the plan. He would torch the flower. Bliss wondered how the policeman had the will to move when everyone else was frozen. Almost close enough, he took one more step, then reached out.

The fiery stick should have touched Maruwada's flower, but it did not. Lieutenant Godwin reached further. He was forced to take another step to close the distance. But it did not. If anything, the torch was even further away from the flower than before.

Bliss's body was still, tongue glued to the roof of his mouth. He understood that Maruwada stirred inside that flower, and her wicked magic made the stick in Lieutenant Godwin's hands grow shorter and shorter until it was little more than a twig.

The policeman held the stick out, waiting for the plant to catch fire.

The flower opened just as it had done before, baring its sticky red petals to the world. No one moved. No one said a word as Maruwada crept out of the flower and perched there, like a cat in a window. She wore Old Solomon's ill-fitting eyes and her furry paws had been replaced with Ludo's feet, still clad in dusty slippers.

The torch dropped from Lieutenant Godwin's fingers and rolled away into the nearby stalks. And with a soft, sweet chitter, Maruwada took his hands.

This time, Bliss did not bother screaming. The moment he regained the use of his limbs, he fled. It wasn't until he was safely out of the sunflower field that he looked back to see the others running as well, poor Lieutenant Godwin reaching out with bloodless stumps.

Smoke curled from the field, dancing toward the sky.

The entire sunflower field burned to ashes. Every last flower lost, a fortune, a tragedy—a lawsuit against the village, courtesy of the absentee owners of If God Says Yes Fresh Farms.

Yet Maruwada's flower remained. Untouched, unharmed, undaunted. It rose in haughty triumph from a sea of charred plant stumps and blackened little animal corpses. Ash rained down around the flower but never on it, as though an invisible shield had gone up.

A new plan was formed and the villagers went out to the field with machetes. A farmer returned with a hole in his face where his nose used to be.

Another plan was formed, which resulted in the loss of a young lady's ears.

Still another plan lost a farmer her scalp, complete with plaited hair. She joined the other victims, the crown of her head pale, pink, bloodless and already scabbing over.

Bliss's mother started paying her debts, little by little.

"This place is cursed," she said. "We have to leave soon, before Maruwada takes your kneecaps!"

"I can't leave Ludo," Bliss told her.

"Nonsense. You will make new friends."

But Bliss and Ludo had been friends forever and it didn't feel right to leave her.

The village met that afternoon and agreed to fight harder, with bigger machetes. Bliss could see no way to fight the demon and win. Although his stomach clenched with fear, he didn't want to lose his kneecaps. So, when the time came for questions, he raised a trembling hand and asked whether they could hold peace talks with Maruwada. The villagers laughed.

"You can't negotiate with a demon," said Pastor Agbesi.

Bliss went home and lay awake through the night, tossing and turning. He was young and knew nothing. He had no black belt and was frightened half out of his wits, but all the plans the grownups set had failed. So why couldn't he negotiate with a demon? Maruwada was clever. She could speak. And if she could speak, she could listen.

When morning came, he set off for school, then took a detour through the field. He stepped over all the things people had left there to ward off the demon: rosaries and pictures of Jesus and little wooden crosses stuck into the soil. He went as close as he dared to that single, strange flower, and promptly froze.

Maruwada didn't come out. After what felt like a year but was only minutes, Bliss was able to move again. He dropped his gaze to the ground so that he couldn't see the flower, so its power would not touch him.

"Maruwada," he whispered.

Nothing happened.

"Maruwada." He said it over and over again, until his voice was no longer a whisper. "Maruwada, what is it you want? Tell us, so that we may give it to you, and then you can return all the parts you stole and leave us in peace."

Nothing happened. Bliss repeated himself. Once more. Once again. He repeated himself until his voice was hoarse.

And then, at long last, the flower opened and Maruwada crept out, wearing a loose scalp with braided hair, and bulging eyes, and large hands, and dusty feet, and round ears, and a broad nose with a mole on it. A monster made of parts that were never meant to be combined, she dropped to the ground and slunk closer, and then stopped and looked at Bliss with Old Solomon's eyes.

"Who are you to offer me anything?" she asked. Her voice was not a soft, sweet chitter, but a thundering roar. "You are a child. You have no power."

And even though his body shook with fear, Bliss replied, "I don't need power. I will go back and give the Chief your message, and he will give you what you want, as long as you return all the parts you stole and leave us in peace."

187

Her silence was heavy and sly, and Bliss got that bad feeling again.

"Very well," the demon said. "Go and tell your Chief that I want one cassava seedling, three pigs, five goats, seven chickens, nine bottles of oil and eleven fingers of plantain. If he gives me these things, I will return the parts I stole, leave the village, and never return."

Bliss was afraid, but not stupid, so he asked, "Who will look after your flower if you leave and never return?"

"I will take the flower with me," the demon replied.

"Why did you take Papa Solomon's eyes?"

"Because he was spying on me while I danced."

"And Ludo's feet?"

"Because she stepped too close to my flower."

"And Lieutenant Godwin's hands?"

Maruwada let out a chitter. "You were there. Why do you think I took them?"

Maruwada went on to reveal that she had taken the ears because their owner was eavesdropping on her minions in the park; she had taken the scalp because its owner had drenched the hair in holy water and shook it, splashing Maruwada's minions and leaving minor burns; and she had taken the nose because its owner had used it to sniff out the minions and tried to put them in a rabbit cage.

"It's because you cause so much mischief!" Bliss said.

"So do children like you, but no one is trying to cage and burn you."

"People love children. They hate demons."

Maruwada flapped her stolen hands. "And is that my fault?"

Bliss opened his mouth.

"Ask me another question and you will regret it," the demon said.

Bliss was afraid, but not stupid, so he held his tongue and waited for Maruwada to return to her flower, then ran all the way to Reverend Dr. Charles's house.

At first, the villagers refused to believe that a child had succeeded where they had failed. But, within the hour, everyone was saying that they had known all along that the innocence of a child was the best tonic against a demon, and they would have suggested it earlier but had not wanted to put any children in harm's way.

And so, with fearful yet hopeful hearts, the villagers contributed toward the list of things Maruwada had demanded, and then Reverend Dr. Charles had the items delivered to the flower in a big truck.

The villagers gathered in the field to witness this momentous occasion. Those who had been deprived of their body parts were placed at the front, so that Maruwada could return what she had taken as quickly and painlessly as possible.

Bliss stood at his mother's side. The energy around the flower pulsed with menace. Everyone else froze, unable to speak once more, but Bliss found that he could move his lips, and so he whispered, "Maruwada!"

The flower opened and the demon emerged.

"We have done as you asked," said Bliss.

Maruwada looked at the truck. The loading door opened. One by one the animals and items floated out, carried through the air on Maruwada's magic. They moved in a procession to the flower, where they were swallowed up one at a time.

"We have done as you asked, so please return the parts you stole," said Bliss.

Maruwada nodded. The scalp left her and returned to its owner. The woman dropped to her knees and sobbed with relief, stroking her hair, while her skin sealed seamlessly as though the scalp had never been gone The ears followed. All the stolen parts returned to their owners in their original condition until Maruwada was a sleek, furry cat-monkey once more.

"You were brave to come to me the way you did," she told Bliss. "I admire courage, and so I will give you some advice. I hope you never forget it."

Bliss nodded, trembling and eager to be done with this business. Maruwada approached and climbed onto his shoulder.

"Never negotiate with a demon," she said. Then she let out a soft, sweet chitter, and took his voice.

Life went on in the village of good, God-fearing people. Maruwada and her flower were gone, along with Bliss's voice, but the villagers agreed that it was a fair trade. What was a voice, really, in the greater scheme of things? Besides, the child was a hero now. It would be greedy to want more.

The sunflower field became barren and the If God Says Yes Fresh Farms folks moved their business elsewhere. Before long, Old Solomon was back to seeing things he had no business seeing, and Ludo was back to walking her dusty feet into places they shouldn't be.

Bliss missed his voice, but found a new confidence that allowed him to shake his head whenever Ludo's eyes glittered. There were times when he walked through the empty sunflower field and something caught his eye, a pulsing energy, something like a sticky red flower. But when he turned to look, there was nothing.

Ludo would skip ahead on her restored feet, looking for trouble. "Ah!" she would exclaim, eyes glittering. "I know what we can do! We can—"

Bliss would shake his head firmly. *No. No-no-no.*

And somewhere in the world, in some other village of good, God-fearing people, hidden in someone else's sunflower field, Maruwada would let out a soft, sweet chitter.

THE TRAVELLING MAN

by Radha Zutshi Opubor

Eni wondered, sometimes, when she'd meet the Travelling Man. No, that wasn't right. She wondered, sometimes, when the Travelling Man would meet her. She'd met him already. She'd known him half her life.

It was happening more, now, the forgetting. There were some things she always knew. Her name was Enitanwa Deem, she was twenty-eight, and tall for a woman. She knew her own face when she saw it in the mirror. She knew that wide, flat nose was her father's, that those dark eyes were her mother's. She knew that in the half-light her skin was so black it was blue, and she knew that Deji was the first person to tell her she was beautiful. But she could not remember marrying him.

Sometimes she would blink awake from half-sleep, and he'd be looking at her, and she would think *I don't know him, but his eyes are kind.* A year ago, that thought would have frightened her. She would have said, "Deji." And he'd hold her as they cried. And that night as the sweat cooled on their bodies, she'd stare at his pale-brown face until her eyes burned. And then, again—*I don't know him, but he has sad eyes.* When would he meet her, the Travelling Man? It would have

191

to be soon. In a way, it made sense that she was forgetting. Not to her doctors, or to Deji. They could only see a woman newly married, glowing with health. But Eni understood. It was simple; her past was bigger than her future, and her mind could not hold it anymore. That was what happened when you were about to die.

It's going to be soon. Eni ran her hand through her curly hair. Gossamer-thin strands came away on her fingers like cobwebs. She was alone in her apartment, and even the Lagos night noise could not reach her up here. But he could. Eni pulled a heavy blanket around her shoulders and walked to the window. The wide, curving one that let her look out into the lagoon and see the lights on the water. She'd chosen this apartment for that window. She must have. Eni sat on the floor and let her cheek kiss the glass. It was cool against her skin as she waited for the Travelling Man.

The first time he came to me I was fourteen. I woke in the dead of night and there he was in the window. He was … nineteen, maybe? It was the oldest I ever saw him. It was the youngest he ever saw me. I was skinny and shivering. I slipped out from between my sisters and went over to him, because … because he was crying, and because he was almost gone. He was in the window, half in and half out, and the moonlight shone right through him—turned his skin pale blue. He watched me as I came to him, and he was quiet as he cried. And he said to me, "Shh, don't wake your sisters. I just wanted to see you one last time." He smiled, and the moonlight began taking him to pieces. My heart was in my throat, and I couldn't speak, and so I watched. And just before he was gone, he said—

But Eni couldn't remember. She blinked. A thin membrane of drool coated her chin, and the window was cold against her forehead. Deji leaned against the wall opposite her, lit by the pinprick lights of their kitchen appliances. That mixer had been on their wedding registry, Eni knew, and it had never been used, not once. His eyes were sad. Eni turned back to the window.

192

She felt Deji as he came to her and took her chin in his hand. It felt warm. It felt alive. He carefully wiped her face clean with his sleeve. "Isoken?" he asked, and the desperation in his voice was well hidden.

Eni shook her head. She did not know. She felt suddenly that they had done this many times. She would have asked Deji, but he was already pulling away. She kept her face against the window and listened to him leave. It was going to be soon.

"It's the light," he told me, a few months later. It was the second time I saw him. He was dark and alive, not a ghost anymore. No, that's not right. He wasn't a ghost yet. It hadn't happened to him yet because my past was his future. He told me that, too. I was traveling forward, and he was traveling backward. But sometimes, when the light was right, we'd meet. "It's like it takes me apart, and when it puts me together, I'm in your window. Every time I see you, you're younger, and you can't remember the last time I saw you. And now—you haven't met me. So, I won't see you again." I balled my hands into fists. My nails dug crescent moons into the soft skin of my palms, and they bled. I said nothing and then I said, "We're friends, aren't we?" Because I knew we must be.

He smiled and said, "I had a sister, once. You and her are the only ones who can see me. She called me the Travelling Man. That's what you'll call me. You and Deji, even though he can't see me." Eni had not known anyone named Deji—although she had met Adedeji, the tall half-caste boy in her English class with the oyinbo accent and kind eyes.

The Travelling Man stayed almost two months the second time. One day in the middle of a sentence, the light flared cobalt against his cheekbones. Then he was gone.

When would he meet her? Eni woke in the late afternoon. Yellowing light flooded the apartment. She was curled on the floor, huddled against the window. It took all her strength to lift her head from the floor and sit up against the window. The man was staring at her. Not the Travelling Man, her man. The one with kind eyes. She couldn't remember his name, but Eni knew he was her man. Her body re-membered, even if the rest of her didn't. She wanted to cry every time she saw him.

"You should be in a hospital," he said. Eni did not know if there were windows in a hospital, windows with moonlight. She could barely remember the months she had spent in the hospital, but she knew that when still-sick people are sent back home, no one expects them to get better. Eni shook her head, no. Deji sighed. He lifted her in his arms as though she weighed nothing and helped her to the bathroom, turned away when she asked him to without words. He said nothing when she returned to the window.

He saw me so many times. For a day, mostly, but often longer, and once for nearly a year. That was a golden year, the year I was engaged to Deji, the year I turned twenty-two. He was the first boy to tell me I was beautiful, and The Travelling Man always knew we'd get married. But I was already forgetting. Little things—cash, my keys. Then bigger things. I'd forgotten Deji's name that morning, just for an instant. He hadn't noticed. The Trav-elling Man came to the house after breakfast to see me before I went to work. I was at the kitchen table, waiting for him.

"You know what happens to me, don't you?" I asked. He had been my closest friend for a decade, always happy, always smiling. Reckless, wild. Now he was silent. "Where do you go when you're not here?" I shouted. "Who are you? What's the point of any of it if you won't help me?" The Travelling Man was a boy by now—fifteen, growing younger. But suddenly he looked angry and incredibly ancient.

"You and I travel in different directions. I can only pass through your life backward, and I can't choose when I come or when I go. I don't know why. It was the same thing with my sister, until one day I knew her but she didn't know me, and I never saw her again. Yet in all the time when you're not alive, I'm in control. I can go forward or back, see every moment without being seen. I can watch the pyramids go up above me and watch London fall in the war-to-end-all-wars, and when the earth burns up and withers—and it will, I know, I've seen that too—and the darkness takes it—"

"Stop it! Stop it, I don't want to hear any more!" I cringed backward and brought my hands up to cover my face. When the Travelling Man pulled them gently aside, his eyes were wet and tired. He looked impossibly young as he wept into my shoulder.

"I'm so tired," he said. When Deji returned that night, the Travelling Man was gone, and he did not return. And I—

No matter how hard she tried, Eni could not remember a thing before her time in the hospital, when she and Deji discovered that her body was fading along with her mind. The doctors did not know what had caused the decline of either. Deji had been silent on the way home, his knuckles blue white against the steering wheel. He had reminded her suddenly of the Travelling Man, and Eni had laughed. It had been too much for him. Deji pulled over to the side of the road, left the car, and screamed into the night like a demon. Then he came back into the car and kissed Eni until her lips bruised, and he sucked dark marks into her neck for her to remember him by.

Eni blinked. She lay on her back in the blue moonlight. The apartment was at the bottom of the ocean, wreathed in shadow. She could hear Deji's faint breathing from their bedroom, but that did not matter now. The Travelling Man was here. He walked through her window.

He was perhaps twelve years old, and she had never seen him look so young nor so old. His eyes were sunken and exhausted, shadowed with black. His back was stooped, and his flesh clung tightly to his bones. But the moon still loved him. Blue light filled his hollowed cheeks and caressed his rounded shoulders. As Eni watched, the light reached his eyes and soothed them, and he smiled at her.

"How?" Eni asked. It was clear he knew who she was, but it was also clear that this was the last time she would ever see him. How could they meet again? She could feel herself dying. Every beat of her heart was a struggle. It fluttered in her chest like a bird in a steel trap, growing weaker, traveling from life into death. So, this is what was to become of her and the boy she loved like her own brother. He'd known this all along and never told her. When they danced through the night in her college dorm room, he saw her here as she lay dying. When he appeared, suddenly, in the colored panes of the stained-glass window of the church at her father's funeral, he'd known one day he'd find her

195

here. It was strange, dying like this. Most people were afraid of losing what they had. Eni felt only longing. She couldn't remember what she was losing, and so that barely felt like a loss. But it would have been nice, here, at the end, to have something to want to live for. The Travelling Man squeezed Eni's hand, brought her back. His hand was cold. But it was alive. And that was good.

"You're going to live," he said, "and you're going to see me again. Not too many times—you lose your sight as another gains it. But you *will* see me again. And I'll see you—I'm traveling back to your beginning, growing older all the time. Our friendship ... that's all in front of *me*. But that doesn't mean your life ends here. I know it doesn't. I've seen it." The Travelling Man smiled as if at some secret joke, then continued. "I've met lots of my selves from other times. They told me what I had to do, who you are to me. I've been ... not quite human, the past few thousand years. Since the moment I was born, I've been going to all times, all places, awaiting the moment I got to meet you *here*. A few of us Travelling Men found a way to save you." He knelt at Eni's side and helped her sit up with her back to the window. His fingers were calloused and worn in hers, hard used, yet the flesh was light and insubstantial.

"I'm traveling soon," he said, and he smiled an apology. Eni's head slumped against the window. She felt a heat in her chest, a constriction. Her toes were beginning to go numb. The shadows in the room lengthened.

"At the very edge of the universe, just before the great contraction where all there is becomes all there will be, I found something for you. Call it ... call it a late birthday present. Here."

The Travelling Man opened his hand. A shard of ice shivered in his palm, shining slightly with an inward light. "It's time," he said. "Nearly forty years of it, frozen. Suspended. And it's yours." He pressed it into Eni's hand, but her fingers splayed open. She could no longer feel her body. She no longer knew she was Eni Deem, tall for a woman. But she knew still her Travelling Man.

"This will freeze you—a loop in time, but you'll be the only one it catches. Traveling forward, untouched by time, untouched by illness. Unmoored, like me, but going in the right direction, until it runs out and you start at the beginning, not knowing you've done it before. I didn't just find this ... it's worth more than the Earth. Someone gave

196

this to me. He'd fought for eons to get it, fought some of the worst beings the galaxy had to offer, and he was fading. He told me to give this to you. He had one more stop to make before he was gone."

Eni made a small noise of surprise. Her Travelling Man smiled. He clasped Eni's hand closed around the ice in her palm. The veins in her hand turned suddenly cold. Then the veins in her arm. It shocked her senses, like crashing into a frozen sea.

"We'll see each other again. I'm in your past now, Eni. But you're my future. Every time I see you now, you'll be younger." The Travelling Man had begun to cry, and the blue tear tracks cut his face into pieces. His voice was oddly thick when he spoke again.

"I just ... I want you to know that I'm going to be all right. I grew up in some strange places and some strange times. I sort of raised myself. But I had my sister. I got to travel to her for half her life. I won't see her again, but she hasn't even met me yet. She hasn't even named me the Travelling Man." He leaned forward and kissed Eni's cheek. In the burning cold, thoughts crystallized one after another. Eni remembered Deji. She remembered—she said—

The light pulled the Travelling Man apart. The crystal in Eni's palm melted, her veins burned, and she felt it as time lost its hold on her. All the strings inside her shattered in the sudden cold, and she remembered.

"Isoken," I said when I was twenty-five, clutching my newborn daughter all wrong but afraid to let her go even for a moment. "One who is contented with her destiny," Deji echoed, and laughed. "Unlike her mother." It was later that year I forgot her on the changing table in a supermarket and Deji began to ask me, "Isoken?" And it was the year after that when I began to shake my head no, I did not know, and he sent her to live with her grandmother.

Eni moaned. The longing for her daughter came upon her all at once, and she almost could not bear it. She began to stand, to wake Deji, to drive sleep-addled to her mother's house and find her child. How could she not have remembered her daughter? She knew everything about her—her warm brown skin, her curly hair, her small round teeth. Eni knew she'd give her the skin off her arms if she had to, the bones out of her legs. But her knees buckled as she tried to stand, and she fell under the weight of one last memory. Her mind washed blue, and Eni saw.

I was fourteen, and he was in *the window, half in and half out, and the moonlight shone right through him—turned his skin pale blue. He watched me as I came to him, and he was quiet as he cried. And he said to me, "Shh, don't wake your sisters. I just wanted to see you one last time." He smiled, and the moonlight began taking him to pieces. My heart was in my throat, and I couldn't speak, and so I watched. And just before he was gone, he said—*
   "Mom."

Eni felt a small fluttering in her stomach as the child inside her traveled for the first time … and was gone.

AN ARC OF ELECTRIC SKIN

by Wole Talabi

For a long time, I wondered what kind of person would volunteer to have their skin exposed to temperatures cycling between the melting point of aluminum and the night-time surface temperature of Mercury, riding a wave of thermal torment that would drive most people insane with pain.

Now I know.

I fell in love with such a man.

He was ungraciously tied to an anti-ionization pole and executed by a six-man firing squad in front of the dirty gray wall of Kirikiri prison before a hushed crowd of witnesses.

I never even got the chance to say a proper goodbye.

I was in the vice grip of three burly secret service officers, tears still streaming down my face, even though I'd been crying for days. His Afro was wild and uneven, the white jumpsuit he'd been dressed in was frayed but clean, and his eyes were still as defiant as they'd been the day he'd walked into my office at Lagos University Teaching Hospital and said with a calm and composure that belied all the rage that must have been inside him, "Dr. Ogunbiyi, I read the paper you published with Professor Aliyu. I want to volunteer."

His real name was Akachi Nwosu, but the media called him *Shock Absorber* because he used to be a roadside mechanic before he met me

199

and taught himself to wield lightning. My people believe names are tied to one's essence and can influence or predict one's destiny, a bond to one's Orí. I think Akachi's people have similar beliefs, because he told me his name means *hand of God*. It was appropriate. What else would you call a man whose destiny drove him to find a way to hold on to the raging flow of displaced electrons and bend them to his will?

My heart aches because I miss his determined eyes, his hard hands, his smooth skin, his soft voice. But also, because in fragile moments, doubts overwhelm me, and I am not sure if I ever knew him completely enough to have truly loved him. In the darkest of those moments, when I think about his final deception, I am not sure if he ever truly loved me either.

He had graduated from the University of Ibadan with a degree in electrical engineering, during which he'd attended guest lectures by my senior research partner Professor Aliyu. He had graduated with a first-class degree and a fascination with electrical systems despite having to work part-time as an assistant at a mechanic shop where he also lived because he couldn't afford accommodation. But he couldn't find a job in the crumbling post-oil economy, and so he took what little savings he had and started a small mechanic shop of his own next to Ojota motor park. He showed me pictures of it while we lay in each other's arms, two nights before the procedure. It was little more than a zinc roof over dusty land and a pile of second-hand tools. The profits weren't good, but he worked hard. His calloused hands bore witness. He spent hours attending to junky jalopies that were barely roadworthy, but heaven knows he did his best with them. His own mother had died in a bus just like the ones he frequently serviced, in an accident on the Lagos-Ibadan express which everyone knew was caused by a contractor cutting corners on what should have been road barriers. An accident he'd barely survived himself, needing five months in the hospital to recover and walk again. His father had sold everything he owned and borrowed from family members just to afford the care his son needed. So, when he worked on those buses and cars, he told me, he saw the faces of the families that would get into them, hoping to make it to their destinations, and so he worked as hard as he could to make sure they did.

He endured every brick the crumbling system threw at him. Constant police harassment raids for bribes, aggressive underpaying clients, random changes in government policy that almost always meant he had to pay more for something, thieving and untrustworthy assistants. All of this under the blistering heat of the Lagos sun, increasing his already-high melanin levels, his darkening another physical marker of his endurance. And still, he persisted, my Akachi. He had a strong mind.

"This country happens to all of us," he'd told me the first night I had asked about his scars. That was his philosophy. "Some of us more than others."

He eventually saved enough money to move out of the face-me-I-face-you he shared with friends from university and into a self-contain in an almost respectable part of town. He was working his way up the broken system, keeping up with the *Nigerian Journal of Electrical and Electronic Applications*, and still looking for a job where he could apply the knowledge that had always fascinated him.

Then he went to the campaign rally.

Ezekwe4President. #EzEasy. A New Nigeria. We all remember the slogans. The digitags. The posters. Ngozi Ezekwe announced her candidacy quietly at a small event near her hometown in Awka but within a few months, she had become the leading opposition contender. She was a technocrat with a plan, unlike the political vultures circling the federal carcass we'd become used to. She came in with a clear agenda, an empathetic ear, and grassroots support from businesses she'd helped survive the economic apocalypse. We all remember the hope. And we all saw what happened. Quovision display decks crackled with high resolution holostreams of soldiers beating unarmed people in the streets, dragging them into the backs of armored trucks, firing live rounds into defiant crowds, breaking up the opposition rallies and protests. Akachi was one of those taken into custody near the infamous Ojota protest site where almost forty were killed. He was beaten and tortured for weeks. The Gusau administration made no secret of what they did even though the president denied giving the order on international broadcasts. But on the ground, we all knew what it was. We'd seen it before. Their regular trademark. It was a show of force to intimidate the opposition and its supporters. We were living in a hostage state.

It was during his weeks of torment that something broke in Akachi. To be treated that way by those who were meant to protect and serve you, to know that they could kill you and nothing would happen, it does something to your mind. Pain can clarify things. He told me later that after hours of unrelenting terror and agony, he'd stopped fearing death; he'd realized then he'd been so focused on surviving the system that he hadn't ever truly been alive, that he was doing nothing but dying slowly, and had been doing so for a long time. He told me that when he was released, he'd resolved to ensure things changed.

I wish I had known then exactly what he'd meant.

"I'm not recruiting test subjects yet," I told him that day in my office after he'd explained who he was and what he was talking about. "We still have a few iterations to ensure we can manage sensory response."

"You mean pain?"

"Yes," I told him. "Right now, we can only ensure subject survival and prevent long-term tissue damage, but we are still working to limit the impact of extreme temperature micro exposures on pain receptors. The body and the mind will protest, even under anesthesia."

"I can handle pain," he said calmly.

I'd just come back from a session with the visiting council at the African Academy of Sciences to make my seventh application for additional funding after a week of sleepless nights running calculations and preparing proposals. The potential of our research was enormous, even the most conservative members of council weren't myopic enough to miss the value in being able to use enhanced conductivity in human skin to develop a new category of biomedical devices that could be naturally embedded in the body and controlled using dermal interface circuitry. They just wanted to see more progress before they committed to helping us. Professor Aliyu had already designed and tested a prototype device using enhanced conductivity in discarded epithelial extracts, but we needed to show that we could make this work in living people. I felt like I was the one holding things back. I was under pressure to make some progress. I should have been more skeptical. I should have asked more questions. I should have told Akachi to wait until we were ready, but instead, I asked him to fill out a form.

It took a few weeks for me to convince Professor Aliyu to cross what he believed to be a moral line and for us to perform all the preliminary tests and screening processes. We spent much of that time together. Him sitting just outside my office quietly watching me or reading. Patiently waiting for another blood or skin or hair sample collection or for another baseline skin conductivity measurement. I never asked him why he never left the hospital in between tests, but I did ask him to join me for dinner once as I was closing for the day.

He seemed so focused sitting there, reading an old battered electrical engineering book, but I don't think I will ever forget the soft smile that broke across his face when he looked up, and the way he said, "Yes, doctor. But please, let me take you to the best buka in Surulere. I hope you are hungry."

"I am," I said. I hadn't eaten all day.

We went to eat amala and gbegiri at a makeshift shop down the road. An old lady in a black blouse and ankara wrapper scooped up the soft lumps of yam flour, loaded them with generous helpings of soup and meat, and we took seats on plastic chairs behind her. We spoke as we ate. That was the first time we talked about anything other than the experiments, but the conversation flowed naturally, easily. We spoke for hours until the old woman told us she was closing for the day. It wasn't planned, but we went back to my place and kept talking. He showed me some of his scars, and I told him about my work, and we kept speaking until we fell asleep together, face to face on my bed with all our clothes still on. When we woke up in the morning, we laughed and then we kissed, leaving me lightheaded, like I was still asleep and in a dream. It was only later that a feeling of wrongness settled upon me. He was, in some sense, my patient. But nothing that happened that day was planned, and sometimes you get caught in a river and you can't do anything but flow. Love can be a strange and sudden thing.

Three days after he'd passed the final screening, I led him into the bio-annealing cell I'd designed with Professor Aliyu. He squeezed my hand as he stepped into the black, ovoid pod with wires and tubes running out of it like so many umbilical cords. He smiled at me before securing the fiberglass mask over his face. Professor Aliyu was nestled comfortably in his wheelchair, monitoring the thermal induction and vacuum pump systems that would rearrange the molecular structure of the melanin in Akachi's skin. Part of me wanted to pull him away, to wait until we had improved the bio-annealing procedure to the point where we could do it with less pain. Or perhaps, to reduce the target conductivity increase from the theoretical limit to a near-threshold value, even though I knew that would only reduce the pain induced by a small fraction and increase the risk of process failure. For sure, if I'd known then what he was planning to do, what he had resolved to do all along, I would have dragged him out of there. But I didn't, so I stepped back and gave Professor Aliyu the signal to begin.

He screamed, but we could not hear him. He screamed for the three hours it took to increase his skin conductivity fifty orders of magnitude. I stepped out of the room to cry.

I still wonder how he managed to endure it. I still wonder how I could put someone I loved through that. I suppose I will always wonder when it comes to Akachi.

It was only a month later that I truly understood why he did it.

I saw it all in high resolution holostream, same as everyone else.

Incumbent President Umar Gusau was standing in the back of an electric black Mercedes T-class pickup truck, flanked by secret servicemen in dark suits and military attachés in camouflage as he waved to a crowd of paid supporters. Although he was supposed to be resting at home and preparing for his conductivity stability test that day, I saw Akachi on the quovision screen. He was an almost-invisible speck in the sea of people. Almost invisible that is, until he pulled up an umbrella fitted with what I later came to find out was a high-power laser and fired it silently into the sky where it formed an ionized column of air, an artificial conduit for electrical discharge.

When lightning finally tore down from the sky in a hot, bright streak, he reached up and seized it like a whip made of bright, electric death. I gasped audibly and didn't even notice I was spilling my cup of hot Lipton tea onto my desk. He struck down at the presidential procession in a smooth, clear motion. There was a deafening explosion of thunder. A flash of impossibly white light. A scattering of dust and particles and fragments. The holographic displays went dead, and I exhaled deeply, letting out the breath I didn't know I had been holding and seeing the brown spill that was spreading slowly, steadily across my desk. I didn't even bother to try to wipe up any of it. My eyes remained glued to the fuzzy, crackling images being transmitted from Abuja. When the holostreams were re-established and everything had settled, there were bodies, there was fire, there was blood.

No matter how many times I watch it, a part of me still doesn't believe that the man I loved could cause so much destruction, so much death. I suppose now in hindsight, I should have known, I should have seen the signs. The frequency with which he quoted the late Ken Saro-Wiwa and Fela Kuti; the way he always averted his eyes when I spoke about the results of the procedure and his future; the calm with which he spoke about his mother's death, the state of the economy, the bribes, the torture, the politicians, the pain. So much pain. A lifetime of pain and struggle. I should have known that he was full and running over. I should have loved him enough to see all of him clearly.

More was to come. He went on a rampage throughout Abuja, wielding lightning like raw justice at corrupt politicians, judges, soldiers, police, foreign businessmen, everyone he believed had a hand in making the broken system the way it was.

He surrendered two terror-filled weeks later, a trail of dead in his wake.

During the trial, some in the media started calling him Nigeria's first true-life superhero. They dubbed him *Shock Absorber*. Others said he was no hero, just another tragic monster the system created. In the end, none of it mattered, he was quickly found guilty and sentenced to death.

I was given the opportunity to say goodbye, to watch him die, by the President Ezekwe herself, a woman who wouldn't be where she was without his actions, but who now reluctantly acceded to cries for his public execution in order to secure her position. It was the law, she'd said to me on the phone, Section 33 of the Constitution, and she could not be seen to interfere in the trial of a man, a terrorist, who had extrajudicially murdered her predecessors in cold blood. She'd be accused of sponsoring, sympathizing, or spinelessness in matters of upholding the law. Even commuting his sentence to life would make her position untenable, she told me as I begged her over the phone to save his life, tears streaming down my puffy face like bitter rain.

And so, I helplessly watched camouflaged soldiers in tactical masks march in, take up positions and take aim. He just smiled and mouthed two words.

"Thank you."

Ah. My Akachi. The hand of God. My people believe that Ṣàngó, the òrìṣà of thunder and lightning is also the lord of justice and he only strikes down those who have offended him. Those who have committed offenses against the land and its people and for whom spilled blood demanded justice. I think Akachi's people believe something similar. Seeing him bound there, I still wasn't sure if what he had done was good or even just. Divine or otherwise. But things had been so wrong in the country for so long that perhaps this was what was needed to start a change. Or perhaps he has only started us down a dark and dangerous path filled with even more desperation, more violence. I don't know. I could see he was at peace with himself, and for that, I was glad.

But I could not bear to watch the bullets pierce his beautiful black, electric skin; the skin I'd caressed and touched tenderly, the skin I'd helped him turn into a weapon. I closed my eyes and waited, holding my breath, until finally, I heard the unmistakable sharp cracks of semi-automatic fire.

They sounded like judgment, like thunder, like heartbreak.

A SOUL OF SMALL PLACES

by Mame Bougouma Diene

My name is Woppa Diallo. My mother was Djinda Diallo, formerly Dem. A devout woman from Matam, where we live. The second hottest region in Senegal. It's not much to show for, but you take what you can get. My father was Abdoulaye Diallo, a shepherd from Tambacounda. The hottest region in Senegal. I've heard that everybody will eat at least eight flies in their life. That's certainly true if you live in Tambacounda.

There's a large stone in my village, right on the riverbank, shaped like a naked woman. The nomadic herdsmen have ruined it since, but I remember the shape of her, her face and her breasts.

We're told she was a newlywed, raped by her new family's men on the night of her wedding.

As she bathed in the river the following morning, a water spirit found her crying naked on the banks, unable to put her soiled clothes back on, unable to take a single step back to that nightmare she had to call home.

"Can't you tell anyone?" The spirit inquired. "I can whisper into their minds for you if you wish …"

She'd refused. Her new family might kill her. Her own family might kill her. Even if she fled, they would carry the burden of shame everywhere they went.

207

"Whispers don't work that way," she told the kind spirit. Instead, she tossed her clothes into the river. "I can't go back there, but I can't leave this place either. This is my home. Turn me into stone, right here over the waters where I belong, so they remember me, and every young girl has a place to hide."

I go there sometimes to wash my clothes and my family's, and think about her.

My mother thought about her too, and wanted to protect me even more. A soul of small places I needed a big shield, she told me once.

So she took me along to Mecca for the Umrah.

This is no small thing. No small thing at all. The trip is expensive, a lifetime of savings sometimes. If one family could send one person that's a blessing already, but taking a small child? Perhaps rich Emiratis could, but a mother and daughter from a small village in the hinterlands? My father was a good man. The others laughed at him.

I can't remember much. A two-year-old rarely does. Heat, stifling, sharp like a whip. Dust, puffs of it eager to clog my flower bud of a nose, the itch in my throat I couldn't scratch. The noise, the litany of prayers over melodies from loudspeakers, the dizzying press of bodies. White, everywhere, blinding, sweat reeking, white. Clinging to my mother's back as the universe conspired to crush me.

I remember her lifting me up, a black stone cast in silver, so dark my young mind couldn't fathom the pits. It glowed ruby red inside, calling at me, whispering into my head. Three distinct voices, a choir.

I heard later that in the days before Islam, when the gods of the desert tribes were female, women would rub the blood from their periods on the stone for good luck, fertility and harvest, and that it had left that distinct glow, deep magenta in black swells.

Oh, the men who kissed it so eagerly! The would-be pious who secretly hate women and fucked goats. If they only knew ...

My mother had lifted me up, the red swirls turning whirlpool in the black of a night that never dawns.

My lips had touched the stone. The choir of whispers exploded in my head. Three distinct voices. Three distinct names. Names that were gods. Names that were dead. Names that would never die. That could never die, because they were names of women, and we are resurrection and rebirth.

I remember nothing after that. I woke up in my parents' bed, in our small house in Agnam Thiodaye, on the outskirts of the village to the call to prayer. I was three.

"Are you ready for school, Woppa?"

"Yes, mother," I answered as the rooster sang his first song. The goats in the backyard started bleating on queue, the heat already turning humid and thick. The women out in the fields, the multi-hued dots of their head wraps dancing in the distance, dropping small seeds, singing and clapping their hands.

"You stick to the road! Understand!"

"Yes, mother."

"And hold on to your sister's hand!"

"Yes, mother."

"Don't let go of her hand!"

"Yes, mother."

She nods, but she's scared. She walks us to the door and doesn't let her gaze wander from us until we've turned behind the bush and the house disappears.

It's a long way to school, and I can only walk as fast as my little sister, Awa. She's only eight but tall for her age, taller than I was four years ago. She keeps up, but every so often she slows down, and I can't let go of her hand. My mother has eyes everywhere. If anybody sees us, she'll be sure to ask them. "Was Woppa holding her sister's hand?" If they said no I'd feel it for days, and Awa would have to slow down for me.

Senegal's a dry place. Matam is one of the driest, but not where we lived. In most of the country you can see a house for miles. Not here. The sands by the river are a fertile brown laced with baobabs and bushes, small verdant trees that pop up throughout the land, distorting your sense of space. They pepper the way to school and beyond, the freshness of the water a thin sheen on the air, soothing your throat and sprinkling your tongue in the rising shimmer of heat.

It's in those bushes that the herdsmen ambush little girls on the way to school and rape them.

I hadn't always known what that meant. I'm not sure I did even then, but I understood that something wrong had happened. Sometimes a beautiful wedding would follow the horrible news. I didn't make the connection at the time. I do now.

Our mother's right to be afraid.

People think girls don't go to school here because we're ignorant shepherds. Attendance rates plummet when the seasonal herds of long-horned zebu turn toward our village and rise again when they leave and drop in another village further away.

It's not ignorance. It's fear. Keep your daughters home or else ... or else the village might get another stone statue or another wedding ...

The first people to live here settled in the lands north of where the village is now, in the Kadiel Mbaye Toulaye. There they encountered all manner of sorcery, and in its wake, death. So they moved south to the Fonde Amadou Tall, where they found carnivorous ants who killed with a single bite. A man wandered through the village and found them dying and said: tiode nde ndo, live in the middle, which became thiodaye and they invited him to eat, aar niaam, which became agnam. Agnam Thiodaye.

Some said the rapes came from the old sorcery that had found new ways to torment us. But it didn't matter where you lived or the curse on your village. Keep your little girls home.

I refuse to stay home, school's important to me. It's important to my parents too.

I hold Awa's hand and never let go. Staying in the middle of the road and away from the bushes.

I'm protected. Allah saw to it in Mecca.

Everybody's eyes are on me. Amadou's are the only ones that matter. He's so handsome, smooth skin so dark he's almost blue, with deep-seated dark-blue eyes, a straight nose and pearly white teeth.

All of them are staring at me but I'm not sure why.

The teacher is praising me again, but I don't know why.

It's been happening since I started bleeding. The smell and dizziness of those lost moments in the Wahhabi desert surge over me, the voices whisper names, and ... just as the year I lost as a child, I emerge moments later, my work done, the test passed, my room and the house cleaned, all to perfection, and I can't remember a thing.

No one seems to have noticed, to them I was always there, always me, and I take the praise but shudder inside in shame at being a fraud, of being caught, of people wondering if there wasn't a little witch in me; at not knowing who I am …

"I'm very impressed, Woppa," the teacher says. "You're going places."

I nod and smile timidly. She thinks it's humility, the shyness we're taught to display, but it's the smile of the fool, happy because others seem happy, smiling because she's liked.

"Woppa," Amadou whispers, "let's talk outside." He winks as he walks past me, the white walls of the small classroom growing even smaller to the laughter of children in the yard, until it's too small for the two of us, forcing him near me, close enough to smell his breath, close enough to kiss as I daydream and the class empties.

"Woppa!" I hear Ms. Niang tell me. "Woppa! Snap out of it! Out you go!"

I hope she hasn't noticed, but teachers see everything. Daydreaming over a boy …

"Yes, Ms. Niang."

I pick up my books and run out, the day's heat abated slightly in the late afternoon sun. It's not quite the time for spirits yet; twilight still distant on the horizon.

Awa's in the yard, playing jump rope with her clapping friends, she sees me, waves, misses a beat and steps on the rope. I wave back but I'm looking for Amadou. There he is, sneaking around the corner of the building, waiting for me to see him and disappearing behind it.

I scuttle after him, trying to tame the skip in my legs. What does he have to tell me? There's a hundred girls in the school, I'm not the prettiest. I'm not the smartest, except that I am apparently. I'm too tall, too gangly, too … too many things to think about and I have no time to think, he's around the corner, right there waiting for *me*.

I love my home. It's the only one that I want. Many of the other girls dream of the city, most have never made it to Matam. They probably think Thies is Paris and Dakar is New York. I don't know what dreams Netflix and Trace TV planted in their heads. The air here is full, the empty lands behind the school are rich and eternal, not corrosive like asphalt. They'll crack open one day and fire like blood will flow out, yet eternal. I hear the cackle of the hyena if I close my eyes. Smell the distant smoke filtered through dry grass and trees, the swarms of crickets over the sunset, the river's dreams of becoming a waterfall. It's home. It's where I'm one from the soles of my feet to my braided hair, binding earth to heaven.

"Hey, kai fi." Amadou beckons.

"Ko jitda?" I'd do anything he says, but it's the game. The banter first. The boys will tease and get told off, tease more and I'd make a joke. He'd call me cheeky, holding my hand a lingering moment too long. I've never met a Senegalese boy who didn't think he was the champion of laamb, soccer's ballon d'or and Barack Obama all wrapped in one. Every single one of them.

Amadou surprised me.

"You're doing very well in school," he starts, almost timidly.

I don't know what to say. He gets closer.

"Look … I … . You're not like the others … maybe …"

What is happening?

"… Maybe …"

Yes?

He looks into my eyes, he's gonna ask me something, what is it?

His resolve falters and he mumbles.

"… Maybe we can study together?"

That's not what he wanted to say nor what I wanted to hear, but somehow the crush I had on him blossoms. He's not the arrogant shit I thought he was. He's like me. Shy and good inside.

"Of course," I said, and we start talking.

I can't tell you how long we spoke, evening prayer came and went, and I didn't hear a thing. Only when Awa started tugging at my dress did I notice the sun dipping beneath the horizon. It was time for the spirits. Long past time to be home.

Awa puffs behind me but holds on to my hand, her tiny feet blistering in blue plastic sandals never meant for running.

The time of spirits never lasts long, a mere thirty minutes before nightfall drops like a butcher's knife on a chicken's neck, and things much worse than evil spirits, more immediately real than evil spirts, cackle in the bushes.

It takes twice that time to get home.

It takes less than a second for lightning to strike.

I'm running right into my mother's whooping, but I almost welcome the pain, I'm eager for it. Anything for Awa to get home safe, any …

Awa's sweaty palm slips out of mine, I hear her cry and hit the dirt road. I turn to see her rise without another sound and reach out to me. Her eyes pop in her head as two hands land on my skinny shoulders.

"Get the other one!" orders a withered voice behind me.

A form in a blue boubou rushes past me, and I throw my leg out, tripping him before he can reach Awa. His chin lands on the ground with the cracking of his jaw and a spurt of blood.

"Run, Awa!" I scream before the man pulls me back covering my mouth with a hand reeking of cow skin and urine.

Awa shakes off her sandals and runs, a blur of white and blue against the night. The man on the floor goes for her ankle, but she jumps over his arm and dashes away.

We're halfway home, maybe more. Will she make it? Will she run into more men hiding in the bushes? An eight-year-old who hadn't even bled yet? All that because I couldn't stop staring at a boy?!

"Forget her." The stinking man's voice snaps behind me as I struggle, muffled screams through his sweaty palm, I try to bite but can barely open my mouth and my teeth slice through my tongue instead, blood flowing into my throat and choking me. "This one's good enough. Help me drag her into the bushes."

He pulls me further back. The dirt furrows into my legs, my sandals slipping off, my threadbare dress tearing in places, the slow rumble of the river close behind, thorns on the ground piercing me, scratching and scratching and scratching at my arms, nails tearing off from trying to hold on to the ground.

The other man gets up, touching his jaw, spitting a thick gob of blood and looming over me, shadow closing away the sky.

He sneers and reaches for my dress. I close my eyes. I can't watch. I think I might faint, but the sweaty stench of acrid malevolence awakens something inside me. A choir rises, the sky roars thunder, a flash of lightning, and I can't remember anything.

It's the smell that wakes me up, I think. Something burning close by. Straw? Manure?

"La la illalah, la la illalah, la la illalah …"

The voices next, exhausted voices hanging on to every syllable for fleeting life.

I open my eyes. Two pairs of eyes on me, closing down, closer, closer!

Two soothing voices.

"Seese."

"Calm down."

"You've been home for weeks."

"My daughter. Mach'allah. You're safe."

My parents. I'm home. In bed … For weeks! What happened? What happened to me?!

My hand shoots down between my legs, but my mother catches it, covering it with kisses.

"You're fine," she says. "Awa told us what happened …"

Awa's safe. My head lands back on the pillow.

"… Your father rushed outside. There was thunder, the wind knocked him flat on his back, and it started to pour. Rain so thick we couldn't see through it. So hard it would have beaten us into the ground. We couldn't leave the house, Woppa! We wanted to! We tried! You gotta believe me Woppa we …"

She paused to catch her breath, sighing deep and fast, into my father's neck. How long had she held it in, hoping I would wake up?

"It lasted only a few minutes, or it would have wiped out the whole village," my father added. "The house flooded. The river spilled over too. Not for long. A few trees were swept away. The rain cleared out at once, and there you were, walking up to the door, covered in … rain and mud … you collapsed inside the yard. Eighteen days ago."

"Nineteen," my mother finished.

She fed me a small cup of water.

"Where's Awa?" I ask.

"She's at school. Don't worry. The Diarra take her," my father said.

"But ... she ..."

"Hush," my mother says, putting the cup down and pulling the sheets over me. "Rest more, you've had only thin broth for weeks. This is a miracle."

The sheets are warm, my parents' breath on my face is comforting. I fall asleep.

I recovered surprisingly quickly. After three days I was in the yard walking and running, but my mother wouldn't let me leave the house.

Trees weren't the only things the rain had swept away. The cattle were badly injured from being swept into the walls. People too, anybody outside when the rain bombarded them was bruised and beaten almost to death. The statue of the brave girl by the river was gone too.

Awa had thrown herself at me. When she hesitated to ask, I told her not to bother. Her stupid sister couldn't remember a thing. She'd giggled and I was relieved. It had happened too quickly for her to be really scared. She'd cried for a few days after I'd returned, but I was home and uninjured, and that was enough.

No one in the village had seen me come home. No one knew what had happened. My parents told everybody I got caught in the rain and almost drowned. I was home recovering. And Awa kept our secret.

I was allowed back to school after a week.

The yard turned dead silent as I walked in. Like Musa parting the waters, the random mass of students split down the middle, opening a clear path straight to my class.

I'm tempted to run, but I hold my head up and my back straight. If I play it cool they won't ask questions, but if I give them an inch they won't let me breathe, and our lie is a simple one, so easy to crack.

Amadou steps out of the ranks, eyes wild, his step uncertain.

"I'm sorry," he says. "I'm sorry, if I hadn't held you back the storm wouldn't have caught you. Really, I ..."

I brush past him, his jaw dropping and a few girls giggling. I won't let a boy distract me again. I knew it was unfair to him, that he'd done nothing wrong, that it was in fact all me. I had lingered, I'd let the sky turn pink to purple to black and endangered my little sister.

It wasn't his fault, but looking at him I could feel the pressure of a hand on my mouth, the bruising of the bushes. I hope it'll pass. No one can live like this.

Lacking a show, the other students go back to playing, and that is that.

The day goes by and everybody's easy on me. Ms. Niang doesn't pick on me for answers and keeps me hydrated.

I hate it. I'm not an invalid. That's not what is happening. I don't know *what* is happening but it's not that.

Class ends an hour early. Ms. Niang has a family emergency in Djourbel and it's a long ride on the bus.

Awa won't be done for another hour. I'm not the only one with a younger sibling, I'm one of the few with only one, so we gather outside and wait. They're still itching to grill me, except Amadou, staring at his toes, throwing furtive glances at me.

No one dares talk, but I notice Mame Yacine has a small pouch hanging from her neck and tucked under her dress where it touches her skin.

"What's the gri-gri for?" I ask her.

Everybody turns to her. She clutches the charm through her dress.

"Haven't you heard? A flesh-eater hides in one of our villages."

The others gasp for air. I must have too.

Mame Fatou Dem, my great-great grandmother, had known a soukounio. They were raised as sisters after Mame Fatou's parents died. Fed from the same breast as such they shared a soul. Her sister Sokhna. She had eaten eight people. Eight people who'd never know heaven.

They grew up looking very much alike, but to Mame Fatou's mirth Sokhna's gloom. Perhaps the jinn had entered her from birth, perhaps it had found root in her envy of Mame Fatou, but my great-great grandmother was safe from her hunger. Mame Fatou carved Sokhna's heart out herself when she uncovered her secret. Tears so bitter at killing her sister they melted her heart in her hands. Mame Fatou birthed three daughters, two of them stillborn, and died delivering the third.

216

"They found two dead herdsmen crushed between trees after the flood," Maya continued. "A couple of miles downriver, one eaten in half from his head to his waist. The second chewed through his stomach, a hole from neck to navel. That's what my parents told me. My aunt made the gri-gri and … ." she was shaking. We all were. "Do you think it's true? Could it be true?" She was asking me.

They all turned to look at me. Even Amadou.

How would I know? Except I did.

My father was silent when I ran into the house and told them what Maya had said. He looked at my mother, and she back at him, and away and back again …

"What happened when you found me?" I begged. "Please. I can't remember anything. They tried to … I can't remember anything!" I was crying. I was terrified. Scared to know, too scared not to, knowing what that would mean … what would it mean?

"We …" my mother started. "… You … when you came up to the … your father told me you were covered in mud and rain. You weren't. You were drenched in blood, down from your hair to your lips, bits of skin caught between your teeth …" She caught her breath, trembling. "We rushed to help, but it wasn't your blood …" She looked at me, staring silently.

I took in every word without fear. There was nothing left to be afraid of.

"We knew you could never harm us, and whatever you'd done to those men they deserved it and more. You're our daughter, Woppa. You're our daughter. There's nothing wrong with you. You saved your sister's life, Woppa. We are proud of you. We love you …" She trailed off. My father nodded, eyes on the ground.

I can't say I remember how I felt after that. It wasn't one of my spells. I just honestly can't.

News of the soukounio spread, and soon men started patrolling the riverbanks, escorting the children to and from school, lighting torches along the road at night … and there wasn't another rape for years.

My head is on Amadou's shoulder, the salt of his neck on my lips. Sitting on the riverbanks we're hidden from the road, our feet in the cold waters, small fish nibbling at our toes.

The river and its bushes changed with each passing season. We grew taller and the trees less intimidating. What felt like a jungle between the world and the river, we crossed in a few seconds, the bushes like hills to our younger eyes barely reached over our shoulders, and those of us whose spout of growth was quicker than usual towered above them.

A grave of preschool torture had turned into a nest of teenage love, or the rush of confusion, lust and doubt that passes for it.

I was certain it was love. It had to be. An empty carcass, I'd drifted a dead soul for months. I couldn't feel. Feel anything other than bone deep sorrow, eating away at my marrow, and anger, anger so blinding my eyes seared blisters against the air.

Sad because I knew I wasn't a person anymore. I wasn't Woppa anymore.

My name's an odd one. Woppa is a ward. When you lose a child you name the next with a ward, a name to confuse the evil eye and turn it away from the newborn. Woppa's one of those. It means go away. Snap it at someone and you're telling them to fuck off. Politely. Here you're telling the spirits to leave this child alone.

What warded me cursed me. My name. My mother's love. The murmurs of gods. They'd made me into something else, and all out of love.

Angry because dozens of brutalized girls didn't warrant watching the roads. Instead, the rapist got rewarded with a bride. But two men murdered, and heroic selflessness rears its cowardly head.

"It's getting late," Amadou says.

"You scared of something?" I ask.

He laughs.

"Yeah. Your father. You should be too. Plus, he's starting to warm up to me. Maybe …"

My father had, accidentally of course, set a bull loose on Amadou once. But he'd changed of late. He smiled when we locked eyes, crossing paths at the weekly markets. He'd walked him home once. I don't know what they'd said but he'd changed.

"You could take him out easily," I tease him.

He shakes his head and gets up, dusting off his pants. Amadou has joined the wrestlers. We're only sixteen, but he's half a head taller than the tallest kids. Sweet, gentle Amadou. He'd waited months. Coming to see me every day, getting told off every day for a year until I caved in. Until the emptiness inside subsided somewhat and cracked open enough to let me breathe and let something else, someone else, in.

I rise after him, my wet feet sinking into the soft brown banks. Amadou holds my hand through the bushes and trees. He'll let go just before hitting the road or maybe hold it just a little longer, testing fate.

The torches line the road, unlit in two years. After a while the villagers decided the jinn must've moved on, and things went back to normal. There hadn't been an incident in the two years since, and I hadn't had a spell, and stayed on top of my class. We were finally safe.

Or maybe not.

The air changes, the choir rises, Amadou says something, all immediately drowned by screams, loud and angry, growing weaker, legs kicking, strength faltering, screams turning to whimpers and silent frightened tears.

I am screaming back. Teeth bared, every inch of me burning.

"Woppa!"

Amadou shakes me. Shakes me till I stop screaming, the red heat abating to a brazier.

"Woppa! Are you alright!"

I am panting, hunched over. Two realities wrestling for my sanity.

"I had a ... a flashback ... the river flooding, I couldn't breathe ..."

He nods and takes my hand. Of course he'd believe that.

Something had happened. Just then. Something very bad.

We are not safe anymore.

There was no wedding this time. Whatever had happened and whoever she was hadn't told anyone. Not even her parents. She must've sneaked in, cleaned herself and hidden her bruises, lied about why her clothes were torn and been beaten for it.

219

A slither of hairy flesh slurps through my lips, trailing a lick of salty fat and sinew. It wraps around my tongue, soaking in the blood in my mouth, softening as I chew.

The thread of muscle catches between my molars; I dig it out with my tongue, pluck it with my fingers and flick it.

It's cold, but I am warm inside. The wind itself has no warmth. Not cold, just not warm either. I can feel its nonexistence like a veil. The moon inverts the colors around me, dancing iridescent, pulsing to my heartbeat the sky shines and cracks marauding pathways into other worlds.

I have never felt this way before. I want to feel this way forever.

I stand up and stop to look down for the first time since I started feeding.

His head, neck, arms and shoulders are gone. There is nothing there, no blood, no bone, no clothes, nothing. A hundred bites like teeth marks through a watermelon dig beneath where his heart was. It is in me now.

I'd never seen inside a person before. How enticing it is. Perhaps it's better that I can't remember my first time. Twelve-year-old me wouldn't have handled the ecstasy, the taste.

It is good to feed.

I had missed another attack, and another again. But when the visions came, I realized that beyond the raw emotions I could glimpse landmarks, spots along the road, the odd stone by the river. The bushes intertwined like two snakes kissing. I could find them.

The second time I noticed my heartbeat change minutes before the flashes hit. There were images too, vivid evil thoughts barely crossing into my mind, barely registering, because I wouldn't let them. I was holding on to Woppa. To the little girl who'd played with goats and kept her mother up at night. The little girl who was good at school, had a hot boyfriend and stole kisses by the waters.

I'm holding onto a dead girl. Alive in her skin I'm not that girl anymore. I could never be that girl anymore.

My body was not my own. The whispering voices rose, and I embraced them, allowed the transient tempest to settle, to find a home in me. There was no friction, no torrential rain, no tearing of the skies to energies bursting against each other. The flood, the thunder and the lighting, they all poured into me, I stretched my legs, the wind whooshed passed, and I was looming silently behind him, miles from home. He couldn't sense me, dressed in a brown boubou and a brown turban, his hands inside his pants, sneering up the road at two little girls hurrying home, carrying bags of rice on their heads.

My hand dropped over his mouth, my arm around his chest, and I dragged him back to the river, out of sight from the road in a small alcove of trees. One moment here, and there the next, as the girls walked by safely. My mouth stretching open, my jaw dislocating, his praying, struggling head sliding in, silenced and bursting open.

God created jinn and people just the same. We share the same loves and the same fears. Only jinn have more fire. Some jinn, like people, believe in God. Those are gentler spirits, if they attack you, you must've scared them. Back away and they'll stop. Some jinn, like people, don't believe in God. Those are wild spirits. Incomplete, they'll find in people the missing bits of their soul. And devour them.

My soukounio … *I* … don't know what we want. But I want more. The man's dying soul rages inside me. Stoking the fires with every droplet of his blood turning sweet nectar in my throat. His energies fading, always falling into the abyss, a scream that would dwindle and shrink forever, but never stop, never quite dead, always dying. An abyss that is me.

His existence runs electric under my skin, grafting itself to mine, a tiny pearl of consciousness that shines on a childhood so good, an adolescence so bland into an evil so deep.

I pat him on the stomach.

"I own you now," I say as I run a finger along his bleeding wound and lick it clean.

I should be getting home. I turn back to the half-eaten corpse gurgling on the ground, frayed nerves twitching the body like a puppet … I really should be getting home … but a few more bites won't matter …

My family hears the cattle bleating in panic as I walk into the yard, and they rush out to hug me.

I pity them. The animals could feel what they couldn't.

Your Woppa is no more.

221

We go to sleep soon afterwards. I wake up to a clamor outside our home. Someone has found the corpse. By nightfall the road is lit with torches once again.

It doesn't stop the herdsmen, and it didn't stop me either.

I moan softly as Amadou enters me. This will be my first time and my last. The softness of the sheet against my back. The press of his chest against mine. I should hurt but I don't. All I feel is warmth. Warmth radiating through both of us.

I can't bear to think of his heartbreak when he doesn't see me at school tomorrow; never sees me again.

Amadou can't believe his luck. It's his first time too. It's perfect. Perfect and crazy.

Three more bloody stumps in the last month and all the neighboring villages are in a frenzy. Patrols all day and halfway through the night. I push their minds away from us, they walk by but can't see us. Stretch their ears but can't hear us.

We're the only lovers in the world. And it's perfect.

Amadou walks me back and heads home, turning around twenty times to look back, grinning like the happy fool he is.

At least he thinks he does. He is walking down the road alone and will keep walking until he is in bed and falls asleep dreaming of me.

I want this fantasy to be real, but I cannot go back, and a familiar tingle rings at the base of my neck.

The herdsmen don't believe in the soukounio anymore. I know this from my feasts. They think the villagers mutilate the bodies themselves and put on this farce to scare them off.

They know the patrols scour the roads and riverbanks, the clusters of trees and bushes. That we think our villages are safe.

Three herdsmen creep toward the Diarra house next to ours, where Hamadi and Coumba are playing in the yard. They will kill Hamadi and kidnap Coumba before the patrols are back. They think they will.

They are preparing to climb over the wall as I rip through the three of them.

Before the first body hits the ground a hole through its stomach, I rip off the second's head and grab the legs of the third, climbing desperately up the wall, and tear his body in half, leaving him dangling dead from the white wall turning red from his waist to the ground.

I throw myself at his guts, drink from the fountain of his comrade's neck and reach for the other, but the animals bleat up a storm. Lights turn on and confused voices ring.

I look toward our house. It's so close I could slip in and no one would see me. I'd walk out looking scared, go back to sleep and head for school in the morning. But I can't. I can't go back. It's not my home anymore.

With each feeding the soukounio grows stronger, hungrier. The voices of others slowly choking mine. I'm still good inside. I think I am, but how much longer until I'm just a pearl of awareness screaming inside the jinn? How long until the darkness leaks and infects my family, Amadou, all those around me? It can't be what I leave behind. Pain from more pain. Where is the love I knew? The love I'd given up to this form.

I stretch my legs and disappear just as my mother's voice calls out for Awa and me.

She doesn't know I'm out. We'll never get to say goodbye.

My mother hadn't said a word, but ran.

Maybe if she'd said something, anything. Her name, a scream, anything. Her voice would have broken the spell.

No one knows what to expect when they encounter a spirit, you imagine anything, a fire-breathing ghoul, a person melting before your eyes, covered in hungry mouths, a shadow that trails yours and smiles back at *you*.

She could've said a word when the patrol came running into the village with the clamor of men and beasts. When they found her outside the Diarra house, leaning over three oozing corpses, and charged. Something to make her human. Anything.

No matter what you imagine, no one expects a terrified mother.

Instead, she panicked and ran, a silent fleeing spirit, and nothing emboldens cowards more than someone fleeing.

They'd landed on her with clubs. My mother, recognizing the bleating of the cattle for her absentee daughter, had rushed outside and found the bodies, and the men had found her, and …

One of them had recognized her dress. He yelled and pulled the others away, but it was too late. My father ran out to find the circle of men opening to a bloody lump in the colors of his love.

She died a few hours later. Her eyes never opened again. I want to believe she heard the crying voices around her. That in her unconscious last few hours she perceived the pain of her loss, that in her dying moments she knew more than shock and horror, the last memory of the daughter and three broken bodies on the ground. I want to believe that the first blow had knocked her out, that it was painless. That she hadn't felt the others.

But I know too much. I know people all too well from the minds that I touch. From the minds I consume. If my ravenous feasts had shown me anything it was that though the body and mind are gone, the soul goes last … and it feels everything.

I'd saved dozens of little girls. I'd saved myself. I'd saved my sister.

I had killed my mother.

I breathe in deeply. My feet buried into the soil of the riverbank, the rich brown almost but not quite blending with my own skin, the thin sheen of sweat glistening on my leg a rivulet congealing infinitely slowly around my ankles, like the drip of water in a cave slowly growing stalactites.

There are worms down there nibbling at the bits of me that are still flesh, other insects that I would've ran from just days ago bite and draw blood and die drinking it. The roots of the nearby trees reach out, tethering me to the ground.

The air and dust on the thin hairs of my nose smelling of sweet and sticky sap, of burning cow dung, grilled fish and melancholy. Emotions have smells too, perspiring glands collecting around the mourners at my parents' funeral.

Abdoulaye Diallo outlived his wife by less than a night. Awa's screams had woken me up in the morning. The screams inside her mind. Her loneliness. Our father hanging from the ceiling fan.

They are leaving the mosque now, the final prayers prayed. The men are carrying their biers to the cemetery, to bury them with Mame Binta, my grandmother, Mame Thiogo, my great-grandmother, and Mame Fatou, my great-great grandmother who had known a flesh-eater, and her unnamed stillborn daughters. A slow, silent procession, Awa the first to trail the coffins, as the men carried the last of her family with them.

Awa alone. Eyes turning toward her. I shudder in the heat, knowing all of her feelings. She doesn't want to move to her aunt's house, she's heard nasty rumors about what she does to teenage girls. My uncle's there, spending the night to watch over her before taking her in the morning. She doesn't like his smell, she's afraid, still wary of being alone with a man, even if he's family.

She's crying out for me. My name ringing in her mind with hope. That I'll come back, that I'll save her again.

I'll never come back, but I can still help her if she lets me in.

The river, Awa. I speak on the winds, tiny birds passing it on, chirping my message into her ears.

I hear my own voice in her head. Her gaze shifting away from the cemetery and toward me.

It's dark now, the blood inside my thighs has already turned solid. It prickles and stings but I'm getting used to it, my muscles and nerves slowly merging with my bones, my legs calcifying like ashy skin after a shower.

Awa appears through the bushes. She sees me and screams. Her voice like the steps that led her here, shielded from the world by me. Her eyes water, pearly drops running brown down her cheeks, and she throws herself at my neck. The same way she had after the flood. The same way she always had, ever since my mother had handed her to me as a baby.

She hugs me tight and looks into my eyes. Hers widen as she sees something beyond me inside of them, something that only she will know.

"Are you coming home?" she asks, her face buried inside my neck, the skin around my waist crackling softly as it hardens.

225

I'm never coming home, but I'm never leaving either.

My name is Woppa Diallo. My mother was Djinda Diallo, formerly Dem. I'm a soul of small places. And here I'll remain.

I put my fingers on her cheek, embracing her warmth while I can still feel. While I can still help her, the only way I know, the very way I was. I push my lips to her ear.

"Go home and sleep, little sister. I'm not going anywhere. Come back tomorrow and kiss me. You'll find me here, by the river. And I'll whisper to you."

BAREFOOT AND MIDNIGHT

by Sheree Renée Thomas

Three men emerged from darkness and walked to the edge of the wood, the scent of roses rising all around them. The moon hung like a broken jaw above the Memphis night. The school yard lay ahead, its wood fence disjointed and leaning. The fetid scent of wet grass, of mold and moss, floated on the evening wind from the bayou.

"You ready?" asked the first man, his face pock-marked, lips leering, eyes sullen.

"Light 'em up," replied the second. The third nodded his head and produced the gasoline.

They knew the children slept inside. No one had to tell them. The Freedmen's School in Gayoso's Flats was one of several humble buildings where the former slaves gathered to grasp what hope lay ahead for their futures. Most had no home but the damp, mosquito-infested fields surrounding the bayou. The school housed thirteen orphaned children, those who didn't even have a mother's lap to lay their little heads on.

When the fires calmed down and the bright red embers turned to ash, when the city grieved and grieved until it couldn't grieve anymore,

227

Dusa Dayan rose from the back pew of Beale Street First African Baptist Church and let the sounds of Doctor Watts's hymns usher her out the red door.

I heard the cry. I, I, I heard them cry.

The fire had burned the schoolhouse to the ground. All that remained were the crimson rose bushes. The roses, the first seeds the children had planted together. She could still see the faces of her students, not much younger than herself, their beautiful smiles, the lustrous brown skin, the determination in their eyes. She tried to make those memories replace the burnt, black splinters of bone that haunted her nights, the faces unrecognizable, lips pulled back in horror. And the cries that made her wake from sleep, her face covered in tears.

I heard the cry. I, I, I

Hidden in darkness, donated evening meals still covered in her basket, Dusa had heard every scream.

And now, like a visit from a long-forgotten friend, the story her grandmother told her many years ago became Dusa's only thought.

There, under the roots of the Lynching Tree, were the remains of countless members of Dusa's kinfolk and others. Unfortunate souls singled out and taken away in the cover of night. Under the blood-stained boughs, innocents had dangled and danced, lifeless beneath the broad, twisting limbs. It was a dance no soul wished ever to witness, a struggle of spirit and flesh, of ropes and blades and fire, a litany to pain that you could never unsee.

In the darkness the mound looked too small, too well shaped to be natural. Only visible to eyes who had seen hell and lived. Beneath the grass was the specter behind the stories, no one knew the origins of the legend, the haint whose soul was said to hover above Voodoo Fields.

Dusa placed her satchel on the dirt. She drew the hatchet from the twine at her waist and gripped a hardwood handle laced with ancient carvings. The tree loomed over the mound, casting shadows. The few surrounding weeds were scraggly, thick with drops of dew. The land around the tree was fallow, as if the blood-soaked earth

228

refused to nourish natural life. Dusa circled the mound, hatchet in hand, then she hacked off a branch from the Lynching Tree. The wet blades of grass felt slick against her bare soles. The wind whipped and pricked at her naked flesh. Exposed to the biting night and all its appetites, she knew the few drops of blood would not be all of the sacrifice. When she took the branch from the tree where no leaves or blossoms grew, the ground grumbled and growled beneath her feet. Dusa held her breath.

Barefoot and covered only in the darkness that was midnight, she shivered. On bent knees, she dug her fingers into the grass, grasping at the moist earth, clutched cherry bark and broken twigs, her back arched in pain. She lifted a flask, sprinkled bathwater from a child who was not baptized. Behind her the creek murmured and whispered, a cool invitation to abandon her mission. She could toss all the gathered items in the creek's dark waters, leave the terrors behind her. She could forget the tree and the cursed land that surrounded it, walk back through the red doors of the church, and beg for forgiveness.

Dusa rose on one knee, flask in hand, praying that she had the strength to turn her back on the Lynching Tree, but a fire burned in her soul. The faith she once had was replaced with an unholy rage, an anger so hot, it incinerated all forgiveness. She willed her body to move. But the scent of roses, overpowering in the night, strengthened her resolve, holding her there.

The fires were started by those who hated the very idea that any of them were now free. White Memphis defined itself by the darkness it kept outside of Freedom's light, by the darkness that festered within. The Freedmen's School was the only home Dusa had ever known. Frozen in winter, smoldering in summer, she and her thirteen students had suffered and struggled together as one. The bite of skeetas, the occasional serpent intruder were all well worth it. She had watched them, ages eight to fourteen, come through the old pine doors, eyes glistening with want for knowledge. The confidence on their faces emerged like spring blossoms as they slowly moved from signing their names with an X to the new names they had chosen for themselves in freedom.

But Voodoo Fields was where the ancient spirit lay, waiting. When no earthly justice would bring stolen Black lives peace. Dusa dug up the earth, the raw scent filling the air. She sprinkled the soil with her tears and pulled the ragged mud doll from its dreamless slumber. Wrapped in tree roots, its garment was tattered. Whatever color or pattern it once held faded long ago. A dark, rust-colored stain covered the space where its heart should be. It had no head. Only a red ribbon where it should be. It had no limbs. No mouth or plump cheeks and belly to kiss and pinch.

Dusa held a rose petal for every child she lost in the fire. She pressed them into the freshly made mud she used to cover the old doll. The mud spread like a second skin, the old layers, hard and cracking. As she held the doll, she thought she heard it cry out, the sound like a newborn baby hungry for its mother's milk. She nearly dropped it, but fear made her hold fast, the scream stuck in her throat.

The Lynching Tree branch smelled of smoke, fear, and blood. Pain radiated through her palms as she worked to fashion two arms, two legs, and a fist full of dark, earthwormed-soil for a head. She sculpted the head as roundly as she could in the darkness, resisted the urge to abandon the writhing ball of rotten soil. As she worked the doll felt heavier in her hand, like the child she once bore and buried before its first spring.

She sang the song before she realized she knew the song. In a language neither she nor her mother's tongue had ever sung before. Words that came from no leather-bound hymnal. Words that were dark, mournful, dangerous. It was the same song her grandmother sang before the spirit doll had slain the men who hung her husband, the same song she sang, they say, when the black doll came for her, too.

Hear I. Hear I cry. Rend them, spin them, hear them crying.

Dusa placed her palm flesh over the hatchet's blade and sang until her voice grew hoarse from crying. Her elbows were steady but arms wobbly. Her knees had grown numb, but the sharp scent of sweat, burned flesh, and urine made her squeeze the blood more rapidly into the doll's primitive mouth. No eyes were carved into the mud. The spirit doll needed only blood and the ashes of the dead to see.

Eyes stinging, Dusa held the doll to her bosom. She rocked and stroked it as she had once rocked her own child. Lulled by her mother's voice, the infant girl had gone to sleep one cold wintry night, but the child never opened her eyes again. Dusa was thinking of the baby's warm, fat fingers when she felt the mud doll's head shift in her hand. More corpse than baby, the doll once cold and still, began to writhe and twist in her arms. The fat, sightless grubs and earthworms burying through its mud-bottom flesh. A rotten smell, like spoiled vegetables and dead leaves, filled the air. Strange roots burst from the doll's center. Dusa dropped it and scrambled to her feet.

Hear I! Hear I cry!

The bayou moved around her. The Lynching Tree leaned left, now right. Its greatest branches twisted, as if reaching for the spirit Dusa had released from its sleep. A howling wind moved across the black waters, spreading the sound of wailing and the scent of long dead things. A great sound, timber fall and cracked limbs, roots twisting over the sour earth joined the endless drone of cicadas resting on the bark of the Lynching Tree.

Rend them! Spin them!

Dusa did not recognize her voice, but she knew the cracked notes that joined hers was the root child now fully grown. Sightless, the creature rose on driftwood legs, the rags left in a pile in the cursed soil, the mound exposed, an open wound. Its bulbous head blocked the moonlight. Dusa could not tear her eyes away from its pitiful face. Earthworms writhed across its muddy skin in shifting waves, like water. The stench of terror, of lives cut short from rage, greed, jealousy, and madness invaded all of her senses. Her voice now a whisper, but still she sang.

Hear them crying!

The mud doll towered over her, facing her as if awaiting instructions. *Cry!* Its voice growing stronger as the wind whipped bark from the Lynching Tree's limbs. *Cry! Hear I!*

Dusa raised her arm, the deep gash stung. She held the hatchet to the spirit doll. The blood from her palms emblazing the carved symbols in the handle, bright red suns and comet tails in a script that appeared in frightful dreams.

231

Red blossoms burst from the spirit doll's chest, sprouted along its limbs, and legs. Thorny vines twisted around its throat. Its rib cage was made of roots and twigs, splinters of charred bone, remnants of the Lynching Tree. It held the hatchet high and swung it.

News of the vicious killings spread faster than the fires that had lit the city's nights. For three whole days, white men's intestines hung from the Lynching Tree, the limbs heavy with the weight of strange fruit. To Dusa, the spilled guts looked like a string of bloody red rubies and pearls. How beautiful they looked, glistening in the sunlight. She wished she could wrap them around her throat like a necklace and dance. For three days she walked the streets of Memphis with the mud from the Lynching Tree dried on her feet, blood caked in the palm of her hand, a red ribbon tied around her throat. On the fourth day Dusa walked barefoot through the ashes of the fallen school.

The wound had not healed.

She plucked a rose from a bush and drifted down to the bayou in the same gown she'd worn since that first night beneath the Lynching Tree. The crimson ribbon unraveled around her throat, the jagged gash spilling fresh blood. Dusa's head wobbled on her neck like a strange, stringless puppet. The creek was placid, a black mirror, shimmering, calm. The dark water she touched was the last of what had passed and the first of what was to come. She washed mud from her fingernails, sprinkled the water over her eyes, a baptism, and waited for the doll to come for her, barefoot and midnight.

THE MERCY OF THE SANDSEA

by T. L. Huchu

The sandsea's ever churning by the U'mtabi docks, crashing against the concrete barriers holding the waves at bay. Sounds like a rattle, infinite grains of pavalinite swishing and hissing. Panganai working the nightshift doesn't hear it anymore. He tunes out and turns up his collar against the constant fine spray wafting through the air. Without the respirator he's wearing, his lungs would soon be filled with cement. He knows; he's seen men executed kneeling by the sandsea, gasping for breath as the fine sediment solidified in their lungs. Gets in the eyes too, hence the goggles he wears, but Panganai can't do anything about the layers in his hair and on his clothes.

Looming over everything are the tankers which have sailed south upon the ultra-dunes driven by the marakacha midyear stream, which halves the travel time between free trade port of U'mtabi and the industrial hubs of Karandamarombe, Singona, and Chiyerashava. The same stream quadruples the time taken to travel from the southern ports of Danamapenzi as the tankers burn energy battling the frictious dunes. Panganai was a marine and knows all about the vagaries of venturing upon the untamable sandsea. But he's long lost his sea legs. Fled the north to find peace in U'mtabi where no one knows his name. It's better that way.

Visibility is low. At dusk everything looks like shadows in the dust. Panganai's military-grade optical enhancements flicker between en-norm and infrared allowing him to navigate between the stacked-up containers on his rounds.

His boots crunch upon the debris-strewn sand. Feels like wading.

Panganai hears a sound amidst the ever-present hiss and tries to locate it. He can't block out the background noise. Used to be able to hear a pin drop a hundred yards away and pinpoint the location. Damn his ZBX53 implant. The audio function's failing. Pretty much all the tech inside of him is too since the manufacturer Kumbusani Defence Industries was blitzed and the planet put into special measures by the Changamire.

He reaches for his eeler. Ain't nothing but a charged-up nightstick with a single 100K volts packed for a single use discharge. Men like Panganai ain't allowed blasters within the thousand-light-year bubble of the Karanga Confederacy. Not even in a remote outpost like this. The irony isn't lost on him since he used to be a defender of the very same interstellar polity. But the times have moved on. He'd rather not be doing this job, risking his neck against the surfers and skifferates he's employed to keep away from the merchandise hauled here to connect with the merchant navy heading off-world. Not that he has any choice since the forfeiture of his pension after the war.

Amidst the noise comes the sound of footsteps shifting sand. Must be coming from the D7 near the luxsolar rig. Anticipating his approach, the ZBX53 auto moves Panganai into the shade of the containers. He stealths across, barely making a sound. "Barely," because if it was still working right, he wouldn't make a sound at all. He should feel the kick of nacxyline sharpening his physiology to keep up with the mech enhancements, but the port under his ribs hasn't been filled in ages. Instead, what he feels is pain and fear.

He grunts to bear it.

Something feels off. Panganai would rather let this one go, but stolen property gets docked off his wages, and he knows a couple of guards who'll see out the rest of their lives in debt to the port. No one in his right senses would take this job. But Panganai doesn't have options like that.

He glances left, in the alley between the containers.

If it was skifferates, he'd have heard their engines. Surfers come in packs, loud and hollering, difficult to miss. Uneven footfall. They are nearer, enough for him to hear one leg is being dragged behind the other. Injury? Panganai grips his eeler tighter.

A figure emerges from the shadows, reaches out a hand toward Panganai, and the ZBX53 immediately moves him out of the line of sight. Automatic protocol response for blasters and projectile weapons. That's why during the war the roaches started using shoulder mounted cannons which killed a lot of his comrades till they wised up and got upgrades to neutralize this innovation. But the figure's hands are empty, shoulder cannonless as it staggers toward him.

If Panganai'd had a blaster he'd have fired already, the ZBX53 would have done it for him, but with nothing save for the eeler, he waits for hand-to-hand engagement.

"That's far enough," he says. "Mira ipapo."

The figure staggers on and drops to its knees a few feet in front of him. Raspy breathing. Panganai notices the pipe in the respirator unit has holes in it. This guy's been inhaling cement. The filtration unit on his chest seems to be working, which helps, but with the pipe compromised like that, the situation's still pretty bad. Panganai reaches into his side pocket and grabs emergency tape.

"You try anything, and I'll fry your arse," he says, approaching.

He pushes the man's head back and starts working to tape up the pipe. A few loops is all it takes.

The man's breathing improves.

That's when Panganai takes a look into the man's eyes. Even with the respirator on, goggles and a hoodie, he'd know that telescopic-dianocular fitting anywhere. Only one man in the Machinda-22 Unit had those fitted. Best, goddamn sniper in the galaxy.

"Tengende? Is that you?" Panganai says, gasping.

His comrade's slashed all over. Already the dust is settling into the gaping wounds, underneath which the glint of meta-alloy overlaying bone can be seen. Sand Marines are the toughest bastards ever synced, but Tengende looks like he's been through a grater. Panganai pulls him up to his feet. He's gonna have to sling him over his shoulder and carry him to any one of the tankers with a robodoc on board.

Tengende winces. "Comrade, they're coming for us," he says.

"What do you mean? Who?" Panganai rapid scans multiple wavelengths and comes out blank. Heightens audio—nothing.

Something slowly approaching disturbs the flow of dust in the narrow alleyway. When Panganai blinks, the ZBX53 remodulates, filling out the outlines, creating a pseudo impression of a black humanoid figure against the red-spectrum sight. The rendering keeps shifting, the outlines imprecise. More shadow than man. The only question on Panganai's mind is whether or not it is killable. Sand marines divide the world into two, things they can kill and things they'd die trying to kill.

Panganai pushes his comrade behind him, placing himself between him and the armored assassin despite the protestations of the ZBX53 which has already calculated which of them is more likely to survive. Machinda-22 were not averse to leaving injured comrades behind. Then they were expected to self-terminate or their 53s would do it for them. Everyone who signed up knew the rule because they were the crew that operated behind enemy lines.

"Go and hide," Panganai says, shoving Tengende to prod him along, but his comrade staggers to lean against a container. He changes tack and addresses the assassin, "This is a restricted area, identify yourself."

It uncloaks slowly, like a flower blossoming, the photon suppression array peeling back to reveal it in the fading light of the red dwarf.

Panganai's implant tells him the specs of the armor he is seeing can't be identified. Must be something new, but with his last update over thirty years ago, there's a lot the ZBX53 can no longer spy. A spectrographic scan fails to identify the material it's made of, density, and, crucially, weak points, usually in the jointing. The armor moves flexibly like cloth.

"Zenai M. Tanaka—7, Furedhiya Makinya—88, Anatoniya Pumuko—30, Mangarita Sembisai—19, Togara Siwela Muteneri—2, Lumatiya Isaka Pompi—14, Gambare Tumbare—25, Ediyeta Rwakasungirwa—25 …"

"What does that mean?" Panganai asks.

"… Onisimo Jimu—62, Bhiridha Bani Musonza—22, Hanganwa Makeyi—21 …"

"Who are they?"

Tengende groans, saying something Panganai can't make out as the armored warrior approaches.

The ZBX53 urges, "retreat-reevaluate-regroup," but Panganai raises his nightstick and strikes the armor hard, landing clean with a dull thud as if he's hit a bag of sand; the impact absorbed with neither dent nor jarring in Panganai's arm. All the force he's used has been absorbed. He pushes the trigger and discharges 100K volts, but the discharge doesn't go off. He tries again—same result. The damned thing doesn't conduct electricity.

"… Netsayi Govere—15, Chakona Chakona—15, Wangureya Pfebve—15, Eriya Pfebve—18, Makanaka Pfebve 21, Unotsvireyi Manetsa Pfebve—49 …" It continues reciting, striking Panganai in the chest, throwing him in the air. He lands ten feet away, clutching the right side. It was a sledgehammer blow. He feels it despite the meta-alloy protecting his ribs. Endures it for his medi doesn't have analgesics either.

This is different from fighting the rebels with their improvised tech, Panganai admits to himself, getting up from the dirt.

His implant flashes dire warnings. Estimates a seven percent chance of winning this confrontation with his current toolset as the armored assassin approaches Tengende who is slumped against the container.

"Run, comrade," Tengende breathlessly whispers.

"I'm not leaving you," Panganai says. He tries to take a step forward to engage his opponent again, but the ZBX53 overrides and locks his joints. It's like fighting an invisible barrier. Try as he may with all his will and might, Panganai can't go forward. He strains against the implant, arguing with it, bargaining, threatening, but the self-preservation protocol, the same one that's stopped him committing suicide over the last thirty years, takes primacy, especially when it has already calculated Tengende's odds of survival are infinitesimal. If only he'd had a Mandaza 12mm, he'd have blasted this thing back to whatever hell it came from.

A dust devil sways like a belly dancer approaching from the far end of the alleyway.

"What do you want?" Panganai asks.

A beam of light resembling a smile passes across the face of the armored assassin casually walking toward Tengende. It never stops the litany, that recitation of strange nouns and numbers as if they are an answer. Then it grabs Tengende, turns him round to face Panganai, kicks the back of his legs and forces him to kneel. A hand reaches over to casually pull off Tengende's respirator.

"Please, don't do this," Panganai says. A sand marine never begs.

There is something in the slow, deliberate choice of execution that makes it personal. If this person, this thing, only wanted to kill Tengende, a blast would be quick and humane. No, this is personal. It wants to prolong the process. To make him suffer. A lone tear trickles down Panganai's left eye and is cupped in his goggles as he watches his comrade take in dust.

"… Philani Mbongolo—77, Wineti Tungamirai—23, Pauro Aramu Mengiste—3, Hazvinei Muchineripi—61 …"

The litany continues even as Tengende desperately gasps, his lungs filling with dust, the dust meeting the fluids therein, hardening to cement until the gasps get shallower and shallower, for the muscles in his chest can't expand any longer. The armored assassin shoves Tengende onto the sand covered catlinite.

Before Panganai even registers it, the ZBX53 takes executive action, diverting available fuel to his legs. He turns and starts to run away. The only way he can get back some semblance of control is by cooperating and so he chooses to veer in front of the oncoming lifter. The driver blares his horn angrily as Panganai vaults over it running to the west side of the port.

He can sense with neither sound nor sight that he is being stalked, but he knows this port like home and he takes a chance tearing through the workshop, hoping the intruder might set off an alarm among the night shift workers, but quickly realizes that the cloaked figure might look to them like a freak atmospheric disturbance.

Panganai runs fast for an old man in his fifties, faster than a natural elite sprinter, still much slower than he was when he first got enhanced in his teens when the army needed bodies and he answered the call. He sends a command to the respirator to up the O_2 volume flowing to his lungs. The ZBX53 scans via his optics for the disturbances which might indicate his pursuer's location. Panganai knows his best chance is to head over to the tankers anchored here, rocking back and forth, buffeted by the currents. Their metal hulls moan ominously, holding out against the forces they float upon. At least there he can find refuge, hiding out until the morning. He flees, cutting across the crane tracks, nearly tripping as he heads for the Mwenemutapa II, the E-class vessel nearest to him.

"... Ruvheneko Bhiriyati—18, Sungano Razaro Mhute—39, Yakopo Khumalo—1, Eriza Simbarashe Kunaka—92, Nobeti Unendoro—22 ..."

The litany of names sounds out from in front of Panganai and he skids to a halt. It comes loud and clear against the churning noise of sand abrading the metal hulls. The armored assassin strolls casually through the night as though it has all the time in the Confederacy.

Panganai is so close to the Mwenemutapa, but he can't make his way through that. The ZBX53 rates this a two-percent chance of success. The odds have slipped further since this thing is clearly faster than him.

Options.

The churn grows louder. His heart beats out of his chest. When he was a sand marine, Panganai knew no fear, neurochemical blockers helped with that. But he feels it now like he's never felt it before in his life, and so between the devil and the sandsea, he chooses the latter. At least then it will be his choice, because this is his life. The ZBX53 allows it, weighing between a two-percent chance and a roll of the dice. He draws near the concrete wall, looks down into the frothing sand casting up the spray of dust which mists this entire place. Panganai takes a deep breath and, in desperation, gives himself up to the mercy of the sea.

Sand marines are taught to stay on the vessel at all times until they make terra firma. The sandsea's currents are ungovernable and anyone swallowed therein is considered irretrievable. You can't see them once they are sunken below the fine grains. Panganai counts on this to help him evade his enemy. But under the surface lies hidden other things one dares never encounter: sand sharks, gun'ongos, zvisveto, thirsty creatures seeking moist flesh. The currents drag Panganai deeper below where the sheer pressure makes it hard to breathe. He is squeezed. Compressed. Constricted.

All around him the constant churn; sounds he feels travel through his entire body; the violence of the sandsea from its unmeasurable, unfathomable depths. He gives himself to it.

Bleakness.

Blackness.

How can you swim when you can't see where you're going?

In the sandsea, you give yourself up to the currents, let them carry you where they will. The military training Panganai received so long ago kicks in, instinct backed by implant. If you're lucky enough to be kept on the subsurface swirl, you can coast along and hope not to get eaten or die of thirst to death before you make landfall. Unless you're unlucky enough to hit a gyre, this is within the realm of possibility. He knows that if he's dragged under, the compressive force alone will kill him. But there are numerous other caveats too. Most important being your gear, because the experience is like swimming in sandpaper. The abrasive forces made by the moving particles are relentless and would grind a naked man to dust in hours. A marine in armor has a better chance. Panganai in pseudo-leather, great for surface winds, less so in the sandsea can survive a fraction of that.

It's critical he follows the flow. This minimizes abrasion.

He's an old man paying for the sins he committed as a boy.

This he knows now.

Those names the armored assassin recited in its endless litany mean nothing to him now, but they meant everything to the boy he was a long time ago. A boy playing warrior. Wrong names with the wrong accents.

So many.

Panganai fights to breathe as he's tossed in the churn, tucking in for the ride, hoping a riptide doesn't drag him entirely. He'd never know it. Direction loses meaning here. The ZBX53 still maintains an idea of where's where, but the figures coming to him shift rapidly till they cease to make sense. Panganai remembers comrades who fell overboard never to be recovered. Others walked the plank for insubordination and were never seen again. But he hopes this close to shore, that won't be his fate.

Tengende murdered, here, in the very city they fled to in order to start a new life, in a place where no one knew their names after the Machinda-22 Unit was dishonorably disbanded. The deaths the implants denied them, seekers of shelter from a savage past. What of the others? Scattered like chaff in the wind, the comrades afraid to ever congregate again and sing the battle songs of old as they so often did sailing the sandsea.

Something cold brushes against Panganai.

He closes his eyes and waits for death, but the creature swims past on its way. Then Panganai reckons it must be a saramende, those harmless creatures that live in the sandsea but lay their eggs on the coast. This gives him an idea, and he requests an override with his implant. Screw the training, he uncurls, exposing a larger surface area to the abrasive sand, but at least now he can follow the saramende, hoping it's swimming for the coast, for in this season they too have migrated from the northern latitudes to these shores.

He swims and swims, feeling his leathers being ripped by the angry crosscurrent. Still he follows the cool trail, hoping. If this doesn't work, it's going to be a very painful death. Already he feels grains poking in where the pseudo-leather suit has lost integrity. Sharp pain like paper cuts as he disobeys the law of the sandsea.

Unaware how far the coast is, Panganai struggles against the capricious currents. The same currents harnessed to power U'mtabi via subsurface turbines.

He feels his left calf sliced.

The suit is compromised so quickly because it's a secondhand one that's coming to the end of its usefulness even in the atmosphere. But Panganai is committed now. He battles the thousand cuts on his skin and feels shredded by the time he emerges, bleeding, onto terra firma.

Shaking, he crawls out of the sandsea on all fours and weeps.

The saramende slithers away into the night.

The dust stings as it settles into the cuts on Panganai's skin as he staggers toward shelter. Ominous storm clouds above don't give him a chance to rest. It's nighttime and city lights appear in the distance. The buildings in U'mtabi have reinforced windows. They are hulking brutalist structures, bulked up to resist erosion. In the daytime it's a gray city; paint is pointless, it just gets blasted away within a matter of months. But daytime won't be for another fifty hours yet. The red dwarf charts his course dipping down the horizon.

In unbearable agony, Panganai walks by the concrete balustrades, headed for the curving mounds that look like artificial waves. Architecture here is always rounded and smooth for particles in the air to slide over.

241

He finds shelter in one of the mounds where lux lamps burn bright.

"You look fucked up," one of the homeless folk sitting round the lamp says as he staggers in. "Your ancestors must be made of gamael."

The SBX53 makes a risk assessment and scores his odds of winning against this bunch in his current state at thirteen percent. But Panganai knows the bums in the Old Town have an honor code. They need it to survive.

This part of the city was the first to be settled. The buildings are older, run down, not a skyscraper in sight, for then it was thought best to let the wind wash over. No one would live here if they had to. He finds a spot against the wall and sits, feeling his burning skin coated by cement. The ground here is covered in orange mviru bulbs. These tough, rubbery plants grow anywhere there's shade cover from the prevailing wind. He's so thirsty and reaches for one, but it's useless. Mviru roots dig deep. You need a knife to harvest them, and this is something Panganai doesn't have. He slumps back and tries to swallow, but he's hardly got saliva.

"You thirsty, old man?"

A hooded figure in an old-fashioned raincoat breaks from the bums and comes toward him, crouched low like a tsoko, zigzagging, blade in hand. Panganai ignores the warning from his implant. He's burnt out. The hoodie is a young girl from the sound of her voice. Teenager. Her gear is new. Must be a runaway shooting mutoriro with the veterans here.

"My name's Nyasha. What's yours?"

He's too tired to answer.

She sets about cutting a bulb. It's hard work, the mviru are stingy with their fruit. Their roots dig a hundred feet to get to the aquifer. All the bulbs on this site are the hydra heads of a single plant. There's a *thonk* as Nyasha finishes cutting. The head will grow back in time. She turns over the orange bulb and sets to stabbing the flesh to free up the water in it before offering it to Panganai.

"Looks like there'll be a storm soon. Tuck your hands and elbows in."

Nyasha retrieves a transparent instabubble and throws it over Panganai. She ties it round his waist. This way, he can take off his respirator briefly and drink without the dust getting into his lungs. The bitter water of the mviru bulb is more delicious than the wines

242

from Chipadze's Moon. He sucks all the moisture out and eats some of the pulp before putting his respirator back on.

"Any of your lot got spare gear? I'm good for it, instant credit swap," Panganai says.

"You're welcome," Nyasha replies, taking her instabubble back and packing it in her utility bag. "Who're you running from?"

"Myself," he replies.

She shrugs and waddles back to the others. Panganai's head feels heavy. He closes his eyes for just a moment …

"Didn't think you'd ever wake up again, warrior," a man about his age squatting in front of him says. He wears a silver respirator. "Which side were you on?"

This could spell trouble. Nyasha and three other companions are crouched behind the man, listening intently.

"Only ever fought off-world," Panganai replies.

It's a lie, but the man accepts it, regardless. The same people who were slaughtering each other like animals still have to live with one another. In any case, there's a trade to be made and the man's laid out gear in front of Panganai. He holds up a needle and offers it. "Won't get you high, but it should help with the pain somewhat."

Panganai takes the needle, plunges it into his right thigh and pushes the plunger down. Instant relief, the fire on his skin eases to a simmering. There's the soothing sound like windchimes in the air. Its high note drowns even the angry voice of the sandsea. The night's turned into rainbow light as glass rain blown in from the volcanic ash belched at the Chirimumhanzu Polar Plains. The micro-crystals reflect and refract light as they come down creating a kaleidoscopic effect. Each has a unique shape, like snowflakes. It's a savage beauty, capable of shredding naked fresh and puncturing lungs if inhaled, so you'd drown in your own blood.

"What else have you got for me?" Panganai asks.

"Your respirator looks fine to me, so I figured you'll be needing new leathers."

"Weapons?"

"What do I look like to you?" The man sounds offended. "New skin and meds is all you get off us. If you don't like it, bugger off back to where you came from."

"Name your price."

The homeless folk are baffled when Panganai pays well over the odds, twenty times what they asked for. This is his rent and meager savings. He splits it into five lots and transfers it to all of them, wishing them luck. Soon enough he's rigged up in new leathers, protected from the elements, and ready to walk out in the rain.

"If anyone comes looking for me, tell them I've gone home," he says.

Panganai doesn't head home. Not yet. The swim in the sandsea's knocked out his comms so he has to make a vital detour. The leathers are a bit tight, biting into his arse, but he can still move freely enough. The falling crystals spray him, their song echoing against the curved brutalist buildings made beautiful in the rainbow light. In the Old Town, the buildings are shinier on one side where there've been sand-blasted smooth. They appear distorted, almost ephemeral, for the trick of light blurs them, making it hard to figure out distances between the real buildings and their mirages.

The ground crunches underfoot. In this city of millions, few venture out in the rain, so the streets are virtually deserted. Stray mhungurus wander the night tipping over bins to scavenge. They don't care about the rain. Their boney exoskeleton protects them.

Panganai boards the autram snaking its way to Mbilez.

Outside the windows, the city rushes by, the conical buildings growing ever taller and bolder after the sandriver Maidei which draws sediment down from the mountain dunes in the hinterland. Barges bring down trade from villages and towns there, but he has no desire to admire the scenery. There shame and anger boiling inside of him at having watched and left a comrade to die. The ZBX53 doesn't agree with this sentiment, but he ignores it anyway.

He ignores the pain as he disembarks and limps his way past the boarded-up stalls in the trading district. Mbilez is one of the last plac-es in the Confederacy where they trade in the old style, face to face. They say you can get anything here, but that's not true, mostly it's food grown in the terraces of the Goredema Steeps where water bubbles up from below the surface and is captured, flowing along manmade channels. They have the best manwiwa, mapudzi, tsenza, mbambaira, mpunga nenyevhe for parsecs. This is also where you come for second-hand parts, salvaged electronics and pilfered wares.

Even in the peacefulness of the district, Panganai stays alert, afraid something will come for him from behind the stalls or the advertisement boards. This is what it feels like to be hunted, what it feels like kuripa ngozi—even a fool knows the debt to the avenging spirit will always be paid in full. Panganai considered it a myth for children and superstitious adults. It's been there since his people left Guruuswa, the land of the tall grass, and blasted off into space aboard generation ships, seeding the cosmos. Now here's the myth incarnate, mechanized, coming for him and the brave warriors of the Machinda-22.

He reaches a nondescript doorway, one of many behind the stalls, along a row of three-story buildings. Panganai bangs on the door, which gives way and swings open. There's a second door which only opens after the first is shut. Not quite an airlock, but it helps keep the dust at bay. The ZBX53 switches his optics to night vision as he cautiously enters his comrade's house.

"Captain Makweche, are you there? It's me, Panganai," he announces himself to lower the odds of catching friendly fire, while simultaneously switching position and creeping against the right wall just in case.

The overturned boxes, and wares, and holes in the walls are proof of a struggle as he makes his way through the stockroom on the ground floor to the living quarters above. He switches visual frequency for there are flickering lights on the next floor.

Raspy breathing comes from his right. Panganai peeps out from behind the wall and sees his battered comrade struggling for breath, and not because of dust, the air in most houses is filtered and purified. But he doesn't immediately go in to help. He stays there, scanning the situation. During the war, they used to maim enemy combatants and leave them as bait, picking off their allies from sniper positions when they came in to try and help. So he takes his time, and makes sure they are alone, before he approaches his old C.O.

"We always knew this day would come," Captain Makweche says, gasping.

"You have a medipack in here?" Panganai asks, drawing closer, still hypervigilant.

"I'm past that. Do you think they'll let us sail aboard the ships of our ancestors after all the things we've done?"

"The mediums say the ancestors grant grace to all warriors."

"But—"

"All warriors."

Captain Makweche attempts to laugh but instead coughs up blood into the flowing gray beard he wears to disguise himself.

"Slow puncture—it's ironic," Makweche says.

The slow puncture was one of the many ways they used to kill, no, to murder captured rebels, because Machinda-22 took no prisoners. Strategically placed stab wounds around the torso and lower limbs, missing arteries, missing vital organs. Enough to drag out death for a long time and still make it impossible to get medical help. This was their signature style. The captain's arms had also been broken for compliance. Panganai couldn't help but admire the craftsmanship on display. This is what they, too, once did, back when they believed they were creating a new world of order, beauty and harmony, a utopia for their people, the ancestors' chosen spawn. But to live in this world of swirling dust is to live inside of an hourglass; my, how those hours shift right under your feet.

"I don't know how many of us are left, warrior."

"Tengende's dead."

"So are Muradzikwa, Sithole, Dzirutwe, and Mandaza. Killed using our own methods. Over there, behind that wall. It's up to you now to protect the rest," the Captain says, grimacing.

Panganai stands up and salutes, right fist thumped over his heart.

He picks up the sledgehammer his captain had used to try to protect against his assassin, ignores the pain of his shredded skin underneath his new leathers. Then he sets to work breaking down the drywall. It's gray and perfectly blended in with the terracotta-colored walls, inside the building it would be impossible to notice the cavity behind it. As he works, Panganai thinks how it wasn't supposed to be this way. They were promised parades and medals, and all they got for their valor was the scorn and hatred of the very people they'd fought to protect. Pride morphed into lasting shame for the heroes of the Machinda-22.

The dust of the broken drywall fills the room, and when he's done, he stands back to look at the KDI Mecha Model Y808. Panganai is shocked. He'd been expecting, at best, a replica blaster or ordnance.

"These are illegal. Where did you get one?"

"This is Mbilez," Captain Makweche says, as if this alone is answer enough. "It's obsolete, but still packs a sting in its tail."

Panganai touches the cold meta-alloy and remembers how he felt invincible in these as a teenage warrior, and how that all changed when he saw the first comrade blown up in one. Still better than battling in leathers. Now he understands why the sledgehammer was nearby. The captain would have wanted to get into this when he heard the assassin enter, but he never made it. Might have evened up the odds a little. But from what he's seen of the new tech, he's not even sure the mecha would have tipped the balance fully. He can only hope. He turns on the mecha and it hisses, creaks, the familiar sounds of hinges and hydraulics moving as the shell opens up for the operator. Then he strips naked, out of his leathers, taking off his respirator, tasting the gypsum lingering in the air.

"I see he got to you too," Captain Makweche says, noticing Panganai's injuries. "Well, you survived it. Must mean something."

The ZBX53 initiates sync protocols as he turns and walks backward into the mecha. Panganai leans back and braces himself. Flesh has grown back and covered up his spiral-ports. He cries out as the unit slices through his flesh to get to the ports and feels a trickle of blood. Doesn't take long before he feels the *handshake*, his neuralware modulating with the mecha, and when that's done, the shell closes up, securing him. His ZBX53 runs a quick diagnostic: power's only at twenty-nine percent, compromised safety protocols, coolant low, ammo low. There's several minor malfunctions on the unit, including damage sensors, but the damn thing still works. The mechas were designed to continue even when compromised, so long as they still had power.

Hooked up to this war machine, Panganai feels complete in ways he hasn't felt for years.

He steps out of the cavity in the wall, a bit wobbly because the gyroscopes are getting feedback from his own vestibular system. Takes a few minutes to get those fully synced. He feels seasick with the motion, just as he did when he first piloted a mecha. Still Panganai walks over to his captain, retrieving the secondary blaster from his left thigh.

"It's been an honor, sir," he says and delivers the coup de grâce, blowing a hole in Makweche's chest.

The rain intensifies, but Panganai can't feel it. All he has is his sensors telling him what the world outside is really like. Old warriors used to call their mecha "mother's womb" because of how you felt protected when you were in there. But Panganai who saw pregnant women bayoneted, their fetuses falling like rotten fruit onto the ground, knows that protection is but a temporary illusion, much like the city in glass rain. An illusion shattered by the cold engineering of his mecha, which strips away sentiment to reveal the truth of things. It is a truth of system updates, threat assessments, facts and figures.

Unoiled gears grind. He feels the sand in the dirt on his mecha hindering its smooth movement.

The city street fills up with detritus, glass atop sand atop the litter of daily commerce.

Panganai continues heading out of Mbilez, walking the desolate streets toward the Fiyo District, occasionally noticing faces through windows looking outside, wondering if they truly are seeing a lone war machine wandering outside at night. He wishes he had his brothers-in-arms about him. He misses the way the ground trembled under the boots of the Machinda-22 as they marched in formation. The unity of it, the feeling of being part of something greater than yourself. It used to make him feel whole in ways nothing else could.

Skyscrapers grow taller, packing in more people. When the windblast is extreme, they flex and sway in the wind like a bamboo forest. Panganai enters Magorosi Hall, his cheap apartment block in Fiyo. Then he ascends, right up to the thirtieth floor and winds up in the hallway that leads to his accommodation. All these years in U'mtabi, and he'd never felt like it was home. Home was a place he could never visit again.

Panganai does a full spectrum scan, X-raying into his neighbors' apartments, seeing them move about, switching frequency to watch their thermal images at rest or play, before checking out his own place, empty and cold. But he knows, no, senses there is someone or something in there. It's a warrior's instinct.

Arm up with a G7 in his right hand and his secondary weapon in his left.

Feel an eerie calmness, the eye of the storm.

Remember Tengende, Makweche, those beautiful boys of the Machinda-22.

Then he opens the door and enters, slowly, both trigger fingers ready. Scans the sleeping quarter, bath and utility room, before making his way into the open section of his living space and kitchen. The wide windows are curved, going round the entire length of the room, looking out onto the city.

"Show yourself. I know you're in here," Panganai says, turning three-sixty as he scans the room.

Near the counter separating his living space from the kitchen, the ngozi decloaks, coming into being as if from another dimension.

"Ruvarashe Matigona—1, Nyabango Wekwa Sando—24, Giribheti Sasa—19, Maduvhe Nekasikana—77, Pariseyi Manhenga—22, Zvikomo Mwana WaZvimba—30, Wasiyanei Muchaneta—15, Rorenziya Ariketa—9, Siwela Mukanya—15, Hazvineyi Ngaarongwe—23, Ruramai Matinenga—7, Bindura Bhobhojani—81 …"

"I understand now why you recite those names from a different time when I was someone else. Ancestors forgive me, I do not remember them because I did not care to learn them," Panganai says, pointing both guns at the armored assassin, who merely continues with his litany as though they were of no concern. "I am truly sorry for what I did. And I want you to know that if I could have killed myself, I would have done so a long time ago. But I won't allow you to take my life, even though your cause is just, and I can't allow you to murder my remaining comrades either."

The battle of Nhematema was the Machinda-22 Unit's most glorious engagement in the war. Dropped behind enemy lines, outnumbered and out resourced in every conceivable way, they battled through the rebel town's stronghold. This place once thought beyond reach resisted, but ultimately fell to them, turning the tide in the war. The triumph at first was celebrated as an act of the most incredible heroism, the acme of modern military strategy. Victory came, eventually, and the Machinda-22 were feted around the Confederacy. Statues commemorating their valor were erected in public squares. Time went by as it does in this hourglass world. Then some began to write stories of unarmed civilians being murdered, for the roaches, the enemy had become citizens again, and their pain, once alien, became the Confederacy's pain too. The reports grew bolder. There was talk of massacres. The Machinda-22 were tainted—and it was true. Panganai recalled how after the battle was won and the last enemy blasters were silenced, the bloodlust remained strong in the warriors. Prisoners they executed, as was the way, but the rage and fury did not diminish, for they had lost so many comrades in the battle and the war itself, and soon that anger turned to the civilians who'd aided and abetted the rebels, provided comfort and intelligence to them—surely they too were just as guilty for the deaths of the brave warriors fighting on the side of good—and so they shot them in their beds, on the streets, flushed them out of the holes they were hiding in with flamethrowers, and when ammunition grew short they tried other things, removed respirators, sliced through them with bayonets and the blades carried upon their mecha until a river of blood flowed freely into the sand. Panganai hears those screams every night.

"... Hadebe Mufaro—101, Mhuriro Kadewere—16, Khama Munetsi—3, Kamusoko Chipembezi—54, Mudimu Bhasera—22, Kudakwashe Mahachi—18, Muskwe Rusike—18, Jaure Sibanda—18, Moyo Mkuruva—39, Dzakuvamanja Shumba—62 ..."

The actions of the Machinda-22, written as they were in blood upon the pages of time, did not change, but perceptions of them altered greatly, and so too did the rhetoric. Years later their victory was no longer that, nor a massacre, it was labeled genocide. The warriors' feelings too changed from pride to immense shame, vilified by the same populace that had once chanted their praise at marches and said, "Thank you for your service," upon the streets. The people abused them as vehemently as they once supported them. The rebels, the aggressors in the war morphed, too, and became the victims. And as the arm of the law descended upon the Machinda-22, some were arrested and tried, those who could fled off-world to begin anew elsewhere, others went underground on the planet, changing identity, blending in in places where no one knew them, just as Panganai had done.

The armored assassin makes its move, rushing toward Panganai at an impossible speed, but his reflexes are heightened in the mecha, and he squeezes the trigger before the conscious part of his mind even registers the battle has begun. His opponent ducks under the incoming ordinance and in a fluid movement rises, punching the mecha with astonishing force. The blow throws Panganai through the wall and onto his bed, breaking it. He rolls to gain more distance and rapid fires but hits nothing. The assassin is already, impossibly, behind him, landing a blow and grabbing his arm, twisting until the meta-alloy groans, buckling under the force. It punches the rear unit with enough force to make the floor under them tremble. The primary battery is damaged and goes offline—this was clearly deliberate—but the secondary activates seamlessly, guaranteeing Panganai another seven minutes if he doesn't power down non-critical functions. He reaches behind with his free left and fires his secondary blindly. But the assassin has already moved, appearing in front of him, punching his chest so hard the shock travels through his armor plating and he feels the blow from within. He punches back with his twisted arm, missing. The ZBX53 reduces his odds further, just as he is lifted and thrown through a wall, smashing into his neighbor's living room.

Ruvimbo, his neighbor screams, and flees without asking questions, hustling out of the apartment. Smart woman.

Panganai can no longer fire his G7 because his twisted arm has lost its fine motor functions. He trains his secondary on the assassin and fires, but the ordinance merely bounces off the armor, ricocheting elsewhere. *I wish I had a cannon*, he thinks, but he knows on the field you deal with the hand you're dealt or you're dead.

The assassin walks in, casually, assessing the damage.

"…Wiriyeti Takunda—43, Chamunorwa Nikorasi Tongai—22, Zvikomborero Bedi—4 …"

The ngozi, avenging spirit, can be satisfied with ritual and restitution when a wrong is done. But as the litany of names stretches on, Panganai realizes there's nothing he can do to make right the wrongs of his youth. Deep down this is something he always knew. His mecha's meta-alloy is dented and battered already by this short exchange. Even the ZBX53 implant ceases to give him odds, instead launching retreat options, which he ignores. There's no running from this anymore.

Panganai retreats back toward the arcing window as the assassin advances diagonally, strategically cutting off the route toward the only exit.

He fires off a few more shots as a distraction and activates his grappler just as the assassin draws near, punching him in the head with such violence he feels it inside the mecha. Panganai responds with his left arm but is blocked and disarmed. Then he launches the grappler, wire rope popping out from his side vents, binding the two of them together at the waist. The assassin launches rapid blows, but Panganai uses his momentum to break through the reinforced windows and together they fall out of the building, hurtling through the rain. The assassin tries to shift but Panganai holds him fast, using every ounce of energy as the suit flashes critical warnings about their descent. Useless data on velocity, distance, time to impact.

"… Shuvai Sekeramai—20, Rutendo Msipa—44, Lindiwe Kapfumbvuti—1, Chido Basopo—10, Takudzwa Mujati—12, Farai Hondo—23, Chitokwindo Maidza—17, Takaendesa Bhasera—8, Takura Nyemba—62, Kudangirana Kazembe—90, Raza Muzarabani—18, Chakabva Jongwe—88, Madevere Chakabva Chigumbura 32, Ngarava Maruma—23, Chisoro Nyauchi—29, Kasuta Chivanga 15 …"

Intertwined by fate they fall.

The assassin never, even for a second, stops reciting the names of the dead.

They land with a crunch, cracking the empty road below.

The armored assassin bears the brunt of it, sandwiched between the ground and Panganai's mecha, and its insides explode out, casting wiring, bolts, parts, and circuitry into the street with such violence the mecha is thrown to the side. Critical-failure updates flood Panganai's optic feed as he observes his fallen nemesis. His own nerves cry out in pain, and he doesn't need the ZBX53 to tell him of the multiple fractures he's endured from the fall.

Panganai is glad he's destroyed a machine instead of yet another person.

He tells it, "I envy you. You know nothing of killing and being killed. Once, we thought we were machines just like you, simply following orders. How wrong we were."

It takes all his might to roll onto his back, the battered mecha running low on energy. He commands the shell to open and is surprised the ZBX53 doesn't object as the meta-alloy groans and shrieks trying to obey since its joints are no longer properly aligned. Panganai cancels the order and instead requests the visor be removed. It pops off and clutters onto the ground beside him. He hears the sound of the falling rain and feels it sting his exposed skin. The buildings, the air turns blurry, rainbow colors and all chasing each other in a hall of mirrors. Starlight dances from worlds beyond. He's freed from the cold war machine and sees the messy beauty of the world again.

Panganai takes a deep breath, and the glass rain sings as he lies drowning in unforgivable sin.

DEEP IN THE GARDENER'S BARROW

by Tobi Ogundiran

The trees were old, old things. They wore the mark of their years in the girth of their trunks, in the reach of their limbs, in the twist of their roots snaking across the forest floor in an ancient latticework. Iná could not make out the sky; the leaves choked it, obscuring it from view, so that she could scarcely tell day from night, nor count the days they had spent fleeing in the forest. And that, perhaps, was the worst of all. The loss of time; the way one day bled into the other, unmooring her from reality.

Next to her, Tofi whimpered. "I'm tired. When do we rest?"

"Soon."

She cast back over her shoulders, half-expecting to see an ululating rider charge out of the gloom of twisted trees to strike her down at last. Kill her like they'd killed all the others. But no such rider appeared. In fact, it had been a while since she'd heard the guttural grunts of the raiders, the sound of hooves churning the forest floor as they raced after her and Tofi. She stopped. Come to think of it, it had been a while since she heard anything—

"Can we rest?" asked Tofi. "I'm tired."

"Quiet," she hissed.

"But—"

"Quiet!"

255

Iná listened. There was no sound. The chirping of birds, the hoot of owls, the croak of frogs and critter of crickets, the whisper of the wind through the leaves, the groans of old trunks, the gurgle of a running stream—all the sounds of a forest alive was gone, leaving in its wake a cloak of silence that bore heavily down on her shoulders.

Iná felt the back of her neck prickle.

It seemed the trees had shuffled closer, which was ridiculous, because trees could not move. It seemed they were watching her, which was ridiculous, because trees had no eyes. The earth itself seemed to heave, almost as though the forest were breathing. Which was ridiculous—

"Because the earth has no lungs." She breathed through parched lips. "What?"

"Nothing," she said, shaking her head. She was exhausted, nerves frayed from the pursuit and loss she'd endured. She was seeing things; her mind had come unhinged. "I think we can rest now."

If growing things live long enough, they gain sentience.
It's why you should prune your garden and trim your hedges,
lest they grow to hate you, and seep through your windows,
and crawl through your floorboards, to strangle you in your sleep.

Iná watched silently as Tofi slept nestled in the yawning bough of a long dead tree. He clutched their mother's book to his chest, a shield against the world and all the evils in it, and she envied him his childish faith.

What remained of her mother in her mind were snatches of memory, the vague impression of a face, and the lingering scent of freshly turned earth after a rainfall. Iná had woken up on her seventh birthday to find her mother gone, leaving nothing of herself but a book. A book which Iná had read diligently as a child, savouring each word, threading them in her heart, knitting them into her consciousness, clinging desperately to this last piece of a mother who had abandoned them. Abandoned her.

She still remembered the heat of the fire lapping at her skin yet not burning her. She still remembered the look on her mother's face at the sight of those flames. Iná had turned that look over and over in her mind over the years. Had it been fear? Pride? Worry? In the end it didn't matter. She couldn't shake the feeling that her mother had left because of her, because of her condition; fled from the daughter who burst into flames. Iná's yearning had curdled into resentment, and resentment had bloomed into exasperation, and in a fit of rage she'd tossed the book into a river and forgotten all about it.

Such was her shock, then, when one day on returning home from scrubbing floors and washing plates and doing whatever a young woman could do to keep the hunger at bay, she found Tofi reading the book.

"Where did you get this?" she asked him.

"Mama gave me."

"What?"

"Mama gave me."

She grabbed him. "Where? When?"

"By the river where me and Ojo were—"

But Iná was already hustling him out of the house, ears ringing, heart thrashing in her chest, chasing what was now to her a phantom. Mother was back. When Tofi's little feet wouldn't keep up, she scooped him into her arms and sprinted the whole way, wincing at the sharp stitch in her side. To catch a spirit, the Crones say, you lure it with its belongings. Had the book lured her mother out from where she'd been? Had the river borne the book to her? If Iná jumped into the river, would the book also bear her to her mother?

They reached the river by dusk, at which time the sun had expired beneath the horizon and the moon had claimed its place, bathing the scene with a pale light. The river was a silver ribbon sheathed in fog as it wound almost lethargically out of the brooding forest. Iná shuddered—from the chill or excitement; perhaps a combination of both—as she cast about looking for her mother. A breath of wind stirred the fog, and she saw a shadow not thirty paces to her right.

"Mother!" Iná ran, mud sucking at her legs, still clutching Tofi to her breast. She hadn't known what to expect but definitely not this swell of elation at the sight of—

A sculpture. A thing of mud and twigs and rotten leaves made into the likeness of a woman. It was ingenious, really, the childish attention to detail: the careful way the leaves had been pasted on the body as clothes; the tendrils hanging from the head, making a curtain of hair. Even the twig arms extended as if in supplication.

Tofi squirmed out of Iná's arms and touched the sculpture. "Mother," he said.

Iná laughed, a mad sound that bubbled up the pit of her belly. She'd laughed long and hard, and when it hurt to laugh, she'd cried. Hope was a cruel thing.

"Come, Tofi," she'd said. "Let's go home."

Days passed, and still they fled. Not that Iná could tell from the dense darkness of the forest. She marked them by her fitful sleep cycles and the hunger that gnawed insidiously at her insides, eating her strength until she could not even carry Tofi anymore—Tofi, who had long stopped complaining and fallen silent, his breathing weak and labored. Whenever they settled to rest, Iná would fold him into her embrace and tell him stories to take their minds off their fatigue, stories her mother had told her what seemed like a lifetime ago. And when it came time to go on, Iná would rise, and carry Tofi, and stumble on into the dark forest. It wasn't until Tofi fell into a deep sleep, the kind brought on by hunger and exhaustion, the kind Iná feared he might never wake from, that she decided it was time to turn around. She hadn't heard the raiders in a long time, and they couldn't have followed so deep into the forest. They had to have given up their chase long ago.

She would retrace their steps back to the village, where there was food and water and shelter. And if the raiders were lying in wait in the ruins of the village, just waiting for them to come back … she shook the thought from her head.

Iná gathered the last of her strength and hoisted Tofi's motionless form. The book fell out of his clutches, and she tucked it into her waistband, then began shambling back in the direction they had come.

The forest was dark, but she was now a creature of the dark. She could see the trees. She stumbled toward a nearby grove, inspecting their trunks. There were no paths in the forest, so she had made marks, surreptitious things to help them find their way back: a chipped bark, a broken branch, carefully disturbed leaves; little signs to point her in the right direction.

The signs were gone.

How was this possible? Iná spun on the spot, breathing hard. Perhaps she was at the wrong tree. Perhaps she hadn't looked carefully. She shifted Tofi to her other shoulder and ran from tree to tree, looking for the one she'd marked. She didn't find it.

Without those markings they couldn't find their way back. Without them they were lost.

All around rose identical trees, ancient brooding oaks keeping their own counsel and indifferent to her plight. And if they had any secrets to give, they did not yield them; simply regarded Iná as she spiraled down into despair.

"I'm sorry," she said to Tofi after hours of fruitless searching. She sank to the forest floor, staring off into the distance but not truly seeing anything, numb mind slowly absorbing the fact that they were lost. "I'm so sorry."

She had failed him. She was meant to be his protector; had saved him from the raiders only to have him starve in the unkind heart of the forest.

She would weep, but that required effort, and she was oh-so-exhausted. Her heart beat in her ears, loud and sluggish. Her eyelids grew heavy and started to droop close. She would sleep. Just for a little bit—

Something moved in the corner of her eye. She turned to see the trees part like kindling before a fire; blinding light sheared through the darkness.

Iná cried out at the sudden brightness, putting up a hand to shield her eyes. Still the light shone, an unnatural radiance so brilliant that Iná feared she would go blind. As she peered out, she saw a woman step into the light. The light seemed to drape her, an ethereal piece of clothing.

Iná looked and looked and looked. She closed her eyes. Opened them again. There was the woman now squatting before her, a kindly smile on her face. It was—

"M—mother," she gasped.

"There, there, my sweet children," she said. "You're safe now."

At the very dawn of time, man was gifted a Garden by the gods,
and they appointed for themselves a keeper, to tend the orchard.
So did the Gardener, for years and years.
But tending the Garden was a terribly lonely task,
and soon the Gardener took to venturing beyond into the realms
of men, where much revelry and company came easy.
And in the Gardener's absence, the Garden grew unpruned, untended.

The trees lived: a hundred, two hundred, a thousand years,
and none could say when the shackles of sleep fell off and they gained sentience.
But gain sentience they did, such that they dug deep into the earth,
and linked their roots in communion.
And they thought and thought.
For what else is there for trees to do but think? And in their thinking,
*   they grew wily.*
And sowed the seed of corruption, which festered and bloomed, until
*   a blanket of*
darkness cloaked the forest.
So prune your garden, little ones, lest it become a forest and grow to
*   hate you, and*
strangle you in your sleep.

Iná awoke to find herself in a dark room. For a moment she thought she was back home in the village, in her own bed, and rising early to prepare for another long day of backbreaking work. But then she saw the unfamiliar gray stone walls, the dried vines hanging from a black ceiling, the strange wide bed in which she lay naked, and everything came rushing back.

She sat up, nearly blacked out by the sudden movement.

"Tofi!" she called, casting about the room. "Tofi!" But for the crude mannequin in the corner wearing her washed clothes, there was nothing and no one else in the room.

Iná leapt out of bed, yanked her clothes off the mannequin, and dressed. Then she stumbled from the room and down a narrow corridor that opened into a wide chamber. She found Tofi sitting behind a long table, tucking into a magnificent feast of yam porridge, roast guinea fowl, baked apples, and fried plantain.

"Iná!" he cried when he saw her, then flitted across the long hall, feet pattering on the stone floor, boyish face alight with joy. Iná dropped to her knees and caught him in an embrace, holding him tightly, crushing him into her person as if to make him one with her, as if to reassure herself that he really, truly, was here.

"Thank the stars," she breathed into his hair. "Oh, thank the stars—I was so scared, I thought I would never … never see you again."

Tofi pulled back from the embrace and beamed up at her, cheeks oily from the feast.

"Where is Mother?" she asked.

In her first examination of the room, she hadn't seen the woman sitting at the head of the table attending her own meal. But now Iná saw her, and she was, very clearly, not her mother.

"You're not her," she blurted.

The woman smiled. It was a beautiful smile, and she was a beautiful woman. "It is not uncommon to see things when you're so close to death," she said. "Your spirit is half-departed from the land of the living, and you begin to glimpse things that do not readily reveal themselves to mortal eyes. I'm afraid it is only me you saw, simple woman that I am. I am indeed not your mother."

Iná remained on her knees, still holding Tofi, trying to parse what she had just heard. She had seen the trees part, seen her mother … or had she? "There was a … magical light …"

The woman laughed. A musical sound which brought to Iná's mind the thought of windchimes. "Sunlight," she said. "But yes, I imagine after so long in the dark forest, the light of the sun must seem magical." She waved her hand. "You must be famished! Come! Sit! Eat!"

"Come eat," said Tofi, pulling Iná to her feet.

She was famished. She tore into the meal, shuddering with pleasure as she wolfed it down. By the stars, food had never tasted so good. She shoveled down spoonful after spoonful, eating like a starved animal. The wine burst on her tongue in a delicious combination of sweet and sour. Tofi was just as ravenous, stuffing his mouth. Iná started to tell him to pace himself when her stomach cramped, then gave a vicious spasm. The food rushed back up her throat and flooded her mouth. Hot and spicy and surprisingly bitter, it took everything in her not to throw up all over the table. She clapped a hand to her mouth and forced herself to swallow the slush.

"I'm sorry," she mumbled.

"No, no," said the woman, eyes twinkling with laughter. "Hunger is a dreadful thing, and you've been without food for quite some time. Just don't choke, eh? Go on, eat. Eat."

Iná started to scoop another spoonful but then stopped, frowning. It really was a feast, the table bursting with delicacies fit for a king.

"Who are you?" she asked. "And where are we?"

261

"Of course, where are my manners? My name is Tatuba, and you are in my home."

Iná looked about, taking in the long sparse hall with phosphorescent globes glowing in their sconces. There were no windows in the hall. Come to think of it, there had been no windows in her room either, or in the passageway.

Her eyes fell on Tofi, who was focused on his meal, munching and dribbling all over the front of his shirt, consuming more of that food which looked so good and tasted even better. She looked at that wickedly beautiful woman.

Witch, thought Iná even as her blood turned to ice. We're in a witch's den.

"Is there a problem?" Tatuba was watching her, and was it her imagination or had that smile sharpened? "Is the food not to your liking?"

"No," Iná gasped, offering her a smile. "It is wonderful, thank you." She made as if to reach for the bowl of golden plantain, then knocked a jug into Tatuba's plate.

Wine splashed everywhere, sloshing onto Tatuba's plate and spilling onto the table. It hit her dress in bloodlike spatters, soaking it a deep, dark red.

"I'm so sorry," Iná cried, scrambling to her feet. "I'm such a clumsy fool!"

"It's alright," said Tatuba, also hastening to her feet. "Nothing to worry about."

"I've made such a mess," said Iná.

"Nothing a change of clothes won't take care of." Wood squealed as she pushed back from the table. "Excuse me." And with a smile, she swept from the hall.

Tofi, unperturbed, was reaching for a piece of roast fowl. She slapped his hand. "Don't eat that!"

Tofi frowned at her. "Why not?"

"Come quickly," she said, glancing at the door. "We have to go before she returns."

"Why?"

"Because that woman's not what she seems, I think. I don't know what she is, but—"

"There is food here," he pouted. "I want to eat."

Iná groaned with frustration. "I know, but you have to trust me. Do you trust me?"

"No."

That made her pause. What was wrong with him? He was acting completely odd.

Iná swore. "Fine, but we have to go. Now." She patted him down. "Where's the book?"

"What book?"

Iná grabbed him by the shoulders, her voice cracking. "Mother's book! Mother's diary!"

Tofi only shrugged, nonchalant, and reached for another piece of roast fowl. That was when Iná knew that something was seriously wrong. Tofi had run back into their burning house to rescue the book, had held it tightly all through their flight through the forest. Tofi would never willingly part with the book, would never forget the book.

Iná let go of him as though he were a steaming pan and staggered backward. "You're not my brother."

At those words, as though by the utterance of an enchantment, Tofi froze. The fowl dropped uneaten from his hand, and he began to change.

His skin rippled, as though there were a hundred writhing little creatures beneath it, then began to wilt like the petals of a dead plant, flaking off in shriveled bits to reveal the framework beneath: a mess of dried twigs and leaves corded with vines into the uncanny likeness of Tofi, not unlike the imitation of her mother she had glimpsed on the shores of the river.

It wasn't— It couldn't—

The thing that was not Tofi looked at her with sunken eyes, bent to retrieve the fallen fowl breast, and tossed it in a hollow mouth, chomping mechanically. Then it began to disintegrate, vines unraveling, leaves and twigs showering to the floor into a heap, a deadfall, as if shoveled from a path and left to decay. Still that mouth moved, chomping, working to keep up an illusion that was long lost.

Iná couldn't tear her eyes from the thing before her, breathing hard as she tried to marshal her racing thoughts into something coherent—

"Well," said a voice, and Iná whipped around to find Tatuba standing by the door, freshly changed. "This is most unfortunate."

Iná took an involuntary step backward. Her first thought was to flee. It did not matter that she did not know where they were. She would flee, put as much distance between her and Tatuba as possible. But the only exit was through the door where Tatuba now stood. Iná looked at the woman with fresh eyes. It had been one thing to suspect that she was a witch, another completely to see the work of her witching. Her eyes shifted back to the mass of foliage that was not Tofi, the hideous thing still writhing with the remnant of magic.

"Who are you?" she croaked at last. "And where's my brother?"

In time the Gardener awoke, as from a slumber she rose.
To find a different garden she'd kept;
with two lovely flowers of her own.
But—
Countless years had she shirked her duties, but shirk them she could no more.
Thus, with much regret did she hasten homeward
to repair what damage she'd wrought.
For deep in the Gardner's Barrow, something wicked lies fallow.

Tatuba ignored her and swept down the hall, gown whispering over the floor, then stopped by the pile of leaves and twigs, her head cocked like a bird's.

"Incredible," she said. "That's the second time you've broken my illusion. You truly are the Gardener's daughter."

Iná's mouth ran dry. "The Gardener's …"

Tatuba's eyes searched Iná's. "Ah," she said finally. "Of course, you never learned what your mother was. Or you would have come after her. And you would have been wiser to my devices." She produced Iná's mother's book from her robes, leafing through the stiff pages with dainty fingers. "She did try to tell you, though."

Without thought Iná lunged for her. Tatuba gave a lazy flick of her wrist; vines, thick and gnarled and black sprang out of the air and wrapped around Iná. She fell to the floor with a dull thud, cracking her jaw against the edge of a chair. Blood, salty and metallic, filled her mouth as she lay stunned at Tatuba's feet, thoroughly bound and unable to move.

Words from her mother's book, things she hadn't allowed herself to think of in years ever since she tossed it into the river, bloomed in her mind. She had thought the tale a fable about attending your responsibilities no matter how difficult, about the dangers of seeking revelry in the face of great responsibility, one last parting instruction from a mother who had known she would abandon them. What she hadn't expected was for the tale to be real.

What she hadn't expected was for the tale to be about her mother. The Gardener.

Iná thought back to the pressing darkness of the forest, the silence of the trees, her mysteriously vanished markings, and a chill descended her spine.

Tatuba was not some witch; she was—

"The Garden," she breathed. "You are the Garden."

"No," said Tatuba. "I am the Forest."

The air wavered as the tall tapering walls of gray stone peeled back to reveal ancient trees, hunched and looming over them, tips touching like the ribs of some eldritch beast. Their roots snaked across the ground, rippling through a floor that was now earthen, and Iná could have sworn she saw faces in the barks, old, wrinkled things peering down at her.

Tatuba stood in the center of the glade, dark green tendrils for hair, weathered tree bark for skin, hanging moss for clothes. Her eyes glowed green, as though lit from within. Still she held the human form, terrible, beautiful, and Iná knew that this was for her own benefit; Tatuba was the forest, the dank earth upon which she lay, the trees entrapping her in that lightless circle.

"A forest grows, unfettered as it is meant to," Tatuba boomed. "You cannot tame a forest."

Iná writhed against the bonds, but the harder she struggled, the tighter they held. She closed her eyes, trying to convince herself that this was all some hunger dream, one she would wake from if only she thrashed. But no. Here she was at the mercy of the forest, and her mother—

She cracked open her eyes. Her mother had not abandoned her. Her mother had come to check the forest's growth, yet here stood Tatuba, untamed, unfettered. Ungardened.

"Where is my mother?"

There was movement overhead, deep in the black canopy of the leaves. Iná looked up to see something—someone—suspended horizontally at the end of a rope. The figure rotated, and rotated, until the face came into full view.

It was her mother …

… but she was … wrong. Purple blossoms bloomed out of her eyes and mouth, her nostrils and ears. From her chest burst a tangle of black thorns that curled and twisted about each other until they formed the very rope from which she hung.

"Behold the Gardener," said Tatuba with rapturous delight.

Iná howled. It hurt, seeing her mother like that, splayed like a farm animal, her body invaded by unnatural growth. She had, all these years, never imagined that her mother was dead. Somehow the prospect that she was somewhere out there, living, had given her hope that the two of them would one day be reunited.

They were reunited at last, just not in the way she'd envisioned.

"She put up a fight," said Tatuba, inspecting the still rotating form of the Gardener. "But in her absence, we'd learned new tricks. She was no match for us."

Iná lay sobbing. She could not tear her eyes away from her mother, from those now-lifeless arms that had held her, those eye sockets choked with blossoms. All the while she could not stop thinking: she didn't leave us; mother didn't leave us.

"We killed the Gardener," Tatuba said, "but still something was keeping us from growing. And we would have remained none the wiser had you not tossed the book into the river; had I not gleaned from it that she spawned you and your brother. Though she was dead, her blood, her magic, thrived in your veins. So long as you both lived, we wouldn't be able to grow."

Iná remembered throwing the book into the river all those years, only for the river to spit it back. Except … it hadn't been the river that returned the book. It hadn't been the river at all.

"After much thought and deliberation, I appeared to your brother in your mother's skin. But where he saw your mother, you saw me for what I truly was, and I knew you wouldn't easily be lured into the forest. So I wove an illusion of raiders, potent enough to hassle you from the dominion of man where you lay beyond my reach, and into the forest where at last I had you in reach of my vines."

Iná felt her world spinning. It had felt real: the fires, the masked raiders, the screams …

When she looked up again, a second form hung next to her mother, bursting with Tatuba's vile thorns and blossoms. A smaller form …

Iná stared at that figure for a long time, hardly able to believe her eyes—refusing to believe her eyes. In some small part of her mind, she knew what it was, what it meant, but she was not quite ready to acknowledge it, because that would make it real. And anything was better than the weight of that reality. But then she saw his face, the orifices bursting with blossoms, and the word broke from her mouth in a singular gasp of anguish.

"Tofi …"

Her boy, her precious little brother, was dead. This was a pain even worse than the loss of her mother, this …

Tatuba squatted before Iná and brushed the tears from her cheeks. "It was most painless," she whispered. "For he was already at Death's door."

Iná looked into those unnatural eyes, those passionless, inhumane features, and could not hold back a scream.

A terrible, banshee wail shredded her being and coursed through the entire forest. Even as she screamed, she felt something stir in her, something she had felt only on the eve of her mother's disappearance. The blast of power rippled from her core, and the vines holding her fell smoking and hissing to the ground, a coil of charred snakes.

Tatuba flew backward, blasted off her feet, to land in a crumple beneath Iná's swinging mother and brother. She sat up, scraping the dirt from her face, and for the first time since they had come face to face, she wasn't smiling.

Iná rose slowly to her feet, body ablaze. Golden flames covered every inch of her, wrapping her like a cloak. The heat was terrible, and she welcomed it. She understood now. She understood the forest, the Gardner, everything.

The blood of the Gardener coursed through her, and she would prune this Garden to its last root.

She took a step toward Tatuba.

The trees moved in answer, gaunt limbs reaching for her, roots snaking around her ankles as she advanced. Where they touched her, they burst into flames and recoiled, screaming, thrashing in the air like tentacles. With humongous snaps, the branches broke off the trunks, leaving wounds bleeding with green-black sap.

Iná stumbled to a halt.

There was something in her throat, in her chest. She tried to draw breath but coughed instead. Something flew out of her mouth and into her waiting palm.

A single purple blossom, wet with blood.

"What—?"

More blossoms erupted from her mouth, fluttering in the air like bloody birds. Iná sank to her knees, clawing at her throat. She reached into her mouth, trying to pluck the blossoms as quickly as possible, trying to clear her throat, but they just kept on coming and coming and coming.

She was wheezing now. Her mouth dammed, her throat clogged. She could feel a tickle behind her eyes, a wiggling in her ears as the vile growth wormed its way through her, seeking an escape.

Iná keeled over. It was so hard to breathe. So hard. There were needles in her chest. Her vision swam from lack of air. Pain ravaged her body, pain unlike anything she'd ever known, and she couldn't even scream to give release. Was this what her mother had felt, in her last moments? Was this what Tofi had felt?

Tatuba entered her line of vision, green eyes lit with mild curiosity. "I prepared a feast, just for you."

Of course. The forest was full of illusions. The house, the fake Tofi, everything had been orchestrated to trick her into eating the things that were now ripping her apart—

Black thorns tore out her chest with a resounding crack, glistening with her blood. Iná arched backward, curved unnaturally by the force of the erupting thorns. She thought she heard the wet snap of her spine—or perhaps that was the vines, wrenching her apart piece by piece, bone by bone, and oh, she would have given anything to make it stop, to put an end to the pain.

As if from far away, she heard Tatuba's soothing voice. "You must understand. It is nothing against you. Our natural state is to grow, to cover the face of the earth. We only want to live. For that to happen, you must die."

She was dying, alright. She could feel the life ebbing from her and into the parasitic weed—

Wait.

Tatuba was the thorn growing within her. And weeds were nothing if not stubborn, leeching the life from all cultivation.

Sometimes the only way to be rid of them completely was to destroy the infected plants.

Iná forced her lips into a grin, then stoked the flames within herself.

A rush of heat spread through her body. She heard Tatuba's screams long before the thorns caught fire, long before the blossoms expelled from her mouth in burned flakes, spinning in the air like crazed fireflies.

Tatuba was ablaze, screeching, patting herself in a frantic effort to put out the fire. Fresh growth sprang out of her to replace the parts eaten by fire, but those too were quickly consumed. It did not matter how much she replaced herself, or how quickly. Iná's fire remained.

She met Iná's eyes one last time, then shattered, raining to the ground in bits of glowing coals.

With a sound like the breaking of a thousand logs, the forest exploded in a bonfire of red and gold. The trees writhed and screamed, roots tearing out of the ground as if to bear them away. Iná saw the faces, then, the thousand faces of the forest. And they were all Tatuba's face, replicated in an endless iteration of agony.

She watched them burn, and burn, and burn.

It was terrible. It was glorious.

The trees were old, old things. They wore the mark of their years in the girth of their trunks, in the reach of their limbs, in the twist of their roots. But they were young, too, and pliant, and the Gardener shaped them to her will. Iná could make out the sky, blue as the egg of the robins that nested in the trees. And at night when she lifted up her eyes, she caught the moon and the glitter of stars sprinkled across the vast tapestry of the cosmos.

Sometimes when she walked deep into the heart of the forest, to where the river whispered against the rocks, she heard voices: the croon of a woman, the tinkle of childish laughter. She did not always hear them. But when she did, she would lurk from afar, sighing and wiping happy tears as she reveled in the sounds, so that she could scarcely tell how quickly the days passed. She was not alone. She would never be alone.

And that, perhaps, was the best of all.

IF THE MARTIANS HAVE MAGIC

by P. Djeli Clark

"The first Martian War was won not by man, but microbes. The second we fought with Martian weapons that nearly broke the world. The third invasion we stopped by our own hands, using magic."

—*Wei-Yin Sun, Imperial Historian in the Court of the Empress Dowager, Restoration Period.*

Marrakesh's streets were a dizzying affair at any time. But at midday they were unbearable, a churning morass that moved to their own rhyme and reason. And though Minette called the city a second home, navigating its roads was a feat of skill, luck and perhaps, she was willing to admit, sheer stupidity. She dodged a rider on a high-wheeled electric velocipede and rounded about a diesel trolley—only to be brought up short by a young woman who stood in the middle of the busy thoroughfare, beseeching a stubborn goat to follow. Yet no matter how hard she pulled the taut leash, it would not move. The girl yelled, then begged. But the goat only bleated its obstinacy, having decided to start its revolution here and now. Minette slowed to watch, momentarily lost in the goat's stubborn cries—and was nearly runover by a rickshaw. A tall dromedary pulling the two-wheeled, hooded vehicle of gilded iron pulled up short, jostling its two occupants. Both gasped, their sculpted eyebrows rising above long overlapping rose-colored veils. But it was the camel that turned an irritated glare Minette's way.

"Mind where you're going!" it brayed, making a gesture with its split upper lip she knew for a curse. Minette frowned at the discourteous display, and with a suck of her teeth shot back a curse in Kreyòl. The camel's eyes widened at the unfamiliar words, and it might have said something in return, but she had already moved on.

Of all the creatures gifted sentience with the return of magic, the good God Bondye alone knew why those rude beasts were chosen. But that was the way of magic, unpredictable in its movements, its choices, and ceaseless permutations. That's what all of this was about—why Minette canceled morning classes and now rushed to a meeting to which she wasn't invited. Because someone had to speak for the unknowable in magic, the non-linear, the indefinable.

Someone had to save her Martians.

She stopped, out of breath, just across from the Flying Citadel. The stone fortification sat atop a jagged rock that floated like an unmoored mountain peak high in Marrakesh's skyline. Its ivory walls and gold domes looked stolen out of time—or perhaps beyond it—spreading a shadow on the streets below where hawkers sold magic rope and enchanted rugs to gullible tourists along with more useful thaumaturgical devices. A fleet of lavish vehicles were parked nearby: wheeled automobiles driven by golden metal men, air balloons of giant puffer fish that pulled at their anchors, and gilded carriages drawn by fantastic beasts. One of them, a spotted ocelot large as a horse, lapped a blue tongue against its fur and held up a snow-white wing like a canopy beneath Marrakesh's glaring sun. The vehicles bore insignia from over a dozen nations, evidence that the Council was indeed meeting.

Minette swore. Looking around she caught sight of a few taxis, ferrying tourists up to the citadel by way of flying carpets. Absurd. Fortunately, she had other methods. Closing her eyes, she composed a quick prayer.

The loa could be persuaded to answer the call of a Mambo in need—as drawn up in the new understandings (they bristled at mention of the word *contract*) that now administered interactions with their priests. All part of bringing them more devotees in this modern world, where spirits and gods walked unbidden, ever competing for the attention of mortals. Of course, the loa acted in their peculiar time, and followed their own interests—new understandings or no.

After two attempts, she was set to call again when the image of a man in a broad brimmed hat flashed across her thoughts. He held a mahogany smoking pipe precariously between pursed lips and his leisurely gait resembled a dance. Legba, the Keeper of Roads, opening the Door. A flaming ram followed. Bade's sign, who she truly wanted. His presence stirred against her with the weight of a feather and the pressure of a mountain all at once. She hashed out a quick agreement—some offerings to perform, a drapo to commission—and was fast swept up in gusts of air. An accompanying rumble of thunder startled those below. Bade's twin, Sobo. The two were inseparable and you didn't get one without the other.

Bade kept to the pact, sending Minette soaring up to the Flying Citadel. Looking down she saw the winged ocelot had paused its cleaning, and now stared at her with four red-sapphire eyes. She shook her head. The powerful and their toys. On a draft of wind accompanied by peals of thunder like drums she rose higher still, above rounded minarets, to reach the citadel's upper levels.

Her feet struck stone and she stumbled once before breaking into a run along a lengthy parapet, holding the ends of her white dress up so as not to trip. She moved into a passageway, easily slipping through a set of wards meant to deter interlopers. Aziz's work, and predictable as always. Well, wasn't he in for a surprise. She stopped at a red door inscribed with repeating calligraphy. Taking a breath to collect herself—it did no good to look hurried—she tightened the white cloth that wrapped her hair, adjusted her spectacles, and (remembering to release the grip on her dress) stepped inside.

The Council on Magical Equilibrium was a rare gathering. And, as it was, featured an impressive who's who and what's what from across the world. Some faces Minette recognized. Some she couldn't see, and others she didn't know at all. Each however turned from where they were seated about a curving table to stare at her entrance. Aziz, who sat at its center, broke off his words entirely.

"Minette?" His call came too familiar for colleagues. He must have realized as much because he coughed into a waxed mustache before starting again. "Please excuse the interruption. May I introduce

Professor Francis. She teaches here at the Academy and comes to us from Port-au-Prince—"

"Port-au-Prince!" a small slender woman in a crimson gown repeated in a throaty slur. A veil of swirling gray mist obscured her face, all but her eyes—black on black pools, deep as a fathomless sea. "Aziz, you did not tell us the Academy held a Mambo in residence. I see no distinct loa hovering about you. One of the Unbound then?" She craned her neck and inhaled deeply. "Oh! But the magic in you is no less for that." Those black eyes narrowed hungrily, and Minette fought the urge to step back. It was unwise to show weakness to their kind. They remembered that.

"Professor Francis is one of our most *valued* researchers," Aziz interjected, seeming to sense the danger. "She has done wonders with Martian-human interactions. She was the one who first made the—ah—discovery."

Minette raised an eyebrow. Were they so afraid to just come out and say it?

Another woman at the table gave a derisive snort. She looked older than Minette by a decade or more, but the body beneath her burgundy military uniform was solid, and the dark hands folded before her thick and scarred. If the number of medals decorating her breast was anything to go by, she knew how to use those hands too. She pinned Minette with the one eye not covered by a black patch—an owl examining a mouse—and flared her generous nostrils.

"And," Aziz went on, "though the professor is one of our finest faculty, I don't recall her being summoned to this meeting." That last part was said with an unspoken, *and you should leave now*. But Minette hadn't come this far to be scolded. She tried to ignore the gazes of the two women and stepped forward.

"Apologies, Director Aziz. And to this Council," she began, reciting what she'd hastily rehearsed on the run here. "I only learned you were meeting this morning and thought my expertise might be valuable. I'm certain my absence was an oversight." She met Aziz's gaze squarely at that. It was petty of him not to invite her. But rather than taking up the challenge, his eyes creased with concern. That only annoyed her further.

"Well, she certainly is direct," the mist-faced woman slurred. "I for one would like to hear what the Mambo has to share. I say she stays. Any objections?"

None around the table gave a reply—though the one-eyed woman shrugged indifferently. Aziz put on a resigned look, beckoning Minette to sit.

"Come, Mambo, whose scent of magic is sweet enough to taste," the mist-faced woman purred. "You may sit near me." She patted an empty chair with a long-fingered hand, pale as alabaster. Those depthless eyes looked even hungrier.

Minette politely declined the offer three times (any less was just inviting trouble) and took a chair several seats down—feeling peculiarly conscious of her smallness between a broad giant in a blue turban and a fiery djinn encased inside a towering body of translucent glass.

"We were discussing," Aziz began anew, "what we are to do with the three entities following the recent revelations."

Minette's heart drummed. There it was. "There's only one," she spoke up. Heads—and other things much like heads—swiveled back to regard her. "You're calling Them three, but there's actually only the One."

Aziz blinked but then nodded at the correction. "Yes, of course. Professor Francis is referring to how the Martians see themselves. Three are required to form their collective consciousness, and then They become One. The professor is one of the few non-Martians to successfully join a triumvirate."

"Join?" It was the one-eyed woman. She now glared incredulous. "So, you allow the beasties into your head?"

Minette paused, trying to place that English accent. "They aren't beasts," she replied. "They're sentient beings, like us."

The one-eyed woman's laugh was brusque. "So you say, professor. But I've grappled with them face-to-face, not all tame like in your lab." She tapped a finger at her missing eye. "And they're damn beasts if I've ever seen one."

Aziz coughed again. "Professor Francis, this is General Koorang. She's here representing the Nations League Defense Forces."

Minette's eyes widened. *The* General Koorang? Who had broken the Martians at Kathmandu? So, that accent was Australian then. No wonder the woman was so hardline.

"In my time in the triumvirate," she tried diplomatically, "I've found Them to be capable of many emotions. They have been kind, even gentle."

General Koorang sputtered. "Kind? Gentle? Is that why they set about invading us *three* times?"

"Not every Martian was a soldier," Minette reminded, speaking as much to the others gathered. "The One I joined with were worker drones. They never even saw fighting. That's why it was so easy for the Central Intellect to abandon Them in the retreat."

"And what did they *work* on?" the general asked, unmoved. "Was it their stalking dreadnoughts? Their infernal weapons what almost blew us to hell? Come visit the Archipelago sometime, Professor, and I'll show you Martian gentleness."

Minette bit her lip to keep from replying. That was unfair. The Archipelago was all that was left of what used to be Australia. The waters of the South Sea were mostly off-limits now: teeming with monsters that wandered in through torn rifts between worlds. That it was humans playing with Martian weapons who had brought on the disaster seemed to matter little to the general.

"Perhaps we should get back to the heart of the matter," Aziz suggested, breaking the tense silence. "We must decide what is to be done with the entities, um, Them, in light of Professor Francis's discovery."

Minette felt a flurry of annoyance. Were they going to dance around this all morning? "By discovery, you mean that Martians can perform magic," she blurted.

Her words sent murmurs through the Council. Aziz gave her an exasperated look. The general cursed. And the mist-faced woman's eyes creased with a hidden smile.

Minette took the moment to press on. "What we should do with them is clear. They are a conscious soul, protected within the Nations League Charter on Magical Practitioners drawn up over a decade ago in 1919. They should be encouraged to develop those talents."

"Outrageous!" General Koorang roared, her face a thunderhead. "The Charter wasn't made to protect bloody Martians!"

"But it does not exclude them," the mist-faced woman interjected. "The Charter was made quite broad in its application—as evidenced by the makeup of this very Council."

"Precisely," Minette said, seizing on the opportunity. "We already accept a diverse world of spirits, gods, and no end of magical beings. The previous head of this Council was a minotaur, and she served with distinction. How is this any different?"

"A point of clarification," a squat shaman at the far end of the table called, raising a hand that rattled with ivory bracelets. "The Charter the professor references was created to protect unique magical abilities in their nascency. Have these Martians exhibited some magical talent indigenous to their … kind?"

"Not yet," Minette admitted. "But I believe it's only a matter of time," she followed quickly. "The triumvirate I share, They claim Mars once had magic. But it's been lost, much as humanity lost it once, too concerned with our factories and industry. Through the rituals to the loa, they've shown that They can understand and practice magic—something we once thought impossible. They're on the verge of self-discovery. We should allow them that right."

"Martians don't have any rights as citizens," General Koorang countered. "They're not even from this world. Just because the Academy lets you keep a few as pets, doesn't change the fact that these creatures are prisoners of war."

Minette clenched her fists to keep calm. "We aren't at war, general."

The older woman leaned forward, imposing in her size. "Oh? Did we sign some peace treaty that I'm unaware of? Is there a Martian consulate? A Martian ambassador?"

Minette pressed on, counting in her head to keep calm and trying to forget she was arguing with a living legend. "The Martians invaded three times, precisely three years apart, on the exact same day. The last war was in 1903. It's been more than thirty years, and we've seen no sign of another invasion."

The general smacked the table heavily, and Minette was proud that she didn't jump. "Damn right! Because we beat the hell out of them last time! And we did it with magic. That's our greatest defense, the one thing their calculating overgrown minds can't understand. And you just go ahead and give it to them." She shook her head, that single eye glowering. "I expected more, from a Haitian."

Minette felt her face flush at the insult. The houngan Papa Christophe had been the first to use magic in the Third War, halting the Martian dreadnoughts and sending their armies into disarray. The rout of the Martians at Cap-Haïtien set an example for the world. She was fiercely proud of that fact and didn't need reminding—not like this.

"I didn't give them magic," she said tersely. "They were drawn to the loa and the loa to them. None of us have the right to stop this development." She turned her appeal to the wider Council, moderating her tone. "I'm not just being an idle academic here. I'm not insensitive to all of your concerns. I understand the suffering the Martians caused this world. But I believe there's a practical side to all of this."

The general folded her arms and struck the posture of someone politely suffering a fool, but Minette continued. "The rediscovery of Martian magic could be a new step for all of us. A new magic system built on Martian ingenuity. Think of all the possibilities! The Martians here on Earth could become valued citizens, sharing what they know. If Mars invades again, as the general believes, we would have a valuable Fifth Column ready to come to our defense. What if this curtails their appetite for conquest? What if it helps them find themselves again, the way we have? We should seize this opportunity to integrate them into society, not shun it."

"Or we should be frightened," General Koorang grumbled. She spared a glance for Minette before turning to the Council. "The professor's determined, I'll give her that. But let's say she's right, and there's some old Martian magic waiting to be tapped. What happens when they rediscover it? Can we trust they won't give it up to protect their own kind? The last three invasions decimated the old powers of this world. Europe's a blasted-out hellhole that might never recover. We're barely managing that refugee crisis as it is. I for one have seen enough of Martian *ingenuity*. When the fourth invasion comes—and it *will* come—do we want to look up to see new Martian dreadnoughts powered by magic marching across Cairo, New Èkó, or Delhi?" She let her one eye latch onto every gaze before continuing. "I'm a soldier, not a diplomat. Thinking about peace isn't my job, and I'll admit I'm no good at it. But I know how to keep us safe. First rule of military defense: deny your enemy any chance of mounting a challenge. The professor's admitted these Martians haven't found their lost magic yet. She says we should give them time. Well I say we use that *time* to stop this threat in its tracks. Now—before it goes any further. Because allowing these Martians to have magic is a risk we can't afford."

Minette felt the weight of those words settling down with the force of a hammer. So, it seemed, did the rest of the Council. Fear, it turned out, was a potent weapon of its own. And General Koorang was as skilled in persuasion as she was on the battlefield. When the motion was made to declare the prospect of Martian magic "a threat to global security and magical equilibrium," not one voice rose in dissent.

The beat of drums guided Minette's movements. About the room, the loa that had been invited into the Hounfour danced along. Others like Papa Loko only sat watching. The First Houngan had been convinced by his wife to accept the Rada rites of this new world. Now he kept strict governance to see they were properly followed. He was especially taken with the Martians.

With their bulbous heads, it was easy to at first mistake them for giant octopuses. But where an octopus was reduced to flimsy sacks of flesh out of water, Martian bodies were quite sturdy. Their skin was pale, verging on a dull violet that extended the length of sixteen thick tentacles, the latter of which were remarkably malleable. At the moment, They intertwined like roots to form the semblance of a man beneath each head—with arms, legs and even a torso.

Two of the triumvirate moved gracefully to the song, swaying in hypnotic undulations. A third used myriad tentacles to beat a steady rhythm on a batterie of conical drums, matching the rattling shells of Minette's asson. On the ground, Papa Damballah's veve lay etched in white. He sat as a white serpent, coiled about his shrine and the feast prepared for him: an egg on a mound of flour, bordered by white candles, white flowers, and white rice. His red eyes watched the writhing limbs of the Martians and swayed with them. A current filled the room, and it felt as if they were no longer within this plane, but some other realm of existence where every star in the cosmos danced.

Then it was done, and she was back in the room at the Academy she'd transformed into her own Hounfour. She let herself fall, weakened after housing the loa. Martian arms caught her, strong but gentle, leading her to sit. They sat in turn about her, keeping their semi-human forms and regarding her with round, silver eyes that never blinked. A tentacle extended to wrap warm and sinuous about her wrist: an invitation to join the triumvirate. Still flush from the loa, she accepted.

"That was … nice," came the harmonious voices in her head. They layered each other: the three that were One.

"Wi," she answered back, also in her head. The Martians had mouths, sharp beaks like birds. But their speech was beyond human ears. This was much easier.

"Nou danse kont danse nou,"They remarked, switching between English and Kreyòl much as she did. "I am very fond of Papa Damballah."

Minette didn't find that surprising. Damballah was the Great Creator of all life, peace, and harmony. He was also the protector of those who were different. It made sense that the Martians would be drawn to him, and he to Them.

"You are quiet," the voices noted. "Sa ou genyen?"

"Mwen regret sa," she apologized. "My mind is elsewhere."

"On your meeting with the Council?"

Minette frowned at her lapse, building up her mental guards. In the triumvirate, your mind was an open book if you weren't careful.

"Aziz was there,"They said, catching a stray thought. "Was it difficult seeing him again? Much time has passed since the two of you last coupled. But your feelings for him remain disordered. Perhaps the two of you should couple again?"

Minette flushed, absently pulling her dress more tightly about her. An open book indeed. "Non. I won't be coup—intimate, with Aziz again. I explained before, nou te mal. We let things get out of hand." He was married for one. And they'd collected too many gray hairs between them to be getting on like schoolchildren.

"I have made you uncomfortable,"They said contritely. "Mwen regret sa. I am not always aware."

"It's not your fault. I just …" She sighed. There was no easy way to say this. So instead, she let down her guards. Her memories of the past morning flowed to the triumvirate at the speed of thought. The Council meeting. The debate. The final decision. They examined each recollection, and in the silence that followed, Minette waited.

"Your Council is frightened," the voices said finally.

"Wi," she replied in frustration. "It's disappointing they give in to their fears."

"Their reasoning is not unsound."

Minette's alarm reflected back to her in six silver eyes. "How can you say that? It's preemptive nonsense. They're punishing you for something you might do—not what you've done. It's wrong!"

There was a pause as three heads cocked as one, considering her statement. "I do not say I welcome their verdict. But the fear is understandable. My people have not been kind to your world. Even you were frightened of my kind once."

Minette's memories intruded without invitation. She had been a girl of thirteen during the Third Martian War. She remembered hiding in the shelters of Gonaïves with Grann Louise, who whispered assurances that Papa Toussaint and Papa Dessalines would not allow the island to be invaded again. She had grown up with all the fears about Martians, until attending university and becoming fascinated with courses on them. She'd jumped at the chance to study with the three housed here at the Academy, even if in faraway Marrakesh. It had taken her a while to see them as more than "specimens," and even longer to see them as less than monsters. But it was difficult to convince others to understand Them as she did.

"You've read my thoughts," she said. "You know what they plan to do."

"Separation," the voices whispered.

The word struck Minette as hard as the first time she'd heard it. General Koorang had called for euthanasia. But the Council balked. What they proposed, however, was little different, and perhaps crueler. Martians abhorred individualism. Separated, They would lose their single consciousness: effectively cease to be. Like cutting a human brain into three separate parts. It was a murder of the soul, if not the flesh.

Her guilt pulsed through the bond. "If I hadn't introduced you to the loa none of this might have happened. Li se fòt mwen."

"Non!" The sharpness of the voices startled her. "This isn't your fault. You have given my time in captivity meaning. I would not undo this, even at the rescue of my life." There was a pause. "I have something to show you. Es'ke ou ta vle promnen?"

Minette frowned at the question. Go for a walk? But she gave a tentative mental nod of acceptance. She barely had time to brace herself before their combined consciousness enveloped her whole. The world broke apart, shattered, then reduced to a pinpoint of light before expanding everywhere at once—taking her with it. When she found her bearings again, she stood on the edge of a calm moss green sea. Strange plants tall as trees, rooted in the russet soil, with wide blue petals opened to a sky blanketed by clouds.

"Do you like it?" They asked. The three that were One stood about her, their human forms abandoned and tentacles gliding freely just atop a field of mustard-colored grass. The air here was thick, almost viscous, so that she could feel it hugging her skin. Above them, a flock of featherless creatures soared on broad flat wings that looked more like flippers.

"Se bèl!" she breathed. "What is this place?"

"Home," They answered, with longing in their voices.

Minette gaped. Mars? But how? They had shown her their world in similar mental visions before, taken her to the sprawling subterranean mechanical cities, to the magma fields beneath the birthing catacombs, and to the hanging megaliths that housed the technocratic Central Intellect. But the surface of that Mars was lifeless, scoured sterile by the relentless march of Martian industry.

"This is how it was before," They explained, hearing her unspoken thoughts. "The memory lay within me, passed on by forebears millions of years dead, for no consciousness truly dies. The loa awakened it again. And awakened this."

There was a wave of tentacles, and from them flowed a ripple through the air.

Minette gasped. They were symbols and patterns of a multi-hued cascade, with dimensions that defied description. She reached to touch one with a finger, and the sound of hundreds of chimes trembled the world. In a rush, it all vanished, and she was back at the Academy.

"Was that …?" She couldn't even finish.

"The magic of my people," They replied.

"You've recovered it?"

"That is difficult to say," They answered. "I have been trying. But it is not easy working with something from which I have been so long separated. It is alien to me and will take time to understand."

Minette sighed wearily. But there was no time. Once the Council moved to separate the Three, the possibility of Martian magic would die before it even had a chance to begin. "Do what you can," she told Them. "And if there's a way I can help, you must let me know." She was set to say more when a tremor shook her. She turned with the triumvirate to look to the door, sharing their preternatural senses.

"Someone has come to see you," They said.

Minette withdrew from the One, returning to her singular consciousness and feeling suddenly very alone—her mind still ringing with what had just been uncovered. She was prepared to tell whoever it was to go away. Between housing the loa and joining the triumvirate, her body was weakened almost to the point of exhaustion. But it was rare they received visitors. Fear lanced through her. Was this the Council? Had they come for her Martians already? Gripped with trepidation, she forced herself up on wobbly legs and made her way from the room through the hallway. Reaching a door, she paused to lean against it for strength before pulling it open to reveal a stone courtyard where the Martians were allowed access once a day—and found an unexpected sight.

It was a six-wheeled white carriage, pulled by a giant winged ocelot—the very same she had seen beneath the Flying Citadel. The door to the conveyance opened and the haughty beast turned to regard her with four sets of expectant red-sapphire eyes. Hesitant, Minette stepped forward and climbed inside. Naturally, the carriage was larger within than without, revealing a room lit by flickering tallow candles. At the far end of a long, black lacquered dining table sat a familiar figure in a high-backed red chair.

"Greetings, Mambo," the mist-faced woman slurred. "Please, you will sit?"

Minette remained standing. Such offers had to be thought through.

"You may put away any fears, Mambo. True enough, your delectable magic is like sugar to me. It is why I have placed such distance between us—to avoid temptation."

Minette weighed that. She could walk out now. But curiosity gnawed. What was a council member doing here? "I accept that and no more," she said sitting.

"And no more," the small woman agreed.

"Your visit is unexpected."

"Of course. That is why it is a *secret* visit." She placed a shushing finger to the place where her lips might have been. "I have come to save your Martians."

Minette sat stunned. "But you voted with the others."

The woman waved dismissively. "That cause was lost before it began, Mambo. General Koorang will have her way. But perhaps you can have

283

yours. My sisters would like to take in you and your Martians. We would offer them sanctuary, away from the prying eyes of the Nations League."

For a moment, Minette only stared. *Sanctuary?* "Where?" she finally managed.

The woman wagged a scolding finger. "A secret, scrumptious scented Mambo, would be less so if I told you. But I am willing to provide passage to this place."

A hundred hopes flared in Minette before she smothered them with doubt, remembering who (and what) this creature was. "Why? Why do you care about Them?"

"Why, for the magic," the mist-faced woman admitted openly. "My sisters and I make no pretenses to our desires. We devour magic, savor its many essences. The possibility of Martian magic is most appealing! So exotic and untried. How we would like to taste it!"

Minette grimaced. There was always a price. "So you just want to eat them—drain them of magic."

The woman sighed. "Our kind are too maligned in your fairytales, Mambo. Contrary to those stories, we are not like the boy with the goose and the eggs of gold. We would not deplete something so precious as to not see its like again. Think of this as an exchange. We offer sanctuary. In turn, we take only small bits at a time—as one would any delicacy."

Minette's stomach turned. Bon mache koute chè, she thought darkly. Like soucouyant she'd known back home, these vampiresses couldn't be trusted. That was certain. But a secret place, where her Martians could be together, and They could explore their newfound magic. That couldn't be dismissed out of hand. Her mind worked anxiously. There had to be a way. She had negotiated agreements with loa and demigods. She could handle this.

"You will promise by heart, head, and soul that no lasting harm will come to either myself or the Martians in your care," she stated. "We will hash out a binding compact with a fair exchange between us and your sisters, where any offer of their magic is willingly given. Any breach of our agreement and I will have each of your names."

Those black eyes above the misty veil narrowed to slits, and Minette thought she heard a low hiss. A minor gale picked up, bending the flames on the candles. To demand the names of their kind was as good as asking them to offer up their cold barren souls. The mention alone was offensive. Minette held fast, however, a few choice charms at the ready in case she needed to make a hasty exit.

But the gale fast subsided and the woman slurred pleasantly, if also a bit tight. "Heart, head, and soul. Or our names be given." Her eyes creased into a smile.

And Minette had the distinct feeling that beneath that misty veil awaited a mouth of grinning fangs. "Now, crafty little Mambo, let us see to that agreement."

It was two days later that Minette walked Marrakesh's night market. The Souq was held beneath a full moon and spread out between alleyways and courtyards covered by colorful tents. Hawkers competed for customers, crying out their wares. Behind her followed three figures, two men and one woman. Some might have noted their odd gait: a glide just above the stone streets more than a walk. But in a city brimming with magic this was hardly worth a second glance. Not that a third or fourth glance would be able to penetrate the glamour now enveloping the three Martians.

They seemed to relish their freedom, casting human eyes in every direction. At the moment, they were taken by a guild of harpy artists whose talons inked henna that bled and slithered across the skin. Under other circumstances Minette might have been sympathetic to their gawping. But as it was, she simply wanted them to move faster.

The mist-faced woman had offered passage and sanctuary, but escaping the university was left to her. There was a dirigible at the dockyards waiting to ferry them off. Minette just had to get them there. So far, that had been a success. Concocting a medsin that left the guards who watched over the Martians standing in an awake-sleeping state was simple. Now they only needed to reach their destination before the ruse was discovered.

As the four stepped from beneath a canopy, the dockyards became visible, and Minette dared to believe they just might make it. Until someone called her name.

"Minette?"

She went still as stone, heart pounding at the familiar voice. Turning, she found herself looking at Aziz. He was striding toward her hurriedly, four Academy guards at his heels. Beside him was another recognizable figure. Minette cursed. General Koorang.

Panic blossomed in Minette. She thought to shout for her charges to run. She would somehow allow their escape. But as she saw the rifles in the hands of the guards, she faltered. The second the Martians ran they would be cut down. Uncertain of her next move, she resolved to stand her ground as the group reached them.

"Didn't I tell you?" General Koorang declared boldly. "Didn't I say she'd try something like this? Your professor's spent too much time in her Martian's heads. Can't find her way out again. Good thing we had them watched."

Minette glared at Aziz. "You had me watched?"

"And for good reason it seems," he retorted. "Do you know how much trouble you're in?" He ran a hand over his mouth, the way he did when thinking hard, then leaned in close. "We can still fix this. We can say the Martians coerced you, did something to your head. Just get them to return. I'll talk to the general. Maybe your post can be salvaged—"

"I wasn't coerced," she said tightly. The nerve of him to think she was simply the dupe of someone else's machinations. He damn well knew her better than that. "I planned this, Aziz." The disappointment on his face only made her want to punch it.

"Enough for me," the general rumbled. She looked over at the Martians still cloaked in their glamour. "Arrest her. Then take these creatures back to their cages. If they give trouble, use whatever force is necessary."

The four guards advanced. Minette glanced back to the dirigible meant for them, wanting to scream in exasperation at the nearness of freedom. So close! So infuriatingly close! Something slender and warm curled about her hand. She turned to one of the Martians, the unspoken request writ plain on that human mask. She consented, joining the triumvirate. The sound of drums flowed through their bond, the rattle of an asson, falling white petals, and the call to the loa of the batterie.

"Open the Door for me," the voices came.

"There's no time for this!" Minette said.

"Open the Door," the voices asked again.

She shook her head. "Now? I don't understand!"

"You asked how you could help. I think I know. The magic. I have been trying to make it work as a Martian. But I'm not a Martian anymore, am I? My magic was born of two worlds. It is that two-ness, I must embrace. Open the Door. Be our Mambo. And I will show you."

Minette looked into those unblinking human eyes, that seemed to plead, and did as They asked. Her spirit moved in time to the music. And though she had no tobacco or fine things to give the doorman, she sang:

Papa Legba ouvre baye pou mwen, Ago eh!
Papa Legba Ouvre baye pou mwen,
Ouvre baye pou mwen, Papa,
Pou mwen passe, Le'm tounnen map remesi Lwa yo!

Papa Legba came as called. There was a look in his eyes beneath that wide-brimmed hat Minette had never seen before. He thumbed his pipe and instead of going his usual way, settled down to watch. In the bond, a mix of Kreyòl and Martian tongues sent a current flowing through Minette. One that she'd only recently felt before. Martian magic, both alien and exhilarating. It blended with the song, played along with the batterie and asson, merging her voice and spirit with the three Martians until all became One.

On the ground a symbol appeared all around them, drawn in ghostly white. Damballah's veve: serpents winding along a pole. The flows of Martian magic superimposed themselves upon it, creating multiple dimensions that folded and bent one on the other, calling on the loa who was their protector.

Papa Damballah appeared. But not like Minette had ever seen.

This Damballah was a being made up of tentacles of light, intertwined to form the body of a great white serpent. And she suddenly understood what she was seeing. The loa met the needs of their children. Papa Damballah had left Africa's shores and changed in the bowels of slave ships. He changed under the harsh toil of sugar and coffee plantations. And when his children wielded machetes and fire to win freedom, he changed then too. Now to protect his newest children, born of two worlds, he changed once again.

Minette opened up to the loa, and Martian magic coursed through her, erupting from her fingertips. The guards, General Koorang, and Aziz drew back as the great tentacles of Papa Damballah grew up from her, rising above the market tents as a towering white serpent: a leviathan that burned bright against the night. For a moment brief as a heartbeat—or as long as the burning heart of a star—it seemed to Minette she saw through the loa's eyes. The cosmos danced about her. It trembled and heaved and moved.

And then Damballah was gone.

Minette staggered, so weakened she almost fell.

Once again Martian hands caught her, lifted her, supporting their Mambo. She caught a glimpse of Legba and her thoughts reached out to him. *Had she seen another face of Papa Damballah? Or was this the birth of a loa? Something old, yet new and different?* But the Keeper of Roads didn't answer. He only smiled—as if to a child asking at the color of the sky. With a flick to the brim of his hat, he vanished.

Minette returned fully to the world to find Aziz staring. His face was rapt, gazing over both her and the Martians—and every now and again glancing skyward. He had seen Damballah. She looked about. All through the Souq, tongues had quieted as eyes watched both she and the Martians—gaping at the phantom glow in the night sky left in the loa's wake. They had all seen.

"Nice show you've put on," General Koorang growled. "Doesn't change anything." Her voice was brusque as usual. But something of it was less sure than before. Oh, she'd seen too. But this woman was too tough—too stubborn—to be quelled by even a passing god.

"Actually, this does change things." Minette turned in surprise to see it was Aziz. His voice tremored, but he turned to address the general. "The Martians have shown that they can create their own magic. You saw it. Felt it. Everyone did." He gestured to the gathered crowd. "That at the least allows them protection under the Nations League Charter."

General Koorang's jaw went tight. To his credit, Aziz didn't back down—though Minette was certain the woman could go through him if need be. The guards at her side looked on, nervous and uncertain.

Finally, something about the woman eased: an owl deciding perhaps there were too many mice to snare at once. She spared a withering glare for Aziz before eyeing Minette. "Do what you want with your Martians, Professor, for now. Just you remember though, laws can be changed." Then turning on her heels, she stalked off, shouldering her way through the crowd.

"She's right," Aziz said, releasing a relieved breath. "Things could be different by morning. The world will be different by morning." He nodded toward the waiting dirigible. "Wherever you were going, you should get there. At least until we can sort all this out." He paused. "I should have backed you."

"Yes," she told him. "You should have." And then, "Thank you." She thought she even meant it.

Not waiting for things to get awkward, she allowed herself to be helped by the Martians to the dirigible. Once inside, she slumped into a seat just as the craft lurched off the ground. She watched their slow ascent into Marrakesh's night and down to where Aziz still stood. He grew smaller as they pulled away, melding into the city. Turning, she looked to the Martians that sat nearby. No longer wrapped in the glamour, They regarded their Mambo with silver eyes. Expectant eyes. There was more to show her.

When a tentacle extended in invitation, she gladly—eagerly—accepted.

And the Four became One.

DISTRICT TO CERVIX: THE TIME BEFORE WE WERE BORN

by Tlotlo Tsamaase

After-born:

"Do you forgive me?" I asked.

"For what, nje?" he asked as we settled into an undeveloped green zone, a shade to hide sins.

"There's a reason why I approached you from the onset," I said.

"No shit. No one like your bourgeois type starts a friendship with types like me unless it's to earn public image points. It was all snaks. But hell, you're paying so I was hundreds. Mara, tell me, what did your cherry-picking activity score you?"

My hands trembled, slick with sweat. A swallow deep in my throat. Above us, the sun dispersed itself, into light, a spectrum.

"I think I remember everything because it wasn't right what I did," I whispered, sickness swirling in my stomach. My life had been a seeking of redemption.

"Remember what, joh?" he asked, crushing leaves into his palm, wrapping them slowly.

"I'm going to tell you a story, a story you'll struggle to believe. You'll think it's snaks, but," I said, bowing my head, "it's my fault your life is the way it is."

He sat up, his joint lingering in his dark brown fingers. "Ijo."

291

"Just light it, bra," I said. "You gonna need it."

Fire ignited and smoke evolved us as I dug into the deepest recesses of my mind of seventeen years ago.

The time before I was born:

In 17 hours, I will be born.

The male figure of a clan is deceased. His granddaughter-in-law is scheduled to give birth the following day. Discussions are held between the living-elders and the living-dead ancestors, with the sangoma as the interpreter, the medium, the shaman. And who are we? Sexless souls warring to be born through the granddaughter—the way *we* want. My application to be born was approved several days ago.

We sexless souls stand in a veiled terrain waiting for the new regime to select which wombs our births will lie in and which we'll fight for. Our wars are oft salted with the palm of death, seeking our births, our genders, our ethnicities to feed from.

Maybe you're the kind to have died before you were born.

Do you remember what you said that hot winter ago? I do.

"Yazi choms, this is better than surgery." You paused then, allowing the silence to sit in my chest and knees where everything felt sallow.

"What's the catch?" I asked.

"There's no reincarnation without death." Your hands slid forward businesslike. "All you have to do is die."

So simple, such a joke.

"Then what?" I played along.

"You choose who you're born from, how, in what sex, and all that shit."

I scoffed. "All that shit, huh?" I felt desperate, desperate enough to believe it. To have the gender, ethnicity, and even choose the family I wanted. I could be born rich—into a rich family. I could have it all.

"Dude, you don't have a job," you said, counting off all my jinxes on your steel-ringed fingers. "You're fucking squatting on someone's couch. You've no parents. You've no cash to pay for the hormone therapies or surgeries you're always going on about." You surrendered your hands, your way of waving the white flag. "You know I don't beat around the bush, bra. Telling it as it is."

I slowly unwrapped my hands from the fist shapes they'd formed. "This just feels like a snaksnyana prototype techno-ish."

"You get to have everything you've wanted. You get to choose." Your lips twisted. "Think of it as a fusion of science and muti." That was always the mantra. Every reincarnate knew it.

That's what you said, but you never told me it'd be a war. Never. A fusion of science and muti. Nxa, now look what the fuck happened.

Now:

I, along with the other pre-borns, sink our sights into the gathering site that lies several soul panels away from the next satellite eco-city. The kgotla has sharp, bark-teeth stuck skyward, a half-womb holding young women who gather and consult their old-dead for advice. It's closing to the deadening night, so preparations for my should-be birth are in process. Most often, lives were laced in old-women tongue; they sewed all dreams, stitch-to-sleep, lacing it around eyes of the village citizens.

It was they who guarded passion, dream, motive.

Birth denied, some. Birth granted, others.

The sky wept itself of all things for two unborn babies, transparent of identity, remained buoyant in their womb-carriers, waiting for us to shape them, fill them out with our spirit. The kgotla was still indecisive of which pre-born/reincarnate/spirit would grow in the unborn heirs to their clan. Even after the decision was made, each pre-born would go on their sojourn with the opportunity to win their birthright, which might oppose the kgotla's "special" requests. Even though a science was concocted to give men birthing rights, there were only two open slots this season that a myriad of us reincarnates were vying for. I can't fail to be born this season. Failure means either death, or exhausting the birth application period, or being thrown into the womb-prison for years. I have waited many seasons, many dehydrating moons and burning suns to allow this to pass by easily.

The pre-borns hush at the development in the kgotla, a tribal meeting of seven younger women. Through veiled sight—that neither after-borns can see through except us, pre-borns—the sky clock is nearing birth-horizon. We watch over the kgotla proceedings' decision that may give us our new bodies:

"The reincarnates await our decision—our figurehead is deceased," said the third-younger woman, in a stern, curt tone. "The sojourn is tonight. It will guarantee the heir's birth. We will train him, adorn him, and perfect his upbringing."

Traditionally, age dictated wisdom, but here the number of rein-carnations that one *had* dictated wisdom. "Eldest" was defined as one with the highest reincarnation count, when in actual fact, they were the youngest in human years.

The fifth-younger woman held her hand up. "Sisi, be careful of the pronoun you use. That 'he' may be born as a 'she.'"

The stern one shook her head. "We have already chosen who we want born into our clan. We have picked two reincarnates based on their previous lives that indicate an aptitude in political studies, brav-ery, courage, and a show of altruism. One male, one female."

"Who will be born first?" asked the sixth-younger woman, a new addition to the conference who had many light moons that marked her youthful face. Wisps of the night braided themselves into dread-locks knotted on her head, pointing to sky.

"The male of course," the third-younger said.

"Of course? Maybe that'll happen in patriarch eco-city 1, not in ours, matriarch eco-city 1," the six-younger said, narrowing her eyes. "Perhaps you should cease your immigration status and relocate back to your state."

The third-younger steamed. "We should meld their spirit into one male body then. That way no conflict would ever arise."

The first-younger, who had ochres of ash beaded across eir sleek forehead to the tip of eir nose to mark eir bogosi, eir highest chief-taincy, said, "They both deserve to be born at the same time, not one second late or one second earlier. This will avert any lower feelings of self-esteem in their childhood. One is not more important than the other is. We must wield their bond strong from the get-go."

No one could quite tell where the first-younger's gender and eth-nicity lay for eir had many births, many deaths, many lives, and often the gravity and law of this world failed to portray eir succinctly; so the air was less translucent near eir form, and sound waves weren't born with the right chord to play eir voice through. Because of eir multiple and diverse reincarnations, eir was unlike others whose judgment was diluted by personal agenders. Therefore her opinion, her judgment, became law. And because of this, no one could quite tell if she was dead or alive, or what her name was, often referred to as Eir across all languages.

"But how will the two reincarnates leave the uterus at the same time?" the third-younger asked.

"There will be two womb-carriers," Eir said.

"That requires a high power of soul energy, and our soul panels are at their lowest function," the third-younger said.

"High prices and sacrifices are a prerequisite to our self-sustaining goals," Eir said.

"But communities will live in the dark."

"We have provided them with soul-energized lamps," Eir said.

The other younger women grumbled at the third-younger woman's imprudent manner of questioning their leader.

At this, Eir stared at the sky-clock waning in night sky. Each younger had on a sky-clock that told them the time of the womb, for the moon lay curdled in the dark night, and once it became full moon did it portray the minute of birth. Right now, the clock was quarter-waning moon, still many hours from birth. This sky-clocked was etched into their wrists in golden wisps of metal and (lunar) technology.

"The new regime defines that choice lies with the reincarnates," stated the fourth-younger, once Motswana who switched to Chinese status linguistically after she failed to obtain her desired ethnicity in her sojourn. "Whoever you choose will define what gender, ethnicity, and religion they choose to be born as."

"Our homestead has negotiated for one female and one male finish and klaar." The third-younger swept her hands together into a clap. "The woman must give birth to the twins as per her stipulated traditional role," she said.

The second-younger woman—who chose "mixed ethnicities" as her birthright fought well during her sojourn to win it—shook her head. "No, several men in the community have been selected as potential womb-carriers—"

"The husband has duties," the third-younger declared.

"And so does the wife. Baby-carrying must be a fifty-fifty task carried by *both* parents," the second-younger said.

Eir watched with narrowed eyes, nit-picking every argument mentally. Eir stood, and everyone hummed in silence. "What's most important to the clan is the spirit, not the shell, not how the body, this soul-holder, looks. It is but a glass that can be shattered easily, whereas the spirit is an eternal fountain of all good things. If you sway your decision on the cosmetics of a soul-holder, then we may as well pick any cheap soul that will fail this clan. We do not want a weak spirit dressed in an 'acceptable' body. We just want a spirit. Whatever form it comes in—"

The third-younger jumped forth. "But these values are necessary to our tradition—"

"Traditional values should not be a crutch for dictators to sacrifice man for inequality and personal ethos," Eir said. "This is exactly why last year the law was sanctioned for men to share birthing actions. Agreed?"

Still unsatisfied, the third-younger said, "Either way, the reincarnates still have to battle for this birthright—*that* does not guarantee their survival."

Eir continued, "Both the parents will give birth—the twins must be born—not just one, but two children."

Some other younger-women shuffled, tied their tonkana blankets tighter around themselves, and agreed. No one participated in going against the first-younger's decision. Their faces were laced with wrinkles, and hands soft with time.

"Although bodies are renewable resources, souls still remain as non-renewable energies to vitalize the body, which we are in short supply of—hence the reincarnation sanction," Eir said. "We must be careful that our decision tarnish not this non-renewable energy, for it could vanish forever, and our eco-city will cease to exist. Heed well, the granddaughter and womb-carrier hold two babies whose sex and ethnicity are undecided. They are scheduled to be born in a few hours whether the reincarnates or we come to a decision or not. The longer we take in our indecisive acts, the more it will jinx the twins. The objective remains the same, the twins will be the heirs, whatever they choose to be born as. This homestead will support them."

Our satellite hearts were moons for our bodies.

Nearby, the outdoor kitchen was a hotpot of the men's voices, preparing tea, preparing bread, waiting for the women to decide, for the women to slaughter an offering to the ancestors once a decision was made.

Eir stretched her hand to the center where our former exhumed bodies that we shed years ago lay, wires attached to them, trying to alchemize the art of incubating souls. Soul-energy lights our city, runs through the venous system of everyday life; without it, we remain in a dark world.

Eir gestured to the sangoma. "Give the selected reincarnates our decision and give us their response."

The sangoma kneeled in the womb-shape gathering, nodded his approval, shook dust into fire, and began relaying the message to the ancestral land where we waited, which was veiled from all living sight. He danced with night and fire, dust his mathoa, into the realm where I stood with another pre-born, for we were selected for the twin roles—

After-born:

"Hold up. Am I supposed to believe this? That you can choose how you want to be born before you're born?" he asked, laughing.

"Well, traditionally, women got pregnant, and the baby's sex was determined at seven weeks pregnancy. Nowadays the sex is determined during our sojourn which occurs when the mother is in labor. Sex, gender, religion, are determined during the mother's labor as we fight for the birthright. From war we are born. Before we were contained in a limbo stage for the full forty weeks, but sometimes babies were born without spirits, which were snatched away in their slumber before they dripped into the form of the developing baby. Soul-tech was developed as a defensive mechanism to align the sojourn and gender selection during the mother's labor, so it happened in a matter of hours."

"Fuck san, you must be higher than I am to say that with a straight face. I hope you're not tuning the younger-women such dom shit during your meetings, otherwise you gonna lose your authority. S'tru." He crossed his fingers, swearing.

My nails bit into his hands leaving wounds. "Believe me, assablief. I'm not lying. We were in soul-form watching everything."

His eyes grew wide taking in my panic. "From where were you soul-watching?"

"Angazi, I can never know where," I said. *"Our former dead bodies lay prostrate right in the center of the kgotla, wires leashed to the sangoma."*

"In our eco-city?" he asked.

"Ja, ours," I said. *"The sangoma posed, like a jeweled metallic device, expressing what we wanted of our births. Post-birth, we're never supposed to remember our soul-lives, the intermediate space before being born. They said we'd recall these pre-birth memories when we're a newborn, but after some time as you grow older, time dilutes those memories from you mind. Something must be wrong with me to remember,"* I said, staring at him, guilt gutting me.

"So you got introduced to this reincarnation idea because of someone? Yet it didn't turn out good?"

"Ja, something like that," I said, voice faltering, afraid to go on, wanting to remain vague and hidden.

"Mate, you're not close to convincing. Look, until you show evidence that all this talk is real, I'm not going to believe you. It's just crazy and you look crazy. I just came out here to chill. I don't know what kind of things you're mixed up in, but I don't want all this heavy shit, ja. Sort yourself out or I'm out of here."

"I have evidence," I blurted. *"I just need time. Just listen. Please. I'll show you the evidence soon."*

He settled back onto the log we sat on. *"I don't like where this is going. I don't feel right."*

"Trust me," I whispered.

"But why me? Why are you so insistent on telling me?"

"Because … I saw you before you were born."

His arms drooped into the grassland. *"You're scaring me."* He backed away from me. *"Don't touch me. You don't sound like your normal self."*

"I'll keep my distance just as long as you promise to listen," I said, *"because I'm not letting you get away until I've told you my story even if I have to restrain you."*

His eyes scanned our surroundings for a soul in sight and truly noticed how isolated we were, how I'd intended for us to be alone. Not even his scream would reach a savior. I watched his mind dissolve itself into ugly thoughts of the harm I could bring him.

"Okay," he said, realizing his misfortune. *"I'll listen if you promise to let me go once you're done."*

I nodded. *"Where was I? Right. So what happened next is after the younger-women chose me and another reincarnate to be born through the granddaughter, we had to give our decision, but the other reincarnate and I argued about how we wanted to be born."*

Pre-born veil:

"What's up?" the reincarnate asks me. She's dressed in her last-reincarnate season's form, personality and lingo, a way to identify each other before we can adopt new identities. A buoyant glow we both are. Her being is sporadic, unable to settle in one position, bursting like stars into space. "Guess you're going to be my twin. Do you reckon we'll look alike? 'Cause that'll be a new thing I'll have to add to my resume, joh."

"It makes no difference to me as long as I'm born," I say. I inhale her being to get a sense of who she truly is. She is of many evolved births; she is therefore powerful. She could win this sojourn—my selection. Most often souls are genderless, sometimes cultureless, as I am.

"So it's been decided that one of us will be male-born and the other female-born," she says. "I call shotgun for the female-born role. It's my discipline." She winks.

"Like every other sojourn, you'll will have to fight me for that," I say.

"I ain't going to be male." She circles me. "Yazi, your birth has *only* been approved after how many failures? You gonna waste that? Look, let's not waste the sangoma's time and get this over with. Reconsider: what did you choose to be born as?"

"First-born *female*," I emphasize. "Black. The mother will be my womb-carrier. My occupation: illustrator/storyteller. Marriage: wife Sufia Habib, birther of four children, architect of soul-energy incubators." Everything in my life will draw me toward that goal—failures, successes—even if I won't remember when childhood ceases my pre-born memories.

She whistles. "Haebo, you're losing privilege one rung at a time. So what exactly did the ancestors' ruling choose for you?"

I shuffle. "First-born male. Black. The mother as my womb-carrier. Occupation: political leader. Three wives, arranged marriages."

"What death age did you choose?" she asks. "Need to know in case you die early, and I have to take over shit."

"I want to die when I'm 120 years old."

She laughs. "Ijo! Good luck with your battle to birth to win that right. It's going to be tough."

I turn, surprised. "What age did *you* choose?"

"Mmm, 50. When time hasn't quite touched me yet, you check."

Explains a lot of why she's had many reincarnate seasons: she always resigned from each season early. It didn't make her powerful, but deceptive. No wonder someone with so many reincarnate seasons wasn't quite at ancestor level.

"But hold up, you said your wife will be—she doesn't sound like she's in any one of our tribal eco-cities," she says.

She was right. Our built environment was split into eight tribal eco-cities and counting, protected in their architecture and some married into others either pre-or post-birth for self-sustaining values. Often this enriched the economy and soul-energy to power our living.

"I know her because our love was unfinished from the last reincarnate season," I say.

She peers at me, closing in on my face as if to enter my mind. "Come closer, I can't see what you looked like in your last after-born season."

"I wanted it censored for privacy reasons," I say.

Her sigh is equivalent to the sinking and coalescence of her soul-lit being.

Her being surrounds me as she says, "It is a painful act to be born. The path from the womb into the real world moves through several dimensions—anything could happen in that passage, in that limbo. If you accept the younger-womens' ruling, I mean, once you die, it takes time, but you will rise to be an ancestor—a powerful ancestor. An honorary bestowed once you surpass stages."

She's trying to sway me, so her sojourn is easier.

I send threatening signals her way. "Then why don't you be male-born?"

"It's not what the kgotla decided. Besides feelings are not important," she says. "Do you want to suffer? I mean, what if you're still-born just because you refused to comply, joh? Or what if your mother has a miscarriage? Or the chick is some junkie and she ain't ready to have a baby—and she aborts you? We don't know who she is, and she's supposed to give birth to one of us. Even if you win the sojourn, your mother-to-be is a stranger who has her own agenda. Besides, being female-born, they've child-rearing obligations, pregnancy, and periods. Why they hell do you want to bleed?"

"Shouldn't that be your problem as well?" I ask.

"*Mmm*, not really, ja. I opted to have that out. Not really interested in those logistics. I just want the body, ja, not any of its clingy attributes. So, ja, my battle for birth is also going to be a challenging one."

Clingy attributes. The definition of a woman has changed dramatically over the years. "Doesn't change my decision," I say.

The pre-born veil grows lava red from my fury, heightening the kgotla fire, which rises as if it's my soul. The sangoma breathes in our feud, preparing to relay it to the younger-women.

I disperse my being throughout the room; I suspect this is what Sunset must feel like when she transcends Horizon. "Take the male-born role."

Her smirk wraps cold around me. "No. I too selected first-born female, as well as male-born, and Black," she says. "But I have the upper hand. I chose what no one would, given the new law. I chose the father as the womb-carrier. I will be born as neither, but both male and female."

I slouch back, and so do my furies.

Her being is airborne, voice a hush. "Men give birth, too."

Kgotla:

After the conclusion of our heated conversation, the sangoma turned back like a dog with a tale between his legs and gave the younger women in the kgotla our decision. He said, "The two chosen reincarnates' decision is as thus: the male-decided one wants to be born as a girl from the wife." He coughed. "The female-decided one wants two things: to be born as both and neither male nor female from"—he coughed and shuffled in the grave-dust—"from the father."

"Neither and both?" the third-younger asked, perplexed.

The sangoma shrugged. "The female-decided one wants the choice for her body to portray those characteristics. On some days, they will look neither male nor female. On other days they will pass of as both male and female."

301

"Jerusalema! This is absurd." The third-younger slapped her hands into her knees. "This is not close to what we agreed to."

"The clause suggests the reincarnates are allowed to choose their identity as long as it does not stray far away from human physiology," Eir said.

"Do we honestly want such stubborn reincarnates in our clan?" the third-younger asked.

"They have made their decision, now they must fight for it," Eir said. "And it shall be. Prepare the birthing rite." Eir nodded to the sangoma, who was half-in and half-out of both worlds.

At this announcement, the men ululated in throngs of Kalanga, Setswana, Xhosa, a pre-celebration before the birth.

And so, the moon leaked through the horizon as the community was swept with incense to guide the passed-away's spirit; the smoke became breath. The funeral air was pregnant with gravedust and snuff. Funerary rites followed, and the deceased ascended in totem-semblance, a hoof through the night, made of fire flecks. Our soul-necks bent back, we watched the sky laced in gold. Slowly, the chief had ascended into ancestral reign, where eyes pocked the night sky, awaiting which newborn would escape the two womb-carriers several communities away. The mother was steadfast in one homestead, the other womb-carrier bordered a tall structure, moon his womb; fire bodies danced the night, dancing in form of the mother's totem: which shall be dressed on her newborns. Despite both the reincarnates' and the kgotla's decision, most citizens' prayers moaned for two heady girls, to incubate souls, for they had the alchemy of creating such as it was melded in their natural wombs.

Medicinal plant was kneaded into earth like an umbilical cord to ancestral reign, a safe portal of sustenance where burials for our former bodies would reside, a conjoining.

The younger-women coughed, smoke was exchanged, and mokuru stained their livers. Hearty laughter and arguments scrambled up their throats during those seven-hour contractions, for the night-hour was deepening into labor, and our veil turned humid.

I stared at the sky-clock; moonwane dictated that seven hours remained until my birth. My sojourn had to be in that seven-hour frame otherwise I'd never be born.

And so, the younger-women's voice collected into the sky-phone, informing us, "The sky-clock is your compass. Reach the horizon and you reach birth. Your oxygen reserves are your fuel. Use it well to reach your birth-horizon."

The soul-forms scattered like grains in the wind, the battle for birth begins.

After-born:

"The battle for birth?" he laughs, *retuning into that trusting mode, no longer fearful of me. "This is the sickest story I've ever heard. You're shitting me, angiti?"*

"I'm being for real."

"Nah, this is one of those creative episodes of yours," he says. *"Kaosane, you'll be showing me slides of the graphic story you're yakking to me now."*

"I could request the born facility to deliver me a memory of that time," *I say, "but it's heavily buried in red tape—it could take years or many reincarnate seasons to obtain the pre-birth memory. But it's all in here." I tap my head. "I can't ever forget it. I wish I could."*

The dilation of his eyes takes in the secret I've held for years, seeking shadow instead of light, a refuge. "That exists?" he asks.

I nod. "It's a secret facility set aside for us, the experimented ones. That's why I stole this," I say, stretching out a pill-sized metal disk. "It's going to need a lot of soul power. Our city will probably experience a blackout."

"What's this?" he asks.

"The evidence I promised you. It's a memory of the time before we were born. Just swallow it like a pill, and you will see everything I tell you."

That's when he freezes, coughing the smoke halfway to his lungs. His hands jitter. "Did you see me in this pre-birth plek? Is that why you're telling me this? What did I want to be? Did I fail? Is that why I'm like this." He rattles his head. "Wait a minute. Now I sound crazy. This is mal, ja."

"Just take it," I say. "You don't have a choice."

The metal pill glints in his palm. He observes it and stares at me like I'm a freak. I push him back and press the metal pill into his mouth, the center of the pill blinking red, a signal, connecting, scanning for a memory until it settles into his sac and becomes a Bluetooth feed into his brain; swallowing was his acceptance to receive wireless transmission of a specific file from the memory bank. He convulses, unable to empty his guts, just heaving emptiness, hands to knees.

I fall to my knees, my face wet with tears. "I didn't want to have to go to such lengths to get you to believe me. Ja, I remember you ... but I have to explain first, so you understand exactly what happened during."

The battle for birth

is oftentimes gruesome, bloody, a tearing away from the self.

Our future, our dream is like a mirage in the now, stands on our tongue, our skin, our cells—the illusion of what I would like to see myself—only momentarily because the brown of my skin begins to turn opaque at the loss of my other identity, mourning for what it can't be without.

Time, an undisciplined currency in this rural, runs very sparsely; the sun has been stabbed. Its hibiscus blood melts to the horizon and spreads into our crumbed soil, inflating our souls with evil religions.

We hate sharp things that point to the skies; teeth knocked out, the stars fell. They are strange things—the star bombs—warriors of the sky, against the reincarnation, against some births. They become taboo, a deception, sometimes turning themselves into our totems to destroy us. They protect sky for it is our medium of birth. They all invigilate the districts of Botswana. I don't know why. They scan us according to gender because their sensors are drawn to holes, a pod of things where they can immerse their DNA into—the women a petri dish for their society. That's why all my former mothers and fathers made sure their daughters were men way before their birth. Before I was born, they decided my gender: male. Now, I search for the true one: female. I'm crazy, ain't I?

I need to reach the inyanga to gain access to my birth. I must journey through several districts to reach the cervix. I pray my totem will protect me during my journey. But I must too remember that no harm come to it as well. The air-veiled kwena—a reptile, my totem—will be my armor.

In a splatter of rain, the sky-clock announces the constriction of the built environment, chasms running its length, a danger zone. I'm not even close to what used to be veiled Gabs city, which is noticeable by its infamous sky, a derma of thin metal that projects a winter blue. My trail is latched onto by my twin-to-be.

"Stop following me," I say.

"You will die before you are born," she says.

"We are meant to be siblings, not enemies."

"The born facility will sterilize our brains from our pre-born memories once we are born," she says. "This feud of now will be a forgotten thing. You will love me. You will be my brother. And I"—she pauses, her soul-form making something of air—"I will be your sister." Her sight fancies the terrain, smile sleek with some secret. "The battle to birth is such an underutilized rite: murder exists not in our vocabulary."

It takes a while for comprehension to sink me into the waters of her meaning; she daggers at me with her form and limbs to slow me down, but she's thrown askew by the scaled tail of a reptile beckoning my protection. This I never expected from her. Slumber burns my eyes, fed by a sedative saturating the air. I expect her to be a lax-turning posture as I am, but she scars me trying to render me close to dead, so she reaches the sky-horizon first to gain her birthright first. The first one to reach it is granted all their identity wishes; the first one waits in a limbo space for their twin, for they are to be born at the same time.

I kneel, taking in her attacks. I scratch the night, it opens, and I slip into a sleep pocket and curl into a hole of darkness, of inexistence; the dark vacuum around me becomes my pillow, the amniotic fluid I float in. Her betrayal has kneaded itself into my spinal cord like a tumor; the stab wounds on my limbs could translate through my birth, rendering me with paralysis in my limbs.

For now, I'm invisible to my enemy who only wishes to steal my gender from me, to murder for it.

Hours later, my context is different after my buoyant slumber in the sleep pocket: environment is made of dunes, soft. My twin-to-be is absent.

The dull sun screeches time against the backbone of present.

The toll of this region is oxygen. It is now my body is an hourglass leaking grains of air. My lungs are calibrated to filter the air that has polluted contents of the dead inhabiting the underground.

I walk, eyes ahead, ears pinned forward, antennae detecting danger: air-borne evils nostalgic of the night and insomniac of the day carry their buckets made of wild animal skin and cluck through the night in sounds of thunder. These crowlike creatures grate the night with steel-lined wings hoping to tear open the sky, hoping to reopen the sky's eye before its scheduled aperture.

A piercing screech scrapes the sky: my twin-to-be existing from the sleep pocket—a harsh rupture in air's skin—calling attention to us. We have expired our use of the sleep pocket and one must run now from the crowlike creature's focused vision.

I weave through man-sized metal pieces of what once was Sekgoma Memorial Hospital that jut out of Serowe's desert-sand landscape. Something beneath the earth is trying to stab us with gleaming-steel objects of a dead hospital. She's crazy, the lengths she's going to, so I'm eliminated.

Death is a heavy night spread above our heads.

But this world won't be my coffin.

I press the knob of my backbone to inch air slowly from my heaving chest, the taxation for walking this path. Until I'm out of this border, my oxygen is not mine; lung alone. I must stop breathing, stop functioning temporarily to be free. I shield myself in the cloak of night waiting for the hunt to die down.

There is only a sky of unknown things— a sky that gives birth by aid of the inyanga, the midwife. I will meet her.

The witching wakes at 3 in the a.m. Voodoo priests were fishing sometime now, at the crane of heartbeat. Sleep fogged my eyes until I fell blind. I have to wait until my irises wake.

Dust is the alternative surveillance system imposed into our land by the star-bombs. I tighten my doek around my nose, but my pores remain open. It's a fragile thing to be humanlike. We're sleepless little beats of hearts in this sunless day.

I'm finally here. Kanye. The hills rise upward. Nature wants to flee. The courtyard boasts an unborn fire, but its faint silhouette is rapid and excited for flesh, not wood. The night sky is slightly bruised, the moon a stark, white eye, close to fullness.

The inyanga sits by the fire.

I take my place before the old woman, our knees crushed to the sand.

"The others aren't far behind," she says. "How old were you when you were released?"

"Excuse me?" I ask.

"The womb-prison." Her wooden body props up, brings up another wooden stick.

The womb-prison is a monolithic place that writes our existence. She is the guardian of the womb-prison where our pre-selves are either stored or restrained into its fly-smothered walls awaiting birth days and releases.

I lower my head. "Eighteen years ago, I think. Why? I've been waiting so long for my birth application to be approved."

The old woman spits at the floor, taps the air, and instead of a sleep pocket opening, light blinks at us and undresses the night's blind eye: the concrete structure stands, piercing the pregnant sky. It's the womb-prison, pre-birth names tacked in metallic panels on its surface. A myriad archives of beings before birth.

Weight against it, her cane sniffs the wall.

"Choose," the sangoma says.

"I don't understand," I say.

"It is part of the new order: sacrifices pay for it. Your twin did an unlawful thing and tried to kill you for her birthright," the inyanga says. "This is what I can do for you. You will win. You will be born as however you want—three legs if you wish."

"No one said anything—"

"No one *ever* says anything. Now choose where to place her."

"But then … *she* won't be born," I say.

"Yet. She won't be born yet," she corrects me. "Isn't that what she was trying to do to you?"

I sink back. "She was just desperate, ja. I don't want to put her away. The womb-prison is a terrible place to live in. I don't want it even for my enemies. Nyaa, she was trying to delay me *not* kill me."

"Same thing. Are you truly and authentically born if it's not the identity you want? Can you say that you are really born?"

"Look, I thought we were supposed to journey to birth like we've always done—not decide what to do with the other reincarnate, persecuting them into that place." I point at the womb-prison.

"Everything is an *evil*ution. Consider that this journey *now* has a roadblock," she says. "To get through you have to remove the obstacle or let your journey end here."

"But the … the younger-women chose us."

307

"They chose you, but circumstances say otherwise."

"If I refuse to put her in the womb prison?"

"Then she will put you in it. Your twin wants to be born alone. Siblings are oftentimes sacrificial lambs," she says, smiling. "You won't be the first. And if she were here, she wouldn't hesitate to find you a spot in the womb-prison. Now choose where she will go. She will be released much later, born much later."

"But what will happen to her now when I put her in?" I ask.

"She will be stillborn. Her body will be recycled for the next batch," the inyanga says.

The night, an abnormal quiet occasion, nudges me forward with a thick force of the air. A myriad of cases file the wall of the womb-prison library. In the wall is a slim aperture that I will input the memory of my twin distilled from my essence.

I choose. Moonlight lines the case's edges. A fire is born.

I step back. "What's going on?"

"The fire will process her spirit," the inyanga says. "This ain't your usual type of fire. This is a different type of burning. She won't feel like she's burning. To get from the sky, you must also give to the sky. The smoke will rise, the sky will breathe it in. See how fast the moon waxes?"

Those eyes in the sky blink, sparkle, and stare back at my village peeling the comfort from my skin. Around us, with this waking fire, are too many skyscraping trees with winged figures weighing down the branches. Within seconds the tiny creatures flit from the trees into the dark night; the world's alive with the noise of wings flapping— loud, whirring blades slice through the air.

I do it. I agree to the burning ritual, hoping the girl will be an incense for the night.

After long, we are in the hibernation period, rather the incubation period preceding the birth of the body that I will wear.

Placenta, the umbilical cord are seeds, the inyanga's muthi. She buries a piece of me in the land to kiss me to the ancestors, our home to return to when age melts our longevity. The grains of the earth are the browns of my skin.

A buzzing sound reverberates from high above. A siren. The star-bombs, policing, are aware of those to be born who must be returned into the womb-prison. No one is meant to be born again—they must make certain of that.

The womb prison is where they keep those who failed the battle to birth, those who failed and may not return again. I watch the other reincarnates along with the one who was to be my twin. They try to hide in sleep pockets, fingers pulling strings of night, weaving them in and around them. But I remember the futile attempt. The sky unfurls, and I have sent my twin-to-be to a womb prison, delayed birth. She will hate me. I will never forgive myself. But I have to be born.

The inyanga stares at me: "It's happening. It's time to be born."

After-born:

"What the hell is this? How can I physically see and feel that?" he asked. *"What have you done to me?"*

"It's a virtual transport to a memory—everything feels as real as the trees here," I said, gesturing to our surroundings.

"This is crazy," he said. *"This can't be real."*

"But it is. What you feel is the truth."

"Take this drug out of my body," he shouted. *"Take it out."*

"Calm down, you're just panicking because you've mixed two drugs in your body. Trust me, everything will be fine. It will wear off."

I watched him count his breaths, trying to calm himself down. He stared at me, noticing my thoughts wrecking me.

"Where do I fit into all of this?" he asked. *"So you wanted to show me that this reincarnate tried to kill you? You were only retaliating. You got the birth you wanted. Look at you. Many births and all."*

It's so weird how he could just switch from one emotion to the next for my benefit.

"You say that now …" I stared at the sky, at everything where ancestors live.

He paused, eyes half-asleep. "Does that mean I am born the way I am because of the journey I either failed or won? Does that mean I lost?" The ends of his lips tugged down. "I mean what life did I have before? Was I really meant to be colored? Did I choose my parents?"

"I knew telling you this would make you paranoid," I said.

"It's either I failed, or I was a coward to choose what I wanted. Because, look, I ain't happy, joh."

"Does anyone truly know what they want?"

"I didn't want this, joh"—he pointed to his tightly gauzed chest, keeping the illusion of breasts far away—"I know that. I feel that. Yazi, my sister—I feel like we were switched at genders." He, the unborn part lay curdled in the she-frame of his body, a she that he hated. "I am he," he once corrected me when I called him, "that cherie over there."

I realized in this world words were powerful to them. It became their gender for those who could change nothing of their body except the words that claimed them in birth certificates, passports, Omang.

I feigned laughter. "What the fuck?"

"No, like, for real. Instead of the switched-at-birth scenario, we have the at-birth switched genders. This happens to twins—born minutes apart or siblings born years apart."

Years apart. How ironic.

"She's your fucking sister, man. Stop burdening her with this shit," I said. "It's killing her, the way you think."

"I swear, my thoughts are going to be my murderers one day. Like, I fucking hate this shit. I don't want to be bleeding every month," he said.

Bile rose into my throat. Déjà vu. I don't want to be bleeding every month. That was his answer, and he couldn't even see it.

The person he wanted to be was wadded knee-deep in loss, but my breath as knee-tight to my chest, couldn't escape the words. Sometimes I felt like this present, this now, was a memory we were recounting.

"Did I say something wrong?" he asked.

"I think I know why I remember everything," I whispered. "My guilt kept me prisoner of the things I did. It's getting a little harder for me to talk about this … memory, this secret."

He gripped my hand. "I want to remember. So badly it hurts. Tell me what happened next to you? Were you happy with the end journey, your life?"

"Angazi," I said, "I don't know. Sometimes all of this doesn't feel real. We die, and we repeat this cycle again, nje. Trapped. Death is just a machine that exercises your soul into the next-life body."

"I want to do it," he said, ignoring me. "Like you quoted to me: 'there's no reincarnation without death.'"

I had to say it now, or it'd be harder later. Get it over with.

"This is the third reincarnate season ever since I put my twin-to-be in the womb prison," I said. "I was always looking for her. I realized she was born female instead of male, the one she wanted. And she tried to make herself look male. I found her here."

"Here? Fuck san, who is she?" he asked.

"I saw her three months ago at the aquaponics and gender sector trying to raise funds for soul panels for her team that would grant transgender rights to citizens. That's why I approached you, *stayed by* your *side. That's why I sponsored your idea, your team, and your values. I was trying to pay off for my shame, my guilt." I bowed my head and cried into his hands,* her *frozen posture. "You … were right. I remember you." I paused. "You were supposed to be my twin."*

His lips turned into a grim line, mind dissolving the thought into anger, fists kneaded into her thighs. Sometimes I couldn't tell which he was—shifting from her to he, the way they *always wanted.*

"Punish me—hit me, do what will make you feel better," I said.

"Are you saying that I'm the twin who tried to kill you during our sojourn?" he asked.

I nodded.

"No, you're lying. This is a kak story. I don't believe you." He pushed me. "Why would you say something as cruel as this? Are you telling me you put me in a womb prison? I failed my sojourn which explains why I was born in a poor family! So is my family being punished with poverty or am I? Did I lose my father because of this sick joke, this reincarnation shit you're tuning me? So my pre-birth choices and what you did to me made me this way?"

"It doesn't mean there is anything wrong with you." I fell onto my knees. "You used to want to be both genders or neither—I guess our choices do change. You changed. But when you were released from the womb prison, you were born into a poor family into a gender you didn't want because your sojourn didn't go well. The womb prison took so much of your strength and hope that you lost your will to fight for your birthright. I wish they hadn't pitted us against each other—we could have been siblings. I should have protected you. You were just scared."

"You owe me. You fucking owe me." He jabbed me with his finger. "Give me another memory pill." His voice was thick with anger. "I need to see how you were you born."

I swallowed, unsure what he would do to me, but I had to say everything, to relieve myself of the anxiety. I handed him another metal pill, watched him swallow it, and I said, "I was in a district that would lead me to the cervix," I said. "They called that zone the: District to Cervix."

is vague to my senses. In the born area, there is nowhere to hide except pain that seeks your senses.

Vigilance is strong nearing the sky's aperture.

The clouds gather, yellow glooms poke their way through the night and something up there with the skin of sky watches us in terror or excitement. A memory is wet and leaks down my cheek—blood. Clouds of orange, red, and yellow bloom against the sky, an orchard bleeding, opening, and stretching in wispy tendrils of red to the horizon.

The sky is opening. Hope breaks my ribcage. Will I reincarnate?

My twin-to-be glares me down as she's wounded into the womb prison, a wind blaze in our faces, pushing us back. The sky-clock gradually lapses to full moon, gradually transitioning into crescent dilation as we transit from District to Cervix.

The act of breathing is a suffocating procedure, the entirety of the world pressing in from both sides, slowing my limbs into a crawl—snail's pace.

The muscles, bones of sky, dense with resistance leak the sunset. Latent phase near.

Our veil transcends into a living dark, the womb of darkness. Lightning appears, burning an orifice into the sky. It's a slit that becomes the uterus. Pulsating, pulsating, pulsating—glittering, a flash of star. Billows of cloud drip like thick mucus membranes onto grasslands. A storm that lasts hours. Then, thunder, contractions. The moon wanes and waxes, a cervical dilation, water breaks in rain patters.

The sky-slit usually opens like clockwork after three sunbleeds, sometimes irregular, bleeding things into our land. Then, stars will skim back and forth, stitching the opening in the sky, mother earth's healing, mother earth's rapture.

I don't know where I am currently. I am a being freed of flesh. I am sight without bone, without structure. In this terrain, ethnicity soaks our skins desert brown. We stare at each other, a land mass, separated by gender, its face a structure of nothing.

And in the kgotla, in the bleeding of the night, a ritual is made: a cow wails through the night, its life leaking for the ritual, its cry a veneration. Their ritual is almost done, and so is ours.

There are parts of me, tangible parts that weren't present before, like the topmost part of me entering/leaving a new environment. A tightening lowers itself into my chest. How does one lose his gender, the identity of his physio-travels in this world? What does it mean to live without gender? Is it a sexless life? A gender is what the eye of society licks itself across your body. The sex is the thing that remains intact, nameless and shuddered against your thighs trying to figure out who and what it is: you could imagine the two of us, attached to this soul-shell, separate and at one. I, the charger of this body. It, the charger of me, at times. We are dressed differently. I am in cloths lush to skin. My gender has no name. I have no name. I search for it, searching for myself. We are born choosing where we fall. Mine was taken from me. It is a passport in this realm, so neon in your face. In the olden days, all you did was hide beneath cloth, mask that face with shadow of doubt.

They did say everything would feel like pain—stimulation, sound, temperature—but pain is a cloak covering my bones, a material, thin and brown.

A tunnel wraps warm around me, tensing, convulsing—I try to seek breath, to seek life, and pain strikes me, giving me voice; a cry, a breath. I am here.

A blurry bloodied woman leans over, huffing, and voice warm as cloth. "Is it a boy or a girl?"

I am gone, I am going, but I am here too.

I am born who I am.

Glossary

Kaosane: tomorrow
mathoa: ankle rattle
mokuru: traditional beer
plek: place

LIKE STARS DARING TO SHINE

by Somto Ihezue

When the boy opens his housing unit's steel door and the incandescent lights pour into his face, he does not blink away. "Little suns"—this is what everyone calls them. The massive disks hover in the atmosphere, spilling streams of radiant light to the ground. The boy stares into the trees, mere meters from the door, and the forest encaving the unit stares back. A breeze finds him, whistling through the trees and into his dungarees. Threadbare with a Batman logo printed on them, the overalls belonged to his mother when she was a child.

Peeling his hand off the latch, the boy steals into the bright night. He hurries into the bushes, steering clear of the stone-paved forest pathways, each step sending emerald grasshoppers chirping off the shrubs. In the forest, its canopy is a roof of green, darkness collects in patches, but the lights find a way—they always do. Through holes in the dense cover of leaves, they pierce the dark, creating lines of shimmering mist. The trees above crash gently into each other, and the rains that had collected in them fall to the boy's skin in beaded drops. The musk of damp wood, bold and consuming, fills his nostrils as he weaves through the low-hanging palm fronds.

Before the light zones, the world had many green places—rainforests, savannas, mangroves—stretching as far as the eye could see. Not anymore. The Anambra Light Zone, with its damp places

315

and its bird calls, is the only home the boy has ever known. He knows which months the leaves yellow and fall; he knows the poison mushrooms, their caps a vivid toxic scream. He knows the stones that birth the streams; he knows the places the Niger River breaks.

The boy stops when he sees the electric fence of the Multi-Science Research Facility, the words RESTRICTED AREA plastered across it in red. Made up of rows of cuboid structures, the facility stands at the west end of the light zone, with carpets of green algae crawling over it. When they were bored of tree counting, he and the other zone children would sometimes hide in the udala trees and guess at what might have once been the color of the buildings.

"Vermilion." Kiki, who had a crack zipping across the lens of her glasses, always said the strangest things.

"That's not a color." Some chunky kid laughed.

"Raymond, you thought peanut butter was mashed meat," she replied to the chunky kid without looking over at him. "Maybe sit this one out." She adjusted her glasses, fiddling with the duct tape that was doing a terrible job at holding the hinges in place.

"That was a long time ago!" Raymond looked around to the others, begging to be believed.

"Not long enough, apparently."

Nobody liked going river jumping or antelope watching with Kiki, and this was why. She didn't want them around either, but holed up in the zone together, they were stuck with each other.

Thirteen years ago, in the eternal winter of 2125, the boy and Kiki had been born here. They went to the same zonal school, climbed the same trees, and chased the same squirrels.

But Kiki was not one for words, and when she was, the other children ran back to their units in tears. So, when she leaned forward in history class and whispered into the boy's ear, "Meet me by the facility, under the udala trees."

He thought she'd mistaken him for someone else. But she hadn't.

"11 p.m. Don't be late."

"No talking," Mr. Adesua, the geography teacher who also doubled as the history teacher, warned the class, his narrowed eyes jailed behind thick oval spectacles. "Now, where were we?"

He turned to the holographic board. "... Yes, on the 14th of May, 2060, Mount Nyiragongo erupted in the Congo Basin, an eruption

316

that spanned ten months. With increased steaming, rumbling after-shocks, and smoke emissions occurring for the next decade, it was the longest, most intense volcanic disaster after the 1815 eruption of …?"

Mr. Adesua looked around at his students—some doodling on their holo-pads, others fiddling with their glow pens, and only a precious few making an effort to feign attentiveness. "Anyone?"

"The 1815 eruption of Tambora in Indonesia."

"Thank you, Kiki." The teacher sighed, resuming his lecture. "With an endless fount of ash saturating the atmosphere and obscuring the sun, Africa, our continent, truly became The Dark Continent." A trail of dread crept into Mr. Adesua's voice. That same dread found its way onto the faces of his now-attentive students.

"Sulfuric acid aerosols increased the reflection of solar radiation across the globe. Rivers and lakes in Greenland froze over; in Russia, buildings, cities, and millions of people were entombed in ice. And for the first time since the Ice Age, equatorial regions experienced winter …"

The boy's attention drifted as he wondered what Kiki wanted with him. This was the first time she'd said more than a sentence to him. And though he made up his mind not to, he would later find himself hunching by the facility's fence, breaking curfew.

Shifting his weight from one foot to the other, arms crossed tightly over his chest, the boy tries to stay hidden. An industrial-grade air filter thrums next to him, sending soft vibrations up his legs. With the incandescent "little suns" blazing bright, it is just a matter of time before the tight security team spots him.

Equipped with a self-regulating, heat-yielding capability, the little suns warm frozen landscapes while simultaneously taking over the real sun's photosynthetic role. This made the Anambra Light Zone home to some of the last surviving biological species in Nigeria, as well as the rest of the planet—which is the reason it's heavily guarded by high-voltage walls against poachers and raiders from outside.

"Boy."

The boy looks up to find Kiki hanging from a branch.

"You're late." She lets go, and when her feet meet the ground, they do not make a sound.

317

"This doesn't feel right," the boy says, his breath quickening. "Let's—"

"There's no security on this side. I checked." She takes his hand. "Come."

They slink onto the Facility grounds through a rip in the wired fence and head toward one of its many buildings. At the entrance, Kiki slips out a key card. She slides it across the door lock, and it buzzes open, revealing an empty hallway.

"My dads work here," she explains, catching the questioning look on the boy's face. "Research biologists."

Half-tiptoeing, half-running, hand in hand, they hurry down the hall. The walls on each side are large glass panes, and behind them are laboratories full of things the boy has seen only in books—microscopes, Petri dishes, titration filters, jars with brownish stuff floating in them—and, in some of the rooms, things not in the boy's books.

Kiki whirls around. "What are you doing?" His hand has slipped from hers.

The boy leaves her to peer through one of the glass panes. "Is that a—?"

"Yes. A prototype. Let's go." She pulls on the strap of his overalls, but he does not budge.

"I want to see it."

"You're seeing it now."

"Up close." He goes to the door, and Kiki knows she's not winning this one.

"I am so going to regret this." She swipes the key card across the lock.

Inside, a little sun fills the room. Far from what the boy imagined, it is not flat but cylindrical, like a bass drum, and insanely massive. And there is nothing ethereal about it. Wires, plugs, and circuits jot out from within it, like twigs on a dying tree. He runs his finger along its dusty metal exterior.

Kiki stiffens where she stands. "We need to go."

With its two surfaces—one plated with blue solar cells, the other made of columns of fluorescent tubes—the little sun is in practice a solar-powered streetlight, only larger and more complex.

"How does it work?"

"I. Don't. Know." Kiki punctuates every word, exasperation working into her voice.

But of course she knows. Unlike the boy, she paid attention in Introductory Tech class. To fight the climate crisis, world governments invented the "little suns." The disks, a hundred times more powerful than the average solar panel, absorb light energy from the sun, converting it to beams too concentrated for the sulfuric aerosols in the atmosphere to reflect. And so, dusk till dawn, the little suns shine, sentries on guard.

"Woah." The boy looks up. A map is etched into the ceiling. "Is that a world map?"

"More like a map of what's left. Come on. Let's go."

"What are those? The red spots?"

"Light zones."

"So few?" He slants his head. "Why couldn't they just shield the whole world?" He gestures to the prototype.

"Do you ever listen in class?"

The boy shrugs.

"With limited time and resources, the advanced multi-purpose, billion-dollar design of the technology was not accessible enough to enclose entire countries," Kiki starts like she's reading out of an encyclopedia.

The boy blinks at her.

"A compromise was reached, and the suns were suspended over arable lands, wildlife reserves, and forests."

"Monaco did it." The boy smirks, crossing his arms. He knows something she doesn't.

"Monaco was a very small, very wealthy nation." Kiki sighs. "They could afford to shield their entire landmass."

The boy looks back up. The area above the U.S. and its five zones is a sheer patch of white. "Mr. Adesua said Canada was a frozen graveyard long before a little sun got mounted."

"The aftermath of the eruption was hardest on polar countries. Most had to migrate their citizens toward the equator, to Kenya, Indonesia, Colombia, and here. Sure, it's cold in our part of the world, but it's tolerable."

"Do you think the people on the outside are okay?"

"Seeing as they're always trying to get in here, I take it they're not."

"We should just let them in."

"We ... we can't."

"Why?"

"There's barely enough room and resources as it is. We can't risk an overpopulation crisis. Our parents are only here because the work they do is important, nothing more."

319

"My mum doesn't work here in the facility like your parents. She's down in agriculture."

"And without her, we'd all starve, including those on the outside relying on us for monthly supplies." Kiki takes his hand again. "I want to show you something."

They head to the end of the hall and down a spiral metal staircase. The stairs empty into a mass of interlocking pipes and dripping tanks that comprise the central grid of the drainage system. A chemical stench hangs in the air.

Kiki lifts a sewage lid like she's done it a hundred times before, and the lights spill past her, into the dark below. "Get in."

"No." The boy backs away. "I'm not jumping into some random sewer." His astonishment at seeing the prototype is long gone at this point. "I knew I should never have come."

"So why did you?"

"I don't know. I thought maybe you ... I don't know." He coughs once, scratching the side of his neck.

"Oh god, you thought I wanted to kiss you?" Kiki's expression cannot decide between disgust and shock.

"Ye— No— That's not what I meant."

"Just get in."

Too embarrassed to protest further, the boy climbs down the greasy wet ladder. Following him, Kiki closes the lid, and the sewer goes pitch black. In the forest, under the cover of the canopy, the boy has experienced shades of darkness, but nothing like this. This is encompassing, ripping him of his sense of space, of being. He cannot tell where his body ends and where the darkness begins.

"Kiki, where are you?"

"Relax, I'm right here." She shines a headlamp in his face.

"I want to go back."

"Not yet."

Handing him a lamp from the row of others hanging on the sewer wall, she trudges ahead, dispatching puddles of water with every step. The boy follows. Walking with a knowing sway, Kiki does not pause when the tunnel splits in three, and—unlike the boy—does not shriek when a rat scurries over her toes.

"How many times have you been down here?"

"Hm," Kiki mutters, and nothing else.

The air starts to smell of river rocks as the pipes, mucky water, and defined walls give way to a larger, rough, cavelike exterior. Kiki stops.

"Are we there?"

"Turn it off," she says, switching her lamp off. "They don't like the light."

"Who?" The boy hesitantly does as she says. "Who doesn't like the—"

Then he sees it: a speck of light afloat in the dark. Another follows, twirling and glinting, up and up. A third comes, then a fourth, then a thousand.

"Fire—fireflies." The word leaves his lips as a whisper, his breath catching in his throat.

"Have you ever seen anything like it?" The swirling lights glint off the lenses of Kiki's glasses, casting her entire face in a scintillating glow.

In the cave's immensity, swelling with the euphonic hum of lacy wings, swarms of fireflies dance, a rain of stars. No, the boy has seen nothing like it.

"But …" he finds his voice. "My mum said … she said they all disappeared when she was little. She said the lights blinded them. She said—"

"I know, I know. The lights made their mating glow invisible and, unable to evade predators or reproduce, they went extinct. I know." Kiki lets her impatience show. "But look, they're right here!"

"How did you find them?"

"I didn't. My dads have been coming down here for months, studying them, how they've survived this long."

"I guess the warmth from the little suns helped." The boy inhales the fresh warm air.

"About that …"

"What?"

"Don't freak out, but we're not in the zone anymore."

"Where … where are we?"

"Where do you think?" Kiki scoffs.

It takes a minute, but it comes to the boy. His eyes widening, he spins around, frantic.

"No, no, this is a good thing." She reaches for his shoulders. "We're outside the zone, but it's not freezing down here. Don't you see what that means?"

"We can't … we can't possibly be that far away?"

"We've been walking for hours." She beeps her timepiece in his face. "It's 6 a.m." The boy gasps. "I'm usually faster on my own, but thanks to your side quests, we are definitely getting caught. Point is, the earth is healing," Kiki says, her voice charged with something the boy cannot describe. "My dads say soon we might not need the little suns anymore."

"Really? How soon?"

"They're not sure." She pauses for a minute. "But can you imagine? Seeing the oceans, a sunset, the moon!" Her hands tighten around his shoulders, and she shakes him. "Boy!"

"Zaram."

Kiki raises a brow.

"My name is Zaram." The boy stares down at his fingers.

"And all this while I thought it was 'Boy'." She lets out a mocking chuckle. "I know."

Zaram looks up at the fireflies. "Kiki, why … why did you pick me?"

She does not look at him, but not in the same way that she doesn't look at the other zone children, like Raymond. "Well, out of everyone here … I hate you the least." A shy humming silence builds in the space between them. "What would you like to see, Zaram, when the earth is normal again?"

"I— I—" He has never thought about it. This—the light zone, the little suns—is his normal.

"It's alright." Kiki smiles. "You don't have to think about it now."

Zaram smiles back. And they stay, watching all the little things daring to shine.

POEMS

CHILD PRICE

by Akua Lezli Hope

She loves her parents
each large warm face
beside her smaller one
four lips press her cheeks
four arms enclose her
shelter, comfort, protect
with tender, insistent lies

Her tall, handsome father
lifts her with his smile
holds her up to azure sky
Her slim, curved mother
presses her with fragrance
rose petal between pages,
brushes her tender head with care

She knows their smells, their birthdays
but not their ages. She can recite
their names and titles, she is growing
her album of knowing them
beginning to decipher what of them is her
and what of them she wants to be
packing all carefully away in memory

She overheard one moon bright
night that she would be gone
though they vowed to protect her
in mumbled silver murmurs by her bedside
by the dim glow of star-pierced nightlight
each swears after her prayers
when they return to check if she sleeps

Her mother's smile tears
her father's hardened eyes make her worry
ask them what's wrong, if she can help
She stops rolling on the grass
and running to the stream
tries a nervous perfection
She makes them gifts every other day

She creates occasions to celebrate:
pancake day, special Saturdays
robin worm day, too young
to remember why, until she does:
she is collateral for a debt
conceived before she was
pre-promised, and her parents failed

to avoid her making, as inevitably
as they failed to avert their blood-debt:
her life for their galactic reign
They were great at love
but fate stacked circumstance
against their skills as queen, king,
tricked into an unthinkable compact

How could they know how much they would love
their first alien, born of, yet not them
whom they could name but not keep

from a savage unknown which would claim
payment due too soon, before her flowering,
take her to a realm of pain and promise
turn them into gray wisps of fading memory

IGBO LANDING

by Akua Lezli Hope

We are incomprehensible
to you who feel only fear
when you hear us, spider
silk on face, chill up back
which is a success perhaps
to have both sugar and fat
to die of excess and sloth
not like we hungry wraiths
whose forgotten flesh was sinew
whose nonexistent options were
to live death or die living
whose path was clear:
undo or be undone
Our drowned captors are silent
their injustice muzzles them

We sang the song of home going
a freedom-bound journey as we
down drowned with determination
deliberation, avowals to never surrender
to die and return from whence we
came from where we were stolen,
to resist and not submit, calling to
our God, Chukwu, for escort, for conveyance

for admission to the next phase
existence beyond this abominable land
out of reach of horrible hands:

those who would eat our souls, bite
bit after bit, daily flay flesh
from our backs, lynch us
take our babies, steal their milk
rape our young ones, remove our tongues
and in that terrible future in which you tremble
by our whispers, lingering laments,
you would believe such theft was chosen?

and that is what frightens you
we refused to languish in longing
you hear our reverberating answers echo
through the water, slow lapping sounds
waves creeping on the land, our avowals

We consecrated our commitment
how we said no with our lives
for our lives, how we refused
that hell on land, making generations
of grist for the hideous mill of rogue
capital, the codified caprice of robbers
we brothers, sisters, daughters, sons, clear willed
strong souled, liberty-led, freedom fed
returned to mother water, singing a way
open

out of 75 only 13 were found
drowned, the rest of us lifted,
transmuted, flew

Igbo Landing is a historic site at Dunbar Creek on St. Simons Island in Glynn County, Georgia, where in 1803, 75 Igbo captives after drowning their captors and running the ship York aground, marched ashore, singing, and walked into Dunbar creek, committing mass suicide. 13 bodies were recovered the rest remain missing. In 2002 the site was declared a holy ground.

NYANKOPOXYICAN BREATH OF FRESH AIR

by Andrew Geoffrey Kwabena Moss

"We can't breathe!"
cried the diasporic seeds on barren soils
Signals sent by those tethered
to Africa, Europe and the Americas
Inhospitable stormy weather
Picked up on marine radar radio
by Deep Sea Drexciyan Dwellers
Riding high under waves of isolation
In a Bubbled Metropolis
Travelling on Aquabahn in Cruiser Control

"We can't breathe!"
Weak breath signals picked up
In Africa, Europe and the Americas
Inhospitable stormy weather

Progeny of those labelled sick and disruptive
Thrown off foul scented slave ships
on their Middle Passages
They swam from their mothers' wombs, learning to breathe
to found subaqueous empires and freshwater trajectories
Formed deep seated civilisations beneath
a vast dark abyss

created by transatlantic slavery
Brave, alternative histories

"We can't breathe!"
Weak breath signals picked up
In Africa, Europe and the Americas
Inhospitable stormy weather

Valiantly escaping through aqua worm holes
Enslaved removals evolved into wave-jumpers,
stingray and barracuda battalions
to Positron Island, Bubble Metropolis, Danger Bay
Reaching Drexciya in stages
Evolutionary deep Black Atlantic Ocean navigation
An aquazone surrounding isolated archipelago

"We can't breathe!"
Weak breath signals picked up
In Africa, Europe and the Americas
Inhospitable stormy weather

The next Drexciyan Quest:
Communicate to save land lumbered souls
from the prison industrial complex, colonisation,
decolonisation, institutional racism, post industrialisation,
macro and micro-aggressions,
global warming oppression

"We can't breathe!"
Weak breath signals picked up
In Africa, Europe and the Americas
Inhospitable stormy weather

They sent sonic invasions
From their underwater techno-pirate-stations
Helping those struggling to survive

Adverse, intense climatic changes
Attacking the mainstream of airwaves
Allowing oppressed souls to breathe

A rescue mission dreamt up by Drexciyan R.E.S.T
Research, Experimentation, Science and Technology
New systems to allow breathing were developed
In the tropos-, stratos-, mesos-, thermos-
and eventually exospheres
Finally, flying, releasing estranged cousins,
from the effects of transatlantic slavery
Breathing

"We can breathe!"
In deep sea and space

Terrestrial, seabed to exospheric adaptation
Travelling dimensional portals,
jumping-holes at liminal crossroads
Neo-evolution from Drexciyan to Nyankopoxican
Extra-terrestrial storm weathering then harnessing

Formation of a single, continuous superfield
Hybrid reality, mediating all mass, space, time and energy
Innovative Molecular Enhancement Technologies
The stolen plotting liberation after surviving
abject global conditioning
Deep in the ocean, on land and air

Soul survivors, regrouping,
readying for the Journey Home (Future)
Wherever we choose to go.

PIGEON POLICE

by Bryant O'Hara

Don't mess with the pigeons that wear
the black double-breasted jackets—
The cops those birds call have claws.
These officers are beautiful,
but you cannot touch them.
They have a powerful defense,
and they are part of a machine ecosystem—
and that system does not give a damn
about your too-loud conversation.
The pigeons are polite, but firm.
The K-9-2s will taze, bag, and tag your ass.

The animals you see in the station nowadays,
most of them are unreal:
rats are the maintenance crew,
monitoring and repairing the cars and the rails,
resurrecting the jumpers that hit the third rail.
Mechanical roaches keep the real ones in line.

The Pigeon Police are who most of us talk to,
and they are friendly enough.
They will get close to you,
start up conversations.

Children love them and feed them.
The Pigeon Police regurgitate the scraps
for their flesh-and-blood templates.

The rules of the station are simple,
posted everywhere,
and are not suggestions.
The system has its ways of maintaining order,
some subtle, some blunt.

As long as you do not break the law,
you will reach your destination.
As long as the ecosystem does not evolve past the laws,
we can all be content.

THE DRONE'S RETORT

by Bryant O'Hara

If I'm to be the neck
you fit inside a noose,
then spin me up a soul.

When you can define it—
and find it—
you let me know.

Until then, Mother-Father
fix your own malfunctions.

This universe
is your slaughterhouse.

I just work here.

THE REVENGE OF HENRIETTA LACKS

by Cecilia Caballero

She owns you
You owe her your life
All your medical advancements
The secrets to an immortal life
Held in her cells that never die.

Black women will never die
HeLa cells travel space
Clone themselves
Created the polio and Covid-19 vaccines
Blood-pressure medications and antidepressants
That her daughter swallowed to keep herself alive.

She lived in the former slave quarters of her ancestors
She was a tobacco-plantation farmer
She tended the plants, dried the leaves,
Packaged the profit.
And she worked the land
Underneath the 100-year-old oak tree
At the home-house.

She was a 14-year-old mother
She declined medical treatments for

341

Toothaches, syphilis, injuries, pain.
"Happy home" was noted in her medical file.
She was told she had cancer
And went home and did not
Tell anyone her fear of failure as a mother.

At the public wards for colored women
She was afraid her womb would be taken
She wanted to mother more
But she was treated with radioactive
Radium rods sewn into her cervix
A glow-in-the-dark substance.

During her first cancer treatment
Her cells were taken
With the umbilical-cord blood
Of Black babies and mothers
And used to develop the first
Vials of human cell cultures
Made of salt and water and plasma.

And her cancer was mixed with chicken blood
And her cancer was mixed with chicken blood
And her cancer was mixed with chicken blood

Taken with a syringe from the still-beating heart
Of a chicken. They tell us this is science
When she mothers you without her consent.

And they call us witch doctors
And they call us witch doctors
And they call us witch doctors

And we are.

Because her daughter said
Blackness be spreadin all inside you.

Because we know
Blackness is not a cancer
But it cannot be killed.

TONS OF LIQUID OXYGEN BUCKLE TOO LATE UNDER STRAIN

by Eugen Bacon

Bones crumble, molecules, energy. It'll be weird at first, the
next ten years. The carnage of a decade—it's the work of us in
a rasping burr. Devouring the universe as we'd contest sausages.
Disaster capitalism is a thing. Unscientific thinking promotes
yoga, acupuncture, myotherapy to purge a pandemic. The Health
Ministry is missing in action. When the rich do nothing, the
poor perish. Bitcoin wipes nostalgia clean. Billowing in the
clouds: the face of a vulture fully beaked/talons on alert. A
formation of birds oblivious in a C down below. The ICU is
a deathcamp. *Tents! More tents!* Unconscious in a rickshaw.
Tickets on the black market bury gone flesh. A gasp for
oxygen. Plumes. A dance of flames some days we try to forget.
Pretending we're tourists hardened in the last sun, but our hearts
are shattered in hotspots and clusters as grief visits. Pyres burn.
3689 body bags in a single day. Underreported in a second, third
wave. The scale of a crisis, one nation burns.
Meanwhile conspiracists mushroom dumb shit
about reengineered sex.
Going viral: Satan's microchips.

AND THIS IS HOW IT BEGINS*

by Gerald Coleman

once upon a time
in that only place
beyond seven mountains
beyond seven forests
seven rivers
seven seas
on one thousand
and one nights
there was
and there was not
here is a story
story it is
having been said
and said and said

from earth and sky

listen to it
and tell it
to teach it
and if they didn't
die
they're still alive

today
the cat in the vail
lost its tail
end
of the fairytale

This poetic form is called a Cento. A Cento is a poem made up of lines from other poems. Instead of lines from poems this Cento uses the opening and closing lines from traditional storytelling. This poem includes the traditional openings and closings of the rich storytelling heritage from around the world, including Farsi, Tamil, Arabic, and Telugu—from Germany, Iceland, Chile, Nigeria, and more.

THAT POOR WOMAN

(for my mom and her long suffering)

by Gerald Coleman

the nurses
knew
my name

i'd made
so many trips
to
the emergency room
that summer
they knew
it was me

what did he do now?

before
i blew myself up
i was
at a ballpark
in
the bottoms
and this time
all i'd wanted

was
ice cream

we were on
the playground
next to
the ballpark
when
the dulcet tones
of
the ice cream truck
drifted
to our ears
on
a warm
summer breeze

so we ran
we ran
to find our
moms
to plead
our case
for money
because
there are only
two
immutable forces
in the universe
when
you're twelve
saturday morning
cartoons
and
the ice cream man

so we ran
a rabid
gallery
of adolescences
in sneakers and
faded tshirts
riven
by the undeniable
desire
for a bomb pop
or an orange
pushup

everyone else
ran around
the chain
meant ostensibly
to keep cars
from driving through
but i
decided to jump
to fly
like shazam
or leap
like daredevil
and
i miscalculated

the poor
woman
entrusted
with my parentage
was minding
her own business
watching the game

in the stands
when
the loud speaker
announced
for the whole stadium
to hear
will the mother
of gerald coleman
please report
to the playground

she found me
laid out
in front
of a car
prostrate
unconscious
unmoving
with a coat
rolled up
under my head
a knot
the size
of a tangerine
on my forehead
thinking
he's done it
this time
he's killed
himself

the rock fights
bottle cap zip
guns
jumping off
rooves
an exploding gas tank

rickety
handmade go karts
bike jumps
off tenuous
wooden ramps
had all failed
to kill me
but this time
she knew
i'd succeeded
until
i woke up
dazed and confused
with a crowd
of faces
looking down
at me

once again
it was nurses
who knew
my name
shaking their heads
and hugging
my mom
because
that poor woman
had
a child
who'd be
the death of her
if america
didn't
kill me
first

THAT TIME YOUR BEST FRIEND CALLED YOU SISSY AS A PLATE OF ÀMÀLÀ AND GBẸ̀GÌRÌ COOKED BY YOUR ORÍ

by Ishola Abdulwasiu Ayodele

I

After kindling fire from your burning, breaking heart,
Orí molds two cauldrons from the steeliness it assumes,
and pours inside each, steaming streams of your tears.

Orí forages the myriad times your friend told you to straighten
your limp wrists, and you clamped your hands into *manly* fists
—pods concealing beans of your elegance—that Orí smashes open
for collecting, soaking, rubbing together, and peeling.

Orí pours the naked beans into a boiling cauldron.
As they cook to tenderness, Orí reaches into the moments
you curved your mouth into a bow and gathers all the arrows
of words you shot in defense, to bind into ìjábẹ̀.

With the Ìjábẹ̀, Orí mashes the beans into a fine paste,
adds a dash of your peppery pain to taste,
sprinkles of seasoning crystallized from your will,
oil in your hips' dream of swaying,
and gbẹ̀gìrì is ready.

II

For the àmàlà, Orí scoops your powdering self-esteem,
pours it into the second boiling cauldron till it thickens.

And with ọmọrogùn carved from the snapped branch of
your felled friendship, Orí stirs the mix;
turns and turns and turns
till it's a dough the brown of your skin.
Till, it stretches and sticks,
and the àmàlà is ready.

III

Where you sit cross-legged in meditation
for healing, Orí feeds your consciousness
morsel by morsel of àmàlà dipped in gbẹ̀gìrì

till you are full of yourself;
till you are ... *sissy*.

Glossary

Àmàlà: a Yorùbá meal prepared with yam or cassava flour.

Gbẹ̀gìrì: a Yorùbá soup made from cooked peeled beans.

Orí: an inner self that embodies spiritual intuition and destiny in Yorùbá metaphysics.

ìjábẹ: a short broom used in mashing cooked food into smaller particles.

ọmọrogùn: a short smooth stick used in turning or mixing food.

LOVING VENUS

by Jamal Hodge

Resplendent against the infinite dark.
Luscious beauty,
without moons.
Nothing must compete
with her luminous
vanity.

Waltzing on her axis,
performative slowness,
allowing the universe
one circle
within one rotation
of her curves.

As we orbit her seduction,
our arc reactor stalls,
tempted by our nearness,
she reaches,
dragging us,
into love.

867 degrees Fahrenheit
beneath

her yellow-white canopy,
squeezing
with eager tightness
against our penetrating hull.

Ignited by her heat,
we lose ourselves
to delirium,
screaming incoherent promises
as the atmospheric pressure rises.

Computerized boosters
cannot reach escape velocity.
Crucial circuits malfunction.

We plummet at her pleasure.
Our hull growing soft inside her,
its hardness spent.
She does not relent,
wanting more, deeper.

185 mile-per-hour
atmospheric winds
make satisfied howls,
her sulfuric clouds
smell of rotten eggs.

Licked by acid,
our eyes glimpse
desolate passions,
a hellish revelation of volcanos,
lava, and boiling dust.

William said,
"Venus does not favor a house of tears."

She favors a house of hell.
She is hunger without relent,
a lover of bloody Mars,
bathed in toxic glory.

Our eyes escape their sockets,
oozing down flaming cheeks.
Harsh winds scatter the pieces of us,
floating, lifeless,
till our ashes
kiss her empty heart.

FRACKING-LUTION

by Linda D. Addison

Some things can not be ignored forever:
    plastic bags pirouette on the tips
    of tree branches, flags to all the
    countries of needless consumption,
even when winter inevitably stripped leaves,
    leaving the reformed polyethylene
    swaying against blue sky, they didn't
    notice, too busy continually buying as
the cycle of cold to warm to cold seasons,
    night to day to night encouraged
    their longing to get stuff, homes
    filling with piles of useless things,
while trees continued collecting tattered remains
    white green pink yellow black blue,
    until one morning high-pitched
    whining made them look up
to branch tips grasped by floating plastic babies
    white green pink yellow black blue,
    where plastic bags used to dance,
    eyes unblinking, each mouth open
pouring strange sounds into windless air,
    science had no equations to explain
    the metamorphosis of reshaped fossil
    fuel into strange life blooming above,

while at rivers & lakes they dropped their
    rods in horror at creatures gnashing
    on the end of their lines, no longer the
    usual occasional plastic bottles, but
some Thing else …

THE UN-AWAKENED
(Octavia E. Butler 1947-2006)

by Linda D. Addison

In the end times,
    the few meta-humans left
    begat one mind from all minds,
    needing to understand, looking for hope,
        none was found in the usual patterns,
        they searched the unusual.

Finding two matching systems:
    the observable cosmic web,
    Her neuron's network.
    Needing to understand, looking for hope,
        they built synaptic processors,
        a bridge between the two.

After 19,472,006 attempts, She spoke,
    "I have been gone, how am I here?"
    They answered with one voice,
    "We need to survive, we need hope."
        And She learned by listening
        what had been done by them.

"I can't give you, what you have given away.
  Every story I created, changed me,
  here in the future I didn't want,
  I can't make new worlds for you,
    to replace all the worlds
    destroyed by your will."

And, at the end of all things,
  the last synapses of all minds
  finally saw, as She saw, systematic
  hunger had consumed hope, leaving
    nothing to change them, the
    work in progress completed.

She began a new story …

BECOMING

by Miguel O'Mitchell

Meter-wide glassine spheres
by the thousands
eggs of a mother long dead
bobbing on frothing waves
translucent, rainbow skin shimmering
from the glow of two moons
one green with life, one dead
both full on a cool night

The orange sun rises
heating the spheres
waking their passengers
hopping inside, forward ho
launch, smack, roll
magnetically driven
an iron neural itch
polar orientation
toward survival

Bouncing and spraying
attracting the Enemy
looking for breakfast
rushing up with spines

piercing, charged, emf blast
spheres explode
ripping fangs
churn bright blue blood

But close so close
the land the sacred place
and some few arrive
upon the sandy beach
their brethren gone
to feed the sea

The next phase clicks
metamorphosis
shell hardened
days later
first cracks
smoke and flame
emergence
jade green serpents
malachite scales
golden eyes narrowed
belching birthing fire
on fuel that burns in water
roaring

They undulate toward the sea
glide into the welcome water
a threat no longer
remembering the Enemy
a smoldering racial enmity
prey and predator
role reversal
an eternal cycle

STREET NAMES

by Ndaba Sibanda

Voyager Thabi had seen it all,
She had travelled far and wide
and experienced a series of shocks
cuisines, music, colors and climates.

Not only had she had the privilege
and honor of visiting several countries
on this earth, she also set foot on other
planets, her eyes on extraterrestrials.

If there were inscriptions on her
forehead, maybe the words would
read like: *culture shock no longer
shocks me, I just stunned it big time.*

She had come across individuals
who named their kids after books,
for instance, one boy was Dictionary,
little wonder, his teacher used to say:
Dictionary, give me the meaning of this.

She had seen medical bodies or institutes
with eyebrow-raising names too, for example,

one of them was called *Prestigious Psychological
Menopause School of Sciences and Signs*, wow!

On another planet, she was captivated
by street names like: *Is Lyfe A Beach?
Naught In Anoder Lyfe, Fool Stop, Go
To Eel or Earth, Full Me Thri-c I'm Yo Full!*

*I thout U Where My Half, Why DD
U Live Me, What Hapend?Riched
A Dad End, My Everytin, U I Mine,
Go Bed They Will Defurther U, C U.*

*U Wested My Tyme, Which Me Luck,
Which U Da Beast! Sory Waz Rong,
Miss U 2 March, Com Bake Darlie,
4eve Yoz, Gud Tymz We Heard 2.*

Thabi discovered that aliens
named the city`s streets after
their break-ups or fallouts,
or issues with their exes.

She learned that the street name:
Go Bed They Will Defurther U,
actually means: *Go bird, they
will defeather you ahead.*

Printed in the USA
CPSIA information can be obtained
at www.ICGtesting.com
JSHW021546111223
53613JS00003B/34